# The Children of the Seventh Son

## Book 2 of The Dark Age

Scott Bury

**Scott Bury**

**The Children of the Seventh Son**

**Book 2 of The Dark Age**

Published by The Written Word Publishing Company
Ottawa, Ontario
www.writtenword.ca
A member of Independent Authors International

Cover image by Marc Laisne
Cover design by David C. Cassidy
Interior design by Samreen Ahsan
Edited by Gary Henry and Joy Lorton
ISBN 978-1-987846-24-9

*For Roxanne, Evan and Nicolas*

*The true lights of the dark age*

# CONTENTS

# MAPS

The Eastern Roman Empire
*Circa 600 Christian Era*

Source: Wikimedia Commons

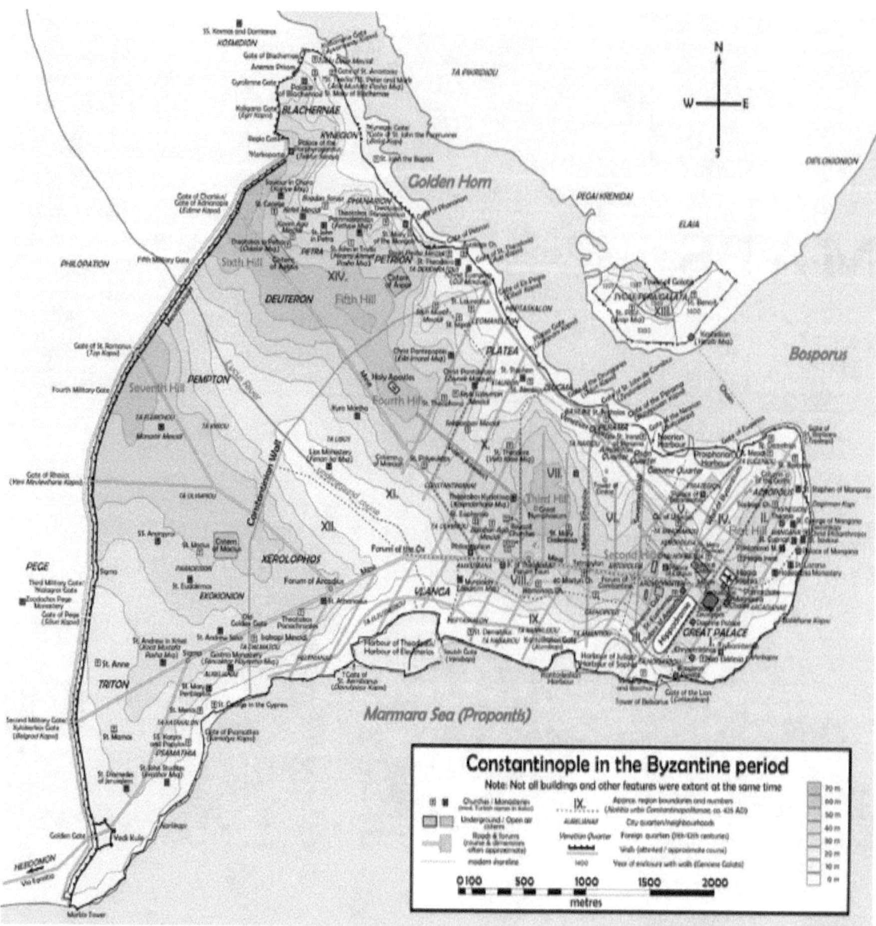


Topographical map of Constantinople during the Byzantine period. Main map source: R. Janin, Constantinople Byzantine. Developpement urbain et repertoire topographique. Road network and some other details based on Dumbarton Oaks Papers 54; data on many churches, especially unidentified ones, taken from the New York University's The Byzantine Churches of Istanbul project. Other published maps and accounts of the city have been used for corroboration.

# Foreword

This is a work of fiction. Or as I prefer to call it, historical magic realism.

It is set in a real place and time: the Eastern Roman Empire of the early seventh century of the Christian era. Most people today know this as the Byzantine Empire. Most people of the empire spoke Greek but called themselves Roman, even though the city of Rome was not part of the Empire at the time.

They called the Black Sea the Euxine; the Sea of Marmara, the Propontis; and the Sea of Azov, the Maeotian Lake.

All the names mentioned in the following pages also come from history, or from the mythologies of peoples who lived in the area of the eastern Mediterranean, Anatolia, Syria, the Balkans and the regions north of the Black Sea at the time, or in preceding centuries. I swear, I chose the name Calanthe long before I watched The Witcher.

The events described in the Interlude chapters are based firmly on historical research. The Avars and the Gepids were real peoples from the Eurasian Steppe who often fought against Roman legions.

The Emperor, or Augustus (in Greek, Basileus) at the beginning of the seventh century was Maurice, or formally, Flavius Tiberius Mauricius, and his Augusta was Constantina. He was succeeded, as the book will describe, by Flavius Phocas, who was then succeeded by Heraclius, whose second marriage was as controversial as will be portrayed.

The Gnostics were a religious group most prominent in the first and second centuries CE, until they were condemned as heretics by the Christian Church. However, some groups persisted, and interest revived in the 20th century.

The Enarei were really a group of Scythian or Sarmatian priests, all men who dressed in women's clothes.

The echidna is a monster from Greek mythology; the gryphon comes from ancient Iranian sources, but appears in the mythology of many different peoples in history.

Ullikummi and Upelluri are gods from ancient Hittite or Hurrian mythology, and the story told in Part 6 is taken directly from their tales. No, I did not make that part up.

Without further ado, please enjoy.

# Part 1

# Andrina

*Year 600 Christian Era*

# The serpent

Javor's left hand found a place to grasp in the soft, crumbling sandstone. His boot slipped once, then caught on the cliff face and he pulled himself up, over a lip of stone onto a rocky platform. He rolled away from the edge, raising dust. He willed himself not to cough and moved forward and upward.

Wishing for the hundredth time that the men who followed him had stayed behind, Javor moved forward to where the cliff rose sheer again, many times the height of a man—even a man as tall as himself. Dozens of deep crevasses cut into its side, canyons as narrow as the corridors in a cheap inn. The sun never reached inside them. Javor wondered what did—and what torture of the earth's bones had produced such a marvel.

"Which way now, Sir Javor?" asked Ionnes, the stout, barrel-chested headman of the little town of—*what was it called again? Cromna,* Javor remembered. *Some little place at the foot of hills in Paphlagonia, whose parish priest had sent to Constantinople for help in exorcising a demon that plagued them.*

Javor hated being called "Sir Javor," too. It was a title that meant nothing. The people who used it did not respect him. They only feared him and hoped to establish their own pathetic perch on some social ladder by acknowledging his superior place on it.

And he hated the fact that the townspeople had insisted on sending a delegation of nine "warriors" with him. "Three times three, to invoke the Holy Trinity. No man can face the evil of Satan alone, my son," the priest had said. Even in the candlelight of the old church, Javor could see the worn threads on his robe, the dirt on his headpiece. More telling was the light of rectitude in his eyes. There was no arguing with a man who believed he heard the word of God.

"Quiet," Javor said to Ionnes. "And tell your people to be quiet, too. We are near the beast's den."

Ionnes looked confused, and Javor realized that, to the people of the town, his accent was stranger and more barbarous than theirs was to him. But they understood when he raised his finger in front of his lips, then lifted his shield and sword and crept into the nearest crevasse.

He had just stepped into the shadow between the high stone walls when he heard a scraping slither from above. Then someone in the hunting party cried out, followed by yelling and panic from the other eight, including Ionnes.

Javor ran out of the crevasse just in time to see something huge, long and dark disappear up the cliff face. Ionnes pointed up after it. His jaw moved up and down, but no sound came out of his mouth.

"Drakon!" said one of the men, eyes wide. *More of a boy,* thought Javor. He could not have been more than 16 years old. His face was long and thin, his thick eyebrows almost hidden by an ill-fitting, old helmet that kept slipping down in front of his eyes. His arms looked thinner than new birch branches, and Javor wondered how the boy managed to hold up a shield.

*I was just 16 when I faced Ghastog,* Javor remembered. *But I was not that skinny.*

"Drakon?" Javor repeated. "You mean, a dragon? Are you sure?"

The boy nodded vigorously. "I saw it with my own two eyes, Sir Javor. A drakon, long as five horses. It took Georgius in its jaws and carried him off like a mouse."

"What did it look like?"

"Big. Big as ten horses."

"You just said it was as big as five horses."

"Like a gigantic wildcat," said another man. This one looked at least like he was fully grown, thought Javor. Short but with heavy arms, used to hard work. He carried his weapons like he knew what to do with them, which was more than the rest of the men in this little party could say.

"What do you mean, a wildcat?" Javor demanded.

"A face like a cat. Eyes like slits, like a cat. An enormous cat!" said the man. *Thomas,* Javor remembered.

"No, like a snake. Have you never seen a snake?" said the skinny boy.

"So it was more like a giant snake than a dragon?" Javor asked. The skinny boy nodded again. Better a snake than a dragon, Javor thought. "Did it have claws?"

"No," said the boy, tentatively.

"Yes it did, Elias," shouted another man, named Cyrus. He was taller than the others, but still shorter than Javor. His hair was grey, but he carried himself erectly. "Great talons, longer than scythes."

"It had no claws, Sir Javor. It moved on its belly like a serpent," said someone else. The little group began squabbling and calling each other names.

"Quiet!" Javor barked, and regretted the way his voice bounced off the cliffs. "You must not attract more attention. There is no way of knowing just how many beasts and horrors are up here. In my experience, there are always more than one."

The men went quiet, looking down at the ground in shame or glaring at one another. "Is that the beast that has been plaguing your town these past months?"

They all nodded. "All right. We must move quietly, now. It has already killed one of us. The next to make noise is that much likelier to be next." Javor shrugged to adjust the shield on his arm and loosened his sword in its scabbard. He stepped out of the hot late-morning sunlight and back into the stuffy dimness of the crevasse. Grit beneath his boots scraped against the stone ground. The eight men left in his "support" party clanked, shuffled, sniffed, panted and swore as they followed.

"We are easy prey, strung along in single file like this," said Cyrus. Someone else shushed him, so Javor did not have to. Once again, he wished he were on his own. They might as well beat on drums.

Underfoot, Javor saw ridges in the sandy floor of a crevasse. Water had flowed here once. *It probably does, every time it rains.* Ahead, the dry streambed bent to the right and widened.

He glimpsed movement on the floor and then something hit his side. He fell against the crevasse wall, bringing a shower of dust and pebbles onto his helmet as Elias sprang past him, narrow sword held high. He brought the blade down, shouting in triumph. As Javor found his feet again, Elias turned toward him, holding something long and limp in his hand. His eyes shone and a grin split his narrow face in two. "Got it!"

Thomas, the stocky man, was at Javor's shoulder. "Got what? That little rock snake? Do you really think a snake as long as your arm carried Georgius in its jaws, armour and all?"

Elias' smile turned downward. He looked at the half of a dead snake he held in his hand in dismay. "I—I saw … I thought," he stammered.

Javor put a hand on Elias' shoulder. "It was a good try." He pushed past, as did the rest of the group, each one laughing or making a joke as they passed the young man.

That was why no one turned when Elias yelled and swung his sword again, clanging it against the soft stone wall. They only turned when they heard his choked-off scream. But they did not turn fast enough to see more than the dark tip of a long tail disappearing up the rock wall, over the edge of the top high above.

"Elias," called Apion, another young man whom Javor thought had to be under twenty. The others shushed him, as if that could help now.

"Stay close together," Javor ordered, but he knew there was no more hope for the men following him. "Cyrus, you bring up the rear. Face backward, walk backward. You there," he pointed at a man with a scar across his face, who had no armour but carried a long spear. Javor thought—or hoped—he looked like a fighter. "You will be beside Cyrus. Help guide him. Look forward and upward. Yell when you see anything.

And if you do, everybody duck low, swords up high.

"Ionnes, you walk beside me," Javor continued, pulling the leader close to his shoulder.

He pointed to two men, who between them might have mustered a single full set of battered, rusted armour. "With the spears."

"Sergius," said one, a short man with thick black hair on his unhelmeted head and wide, fearful eyes.

"Paulus," said the other, another thin man, with a drooping, sad expression.

"You two will be in the middle. You keep your spears pointed up, and you keep looking up, understand? Do not let that thing get another one of your friends."

Sergius swallowed and looked up, his spear waving overhead.

Javor pulled the visor of his helmet down, looking up along both walls of the crevasse before signaling the little company ahead.

They hadn't gone ten paces when Paulus yelled, answered by the others. Javor spun and craned his neck, his vision restricted by the helmet and visor. "Spread out!" he ordered, but it was useless. The men crowded together, their weapons high.

Overhead, just out of reach of their swords and spears, a monstrous snake extended its body, waving above them. A forked red tongue flicked in and out of its triangular head. Its impossibly long black body, covered in deep black scales that glistened with white and dark green highlights, curled and twisted up the rocky wall of the crevasse, holding onto something that none of the men could see.

"It has no claws, Thomas," said one of the men, his voice high and trembling. Thomas had no response.

The snake's unblinking eyes scanned them for what felt like a day, but it could not have been more than a few seconds. Then it opened its maw, let out a sound like iron scraping against granite, and struck.

Men yelled and cried, thrusting their weapons, but the shiny black scales deflected the blades and spear points.

The snake's head rose again out of range, Sergius writhing in its jaws.

He screamed louder, his voice getting higher as the beast rose higher. His blood rained on the others below.

Sergius' screams turned into a choking gurgle as the snake's jaws closed. Below, they heard a sickening crunch followed by a tearing sound. Sergius' legs fell onto their shoulders.

The serpent rose higher. The men below saw its throat bulge as it swallowed their comrade.

"This way!" Javor turned and ran deeper into the crevasse. Around another turn, it widened and split into two branches. "Make a circle. Blades out."

He heard that scraping slither again coming from the narrower, right-hand branch. "Get behind me," he ordered. He drew not his sword, but his great-grandfather's dagger, and lifted his shield, ready for whatever came.

The serpent came out of the wider, left-hand channel, charging at the men faster than a galloping horse. Javor launched himself to the left, dagger out, digging the blade in behind the snake's head.

The beast snapped, twisted and writhed. Javor felt a whip blow against his back-plate as the tip of the serpent's tail struck him. He fell, rolling, holding onto the dagger.

Paulus thrust his spear at the serpent's eye but the animal dodged. Its maw opened far enough for the man to stand up straight in it. Paulus thrust the spear into its throat, catching on something, stopping the snake. Paulus pushed and the snake reared up high, pulling the spear out of his hands. For a moment, the monster towered over the little group. The spear fell to the ground behind it.

Javor regained his feet and rushed the snake again, looking for the wound his dagger had made. The snake's head started down again, its jaws opening wide.

Javor hit it, stabbing the dagger deep into the thing's body, jumping clear as the tail came for him. The head came down and the jaws snapped at empty air.

"Get behind me," Javor ordered again. The narrow crevasse filled with the echoes of yelling men, the smell of sweat and blood and fear, and the stink of an enormous reptile.

The snake's tail whipped down from overhead, knocking Ionnes against the crevasse wall and smashing Apion into the ground. Blood spread across the rocky floor under his head.

Javor's eyes locked on the snake's deep green iris, bisected by a horizontal slit.

*Not like a cat's. A cat's pupil is vertical.*

And a cat's eye does not have beautiful, naked women inside it. Women reaching for me, calling to me. Women singing ...

He felt a vibration against his chest. His great-grandfather's amulet, under his armour and shirt, trembled against his skin.

*Preyatel*— "good friend" in Javor's native language—*is talking to me.*

Do not look into the snake's eye, it said. Do not fall under its spell.

Javor sprang forward, dagger in front of him, aiming for the snake's eye. But the snake struck at the same time, passing Javor. Its fangs sank into Ionnes' leg. Ionnes screamed and fell. Two men grabbed his arms and pulled him away from the monster. Ionnes screamed again as the snake pulled back, its dagger-sized tooth protruding through his thigh. The tug-of-war lasted long enough for Javor to strike his great-grandfather's dagger against the snake's body. The blade split a scale and dug deep into flesh.

The snake reared back, Ionnes dangling from its tooth through his leg. A horrifying metallic noise came from its open mouth.

Javor wrenched his dagger out of the snake. The blade dripped a thick, heavy black fluid. He looked up at the snake's head. Ionnes swung, head down, his flailing arms just out of Javor's reach.

Javor slammed the dagger into the snake's belly as hard as he could and pulled it out again before the monster's body slammed down. Ionnes smashed onto the ground. His leg came free of the snake's tooth with a sickening, tearing sound. His body rolled away and lay still.

Javor pounced, aiming for the snake's eye again. The snake hissed and pulled back. Its tail and body climbed backward up the walls of the canyon.

Cyrus, the older man, slammed a club onto the snake's head. It butted him, sending him crashing against the canyon wall. Its tail smashed down, crushing Cyrus' ribs.

"Here, monster!" Javor called. The snake turned to him again. He looked not into its eye, but at the tip of its snout. The long tongue flicked out. Then the beast turned and retreated up the crevasse, like water flowing upward.

Javor ran after it, the three men left alive following. They rounded a bend just in time to see the last yard of the snake's tail disappearing into a black crack in the canyon wall.

The four men stopped, panting as they peered into the opening. It was higher than Javor's head, but so narrow he wondered how the huge snake had gotten in.

"We have trapped it!" Paulus cried and dashed inside, disappearing.

"Wait," Javor said, his arm blocking the way. Too late. Thomas and Petrus, a thin farmer with no armour, shifted their weight from one foot to the other, alternately looking into the cave and Javor's eyes. "I have been in caves like this before. It is far more dangerous inside. Paulus!" he called into the cave. "Come back now."

Paulus jumped out of the crack, his spear in one hand and something shiny in the other. "Look," he panted, holding up a large golden coin. "The cave is full of treasure."

"Now you have done it," Thomas growled. "Everyone knows you cannot steal treasure from a monster's cave."

"That is just a—" Paulus began, and was interrupted by a deafening metallic shriek. Wind blasted out of the cave opening and the ground shook, knocking Petrus off his feet.

Paulus shoved the coin into a pouch hanging from his belt and turned. The unnatural wind blew his dark hair back and the tip of his spear rose, following the snake's head as it emerged from the top of the cave.

The snake looked down at Petrus and its jaws parted. As it struck,

Javor jumped at the thin man, pushing him out of the way. The monstrous jaws closed on empty air and the ground trembled as the tip of the snake's tail smashed down.

The snake drew back, its pupils widening as if it were surprised and confused. The head moved back and forth between Petrus and Paulus, but skipped Javor. It cannot see me. Thank you, Preyatel.

Javor sprang toward the snout. His left hand found a grip on the edge of a scale. He pulled forward and struck the dagger into its eye.

The tip penetrated. Black blood spurted, covering his hand. The snake reared back, making that horrible metallic noise again, its snout tipping upward. Javor fell onto his back.

He looked up. The snake had reared up above him, looking at him with its remaining eye. Black fluid dripped from the other. Javor tried to roll out of the way, but again was too slow.

The snake struck down, jaws wide. It took Javor up, hissing triumphantly. Its fangs penetrated the iron greaves on his shin and the plate over his chest, but not his skin. His amulet vibrated so intensely, it felt hot against his chest.

The snake hesitated. Its jaws tightened, squeezing air from Javor's lungs, but still the teeth did not break his skin.

Javor twisted. A buckle of his armour dug into his chest. His helmet fell off his head and clattered onto the rocky ground. Below, the three men with him shouted, striking the snake uselessly with knives and spears.

Javor continued to twist until he could bring his arm into position to swing the dagger into the snake's remaining eye. This time, he hit directly in the centre. The blade went deep. He shifted his body further so that he could get both hands on the dagger's handle, then twisted and pulled.

The eye came out of the snake's head with a sucking sound. Javor flung the eyeball away from the blade. He heard a sickening squish as it hit the rocky ground.

The snake whipped back, opening its jaws wide as it shrieked. Javor flew across the crevasse, smashing into the rock wall. The impact knocked what wind was left out of his lungs and he fell from twice his own height to the ground.

The snake's body whipped across the canyon floor, senseless and wild. A coil hit Thomas, crushing him against the rock wall, but missed Javor again.

Javor tried to rise, but his lungs hurt too much. He looked up to see Paulus stabbing at the snake's head again with his spear, but its iron point would not penetrate the scales. He tried to stab into an empty eye socket, but the monster's head moved back and forth too rapidly. It snapped its jaws blindly.

Javor called Petrus as loudly as he could, his voice hoarse and thin. The thin man crept toward him, trying to avoid the snake's writhing coils.

"Help me," Javor wheezed. "Help me get to the snake's head."

Petrus put Javor's left arm over his shoulders, and together they moved toward Paulus.

Paulus dodged another snap of the snake's jaws and struck forward, this time succeeding in getting the point of his spear into the empty eye socket. He pushed, digging it in, pinning the monster to the ground. The long tail attempted to smash him down, but missed because the snake could not see to aim.

"Hold it there," Javor yelled. His breath was coming back. He took his great-grandfather's dagger in both hands again, raised them above the awful head and smashed downward with all his strength.

The blade pierced the scales and bone of the monster's skull, penetrating deep into the brain. The jaws twitched once, the tail spasmed over and over. Javor held the blade down, and Paulus held his spear in the eye socket until the tail's spasms slowed. It felt like hours, sweat running into their eyes, the sickening smell of snake blood and death filling the air.

Finally, the body stilled. Javor pulled the blade out and wiped black blood on the snake's body. He became aware of an itching feeling on his hands. The snake's blood was beginning to burn his skin.

He wiped them on the ground, but it wasn't enough to stop the increasing pain. "Wash the blood off," he told Paulus and Petrus. "Quickly!"

Petrus brought a water-skin, rinsing Javor's hands. Paulus wiped them with a cloth. "The monster's blood is tainted with evil," he said.

Javor could only nod. "We must get out of here while we still can," he said. He used Paulus' cloth to clean his great-grandfather's dagger and sheathed it.

"What about them?" Petrus stammered, pointing at the dead bodies.

As if to answer, unearthly cries, deep roars and more metallic screeching echoed down the crevasse.

"As I said, these things are never alone," said Javor. "If this ... snake was what was taking your village's animals and children, it will not any more. But here in its home, its friends will avenge it. Come on."

His breath had returned. He found his helmet on the ground and put it back on.

"But how can we leave Thomas, Ionnes and—"

"We can't bring all their bodies out," said Paulus. "And it doesn't make any difference to them anymore." He attached his spear to a strap over his shoulder, freeing his hands to take a sword from Apion's still body. Then he picked up Thomas's heavy club. "Take what weapons and armour you can, and let us hurry out of here." Paulus hurried away down the crevasse, the spear bouncing off the backs of his legs with every step.

Petrus stared after him, then turned to Javor. "No. We must give them a Christian burial," he insisted.

He changed his mind when the ground began to shake. Javor took his arm. "Hurry," he said. Together, they ran back the way they had come.

They paused to look over the cliff edge. It took Javor and Petrus a few seconds to understand what they saw was Paulus' body face down, with his spear penetrating fully through him.

"How will we get down?" Petrus asked as the ground shook more violently.

"As fast as we can," Javor answered. He turned to climb down, face into the sandstone cliff, feet seeking steps.

The ground continued to shake as they climbed down. Javor thought they would never make it. Petrus, above him as he descended, whimpered and cried every time the rocks beneath him shook.

But they made it to the rocky bottom, with bleeding hands and bruised faces. They looked at Paulus' body. "He fell on his spear," Petrus said. The point stuck out of his back, with an arm's length of the shaft, covered in blood. Apion's sword and Thomas's club lay on the ground by his side, and one hand clutched the oversized golden coin he had taken from the cave.

Javor pulled a medallion from Paulus' dead hand. It bore not the face of a monarch, but a strange symbol like a twisting path that overall completed a circle. In the middle was a different, angular and familiar symbol.

*The same rune is on the blade of my great-grandfather's dagger.*

On the other side of the medallion was an embossed image of a woman holding a bow. Beside her was an enormous dog. He quickly put it into a pouch on his belt.

The ground trembled again. "Come on," Javor said. He and Petrus ran down the slope to the grassy valley and the town that had sent for him. They only slowed when the ground beneath their feet felt steady again.

Petrus stopped. "What about the others? Can we return to bury them?"

"Only if you want more people to die," Javor said.

"But you killed the demon!"

Javor stepped close, intimidating the smaller man. "There are terrors in those canyons worse than anything you or I can imagine. The snake that was terrorizing your town is dead. Nothing will bother your town anymore, at least for many years. But going up that cliff and into those canyons — that is death."

"But what about their bodies?"

Javor turned away and continued down the slope. "By tomorrow, they will all be eaten."

# Interlude 1

# A good day to be a legionnaire

"Boys, our scouts have found the barbarian camp just over that ridge," the Centurion said.

Tullus Ionicus tightened his grip on the reins and tried to control his breathing. His horse, Albus, stirred under his hips. Tullus could hear his own pulse in his ears.

It was a perfect day for a battle. The late summer sun shone and warmed the cavalrymen's shoulders, but the morning air was still cool. Tullus breathed deep, smelling grass and barbarian flowers and, faintly, the barbarians' cooking fires.

Tullus adjusted his grip on his lance. The Avars had roamed Dacia now for years, as if they owned the place. Today, the Legion would show their Gepid allies who really was in charge: Rome. The greatest civilization, the most powerful empire that ever was or ever would be.

The Centurion gave the signal: a sword flashed downward, reflecting the morning sun. Tullus kicked his heels against his horse's sides, in time with his brethren. He thrilled to feel the horse surge to a gallop.

They reached the crest of the ridge in seconds. Beyond, the plain spread out. In a perfect line, the cavalry troop charged down the far side of the ridge.

He saw the barbarian camp. Men, women and children ran from

cooking fires and tents. In the middle, a whole pig roasted on a spit. A group of women and children ran away, up the far slope toward a line of trees.

They could not outrun horses.

A group of barbarian men ran toward the Legion, raising crude swords and spears in a futile attempt at defence. Tullus aimed his lance and struck a barbarian in the throat, a full yard out of the reach of the man's long arm and sword.

The horse thundered past before Tullus could see the barbarian's blood spurt. Now he was in the thick of the camp, surrounded by tents and panicked barbarians and Romans on armoured horses.

Tullus put his lance into its bracket, tucking it under his left arm, and drew his sword. He swung, satisfied with the smooth motion with which he severed a woman's head from her shoulders. The barbarian fell on the child she carried.

Two fewer barbarians to clutter this land.

A barbarian man, mouth wide, ran toward him with an axe raised. Tullus swung his sword again, carving a deep wound in the barbarian's shoulder. The man fell beneath the hooves of his horse, but Tullus did not hear the sound.

Albus had carried him past the camp now, and was gaining on the women and children running up the far slope toward the trees. He swung his sword, barely feeling the bodies it cleaved. He swung harder and was pleased to see the blade cleave off the top of a barbarian's skull.

He reined in. Albus turned and Tullus took in the scene around him. He saw legionnaires killing barbarians, stabbing them with spears, or using swords to chop off limbs.

The barbarians' tents were burning, and more than one barbarian ran and fell in flames.

One barbarian knelt amid the slaughter, shouting "We surrender!" in heavily accented Latin. The Centurion dismounted, approached and thrust his short sword through the barbarian's throat.

The Centurion turned and shouted to the cavalrymen. "Round them up! These prisoners will be a fitting gift to the emperor."

Tullus sighed. There would be no more killing today. He shook his sword to get some of the blood off before he dismounted.

A woman knelt on the ground, hands together, babbling in her barbaric language. He tore her rough dress over her head and used it to clean his sword.

He looked at the woman. She wept and trembled, but otherwise did not move. She continued to babble.

"You sound like a bitch," he said. "Nice tits, though." He loosened his belt, dropped his girdle and pushed the bitch onto her back.

He was hard, his pulse surging from the thrill of battle and bloodletting. He knelt and pulled the bitch's legs apart.

She screamed and scrambled back, so he hit her head with his steel gauntlet. She fell, stunned, and he got on top. She still squirmed under him, so he punched her face. She slumped back, allowing Tullus to complete the rape.

Finished, he rose and looked around. Other legionnaires were also raping women. The Decurion, Comentus, was raping a barbarian man. Tullus shook his head, laughing, and tried to think of a joke he could tell to tease the Decurion around the supper fire later.

He hitched up his girdle and fastened his belt, looking up at the clear blue sky. *Yes, it's a good day to be a Roman legionnaire.*

# Cromna

They reached the gates of Cromna as the orange sun touched the tops of the trees. Javor saw a sentry run down from his place over the town wall, and a few minutes later, the gate slowly opened.

By the time he and Petrus had reached the entrance, there was a group waiting for them: the parish priest, an acolyte who held up a huge crucifix, and a small party of armed men, even more pathetic than the ones who had accompanied Javor up the cliff. Behind them stood a small gathering of the people of Cromna.

"Sir Javor, you have returned," the priest intoned. He was young, with curly black hair escaping from under the rim of his tall, black hat. He had a round face and a thin beard. The gold crucifix hanging from the chain on the centre of his chest looked tarnished, even in the dimming light. "Were you successful? Did you slay the devil?"

Javor paused in front of Father Theodoric, his eyes scanning the people of the town. Their expressions ranged from hopeful to frightened to despair. Two women in matching tunics, one older and one quite young, held their hands together as if praying. Mother and daughter, Javor supposed. Others held hands. A middle-aged woman clung to her husband's shoulders.

"I killed it," Javor said. He removed his helmet and handed it to

Petrus.

"And ... and the other men who accompanied you?" the priest asked, his voice trembling.

Javor sighed. "Dead. I am sorry."

A woman cried out. The young woman with her mother covered her face. Javor swallowed.

"All of them?" said the priest. His voice was only a hoarse whisper.

"All except Petrus, here," Javor said, putting his hand on the young man's shoulder.

More people cried out. Javor felt like the wailing and anguish twisted his nerves.

"Thomas! Oh, Thomas!" a fat woman wailed, falling to her knees. Others cried for Ionnes, Georgius and Paulus. A thin woman pushed past Father Theodoric. A black scarf covered her head and her eyes were wide and bloodshot. "My Elias? Please, tell me my Elias will come soon." Her lower lip trembled in time with her hands.

Javor had to turn away. "I am sorry. He will not."

The priest made the sign of the cross, three times, and the others copied him. The acolyte fell to his knees, hands clasped, and began reciting a prayer.

"Can we recover the bodies for burial?" Father Theodoric continued.

"There will be nothing to recover by morning," Javor said. "And as I explained to Petrus, going back to those canyons is death. Tell all your people to stay away from the cliffs and the higher reaches of the mountains. There is nothing for you there.

"Now, if you please, I need to wash, and drink some water, and eat something, and rest. And in the morning, I must start back to Constantinople."

Javor pushed through the wailing, weeping crowd, down the muddy street to the priest's house, where he had been billeted. Behind him, he heard the priest call the people to the little church.

A hand gripped his arm and pulled him around. He found himself looking down into a man's angry face. He was thin, tiny, with a broken nose and a nasty scar on his cheek. "How could you let them die?" the man yelled. "Eight men dead and you don't have a scratch on you."

Behind the man, Father Theodoric and the town people watched intently, slowly moving forward.

Javor wrenched his arm free. "I did not ask those men to come with me. In fact, I argued against it. It was your priest who insisted they come. To 'help' me, he said. And they volunteered. None of them was a trained warrior. None of them had seen anything like that snake before. Most of them did not even carry decent weapons.

"I told you all to let me go alone, but you insisted. Do not blame me if your friends died."

"Come, Michael," the priest called. "Come to the church where we will pray for the souls of the men we lost today."

Michael glared up at Javor, his nostrils flaring, his hands opening and closing. He smelled like sweat and animal manure. The priest called him again, and he turned.

Javor watched the town people file into the little church beside the priest's house. Weary as he was, he decided to leave immediately. It would mean a ride in the dark and a night sleeping outdoors, but that was preferable to listening to all these people cry and pray the night through.

He let himself into the priest's house, packed the few belongings he had brought from Constantinople, filled a waterskin and took a loaf of bread and a jar of wine from the priest's cupboard.

The horse he had borrowed in the port city of Tium was still in the stable beside the church. Javor saddled it, took a sack of feed and mounted.

He could hear the congregation in the church, singing a mournful hymn as he rode out of the town, downhill toward the town of Tium on the Euxine coast.

# INTERLUDE 2

# Moesia Inferior

Hunger woke Tullus at dawn, as it usually did. He placed his palm over his rumbling stomach, but that did nothing to ease the pangs. It never did. He rose and picked up his cloak, which he had used as both bed and cover, and wrapped it around his shoulders. The edge was noticeably more frayed than the day before, he thought. There was a ragged hole big enough for his arm to go through, the result of a spear thrust—how long ago, now, since that battle? A month? Two?

Could I have survived on scraps for that long?

He shivered and pulled the ragged cloak tighter. He stumbled between the other prisoners lying by the trench that served the prisoners as a latrine. It was difficult to avoid stepping on or kicking the other prisoners who were still lying on the ground or sitting and shivering in the morning chill—especially as his ankles were hobbled by heavy rope with thick knots.

As he emptied his bladder, he looked at the pink sky and wondered if that signaled rain later. The thought made him shiver again.

As far as Tullus could see, Roman legionnaires lay on the trampled barren earth that had been a battleground. At intervals stood small groups of Avar guards, leaning on spears or squatting, holding their swords across their bent knees. They were coming to the end of their watch and waiting for relief.

Tullus had long since become used to the smell of thousands of men cramped together, with trenches for latrines and a muddy stream for drinking and bathing. But the image of suffering still tormented him.

How many legions had they lost as they crossed the Haemus Range as they ran for territory firmly under Imperial control? Someone had said four complete legions, and that the magister militum, their general commander, Comentiolus, had deserted them, running with his tail between his legs all the way back to Constantinople.

Someone else said the Avars had taken more than 10,000 prisoners, and still someone else had said 12,000.

Tullus shook his head, unable to comprehend such a number. The campaign had had a glorious start. He remembered marching out of Serdica in the Haemus Mountains, one of tens of thousands of new legionnaires in their shining armour and crested helmets and scarlet cloaks. Their spear tips had glittered in the morning sun like waves on the sea.

Now, the thousands of proud legionnaires sprawled, shivered and retched on the former battlefield. They had no more weapons, of course. The Avars had taken them all, and their helmets and armour, too. They had pissed on the standards that had fallen before making prisoners burn them. They fed their prisoners scraps each day, and allowed them to go to the muddy stream to drink. The once-proud Legions clung to life and waited for the emperor to ransom them.

How long will it take? Tullus wondered, again. Not paying attention to where he was wandering, he tripped again over someone who did not protest. As he rose unsteadily, chafing against the rope hobble, he looked down at the man he had stumbled over.

Giorgios, a decanius, leader of ten legionnaires, stared blankly up at him, his hand frozen in an unnatural grip. He had died sometime during the night. Even through the stink of the thousands of men around him, Tullus could smell the last contents of Giorgios' innards that had spilled out of his body.

He glanced quickly left and right, then grabbed the dead man's cloak and pulled it over his own. It was all that was worth taking.

He returned to the spot where he had been sleeping. Theo, a man from Thrace his own age, squatted on a broken log, chewing on a scrap of fat from the night before. Tullus willed his stomach not to growl at the sight, and failed.

He squatted beside Theo. "Giorgios is dead."

"Who?"

Tullus nodded vaguely toward the latrine trench. "I can't remember his patronymic. That decanius from Thrace. Looks like exposure during the night."

Theo shrugged. "Didn't know him." He gnawed some more on the hunk of fat. "I see you took his cloak, though."

"It wasn't doing him any good, anymore."

"Why didn't you take his sandals, too?"

"They're in worse shape than mine." Tullus looked at his feet. At least most of the straps of his sandals were intact, although the sole of one was wearing thin. *Maybe I should take them, too. Maybe I can put these straps on his soles. If his soles are good, that is.*

He looked over his shoulder to see three ragged legionnaires struggling over Giorgios' sandals. Too late.

Another soldier came up to them, shivering. "Think we'll get some food today?"

Tullus looked up at the haggard man. He recognized him from the red scar across his face, still oozing puss. Dimitrios. Tullus could not remember where he was from, though, nor which unit he had served in. Like the rest of them, he was one of the mass. The ocean of suffering. "They usually give us something."

"I'd be happy to wash," Theo said, and spat out a piece of fat he could not chew. "I'll bet that son of a dog Comentiolus is having a nice hot bath right now, and eating grapes."

"He should not have run," Dimitrios agreed. "What kind of general runs away from a battle?"

"A coward," Theo growled.

"A coward and a fool," Dimitrios said. "Why did he give us orders to form up for review instead of battle against the heathens? Why did he send units from one side of the battlefield to the other at the last moment? That was what caused us to lose the battle."

"What caused us to lose was our commander deserting," Theo growled.

"We'll all be back home soon," Tullus said, not feeling the hope in his words. "The barbarians can't be happy about feeding us and guarding us all this time."

"They're not going to let us go. Not without a ransom from the emperor," Theo grumbled.

"That's what I mean. It's been weeks. Months, maybe. I don't know. I cannot remember how long we've been here. But it can't take much longer to bring gold from Adrianople. Or even Constantinople."

"I am from Adrianople," said Dimitrios. "On the road, it's no more than a few days' ride from here."

"It looks like a delegation is coming," Theo said, nodding to the edge of the area where the prisoners were allowed to be.

Tullus watched as a large group of Avar spearmen walked from the east side of the camp. The sunlight behind them shone on their helmets. The silhouette of a single pointed helmet with long tassels hanging from it told him of a single commander. He halted at the perimeter of the prisoners' area and announced something in the Avar tongue.

Several prisoners near the commander rose, looking at the commander, the spearmen and each other, mystified. The commander spoke again, louder. Then Tullus saw someone moving through the crowd of prisoners toward the Avars. It was Basil Angelos, a commander who had always treated the men with kindness even while commanding them to kill and die. Basil stepped in front of the Avar commander and stood, legs firmly planted, looking defiantly at the taller man.

The Avar spoke again. A young Sklavene with long blond hair stepped up beside him and spoke Greek, translating the commander's words. Prisoners near them cried out. Others began insulting the Avars. One ran toward Tullus, Theo and Dimitrios, who caught him by the arm. "What did he say?"

"The emperor has refused to pay the ransom." He choked. Tears ran down his face.

Tullus felt his gut go cold. He turned toward Basil again, who glared at the Avar commander. Two guards stepped behind Basil and pushed him to his knees, but Basil did not take his gaze from his captor.

The commander looked sad. He shook his head before drawing a dagger from his belt and slicing Basil's neck open. The Roman legionnaires wailed as their commander's blood spurted onto the ground in front of him. Basil held his enemy's gaze for a moment when Tullus' heart would not beat, then fell flat on his face.

The noise deafened Tullus as every Roman prisoner cried out. The Avars, silent and stone-faced, stepped relentlessly forward, stabbing one prisoner, yanking their spears out of the dying body before stabbing the next.

Tullus dropped to the ground to struggle with the knots at his ankles. He glanced up to see the circle of spearmen contract around him, then concentrated on the knot again. The coarse rope tore his nails but did not budge. He pushed one side of the rope into the knot and felt a flash of hope as he saw it move a little.

He dug his nails into the other side of the knot as hard as he could. It loosened just a fraction as Dimitrios screamed and collapsed beside him.

Tullus looked up as a shadow crossed his face to see an Avar guard put his boot on Dimitrios' shoulder and pull a gore-coated spear from his chest. Tullus looked around at a sea of dead and dying bodies on the ground, a forest of spearmen stabbing and then stepping further into the shrinking circle of prisoners.

Tullus flung himself toward a gap between two guards, only to be caught short by the rope that still bound his ankles. He heard harsh laughter as he strained his arms to pull himself farther. Blood on the ground smeared his hands and his face.

Someone kicked his side and he rolled away, turning his face up to see the spear coming toward him. He felt it pierce his skin, something break inside his chest, the heat of blood over his body, then a white explosion of pain.

Then nothing.

# Constantinople

Look across the waves of the Euxine Sea. A bright spot comes closer. Soon, it's clear as two triangular sails of a large ship. Two rows of oars on each side rise and dip in a mesmerizing rhythm.

Now look back to the dock at the Neorion Harbour. A compact man with dark hair and beard stands there in a deep blue cloak fastened with a large gold clasp on his right shoulder. The breeze blows the hem to reveal a white tunic. His feet are clad in ankle-high, soft leather boots. His name is Mauricius Macedonius, and he owns the ship.

Behind him is a handsome four-wheeled wagon with two fine brown horses yoked. Two slaves wait behind him, dressed in simple tunics and cloaks. Their feet are bare.

As the ship enters the harbour, its red and yellow sails come down. Crewmen furl them while the rowing slows.

Men emerge from a large building to wait for the ship as it glides up to the dock, graceful as a swan. The ship's crew throw ropes and the men on the dock loop them around stanchions. Others put gangways from the bow and stern, and still more toss bundles wrapped in thick canvas to the men on the dock.

A tall young man with thick blond hair, cut short in the Roman style, strides down the aft gangway. He wears dark trousers and a dark tunic, with a thick and rich-looking cloak with a bronze brooch. A long sword hangs from his left hip and a curious curved dagger is at his right.

"Hail, Javor! Well met," booms the dark-haired rich man. When the younger man reaches the dock, the older man steps forward, embraces him and kisses him on both cheeks. Then he leans back, his hands still on the taller man's shoulders, and smiles.

"Welcome back, my son," he boomed.

"How did you know when I would get here?" Javor asked as a slave carried his gear from the ship to his father-in-law's handsome wagon.

"I always have runners stationed at the port, watching for my sails at the entrance to the harbour," Mauricius explained. "You must admit, Javor, that having such distinctive sails has its advantages."

"Yes, I suppose so," Javor said. As he climbed into the wagon beside his father-in-law, he said, "The red and yellow stripes are pretty, and they make it easy to identify your ships when they come into a harbour. But they also set your ships up as easy targets for pirates."

Mauricius Macedonius patted Javor's shoulder. "We have had this discussion. My ships are also the best-guarded on the Euxine, Propontis and Aegean seas. No pirate dares attack them—particularly with you on board, eh?"

The slave slapped the reins and the wagon clattered off the dock and onto the cobbled streets of Constantinople. The sun was high and bright, and the heat made the smells of the city, the cooking and rotting garbage, horses and cattle and people, sharper and stronger. Javor wished for the smell of a pine forest.

"Why did you come down to the port to meet me, father?" he asked.

Mauricius could not stop smiling. "Well, of course I want to know that you are safe after your mission for the Abbey. I trust you were successful? You met the learned man you wanted to meet?"

Javor hated lying, mostly because he was not good at it. "It's best not to talk of ... missions openly, father," he said. "But yes, I was successful."

Wagons, barrows, oxen, horses and donkeys crowded closer as they approached the harbour gate in Constantinople's legendary high stone walls. The slave at the reins of Mauricius' wagon cracked his whip whenever another vehicle or even a person came too close. "Make way!" he cried. "Make way for his grace, Lord Macedonius." Common people shied away in deference, not knowing that Mauricius was not really a nobleman.

The soldiers at the Gate of the Neorion waved them through without searching the contents of the wagon—not the treatment they gave the commoners. Mauricius tossed a coin to one of the guards, and waved at someone he recognized in another wagon inside the gate.

"What is it?" Javor asked. "Why are you smiling so much? Why did you really come to great me at the dock?"

"I have such good news for you, Javor. I promised my daughter I would not tell you before she has a chance to ..."

Javor's heart thudded in his throat.

"...but I cannot keep my peace. Javor, I am a grandfather. You have a beautiful baby girl." He threw his arms around Javor and squeezed, kissing his cheeks again.

Javor heard a roaring in his ears. The wagon swayed. The sounds of the street faded as if they were far away.

He heard an unfamiliar voice. "I knew it would be a girl." He realized it was his own, but it was hard to hear because of the pounding in his ears.

Mauricius pushed a wineskin into Javor's hands, and lifted another in toast. They drank. Javor choked a little, and Mauricius laughed, slapping him on the back.

"When did it happen? When was she born?"

Mauricius looked up, toward the upper balconies of the low houses near the walls. "I think ... yes, seven days ago. On the solstice."

"The solstice? Just like me," Javor said. His head spun at the coincidence.

Mauricius' grin split his face. "Really? Just like her father? Well, that is ... something."

"How is Calanthe?" Javor asked when he recovered. "Did she suffer much during the birth?"

Mauricius waved his hand. "Oh, you know my daughter. No one ever had as difficult a birth as her. I tell you, it was all over but cleaning up the mess and nursing the baby after two hours."

"Two hours? I do not understand." As the youngest child in his family, Javor had never witnessed a human birth.

Mauricius laughed, a deep rolling chuckle. "All my children troubled their mother for many times that long, Javor. For her first baby, my daughter—your wife, that is—had a very easy time. The baby practically fell out of her."

Javor realized the wagon was not on the way to his home in the Vlanga section in the southern part of the city. "Where are we going?"

Mauricius laughed again. He must be very happy. I have never heard him laugh so often. "Your wife, my daughter, insisted on having Martha, her old nurse, attend her during her labours. So she has been staying with me, in her old chambers, since you left. I tell you, I do not know how willing she will be to return to your home in the Vlanga."

"Oh. Well, I suppose I could stay with you for a few days ... if you don't mind, that is."

Mauricius laughed again. "You are welcome, Javor, please understand that. But Calanthe is your wife, now. You should take her home. You are too soft on her. I love her, of course, as my daughter. But a husband has to exercise some discipline, after all."

"Discipline," Javor mused, looking at the horses' rear ends. "I suppose so ... although I don't mind if Calanthe wants to stay with you. She has known you for much longer than me. And I do not think she really likes my—my aunt."

"That old lady who lives with you? That is because, my son-in-law, no one believes she is your aunt."

"She is also not an old lady. She is younger than you, Mauricius."

"Even more reason for Calanthe not to like her. No home should have two women in it."

"But Tiana does not get in Calanthe's way," Javor protested. "She says nothing about cooking, gives no instructions to the servants—"

"That is another problem, Javor. Why do you not have slaves? They're less expensive and easier to control than paid free servants."

"I have told you. I just don't like the idea of slaves."

Mauricius scoffed, waving his hand again. "You young people have such lofty ideas. But it is your money, Javor. God knows you have enough of it. But you will see one day, and come around to my way of thinking."

Javor looked at the road. He had had this argument with Mauricius more than once. There was no way to change his father-in-law's mind, nor even get him to respect his opinion. "I suppose so," he said.

*But I will never own slaves.*

It was only when the wagon passed through the gates of Mauricius' huge villa on the slope of Constantinople's Second Hill that he remembered to ask: "What did Calanthe name the baby?"

Mauricius laughed again. "Andrina. 'Fearless,' you know."

"I know what that means."

"Really? I did not think your command of the Greek tongue was complete, yet."

"What is wrong with my Greek?"

Mauricius laughed yet again as he took the driver's hand to help him climb down from the wagon. "I tell you, Javor, you still have a barbarian's accent."

Javor felt his face flush warmer. His father-in-law had a casual way of embarrassing him. He jumped down from the wagon without any help, and took his own weapons.

"Come on," said Mauricius, standing on the wide marble steps of his enormous home. "Come meet your daughter."

Mauricius' house was typical for a wealthy merchant of Constantinople. Three stories high, constructed of pinkish-brown stone, clad in front with white stone, it had wide steps on one side leading to an arched entry. Slaves carried Javor's things up the stairs, while others brought the wagon and horses into the ground-level stable.

The two-story high arched entryway led to a marble-tiled receiving room with low sofas covered in velvet and a large carved wooden chair for Mauricius. One wall held his pride, a huge, elaborate tapestry of St. Constantine meeting, as far as Javor could tell, Jesus Christ. Javor did not like it. None of the people looked right to him, and there were too many colours in it.

Mauricius' wife, Calanthe's mother, strode down a column-lined hallway, her glittering, gold-trimmed chiton sweeping across the polished tiles. She was a slender, attractive woman with large green eyes and a long, thin nose. Silver strands accented the rich dark brown of most of her hair. She threw her arms around Javor and kissed his cheeks. "Javor, it is so good to have you back!" she said breathlessly.

"Anna, where is your headdress? Your hair is loose," Mauricius complained.

"Oh, hush. What do men know of clothing?" She dismissed her husband with the same wave he had used to dismiss Calanthe's labour. She turned to Javor again. "Come, Javor. My daughter and I have a big surprise for you." She took his hand and pulled him down the colonnaded hallway.

"Is it the baby? Andrina?" Javor asked and he followed, his feet slipping on the polished marble.

Anna stopped to glare at her husband. "Mauricius, you were not supposed to tell him before you returned to the house."

Mauricius laughed. "It just slipped out."

"Men," Anna said, pulling Javor again.

They ascended a wide staircase to the second floor, where the shutters had been thrown back from the arched windows, letting a cool breeze through. Anna strode down the marble floor, telling slaves to bring food and wine, to prepare a bath for Javor and make up sleeping quarters, to close some of the shutters as the wind was too strong and the sun too warm.

"My dear, I have already taken care of that," Mauricius said, but Anna just waved him off again. They arrived at a closed door. As a slave put a hand on the knob, Anna turned to Javor and Mauricius with a finger to her lips. "Now be quiet. The baby is sleeping, and poor Calanthe needs her rest, as well."

Calanthe's childhood bedroom had always struck Javor as especially feminine and childish—not that he had seen it often—with walls covered in dark gauzy fabrics and the floors with thick oriental carpets that her father's ships had brought from the eastern shores of the Euxine Sea.

The room was dim, with daylight leaking in around the shutters over the windows. Javor thought it stuffy, too, but when his eyes adjusted, he could see his wife lying on her back, under thick coverings. She was plumper than her mother, her face rounder but with the same long, narrow nose, and she had her mother's green eyes and thick, dark brown hair. Her head was propped up on several puffy cushions.

Anna padded to the bedside and bent to her daughter's ear. "Darling, wake up. Look who has just arrived." Her voice was soft as velvet.

Calanthe's eyes fluttered. She groaned, looking at her mother. "What is it?" she whispered.

"Look," Anna said, turning to Mauricius and Javor by the door.

"Mama, I am so tired," Calanthe replied, her eyelids closing.

Calanthe's eyes moved and settled on her father, then her husband. She smiled a little. "Hello, Javor. I have given birth at last. You have a healthy daughter."

Javor strode in and took his pretty little wife in his arms. She remained limp, her arms staying on the mattress even as he lifted her off the bed. He kissed her cheeks, then her mouth.

"Javor, stop that now," his mother-in-law admonished. "You can do that when you two are alone." Still beside the door, Mauricius laughed again.

Javor lowered his wife to her bed. "Where is the baby? What did you call her?"

"Andrina," Calanthe whispered. She looked to the side of the room, where an older woman wearing loose brown robes and a soft cap on her head stood, holding a baby, rocking it back and forth. She was smiling broadly, and could not keep her eyes off the bundle in her arms.

Javor jumped from the bed to take a closer look. The woman, Calanthe's childhood nurse, Martha, smiled at him and pulled a fold of white cloth away.

The last baby Javor had seen had been more than six years earlier, in his distant home village, hundreds of leagues north of Constantinople on the slopes of the Sarmatian Mountains. The child of a very young woman and an older man who lived in his parents' village, she had died at two months of age.

So Javor looked at his own baby, the round pink face and the impossibly tiny fingers that reached up. The baby squeezed her eyelids shut, wrinkled her nose and smacked her tiny lips. She seemed so small, so fragile that Javor did not dare touch her. "Andrina," he whispered, then regretted that his breath might touch her face.

"She is hungry, Lady Calanthe," Martha said, approaching the bed.

"Oh, no," Calanthe moaned again.

Javor strode to the bedside and took his wife's hand. "Are you not well, my love?"

Calanthe pushed the covers down and pushed herself to a more upright position. She pulled her silk gown aside to bare a breast as Martha gently put the baby at her side. "I am very tired, husband," she said as she put her arms around her child. "The birth was very difficult for me ..."

As Mauricius scoffed, the baby latched onto Calanthe's nipple. The young woman's eyes and mouth opened wide and she drew a deep, painful breath. "Oh, Martha," she breathed.

"Please, my dear, do not be troubled. You must relax, lie back and enjoy nursing."

But Calanthe's eyes were closed and her jaw clenched. Javor could see that every muscle was tight.

Anna came close. "Listen to Mother Martha," she said, stroking her daughter's hair. "Lie back, relax and let the milk come. You will enjoy feeding your baby."

Calanthe did not seem to believe them, still clenching her eyes.

But gradually, under the ministrations of her mother and her childhood nurse, her arms and back relaxed.

Javor towered over the little tableau awkward, unsure whether he should say or do anything, until he felt a hand on his shoulder. "Come, Javor. Let the women take care of women's business."

Javor followed him out of his wife's room.

They went to a room off the main courtyard, where the dim light, out of the sun, relieved Javor's eyes. Mauricius' slaves had prepared a bath, towels and clean clothes for Javor. Mauricius poured more wine for them both as Javor stripped and lowered himself into the steaming water. Only when he relaxed in the heat did he realize how bone-tired he was.

Mauricius gave Javor a cup of wine before settling onto a couch against the wall and crossing his ankles. He took a deep draught and leaned against the wall. "Much as this is a happy time for this family, my son, there is troubling news to share."

Javor drank and did not reply. He knew his father-in-law needed no invitations to elaborate.

"The emperor is having trouble with the Army," Mauricius continued. "The wars against the Persians and the Avars have strained and depleted his forces and his treasury."

"I thought we were at peace with the Persians."

"Yes, since Emperor Maurice helped restore Khosrau to the Sassanian throne. But that came after many long years of warfare. Don't forget the threat on the West: the Avars and the Sklavenes."

"I am a Sklavene," Javor said. His throat felt dry, so he drank again. "And I know all about the threat of the Avars."

"Yes, I understand. The emperor cancelled the tribute paid to the Avars in return for peace, which of course meant a renewal of warfare in the Balkans and along the limes," the old term for the Roman border with the barbarian lands.

Javor squeezed his eyes shut. Political discussions always confused him. "How is that troubling?"

Mauricius looked out the door into the central courtyard. "Peace with Persia has allowed the emperor to concentrate more Legions in the West. They have crossed the Danuvius River. General Priscus has destroyed entire armies of Avars, Sklavenes and Gepids in a series of battles at Viminacium. Our legions drove thousands of the Avars into a lake where they drowned. They even killed four sons of the Avar King, what do they call him ..."

"Khagan. The word is khagan." Javor noticed that the water was getting cool.

"Yes, that's it. A particularly barbaric word. Yes, seeing his sons die apparently sent the ... Khan ... Khag ..."

"Khagan."

Mauricius waved the correction away, annoyed. "Yes, well apparently it broke his spirit. He withdrew the remainder of his army. Priscus took twenty thousand prisoners and sent them to Tomi on the Euxine Sea, but the emperor ..." He paused and sighed, looking out the high window.

"What?" Javor asked.

Mauricius sighed again. "The emperor, may Lord Jesus Christ save him, in his wisdom decided to free the prisoners. Without demanding ransom. As a gesture of good will, some say." He sighed yet again.

"That does not sound so bad."

"It is poor policy, and a gesture that was not reciprocated. Another general, a Comentiolus, led the legions against the Avars at Iatrus. The fool then was frightened at the sight of the enemy and deserted his own army. Twenty thousand men between him and the enemy, and he turned tail and ran. It was such a cowardly act that when he reached the city of Drizipera, the inhabitants pelted him with stones rather than admit him."

"He ran but left the legions in the field?"

"When the legionnaires discovered that their commander had deserted them, they fled, too. The Avars caught them at the narrow Sipka Pass and slew thousands. At the end, they had twelve thousand prisoners. The barbarians continued to Drizipera and sacked it. The only thing that prevented them from continuing to Constantinople itself was an outbreak of plague that killed the Khan's remaining seven sons."

"Khagan."

Mauricius continued as if Javor had not said anything. "The Kraik demanded twenty thousand gold aurei as ransom for the prisoners. Maurice refused to pay it."

"What? Why?"

Mauricius tossed his head. "Penury. The emperor is weary of paying huge tributes to barbarians in return for peace. He claims to have no money left after the endless wars in both the east and the west. But do not forget, son-in-law, that he no longer need fear attack from the Saracens, after restoring Khosrau to the Persian throne."

"So what will happen to the prisoners?"

"It has already happened. The Avars slew them all. Every last legionnaire." Mauricius leaned close to Javor. "We must be vigilant and prepared, Javor. The emperor's grip on his purse is costing him support in the city and the provinces. The tensions between the Monophysitism and the Orthodox continue. Even the Blues are grumbling."

"Vigilant about what?"

Mauricius leaned even closer, his voice dropping. "Do not forget the riots that can wrack this city. Or worse. Remember that even Constantine himself did not gain the title of Imperator without a civil war."

Javor stood, letting water drain from his body and reaching for a towel. "In that case, I have some people to see."

# The Order

Instead of going downhill to his home on the south-facing slopes of the city, Javor headed for the old copper market and the monastery there.

The Monastery at Chalkoprateia was not an impressive structure. Situated close to the Basilica Cistern of old Byzantium, across a street from the large, handsome Church of St. Mary of Chalkoprateia, the monastery looked old and shabby. The stone blocks used to build its walls had at one time been covered with white plaster, but the years, weather and the largest city in the world had worn off large chunks and turned the remainder a dirty, uneven soot colour. Walls taller than Javor, constructed of the same shabby material, extended from two sides of the building to enclose a courtyard with a wooden barn, a stable and storage sheds.

Most of the inside of the building was dim and close, but Javor went straight to the audience room of the head of the Order. He stepped through a high, wide doorway into a bright chamber with white painted walls and ornate tiles of gold and white on the floor. Summer light poured in through high glazed windows. An armed man beside the door stamped the butt of his spear on the floor and four men standing around an ornate table in the middle of the chamber looked up.

Javor knew three of the men, but considered only one a friend.

Malleus, the head of the Order, was slim with dark skin, curly black hair and a thin moustache. He wore a black robe trimmed with silver, open over a white shirt, open at the neck, tight black trousers and soft shoes. A silver chain hung around his neck and a slender sword hung in its scabbard at his left hip.

"Javor," he said in a booming voice. "I trust you had a good reason for not coming directly here after you landed?"

Javor hesitated. Four sets of eyes looked at him, and he could feel the eyes of two guards behind him, too. Only two eyes held any sympathy, any understanding of who he was. "Yes. My daughter was born."

Malleus strode to him as a smile spread across his face. "Congratulations, my friend!" He threw his arms around the young man and kissed him on both cheeks. "Well done. A daughter. I trust mother and child are well?"

Javor extricated himself from Malleus' embrace. "Calanthe is tired and weak, but the baby seems well. I suppose. Who is he?" he asked, lifting his chin toward the three men who stood around the table. He knew two: Zeno and Cometus had been Malleus' trusted advisors for most of the five years since Malleus had assumed the office of head of the Order. They wore tunics as fine as Javor's father-in-law, but with simple broaches at the shoulder, marked with crosses. There was no love for Javor in their eyes.

The third was a short, bald man with a thick waist. His throat, chin and the back of his head were covered with short, dark grey stubble, and he wore a brocaded dalmatic over his tunic.

"Ah, yes. Meet Gracian, the new councillor," Malleus said.

"New councillor? I only left four weeks ago!"

Malleus shook his head. "Javor, Gracian has been a part of the Order for over a year. It just happened that he was elevated to this level while you were away."

The new man clasped Javor's shoulders. Javor stiffened as Gracian kissed him on both cheeks. "Javor, I am so pleased to meet our hero. Our champion."

Javor took a step back. "I am not a hero."

"Oh, come now," Gracian said, smiling with his mouth if not his eyes. "Your life belies your words, Javor. Slayer of dragons and witches."

"I only killed one dragon, and that was six years ago."

"One dragon?" Gracian stepped back, eyebrows raised and smiling mouth agape. "My boy, killing a single dragon is an astounding accomplishment. The very spawn of the Devil himself—"

"I do not think you understand what dragons really are," Javor interrupted. "They are not children of the 'devil,' but rather more—"

Malleus interrupted him in turn. "Still, Javor, I must agree, that was a great accomplishment. But let us now focus on the important matter at hand." Malleus settled into a high-backed, gold-coloured chair behind the table. "Tell us about your mission."

"But I wanted to explain about the true nature of dragons," Javor said, looking back and forth between Malleus and Gracian.

*Why will he not let me explain?*

Javor noticed that Malleus had a strange expression on his face. His head moved almost imperceptibly from side-to-side. A warning? He then looked at Gracian, at Zeno and Cometus. Javor decided not to mention the medallion with the rune-like mark, still in the pouch attached to his belt.

He took a deep breath and stepped toward the table. It was covered with maps, as it had been on Javor's first appearance.

Javor loved maps, loved the way they brought order to the world around him. He pulled one map from under others to show the coastline of Paphlagonia on the Euxine Sea. "It did not take long to follow the beast's trail from the town into the highlands behind it," he said. "The cliffs were somewhat difficult to climb because they were made of soft, sandy stone." He found the town of Tium on the coast, then pointed to where he guessed Cromna sat. "The people of the town of Cromna insisted on sending nine men with me. 'Three times three,' they said. Like the Trinity. All but one of them died."

He looked up. Malleus' face was stony, but the three men with him all swallowed at once. "What was it?" the new man, Gracian, asked.

"A monstrous snake. It must have been ... I don't know, forty paces long. It was hard to tell because it never stopped moving. But its head was this big." He held his hands up, shoulder-width apart. Gracias gulped again.

"Did it look like anything you'd ever seen before?" he whispered.

Javor felt a faint buzz of alarm in the back of his head and in his gut, a warning not to mention the medallion.

"It looked like a snake, but much bigger." He shrugged. "It had black scales. And its eyes had horizontal pupils—like a cat's, but sideways."

"That is different from most snakes, Javor," Malleus said calmly.

"Doubtless a sign of diabolical nature," said Gracian, nodding. "Did you find its lair? Was it a cave or a cavern, an entrance to ... the underworld?"

Javor looked at Gracian for a long moment. Terms like "underworld" and "diabolical" were more Orthodox than Gnostic terms.

"Gracian is steeped in Orthodox theology and history," Malleus said. Javor noticed he avoided any mention of Gnosticism.

"It lived in a cave," Javor answered. "Whether that led to the underworld, I do not know. It was a large enough creature to kill men without any magical or spiritual help. Although ...." He hesitated, then went on. "It did seem to cast some kind of spell. Like a dragon. When I looked into its eye, I saw ... a vision and heard voices. Women singing."

Gracian gasped. "The lusting Nephesh made flesh," he whispered.

"No," Javor growled. "There was nothing real. It was a trick to distract me."

"Do not dismiss the mystic power of demons," Gracian said. Javor shook his head and concentrated on Malleus.

"It does not matter," he said. He went to a sideboard and poured himself a cup of red wine. He drank it all before continuing. "The damn fools who came with me died, all but one. They were useless in the fight against that thing."

"Why did they accompany you?" Gracian asked, and Javor had to take a deep breath to quell the surge of anger the question aroused.

"They insisted on coming. The idiots probably thought they could get a little glory from defeating a monster. Then the rest of the townspeople got mad at me when their people died. I left as quickly as I could."

"You fulfilled their request," Malleus said. "You had no more obligation to them. As for the men who died, was it their choice to accompany you?"

"The priest in the town chose them and told them to come. I couldn't make them stay behind."

"It is good that the local priest leads the community," Gracian said.

Javor turned to him. "Why?"

"The Church is the civilizing influence in the world," Gracian answered. "Local priests are typically the only learned men in smaller, remote communities, far from the centre in Constantinople. They can exert a moralizing influence, leading their people to the Truth."

"This priest was an idiot," Javor said, and Gracian gasped at the word. "He sent men to their death. I told him I preferred to go alone. I—" Javor's eyes traveled beyond Gracian to Malleus. He saw a signal that had taken more than a year to learn to interpret. A slight shake of the head, just a fractional movement to the left, combined with a frown of the eyebrows and a widening of the eye. After months of practice, Javor had learned it meant "Shut up now."

Javor took a deep breath.

"Is there anything else you can tell us about the beast?" Malleus asked.

Javor glanced at Malleus again and got the look. "I had to stab out its eyes to blind it before I could kill it."

The colour drained from Gracian's face. He turned away.

"Thank you, Javor," Malleus said, his eyes on Gracian.

One of the other men with Malleus, Zeno, hurried to refill Javor's wine and pushed the cup into his hand. Javor drank, closing his eyes. Slowly, his breathing and pulse slowed. "I am tired, Malleus. I am going home now." He gave the cup back to Zeno, turned and walked out of the monastery without another word.

There was one more duty, though, before he returned home. One more visit to make.

Darko was the son of a Gothic chieftain who had styled himself King. Javor had first encountered the young man as a child, five years earlier in the Alps, when he went on his first mission for the Order, in search of his own great-grandfather's dagger which had been stolen.

Darko's mother was the Gothic Queen who called herself Kriemhild and claimed to have been the fourth wife of Attila, King of the Huns. She had intended Darko as a human sacrifice, in an attempt to manipulate some of the power of the bones of the earth, and bring down the Roman Empire at last. The self-sacrifice of his father had saved the boy from his mother's blade.

With the defeat and death of Queen Kriemhild, and the help of the advanced, secretive Kobold people of the Alps, Javor had returned to Constantinople with the injured Tiana, Malleus, and Darko. Darko's sister, Danisa, Javor's one-time lover and the first to steal his dagger, came, too, as a prisoner. Javor left her with the Convent of St. Mary of Chalkoprateia, the nunnery side of the Order's host abbey. He counted on them to keep her confined within their cloisters for the rest of her life. She was too dangerous to let loose, but Javor could not bring himself to kill her.

That left him with Darko, a seven-year-old orphan. Not knowing what else to do with a child as he started a new life in the capital city, Javor left the boy in the care of the monks. He tried to make a point of visiting regularly, but over the years, the frequency of his visits had decreased at the same rate as his guilt had increased.

I will visit more frequently. But if the Order keeps sending me on these damned missions ...

The monk in charge of the novices, a strict, unsmiling man named Bartholomew, led the now twelve-year-old Darko to Javor. They walked out of the Abbey's main gate to stroll around the Chalkoprateia area, the copper market, close to the Hagia Sophia or Church of Holy Wisdom, the Hippodrome and, of course, the Great Palace.

"How have you been?" Javor asked.

The boy was tall for his age compared to most of the Constantinopolitans. He had thick, curly hair that had not been tonsured, yet, and bright blue eyes like his father. He looked over both shoulders before answering. "Miserable. As always." His head drooped. He seemed to stare at his bare toes.

"Miserable? Why?"

"I hate it at the Abbey," the boy whined. "It's so boring. All they do all day is work and pray. Up before dawn to pray, then work in the barn or sweeping a chapel, then more praying, and more praying. And the food is awful."

"Awful? At least, you get to eat every day. That was not the case for me when I was your age."

Darko rolled his eyes. "Oh, yes, grown-ups always had it so much harder. I hate it, Javor. I wish I was back in Pannonia with the Ostrogoths."

"The Ostrogoths were destroyed decades ago. You are only alive because you are here in the capital."

Darko stopped walking and faced Javor. "Then I wish I was anywhere else!" he shouted. "With the Avars. Out of this damned city. On a horse." He hung his head again.

Javor could not think of a response. They stood there for a long moment, Javor looking at Darko, Darko looking at the ground, as the crowds of Constantinople's streets streamed around them. Finally, Javor clasped the boy's shoulder. "I am sorry. Perhaps you can live with me, now."

Darko's eyes snapped up to Javor's. "With you? I would rather live with serpents than with you."

Again, Javor did not know what to say. "But ... why?"

Fixing Javor in his gaze, Darko snarled, "You killed my parents. You locked my sister in a convent. We only want to be free."

"Darko, your mother killed your father. We both saw it. And she was swallowed by the bones—"

"My name is Ana-Kui, not 'Darko,'" the boy hissed. "And my parents would still be alive if it weren't for you and all the damned Christians."

"Stop swearing. And if I had not arrived, your mother would have slit your throat as an offering to her gods."

"You are the same as all these damned Christians. A liar." He turned on his heel and stalked back to the Abbey. Javor followed until he saw the boy go through the gates, then returned home, sad.

The sun was low in the sky by the time he heard the gate of his villa clang shut behind him. The head servant, a thin, bald man named Gaetan, bowed and said, "My lord," as Javor gave him his chlamys cloak.

"Where is Aunt Tiana?" he asked, but the servant did not need to answer as Javor looked down the hall. A small woman walked with slow, careful steps across the marble floor, one hand on the wall to steady herself. Her light brown hair was pinned back and high on her head and she wore a simple, long white tunic with a blue pattern at the hem. Her only jewel was a single gold bracelet on her right wrist.

She smiled, revealing perfect white teeth, and her green eyes sparkled as she came close. "Javor," she said slowly, her voice weak. Javor knew she was in her mid-thirties, but her voice sounded like an old woman's.

Javor stepped closer and embraced her, kissed her on both cheeks and gently led her to a couch below a tapestry that Calanthe had picked out. He hated it. "Prepare a meal for us," he said to the head servant. "Aunt Tiana and I will take it in the garden."

The servant bowed and left. Briefly, Javor wondered why he did not replace the man. He had freed him from slavery when he had bought the villa from Rutius and Barbara, the owners of the Inn of the Four Winds, which backed onto the house. The house came with four slaves: a cook named Michael, a cleaning woman named Kyriake, Honorius, a groomsman who also maintained the gardens, and Gaetan, who bossed the others around. Hating the idea of slavery, Javor had freed them all, then hired them as servants in his new home. But Gaetan had always struck him as sullen. Javor sometimes wondered if Gaetan resented his freedom. He could not remember the man ever smiling, ever answering with more than two or three words. "Yes, my lord." "No, my lord."

"I am not a lord, Gaetan," Javor would say.

"Yes, sir." But he still would not smile, nor engage with Javor in any way other than as a servant.

Javor returned his attention to Tiana. "How have you been while I was away?"

"Well enough. I feel a little stronger each day."

"You always say that," said Javor. She did not look stronger—if anything, she seemed thinner and frailer than she had weeks earlier, when he left. "Have you been eating?"

"Oh, yes," she said, almost a whisper, and gave him a weak smile. "Of course. Michael is a wonderful cook."

"Not that wonderful. I prefer Barbara's bread." Barbara was the co-owner of the Inn of the Four Winds with her husband, Rutius. The rough inn and tavern was the first place he stayed when he had arrived in Constantinople six years earlier.

Not only did Barbara make very good white bread, which Javor loved much more than the coarse barley bread he remembered his own mother cooking, she had also helped arrange his marriage to the daughter of a rich merchant who had once been Rutius' friend. Of course, that was before Mauricius' growing wealth had led him to aspire to a higher class.

"Come," Javor said, holding out his hands, focusing on the moment before memories of his mother brought tears to his eyes again. He helped Tiana rise from the couch, and held her by the elbow, with his other hand around her back, as they walked down the hall.

"Really, Javor, I can walk by myself," she protested.

"This floor is slippery," he answered, keeping his hands on her until they reached the peristyle garden, an open area surrounded by a stone wall at the back of his house. He could hear and smell the chicken coop, hidden in the corner behind a lattice screen and a low but wide tree that blossomed with purple petals in the early summer.

They sat on low couches, facing each other. Kyriake came out of the kitchen, carrying a small table that she set onto the stone floor between the couches. She was a short, small woman who covered her thick, coarse black hair with a light blue kerchief. She had large, dark eyes, a bump in her nose, and thick lips. After setting down the table, she gave Javor a little bow and then seemed to fade into the background.

Gaetan followed her. He set a tray on the table, giving Javor and Tiana an opening course of olives, bread, a plate of carrots and parsnips in wine sauce. He put cups in front of the diners and poured them full of white wine. "Michael is preparing a main course of mullet with greens. It will be ready momentarily, my lord."

"Stop calling me 'my lord.' I'm not a lord. I have told you that."

"Yes, sir." Gaetan turned away, took Kyriake by the elbow and ushered her to the kitchen.

Tiana's cup trembled as she raised it to her lips, but Javor let her drink with her own strength. She set the cup down and dabbed her lips with a kerchief. "What did you learn on your voyage?" she asked, her voice hoarse.

"Just a new mystery," Javor said. He shoved a handful of carrots into his mouth, took a big bite of bread and gulped down half a cup of wine as he dug into his pocket for the medallion he had taken from Paphlagonia. He nearly choked. "Damn! Why did Michael give us retsina again?"

Tiana chuckled. "You have to get used to it, Javor."

"Why? Why do I have to get used to wine that's been flavoured with tree sap to make it too sour to drink? Who likes this piss, anyway?"

Tiana shook her head as Javor bellowed for Gaetan. When the thin, dour man entered the courtyard, Javor hoisted the jug of wine. "Bring us something suited to human beings, not this swill!"

Gaetan bowed and backed away.

"What do you have there, Javor?" Tiana asked.

To get rid of the taste of the resin-flavoured wine, Javor bit off another chunk of bread. He put the medallion on the table in front of Tiana. "I found this—well, no, actually, another man found this—in the den of the monster I was sent to kill." The medallion weakly reflected the waning light of the day.

Tiana's eyes widened. She reached for the medallion, but Javor took it between his hands to hide it from view as Gaetan reappeared with another jug and hurriedly filled Tiana's and Javor's cups.

When Gaetan withdrew, Javor gave the medallion to Tiana, who lifted it close to her eyes. It filled both her cupped hands. She squinted first at one side then the other. "That is the symbol of Hecate, the Triune Goddess," she whispered.

"Hecate? One of the ancient Greek goddesses?"

"With different names, but very similar symbols, she is worshipped even today, and in many more places than only Greece." The wine seemed to have lubricated Tiana's throat, and her speech was getting more fluid. "She is one of the oldest gods, and her followers are widespread, if secretive."

"She's the goddess of witches and magic, right?" Javor poured more wine for Tiana and himself.

"She is so much more than that." Tiana's voice was stronger, confident. "She is the Triune Goddess, three aspects in one, often depicted with three heads or as three women at once: the Maiden, the Mother and the Crone. She is the protectress, the nurse, the goddess of portals and crossroads, the bringer of light. She is also known as Selene, the moon, as well as the huntress on earth, and the destroyer in the underworld."

Javor hid the medallion again as Kyriake came out and set plates in front of both of them. It was Javor's favourite dinner: mullet and green beans. He shoveled a forkful of fish into his mouth. "This Hecate seems contradictory," he said, his voice muffled by the food. "Protector and destroyer? Is she a friend or an enemy?"

Tiana shook her head. "You know by now, Javor, that gods, demons, archons and aeons do not act either according to or contrary to the wishes or designs of humanity. They act according to their own wishes and plans." She took a small bite, the fork trembling in her hand.

"Then why do they demand so much worship?"

The daylight was nearly gone from the little courtyard, and Gaetan came out again with a candelabrum. Javor again hid the medallion. Gaetan set the candles on a stand behind Tiana, throwing her elegant, delicate profile into backlit relief for Javor, and hiding much of the rest of the courtyard. He noticed the full moon had just risen above the wall. A thin cloud, pulled by a wind he could not feel, passed over its face.

Gaetan went inside again. Tiana watched the door close before answering. "Humanity chooses to worship what they perceive as deities, Javor. Hecate is not the true name of this goddess. That is just a human metaphor for a force far greater than men can comprehend. Hecate is an older power. Her worship arose long before the Olympian gods. She is a chthonic goddess, the force of life, itself."

"Moist Mother Earth," Javor said. "That was the most important god of my people." He drew out his great-grandfather's dagger. Tiana looked at it, then at him, a question on her face.

Javor held the dagger so the candlelight reflected off the curved blade. The handle, he had always thought, was shaped like a fish, and the long blade, made of a dark coloured metal, was engraved with symbols. He pointed to one near the handle. "Is this not the same symbol?"

Tiana glanced at it. "Yes, it is. I noticed that the first time I saw the blade, five years ago."

"You never mentioned it."

Tiana shook her head. "No? Well, there are many different symbols on the blade, and it is not unusual for old weapons, like yours, to bear the symbols of many gods to invoke their protection. For instance," she pointed to another symbol, "That is a symbol of Ashur, the Assyrian god of war." She turned over the blade. "And that one is a symbol of Pallas Athena, the Greek goddess of—"

"War and wisdom. Yes, I know. That much, I know."

"When we first saw your blade, Austinus and I—" She stopped, raising her hand in front of her face, and looked down. Javor saw a tear glisten in the corner of her eye, then slide down, leaving a trail that reflected the yellow candlelight. "I am sorry. I still cannot say his name without crying. Even after five years."

Javor took her hand between his. "I am sorry. I miss him, too."

Tiana nodded and sniffed, staring into the dark courtyard without seeing. After some time, she took a deep breath and turned toward Javor again. When she spoke, her voice was a hoarse whisper again. "When we first saw your great-grandfather's dagger, Austinus and I were more interested, no, fascinated by the other marks, the ones we had never seen before. It took us much time, and searching through many old writings and other sources, to interpret the runes that mention 'the bones of the earth.'"

Javor looked over his shoulder to make sure that they were still alone, then reached under his tunic and pulled out the amulet he always wore. He pulled the fine chain over his head and held the amulet under the candlelight. "Do you see this symbol in the centre?" He flipped the medallion over, showing other symbols. "It's the same as that one."

Tiana's eyes grew wide. Her mouth opened, but no sound came out for a long time. Finally, she said, "Javor, this cannot be a coincidence."

"What do you mean?"

She gulped down the rest of her wine. "Tell me what happened in Paphlagonia."

"It went mostly as I expected," he replied. He put away his dagger, amulet and the medallion, then ate the remainder of the bread and parsnips. "Malleus and the Order received a request from this little town, that they were being plagued by a monster that was killing not only their flocks and livestock, but had started killing people, hunters and shepherds, too." He swallowed the rest of his wine to wash down the meal, and leaned back on the couch. "When I arrived there, the parish priest insisted that a group of men accompany me to 'help' me find the monster. The problem was, none of them had actually seen the monster before, and could not tell me anything about its habits. They had only a vague idea of where it might be found. Of course, it was up in a rocky, barren highland."

"How many men accompanied you?" Tiana asked, her voice beginning to recover.

"Nine. That stupid priest said, 'three times three,' that the power of the Trinity would protect us and ensure success."

"But with you, that would be ten men."

Javor shrugged and chomped down the last of the bread. Gaetan and Kyriake appeared again. As Gaetan poured more wine, Kyriake put plates with cake in front of Javor and Tiana, and took away the platters and plates from their meal. Javor waited until they were gone before continuing his story. "I told you, the priest was stupid. All that he accomplished was to kill eight men."

Tiana's hand went to her throat. "Only one survived?"

"Right. Half the men insisted it was a dragon, but it was more like a snake, but with a head as big as an ox's, and as long as ... I do not know. Very long, maybe ten fathoms. I did not measure it.

"It attacked us when we came close to its nest. One by one, it killed the men. It ate two of them, swallowed them whole. I believe the only thing that kept it from killing me was Preyatel"—the Sklavenik word for "friend," which he had named the amulet that he had inherited along with the dagger. "At times, it seemed like the snake could not see me.

"Its scales were impervious to all blades but my great-grandfather's. I had to stab out both of its eyes before I could kill it. By then, there were only two other men left alive. Then one of the fools went into its lair and brought out that medallion. And that, of course, led to his death."

"What do you mean?" Tiana said, her voice strong again. She sat back, sipping wine.

"The fool thought he was rich and ran ahead of me and the other man left alive. But as I knew would happen, the earth began to shake after the monster died. The same thing has happened every time I have destroyed one of those ... things. You remember five years ago, in the mountains in the north."

"I can never forget," Tiana said, her eyes tearing up again.

"In Paphlagonia, the fool fell off a cliff and impaled himself on his own spear. His body was still clutching that medallion."

The twilight was gone. Javor stood to wrap a blanket around Tiana's shoulders. "Now explain to me what you meant, that finding the medallion was not a coincidence."

"Like your amulet and dagger, Javor, these objects are not inanimate objects. Many have an affinity to one another. An attraction. You were meant to find this medallion."

"Meant by whom?"

"I do not know, Javor. Perhaps by Hecate."

"What does Hecate want from me?"

Tiana shook her head sadly. "I cannot begin to guess."

# A private meeting

The next morning, Gaetan interrupted Javor's training session in the garden. Honorius, holding thick pads that Javor punched and kicked, looked relieved.

"There is a monk at the front gate who insists on speaking to you, sire."

"A monk? Who?"

"I know not, sire. He will only say that he is from the Abbey of St. Mary of Chalkoprateia."

That was enough for Javor. He took a cloth to wipe sweat from his face and followed Gaetan through the atrium and the front courtyard.

Just beyond the gate, on the cobbled street stood a monk in a habit, his hood over his head. "Yes? What is it?" Javor demanded.

The monk said nothing, but beckoned Javor closer. He stopped at the gate. The monk lifted the front of his hood just enough to let some of the morning sunlight illuminate half his face.

*Malleus.*

*In disguise.*

Javor turned to Gaetan. "Thank you, Gaetan. I recognize this Brother. You may go."

Looking disappointed, Gaetan bowed and disappeared into the

domus.

"Malleus. This is ... an honour."

Malleus threw the hood off, his smile splitting his face. He slapped Javor on the shoulder. "Today is an auspicious day, my friend. Get your cloak and come with me!"

"Where?"

"To see a great event: General Priscus has returned from successful action against the Gepids and brings his prisoners to parade along the Mese. You cannot miss this. Come!"

The Mese was Constantinople's broad, main avenue from the Golden Gate in the massive Theodosian Walls, through the Forum of Arcadius to the Great Palace. It was a short walk from Javor's domus in the Vlanga section of the city.

Javor called Gaetan again to bring him a cloak and a bowl of water. He quickly rinsed some of the sweat off his face and neck, threw the cloak around his shoulders, put on a hat and strode uphill with Malleus.

The side streets were already choked with people as they approached the broad avenue. Malleus and Javor worked their way as close as they could to the edge of the Mese.

Javor was tall enough to see over the heads of most of the Constantinopolitans, but Malleus had to stand on his toes and crane his neck.

What they saw, first, was a glorious troop of legionnaires bearing long spears, their armour shining, bristles on their helmets tall and proud, their scarlet cloaks bouncing in time with their steps.

Behind them, the prisoners: dirty men in ragged, torn clothes, chained at the wrists and ankles, shoulders slumped, heads hanging, exhausted and defeated.

"The Gepids," Malleus said. "It is said that Priscus defeated them in four consecutive battles, killing thirty thousand, and bringing back eighteen thousand prisoners."

Javor's mind whirled at the numbers. Thirty thousand dead? He tried to imagine thirty thousand dead bodies on a field, then pushed away the horrifying image. He concentrated on watching the parade of misery and pride.

Malleus leaned his head on Javor's shoulder. His voice was low, soft, his words quick. "I am walking a very narrow path, my friend. The emperor understands how vital the Order's support will be. And I mean the Order, the secret Gnostic Order, not the Order of St. Mary of Chalkoprateia."

Javor kept his eyes on the endless parade of ragged, chained men.

"That means that now, secrecy is more important than ever," Malleus continued. No one else could hear them. Javor concentrated to make certain that he did not miss a word.

"That is because we must be seen to be working closely with the Church and the Patriarch in resisting, and defeating the enemies of Rome. But the position of the Orthodox Church of Rome has hardened against perceived heretics, outsiders and especially Gnostics."

"Then why work with them?" Javor asked, keeping his voice as low as Malleus'.

"Because protecting civilization will require more than the Order and the Empire itself. Remember that Rome faces many enemies. The Sassanians. The Avars. The various barbarians that shattered the Western Empire. All civilizations, Roman and Sassanid, even the barbarians, must learn to resist the chthonic forces together, or we are lost. And I fear we will not find unity."

Prisoners continued to stream past, many stumbling, moving again only when whipped by the Legionnaires who marched, shining and proud along the edges of the Mese. Javor thought about Malleus' words. "What about Gracian?"

"Especially Gracian. Gracian comes from the Church. He is a believer in the decisions of the Ecumenical Council of Chalcedon. Which means he fervently rejects any deviation from the Orthodox doctrines."

"Then why have you made him your second-in-command?"

"The Patriarch insisted. That is what I mean by a narrow path. I must be able to mobilize the full strength of the secret Order—such as you, Javor—in secret, without the knowledge of the Church, yet in coordination with it.

"That means, Javor, that you and I will have to limit our direct communication. And you must never, never mention anything about the Order, Gnostic knowledge or anything about our true nature in Gracian's presence. Do you understand?"

Javor nodded, feeling a tingle in his spine and a weight in his gut.

# Life in Constantinople

Javor and Tiana were finishing their breakfast the next day when Gaetan entered and bowed. Before he could say a word, Mauricius Macedonius strode into the atrium, booming, "Good morning, son-in-law!" He bent to kiss Javor's cheeks before Javor could rise, then turned to kiss Tiana. "And good morning, Aunt Tiana. I trust you are well."

Tiana nodded, giving the rich man a confused smile.

Javor stood, brushing bread crumbs from his tunic. "Good morning. Why are you here?"

Mauricius laughed deeply and clapped Javor on the shoulders. "Are you not happy to see your father-in-law again?"

"No, I mean, yes, I am happy to see you, but I did not expect ..."

"And I bring you a gift, my son-in-law," Mauricius interrupted, laughing.

"A gift?" Mauricius' hands were empty.

"I bring you a wife. Your wife." Mauricius laughed again, then clapped his hands together. "Come, Calanthe. Come here, right now. Do not keep your husband waiting. You see, Javor, I am returning your beautiful bride, my daughter, to her rightful place in your home. Calanthe," he called into the hallway that led to the front door. "Come, come Calanthe. You do move slowly. Come and kiss your husband."

Slowly, Calanthe stepped from the shade of the front wall of the atrium into the bright summer sunshine. She wore a yellow chiton, held at her shoulder by a gold brooch, and covered by a *stola* with rich brocade. Her dark, wavy hair spilled out from under a white veil on top of her head.

Her face was a stark contrast to the cheery colour of her clothing. When she looked at her father, Javor thought she was about to burst into tears. She turned to him and gave him a sad smile. "Good morning, husband," she said in a voice as weak as Tiana's. She came down the two steps from the front courtyard into the house proper, slowly and carefully. Her shoulders drooped and her back was bowed, and she sighed deeply when she had to stand on her toes to kiss Javor's cheeks.

Javor took her hands in his. "What is wrong, my love?"

Calanthe sank onto one of the couches and sighed again before answering. "I am so tired since the baby was born," she whispered. "She rarely gives me any rest."

"Oh, nonsense," Mauricius scoffed. "Martha does most of the looking after the baby, and soon you will have a wet nurse to do all the feeding. It is only for your own health that you need to nurse the baby for the first days."

As if on cue, Martha, the old nurse, carried the baby Andrina, wrapped in white cloth, into the atrium. "You daughter is very healthy, my lord," Martha said.

"I am not a lord," Javor replied, but he could not look away from the baby. Her eyes, an impossibly intense blue colour, seeming to take up so much of her tiny face, were fixed on his, too.

"She knows her father, my lord," Martha said.

Hesitantly, Javor reached for his daughter, tracing the tip of a finger along her cheek. So soft.

Gaetan surprised Javor by dashing across the atrium, then backing up again and bowing as Anna swept in. This day, she wore a chiton the same yellow as her daughter's, but her stola over-cloak was far more richly brocaded, with golden threads and a huge jeweled brooch at her shoulder.

Her veil was far back on her head, revealing so much of her wavy hair that it was almost, but barely not quite, scandalous in Constantinople. Her smile was so wide, Javor could not help smiling back.

"Good morning, Javor," she said brightly, striding up to kiss Javor's cheeks. She took Andrina from Martha's arms, kissed her on the nose and then gave her to Javor.

Javor could feel his heart pounding as he gathered the baby in his arms. Fearing to drop or crush her, he managed to hold her steadily against his chest.

"It is past time your wife and firstborn child returned to your home," Anna said, stroking the baby's head, covered in a fine fuzz. She turned as Gaetan returned to the atrium, carrying a bundle in his arms. Behind him came three of Mauricius' slaves, also carrying bundles. One carried a wooden cradle.

"Shall I take Lady Calanthe's effects to the bedchambers?" Gaetan asked. He looked grumpier than usual.

Javor's mouth opened, but no sound came out. "Yes, of course," Anna answered for him. She strode into the house, turning toward the bedrooms. "I will tell you where things must go. Men are useless when it comes to children."

Javor let out a huge breath when Martha took the baby and followed Anna and the servants. He sat beside his wife and took her hands again. She looked like she was sleeping, slumped against the back of the couch, her eyes closed.

"Oh, stop playing at being tired," Mauricius growled. "You'd think you were the only woman to ever have a baby. All this fuss over clothing and furniture and decoration, that is what is exhausting you. God knows it is exhausting me."

In the nursery, Anna directed her slaves in arranging furniture and clothing, ordering the precise placement of cradle and couches for the nurses. She had even brought new curtains for the window. "You will repaint these shutters," she told Gaetan. "They are in terrible condition, and not at all suitable for my granddaughter."

When the nursery plans met her satisfaction, Anna went to Javor and Calanthe's bedroom, ordering the slaves to install new bedclothes and thick, soft pillows. "And honestly, Calanthe, you will have to get new curtains here, as well," she told her daughter. "These are completely tattered. How anyone can sleep in a room with such poor window coverings, I cannot understand. Javor, really, I know you are a man, but you have to consider your wife's comfort, too."

"Yes, Mother Anna," Javor mumbled, his head whirling with the changes happening all around him.

Next, Anna directed the slaves to clear out a room used to store things Javor did not care about, and install beds and other furnishings for two servants: Martha, the nurse, and Lydia, a small teenage girl with brown skin, thick black hair, large dark eyes and a twisted left arm that was shorter than the right. "This is Lydia, the wet-nurse," Anna said.

"Will she live here?" Javor asked, his throat tight and his voice high.

"Just until the baby is weaned," Anna said. "Then we will sell her to another family that needs her."

Javor had to think to draw a breath. "A slave? I told you, I have no slaves in my house. Too many of my people have been enslaved. I see them all over the city. It makes me sick."

Mauricius patted him on the back. "Do not argue with a woman about caring for children, Javor. We know you do not want slaves, but we are not giving her to you. She still belongs to us. We are only letting you use her. And we will take care of selling her when we're done with her. It will not be your worry for a moment."

"Sell her? She is a human being."

Martha brought baby Andrina in at that moment and handed her to Lydia. The wet nurse held the baby in her right arm. With her twisted left hand, she pulled her tunic from her breast to allow the baby to nurse.

Mauricius pushed Javor gently out of the nursery. "Of course, she is. She comes highly recommended. We would not have just anyone wet-nurse our granddaughter. Come now."

They found Anna in the kitchen, instructing Michael, the cook, in what to prepare for Calanthe and Lydia. "A nursing mother needs the right nourishment for the benefit of the baby," she concluded. "When the baby is weaned, I will instruct you in how to cook for her."

"I know what to cook for a child," Michael protested, "my lady."

"Not as much as I do," Anna snapped. She turned to Javor. "How can you tolerate servants talking back to you like this, Javor? Really, you need to keep them in their place."

"Apologies, my lady," said Michael, bowing.

"Are you satisfied now, my dear?" Mauricius asked.

Calanthe nodded wearily, but Anna said, "Of course not, but it will have to do for now." And they left, refusing Javor's blurted offering of a meal.

Javor sat down, thinking about how much his life had changed overnight. He now had two new servants in his house—one a slave, he reminded himself. And a child.

*Everything is so much more complicated, now.*

At the end of an especially hot summer day, Javor and Calanthe went to the rooftop of their domus, seeking whatever breeze could be found in the great city.

They lay together on a couch, sipping wine as they watched the last of the sunset fade. Beyond the city walls, the calm waters of the Propontis slowly turned from golden to black.

*This wine is so good. Mauricius must have brought it in from Crete or somewhere like that,* Javor thought.

"You know, Javor, I missed you very much," Calanthe said.

"You did?"

She squirmed around a little to kiss him on the cheek. "Yes, of course, I missed my husband. Especially in the last days before Andrina's birth. And when the first pains came, there was no one I wanted with me more than you."

"Did you not want the midwife? Or your mother?"

Calanthe laughed a little. "Yes, of course. And they were with me. But I still wanted you with me."

"But I could not have been with you when the baby was born. That is what your father explained to me."

"Well, no," Calanthe admitted. She rolled over so that she was looking down on Javor lying on the couch. "But after all, my condition was your fault." She smiled and kissed him on the lips. Javor tried to pull her body against him, but she giggled and rolled away to pick up her own cup of wine. "Where were you, Javor? You were gone for weeks. Did you have to be so long? To miss the birth of your first child?"

Javor looked toward the Propontis again. The sun had set, leaving only fading blue and purple glows above the horizon. *Another hot day tomorrow,* he thought. He sighed. "I swore not to tell anyone about my mission," Javor answered. "All that I can tell you is that it was for the Church and the Empire."

"The Church and the Empire? Is there even a difference?" She cuddled up against him again, squirming to find a comfortable position lying against him.

He did not know how to answer that, so he looked at the sky. The first stars began to glimmer.

"Javor?" she asked after finishing her cup of wine. "Will you have to go away again?"

Taking care that his wife would not notice, Javor touched his amulet through his tunic. It was still, quiet. No danger.

"Not for now," he answered. "There is nothing happening now that requires my ... skills."

"Which skills are those?" she asked, snuggling more.

He leaned forward and kissed her hair. He inhaled her scent, sweet and spicy at the same time. He kissed her cheek, and when she turned to him, her mouth.

"Ahem," he heard.

Javor looked up to see Gaetan standing near the steps that led down to the courtyard. He held a jug in one hand. "Will my lord require more wine?"

Calanthe gasped and sat up quickly, her hand in front of her chest, even though she wore a gown that covered her from her neck to her ankles.

"Just leave the jug on the table," Javor growled. "Then leave us alone, Gaetan."

The senior servant bowed just a little and put the jug on the little table beside Javor. He bowed again and walked off the rooftop.

*Is he mocking me?* Javor wondered.

Javor refilled his wife's cup with wine. When she had drunk, he leaned in for another kiss.

"Javor, not here," she protested.

He leaned closer and kissed her deeply. He pulled her closer, feeling her resist, then relax against him. "Oh, Javor," she sighed.

He kissed her neck, pulling at her gown. "No, Javor, not here," she whispered.

"Why not? It is too hot in the bedroom."

"We are outside, Javor."

"No one can see us," he answered, kissing her throat, then moving lower. "Besides, anyone else on their rooftop now is doing the same thing."

"But we are outside," she protested, but did not resist as he opened her tunic and kissed the top of her breast. She helped him pull her gown off, and helped him to pull off his clothes. Her eyes lingered for a moment on his amulet, but then closed when he caressed her naked back and kissed her throat. He moved lower, savouring the feeling and the taste of her naked skin.

They made love as the gentle stars grew brighter, and fell asleep in the cooling night on the roof.

"Just look how she has grown, my lord," Martha exclaimed one morning. "Just look at her going."

At five months, Andrina sat on a cushion on the floor in the open atrium, enjoying uncharacteristic late autumn sunshine with her father and nurse. She had just learned to sit up by herself, and she gazed around the atrium with wide, wondering eyes. Drool shone on her chin. Her round head was covered in soft, dark hair, thin as the fuzz on a peach. She wore a white gown trimmed with blue.

Martha beamed at her, clapping every time the baby girl gurgled, waved a hand or kicked a foot.

Javor knelt in front of the baby, holding out a finger. She reached out and wrapped her tiny hand around it. Javor shook it up and down, shaking the baby's whole arm in the process, and made nonsense words until Andrina giggled. He laughed, too.

He surprised himself when he realized how much he enjoyed playing with his baby, feeding her soft, sweet treats she could gum down, just being a father.

"Hasn't she grown?" Martha repeated. "Look at how strong she is!" she said when Andrina shook Javor's finger up and down and kicked at the same time.

"Yes, she has grown," Javor agreed, and made faces at his daughter until she giggled again.

"Where is my Lady Calanthe?" Martha asked, bending down to stroke the baby's soft head. Andrina turned too fast and toppled on her side. Martha gasped and quickly righted her as the baby kicked and cooed.

"Still sleeping," Javor answered, rising. He frowned as he felt a slight warmth on his chest. He stepped away from Martha and the baby, conscious that the amulet, Preyatel, under his shirt was vibrating slightly. What was it trying to tell him?

"Sleeping? At this hour?" She picked the baby up and hurried to place her on a wooden chair. She began to put small morsels of bread, soaked in milk, into the baby's mouth. Andrina swallowed them eagerly, opening her mouth for more.

Gaetan walked into the atrium, interrupting his thoughts. "A message for you, sir," he intoned and handed Javor a small parchment scroll. He bowed and left.

Javor frowned, annoyed. The scroll bore a wax seal with the icon of the Church of St. Mary of Chalkoprateia. That meant it came from

Malleus.

He broke it open and unrolled it. Written in Malleus' aggressive style, the message had his unapologetic, authoritative tone, without preamble. "Come to the Abbey as soon as possible. Urgent matters demand your attention. Malleus."

Malleus. Javor sighed. He had no excuses not to go. "Tell Calanthe, if she ever gets out of bed, that I am going to the Abbey. I will be back — well, I do not know when I will be back."

Martha looked up, nodded, then returned her attention to the baby, who was reaching up with both hands. "Not yet, my angel. As soon as you finish ..."

Javor found Malleus and Gracian in the counsel room of the head of the Order. Gracian stood beside Malleus' chair, fidgeting with his fingers and looking glum as Malleus paced beside the map table. Both their faces brightened when Javor entered.

"You've come at last," Gracian said. "I did not think it would take you so long."

Javor ignored him, but embraced Malleus and let the slim man kiss him on both cheeks. "It has been too long, my friend," Malleus said. "Months since I saw you. Do you not come to church anymore?"

"Calanthe prefers the Hagia Irene, where her parents attend," Javor shrugged. "It is easier to agree with her."

"Well, it's no closer to your home than we are, but still ..." Malleus' voice trailed off as his eyes turned to maps on the table. "But to the matter at hand. Javor, we have another mission for you."

"Another mission? Why?"

"You know why." Malleus' voice got lower and deeper. "This time, it's in your homeland, Javor. Sklavenia. North, near the Sarmatian Mountains."

"Demonic forces are moving against mankind," Gracian piped up, his voice high and strained. "We have reports, credible reports, of a demonic being, the personification of the Devil in female form. A hag who lives in a house made of the bones of her victims—"

"And the house moves on chicken legs?" Javor interrupted. "You are going to send me on a months-long journey to find a story we tell children to get them to behave?"

Gracian's mouth hung open, but no sound came out. His eyes were wide.

Malleus, on the other hand, looked grave. "It's more than a children's story. Yes, there have been exaggerations, people who conflate what they saw with the stories they heard in their youth. But we have sent investigators, and they have come back with credible reports, as Gracian said."

Javor shook his head and went to the sideboard, which as usual was well stocked with fruit, bread, cheese and wine. He poured himself a full cup. "So, some people think they have seen Baba Yaga. So what? What do you need me for?"

Gracian's voice was hoarse. "The Devil has raised his head in Sklavenia yet again, in the guise of a hag, and it is preparing—"

"Why are you whispering?" Javor interrupted again. "Are you afraid the scary old lady will appear in front of you and eat you up?"

"It may seem like a joke, or a children's story, but this is a serious situation," said Malleus.

"What do you want me to do? Kill an old lady?"

"This 'old lady' has killed entire villages. Your people, Javor. We need someone who cannot be harmed by this kind of evil, someone who looks at things and sees what is there, not what is in an old story. Someone who is immune to enchantment."

Javor popped a little cake into his mouth. Chewing, he said, "No, Malleus. This is not a mission for me."

Malleus stepped forward, arms spread in appeal. "Javor, we need you. Your people need you."

"I would have thought you would welcome the opportunity to return to your homeland," said Gracian, his voice still high.

Javor gulped down the rest of the wine. It was not good, but it was still not as bad as retsina. "There is nothing for me there," he said. "I am sorry, Malleus, but I will refuse this mission. I want to stay with my daughter and wife."

"Don't be ridiculous, Javor," Malleus said. "Stay at home and spoil the womenfolk? What kind of man does that?"

"The kind of man who has already proven himself killing monsters and facing hellish demons. I do not need this, Malleus."

"It is your duty, Javor."

"My duty? I have done my duty, Malleus. Or have you forgotten the mountaintop in Germania? Six years ago?"

"Your duty to the emperor and the Church does not end, Javor," Gracian interjected.

Javor turned to the second in command. "The Church? Do we answer to the Patriarch now?"

"Not directly, of course, Javor," Malleus said, talking fast. He glared at Gracian until his second-in-command shut his mouth and stepped back. "But the Roman Empire is the bulwark of human civilization, now. The walls against which the waves of barbarians break. The bastion of the light against the darkness that is determined to swallow humanity. And the Church is the mortar that binds the walls together."

"If the chthonic forces of darkness are going to swallow humanity, they're not going to do it with an old lady who scares children and has chicken legs," Javor said. "I am leaving. I am going home, to spoil my wife and my daughter. If you have a serious need, Malleus, send for me."

And he left.

# INTERLUDE 3

# Phocas Ascends

*Year 602 Christian Era*

The city of Constantinople is excited. Beyond excited. In tumult.

At the centre of the Roman Empire, the centre of the civilized world, the city is tired, resentful, angry toward the penury of its Augustus, its Basileus, Emperor Maurice.

Weary of new taxes on wine. On bread.

All Romans were weary. Weary of strident and enthusiastic tax collectors. Weary of two decades of sending its young men to wars in East and West.

"The army was starved," the city said.

"The brave legionnaires were sent to overwinter in barbarian lands, without pay.

"They were separated from their lands and their families.

"Without recompense for their labour, for their risks,

"For killing the enemies of Empire and of Christ."

The city, all the citizens of Rome, remember the prisoners. They tell each other the story of 12,000 men of the Army of the West, sent across the Danube frontier to strike a blow against the Avars, the barbarian steppe riders who had swept from Asia, their storms of arrows slaughtering legionnaires in the thousands.

The devils who had captured 12,000 brave Romans and demanded a ransom.

The Blues tell the Greens about the delegation led by Centurion Flavius Phocas, who came from beyond the Danube to Constantinople to plead for gold to ransom the poor, brave legionnaires.

The Greens tell the Blues how the emperor, the Augustus Maurice, refused to pay the ransom. And the Avars demonstrated the verity of their promises, and cut the throats of their prisoners. All 12,000 men.

Twelve thousand brave men.

Twelve legions.

Today, on a windy, bleak, grey November day, Blues and Greens come together to welcome the second delegation of the Army of the West. Flavius Phocas, the Centurion with flaming red hair and beard, pauses at the seven-mile marker outside the greatest city on Earth.

He presents his men's demands—not his own, no, not this humble representative of the courage of Rome. He wants no glory, no reward for himself. Only for the men who defended the City of God, the bastion of the One True God against the forces of darkness.

For the men who served and died bravely, with no regard for their own wealth.

No more than was reasonable.

No more than they could wrest from the barbarians, who lived lives benighted, worshiping pagan gods, devils in disguise.

Phocas, the brave centurion, presented his army's demands to the emperor, and the City, and the Empire.

"Step aside, Maurice, emperor of penury. Step aside in favour of your son, Theodosius, or the brave general, Germanus. Germanus, who defeated the Avars and Sklavenes and Sassanids.

"Step aside, Maurice. Lay down the regalia. Step out of the purple. The people of the Empire can no longer tolerate your austerity. The people of Constantinople will no longer accept privation. The Greens and the Blues are against you.

"We support Theodosius," say the Blues.

"No! Germanus," say the Greens.

Strife. A riot. "Germanus!" "Theodosius!"

The city sees Germanus retreat to the Hagia Sophia, the Church of Holy Wisdom, his wife and family with him for their protection against the strife between the factions, but Constantinople knows, he will need defence against the ire of the emperor who now sees Germanus as a pretender, as a man who could replace him on the throne.

On a late November day as the cold blows over the land walls, Constantinople watches as the Emperor Maurice, with his wife, Constantia, daughter of emperors, and their eight children descend from the Bucoleon Palace to the harbour, where Excubitors take them in a boat across the Marmara Sea to Nikomedia. From the walls, the city sees the eldest son mount a swift horse. The city of Nikomedia tells Constantinople that he rides across Anatolia to seek the aid of the King of Kings. Khosrau, the Shahinshah of Sassanid Persia, who owes his throne to the Augustus, the vice-regent of God on Earth, Maurice.

"We have no emperor!" the city shouts. "We have no one to rule us."

At the seven-mile marker outside the city, Phocas, the brave Centurion, the delegation of the Army, hears their calls.

"Senate and people of Constantinople! Romans," he calls. "Acclaim me as your new emperor. I will undo the tyranny of Maurice."

The Army raises Phocas on his shield and proclaims him Augustus in the same way the Roman Legions chose their emperors in centuries past. During the centuries of civil war. Through the days before the fall of Rome in the West, before the Eternal City was occupied by barbarians.

The Patriarch Cyriacus II places the imperial diadem on Phocas' head. The people adorn Phocas with purple. Four pure white Arabian horses bear Phocas' litter through the great Golden Gate near the Marmaran shore. The Blues and Greens alike cheer him along the Mese, the great main avenue of the greatest city in the world. The people cheer and chant "Phocas Augustus!" in Latin and "Phocas Basileus!" in Greek as the new emperor throws gold coins into the crowds.

At the Hippodrome, the City gathers to cheer. Phocas, the new emperor, watches chariot races celebrating his elevation. He distributes gifts from his new treasury to his troops and crowns his wife, Leontia, as Augusta.

He takes his place on the throne. Now there is only one thing left to do, to cement his place in power.

The city watches, caught between horror, outrage and righteous approval as Phocas' Legions drag the grey-haired Maurice and his family back to the Hippodrome. In the courtyard of the Great Palace, the new emperor sits in judgment of the old.

Bound with purple rope, Maurice, aged 63, kneels on the marble floor.

Legionnaires bring his younger brother, Petrus, the count of the palace, before him. The younger man is also bound, but his ropes are not purple. Dry blood stains his face and his torn clothing. Maurice says nothing, shows no emotion as his brother is put on the block and beheaded.

Maurice's face still betrays no emotion as, one by one, soldiers push his sons facedown on the block, and strike off their heads. Tiberius, Petrus, Paulus and Justin's bodies roll away, their blood staining the marble of the Bucoleon floor.

"Where is Theodosius, your eldest son?" Phocas demands. "Where is the heir to the throne?"

Maurice does not answer. The city holds its breath as they watch Maurice meet the usurper's stare.

At a nod from Phocas, a legionnaire pushes a young woman in front of Maurice. She holds a baby in her arms. It wails, and the weeping woman does not try to quiet it.

"Your youngest son, Justinian," Phocas says. "Tell me where Theophilus is, and I will spare him."

"That is not Justinian," Maurice replies, his voice even. "That is the infant son of his nurse, Epiphania. I thank you, lady, but I cannot allow you to sacrifice your child for mine."

The young woman sobs. There is confusion among the watching representatives of the Blues and Greens. After an agonizing time, another young woman, carrying another squalling baby, is brought before Phocas and Maurice.

The young woman shrieks. Emperor Phocas nods. A legionnaire draws his blade across the baby's throat. Blood flows red, the squalling ceases and the city groans. It had not thought of this outcome, but it knows that a usurper has no choice but to eliminate all rival claimants.

Maurice makes his only response, now. "Thou art just, oh Lord! And thy judgments are righteous."

A legionnaire pushes the old emperor's face down to the block. He does not resist, nor try to rise again when the soldier releases him. He stays still, silent, as the axe is brought down to sever his head from his neck.

The city exhales, not daring to doubt its support for the usurpation.

The first ever in the city of Constantinople. The first violent replacement of an emperor in New Rome.

The city does not dare to think of tomorrow.

Not yet.

# Part 2
# Adam
*Year 603 Christian Era*

# The hut of Baba Yaga

As a child, Javor had always slept on a bed that was little more than a pile of straw, sometimes covered with a cloth. When he first moved into his domus in Constantinople, he was amazed at the luxury of the feather-stuffed mattress in the bedroom. The softness, the comfort made falling asleep unaccustomedly easy. He woke feeling energized.

But this night felt different. As he dropped his dalmatica onto the sofa beside the bed, Calanthe was already asleep, or at least pretending to be. Javor took a last draught of white wine, leaving the cup on a table near the door for Gaetan to collect later.

Wearing only his short tunic, he stretched out on top of the covers beside his wife. The room was too warm from the brazier in the corner for him to want to cover up.

For a long time, he stared up at the ceiling, thinking of his meeting with Malleus and Gracian. *Baba Yaga. They are afraid of the witch that parents tell their children about, so they do not wander too far into the woods. Has Malleus completely lost his courage? His intelligence?*

He thought of the stories his mother had told him about Baba Yaga. Her hut that walked on chicken legs through the forest, turning to present its backside to anyone who came upon it, screaming until the interloper said the magic words: "Turn your back to the forest, your front to me."

Then the hut's secret door would crash open and, contrary to good sense, the traveler could enter. He remembered the story of the little girl—*what was her name?*—who came searching for a needle and thread. Baba Yaga imprisoned her and set her to cleaning the house, threatening to eat her if the girl did not perform satisfactorily. But because of their kindness and purity of heart, the prisoner was set free by Baba Yaga's poor cat and dog.

Javor pictured Baba Yaga as his mother had described her: tall, impossibly thin, with a nose so long it came out of her door long before the rest of her face appeared. He looked down and stepped over her ragged threshold.

Inside, her hut was much larger than it appeared on the outside. It was dominated by a huge clay stove with wide shelves for sleeping on the warmth.

Baba Yaga herself stood in the far corner, holding her arms outstretched from one corner of the hut to the other. She looked exactly as Javor's mother had described: skeletally thin, with arms like dead tree branches and a hunched back. The black kerchief on her head did nothing to control her wild grey hair, unruly as straw in a windstorm. Her nose had a high bump between her eyes, and extended past her face, curving down below her chin to terminate in a wart that sprouted black hairs. The rags that hung from her bony frame had no colour. Grey threads waved from their edges. "Well? What do you want?" she screeched in a voice that sounded like fingernails scratching along rough metal. "Tell me your name and your reason for intruding."

"Ah-ah-ah," was all that came from Javor's mouth. *Why am I afraid of an old woman?*

"I do not have time to wait for fools to find their words." The crone's voice sounded like metal scraping on stone. She picked up a broom and shook it over Javor's head.

"I—" Javor began. *What do I want? Why am I afraid?* Preyatel was still against his chest, calming him. *I have no reason to fear.*

Baba Yaga dropped her broom, which fell to the floor without a sound. She came toward Javor, floating a hand's breadth above the floor.

Her long nose touched Javor's. It felt cold and damp, like rotten cabbage. She smelled like cabbage, too, and garlic and rot. "Speak, fool!" she screamed.

Javor forced breath through his throat. "Why are you killing my people?" came out in a tiny squeak.

Baba Yaga's yellow eyes narrowed, and she drew away. "Do not accuse me, youngster," she cawed. "It is not I who preys on the people of the place the Roman oppressors call Sklavenia. Look to the sky-worshippers."

"Who is killing and eating my people?"

"The sky-worshippers," Baba Yaga repeated. "The sky-worshippers are changing the world."

"Who are the sky-worshippers? And how can anyone change the world?"

She pointed a bony finger downward. "Look at your great cities, young man. Look how they cover the moist earth with dead stone. Look how they smother the fecund soil. Even the city you live in would starve, did the sky-worshippers not bring grain from across the sea."

"Who are the sky-worshippers?"

The hag came closer and her mouth opened wide, then wider. Javor saw yellow teeth, and behind them, another row of white teeth, sharp, winking in the light from the fireplace.

*Why is there a fireplace and an oven in the same hut?*

"Believe in me, young warrior," said Baba Yaga in a voice like a choking horse. "Believe in only me, and your true friend and your own penis. Believe not in the visions in your eyes or your heart. The Earth has turned on humanity because the sky-worshippers have turned on the Earth. Preserve the bones of the earth. Believe only Moist Mother Earth, for she is your only salvation."

Baba Yaga retreated back to the corner of the hut. Javor felt the hut's legs tense, then begin running as the hut rocked from side to side.

The light in the hut began to fail. Baba Yaga fell into shadow and the details of the inside of the hut became obscure. Even Baba Yaga's voice became indistinct. The last he heard was her voice, like a knife scraping on a whetstone: "Trust your gut, young warrior. Trust not what you see in the light of the sun."

# Meeting with Danisa

The convent had smelled of incense, burning wax, boiling cabbage and unwashed female flesh the first time Javor had stepped inside it. The years had not changed it. He settled into a stiff, uncomfortable chair in the tiny visitation room, looking out a window made of uneven glass to a distorted grey sky. He adjusted the dagger on his belt and looked at the wooden screen that separated him from the person he had come to see. The convent strictly forbade men from seeing the sisters of Jesus within its walls.

Tiana had been able to offer nothing to interpret Javor's dream about Baba Yaga. It was a legend she was not aware of.

"Why do you think she mentioned the bones of the earth as well as Moist Mother Earth?" Javor had asked the following morning.

"It may be that you put that all together yourself," Tiana had answered. "Sometimes, a dream is just a dream. A mixture of memories coming together, like ingredients in a stew."

"It is a strange coincidence, is it not, that I should have a dream like that the very day Malleus and Gracian asked me to return to my homeland because of reports of Baba Yaga?"

Tiana shook her head. "There is nothing coincidental about it. Malleus told you something that reminded you of the old stories from your childhood. Childhood memories remain powerful to our souls throughout our lives."

That sounded plausible to Javor, but there was still something that bothered him about the dream.

So he went out in the morning to speak to the only other person in Constantinople who knew about the bones of the earth.

A door opened on the other side of the screen dividing the visiting room. He heard a chair scrape on the floor, then the door closing. On the other side of the cloth mesh window in the middle of the screen, he saw the light shift.

"How many years has it been since we last laid eyes on each other, Javor?" He would never forget the sound of Danisa's voice. She spoke Sklavenik, Javor's native tongue, which he had not used in years.

"Almost seven," he replied in the same language.

"You missed me."

"Sometimes," he admitted. When he closed his eyes, he saw her face, her thin nose, her big green eyes, her brown hair that cascaded down over her shoulders. He remembered how it felt between his fingers, remembered the taste of her lips and the curve where her neck became her shoulder. The sisters probably cut it all off so it could fit under their headdress.

"You still miss me because I was the first girl you ever had sex with, and I broke your heart."

"No," Javor said, turning from the screen to look out the window at the leaden sky. "And yes. You were not my first. And you did break my heart."

"Not your first?" Danisa scoffed. "You've never lied to me before, Javor." He could hear the smirk.

"I do not lie. It never works out."

Danisa was silent for a moment. Then she said "Well, you never told me."

"You never asked."

"Who was your first, then, Javor? Some miserable girl from your miserable little village in the wild? Or some horny old crone, desperate for the feeling of her lost youth?"

*Both*, he thought. *Number one and number two.* "That is not important now, Danisa. I came to ask you something." Javor could hear Danisa breathing, shallow and fast. He hesitated, asking himself yet again whether he should utter the next words in her hearing. *You have already decided this,* he reminded himself. "Tell me what you know about the bones of the earth."

He heard a slow, deep intake of breath. The chair's legs squeaked on the marble floor again. "What are you talking about?" Her voice was strained, as if she were choking.

"I'm talking about your mother, Kriemhild. The woman who called herself the Mountain Queen, who claimed to be the last wife of Attila, King of the Huns. Why did she want my great-grandfather's dagger?"

"Why should I tell you anything? You imprisoned me here, among these stupid virgins."

"You tried to steal my dagger," Javor reminded her. He felt frustration build inside him. "Your mother tried to kill me. She enlisted the help of—of monsters from hell! Tell me what you know."

"You had better lower your voice, or you'll upset the sisters and they'll scold you. They'll sentence you to reciting prayers for hours."

Javor realized he was standing and could almost look over the screen. His fists were clenched and his breathing rapid and harsh. He swallowed and wiped sweat off his forehead.

*Why am I reacting like this?*

The answer came to him in the same instant. *She is doing this to me. She is toying with me.*

He took a deep breath and sat down again. "Tell me why your mother wanted the bones of the earth."

Danisa laughed, a sound sharp and cold as an icicle. "That is a phrase I have not heard for years. I thought it was a fanciful idea."

"Your mother sent a monster to take them, and it killed my parents. She sent a dragon after me. Then she sent you, and you actually took the dagger from me. Tell me what it meant to her."

Danisa laughed her cold laugh again. "Take me out of here, and maybe I'll tell you everything I remember."

No matter how hard Javor looked at the cloth mesh, he could not see Danisa except in his memory. Green eyes, brown hair. She had been so beautiful. He wondered whether life in the convent had changed her looks. Had she become even thinner than she had been at 16? Or was she fat now? It was hard to imagine anyone getting fat on the food the nuns prepared.

"You know I can't take you from the convent. You pledged your life to God."

"I was forced to repeat a bunch of stupid vows in a language I barely understand. I don't care about your god, Javor. And I am thoroughly tired of this dreary nunnery, the tasteless food, the stink of candles. And no sex. Gods, I want to have sex again. I'd even ravish you again, Javor, if I could get my hands on you."

Javor felt his penis stiffen at her words. He could not shake from his mind the image of Danisa, naked on top of him. He wished for a glass of wine. Or water. Or something to smash his balls.

*Think clearly,* Javor.

"That's not possible, Danisa. I am married and I have a child."

Danisa laughed again, but it was a more genuine sound this time, hotter, coloured with regret. "When has that prevented anyone from fucking, Javor?"

*Concentrate on the reason you came here.* "Danisa, I cannot take you from here, but I will try to make your life easier. What goddess did your mother worship? Which one do you worship?"

Danisa scoffed. "Moist Mother Earth, and no other. How did you not know that?"

Javor took a deep breath. "What do you know about the bones of the earth?" he asked again.

Danisa's answering laugh was back to brittle and cold. "I will only tell you this, Javor: the bones of the earth have no more use for you than you have for a flea. If you want to know more, release me from this prison and send me a man with a hard cock."

The chair squeaked across the marble again, the door opened, then shut, and Javor was alone again.

# Return to the north

Javor stepped from the boat onto the dock, the Danuvius' green waters gurgling under the boards. *Drobeta,* he thought. *What a miserable looking town. I'll bet that the people here are just as isolated, just as ignorant and afraid as the people in Cromna.*

Another mission beyond the limes, the Empire's northern border. North of the Danuvius River. Back where I came from.

Malleus' words came back to him. "I am beginning to see a pattern, Javor," Malleus had said as sunlight streamed through the high windows of the Order's conference room, chasing away thoughts of dark forces and monsters in the night. "Chthonic threats at the edges of the Empire, eating away at our weakest fringes."

"There may be a strategy here," Gracian had piped up. "And if so, we must bring the light of the One True God to bear on these dark forces before they bear down on the new Jerusalem."

While Javor had sneered at the superstition of Malleus and Gracian over tales that sounded like his parents' stories of Baba Yaga, they had found new arguments for him to travel north and investigate "strange activity." A legionnaire, or more precisely, a Sklavenik warrior in one of the troops federated to Rome, had arrived, claiming he had seen a dragon.

This was Radek, a small young man with fair hair, cropped in the Roman style. He was thin and wiry, and his head came up to Javor's chin. He dressed in Sklavenik style, with a loose tunic and trousers.

"At great risk to himself, and no little trouble, he has brought reports of a dragon to Constantinople," Gracian had intoned.

Javor wondered how he had found his way to the Order. *Or maybe, he had found his way to Gracian. Which must mean that Gracian is known as a Church leader who is interested in tales of dragons.*

Radek's description of the damage done, even the confusing glimpses he'd had of the beast, were credible—at least to Malleus and Gracian, the *Comes* of the Gnostic Order and the second-in-command of the Abbey of St. Mary of Chalkoprateia.

Their instructions had sounded rational, simple.

"Find what is behind the rumours of the dragon north of the Danuvius, kill it if possible, and report back what you find," Malleus had said.

Even Gracian's arguments had sounded rational. "We must learn as much as we can about the Enemy. The underworld is erupting beyond the reach of God's people. We must learn what the objectives are if we are going to preserve Christian civilization."

"What about the non-Christian civilizations?" Javor asked, and Gracian's eyes widened.

"Our concern is about our own people," he answered.

Malleus put his hand on Javor's shoulder. "Go, Javor. You are our best hope for answers. You know the Sklavenik people. You know the land. Do not put yourself at undue risk. Information is the most important aspect here. Come back alive."

"Of course, I will come back alive. Calanthe is with child, again."

A smile split Malleus' face. Even Gracian looked happy. "Well done, my boy. All my hopes for your wife's successful delivery."

"Another soul for the Church," Gracian said.

Javor looked at him, but could not put his question into words.

Although he hated to lie, Javor knew that Calanthe would be terrified had she known that he was going to try to kill a dragon. So he had told his family that he was again traveling on behalf of her father, Mauricius, to secure new trading arrangements to the north and west.

"So you see? I am taking an interest in your father's commerce. I have to do something with my time, after all."

Calanthe's lips were narrow, her mouth tight. "Does that mean you have to be away for so long?"

"Your father says he needs me to talk with Sklavenik people, and I *am* Sklavenik."

*I sound like I'm lying, even to myself.*

He had told Mauricius to play along with the ruse, and told him he needed passage on a ship to Constantia, at the mouth of the Danuvius, and as far up the river as he could go.

Then, refusing Gracian's suggestion to take a company of warriors with him, he set sail with Radek, the young Sklavene Legionnaire who had brought the reports of a dragon to the Order.

*He's just barely a man,* Javor thought again. *No older than I was when I left my home.*

*I survived. Will he?*

He pushed the thought out of his head.

At least he can speak my language.

In Constantia, Javor and Radek transferred to a barge travelling upriver. They boated up to the once-proud Roman city of Drobeta, on the northern bank of the river.

"I never liked this place," Radek had said when they stepped off the wharf into the palisade. "There's hardly anyone here. There are all these empty buildings, except for the little fort with a few legionnaires. The market is lousy, and no one has anything worth trading."

"It's not Constantinople," Javor agreed.

They bought food for a journey: tough bread that would last a week, cured ham and some fruit. *Apples last a long time,* Javor thought as he handed over a few coins to a toothless woman with tangled, dirty hair at a market stall. *Heavy,* he thought, *but we'll have horses. Too bad we can't get figs or dates here.*

*It's not Constantinople,* he thought again. *It's not even Constantia.*

*It feels empty and fearful.*

Javor chose the two least sickly nags from a herd of five in a corral that looked like it would not stand if Javor leaned on it.

"Fifteen solidi," said the horse trader, a stout man with white hair and bread crumbs in his white beard.

"For those two, I will give you five," Javor said, remembering lessons his father-in-law had taught him. "They are not worth more than a healthy donkey."

The horse trader spat into the rich manure at his feet. "These are the best horses in Drobeta."

"That is a sorry situation. Six solidi then," Javor counted three coins into one hand. He held up three more in his other hand. "The rest, plus another hundred *folles* when I find them fed, saddled and ready to ride tomorrow morning, an hour past sunrise."

The trader sneered, spat again, then took the money and walked into the stable without another word.

Javor and Radek found the town's only inn, a ragged two-storey building made of what looked like rotten logs. None of the walls stood straight and part of the roof had no thatch.

*I hope it doesn't rain tonight.*

A half-dozen people drinking in the public room looked at Javor and Radek with suspicion when they came in.

*What are they so afraid of?*

They bought a meal and mugs of ale. "How far is it to your village?" Javor asked.

"Two or three days' ride," Radek said around a mouthful of bread.

"And you're sure you know the way?"

"I've come here many times. I just don't like it."

They took a single room in the inn, laying their belongings in the corner farthest from the door. Javor stretched out on the straw bed. "Wake me at midnight," he said to Radek.

*I don't trust anyone here.*

Radek rode ahead of Javor, leading the way from Drobeta to his home village, which he called Leleka. Javor took the opportunity to look at him more carefully than he had before.

*He is barely a man. No older than I was when I left my home—was it eight years ago? So much has happened since then. So much has changed. And yet, nothing has changed. This boat trip is a repeat of the one I took seven years ago with Austinus and Tiana.*

*And yet, it's different.*

Javor gazed at the shore of the Danuvius River. The rowers' chant soothed him, strangely, even though he knew they were slaves forced to perform some of the most strenuous work he could imagine.

He watched a falcon soar high above the shore of the river, then bank and land gracefully on the limb of a tree that leaned out across the river.

He pulled his cloak closer around his body. The air over the river was still chilly, even on a sunny day in late April.

*And it will only get colder the farther north I go. I hope that the advancing year warms the air faster than the distance cools it.*

He thought of Calanthe again. She wanted another baby, she had said. Javor had not objected, enjoying her body even though she did not want to remove her nightclothes.

And now, she was pregnant again, even as he left on Malleus' mission to find what had sparked new rumours about a dragon terrorizing villages, gobbling sheep and cattle, killing any would-be warriors deluded enough to imagine they could kill it.

*I would not have believed these stories when I was younger. Until I saw a dragon with my own eyes.*

*Until I saw my parents' broken bodies and faced the fiend that killed them.*

The hawk was aloft again, gliding along the river's shore, seeming to want to continue beside the boat.

*Wait—that's not the same hawk. That's a much, much bigger bird, but far away. Way beyond the edge of the river. It just looks like it's following us. What Austinus would have called an optical illusion.*

*Austinus. His last voyage was up this same river, on a boat very much like this one. Seven years ago, he followed me. No—he followed my dagger. My great-grandfather's dagger.*

The memory of Austinus tightened his chest. He felt a squeeze in his throat. He blinked quickly, looking to the sky. The strange, huge bird had disappeared from view.

"Let's go below," he said to Radek. "The rain will start soon."

They rode westward, the morning sun shining on their backs, on a path along the steep north bank of the Danuvius River. There was a road paralleling the river on the southern side, but Radek's village was north of the limes, the old Roman border on the long river, and Trajan's bridge was the only crossing for hundreds of miles.

They passed above the cliffs of the Iron Gate with the face of some long-dead king carved into it, a hundred feet tall. The going was slow on their old, pathetic mounts. They had to divert northward every time they reached a tributary to the Danuvius until they found a ford across the smaller stream.

The path through the forest opened up to a clearing at the top of a high bluff a little before noon. Below, the Danuvius curved upstream to the southwest, while to their right a bay a half-mile wide sparkled.

"Now we turn to the north," Radek said. "Up this river, the Cerna."

"So, we're about halfway there?"

"No, not yet."

They turned north, the path leading gently lower toward the river level. The hills gradually lowered, but in the distance, Javor could see heights.

The path widened and Radek drew his horse even with Javor's. "You don't talk much, do you?"

Javor shrugged. "When I need to, I talk."

"The mighty warrior. You depend on your sword instead of your mouth."

Javor did not know how to answer that, so he didn't.

The wide bay narrowed quickly about a mile north of the Danuvius into a small river flowing quickly through a forested gorge. They stopped to rest their horses and eat. Radek rubbed the insides of his thighs. "I'm not used to riding a horse for so long," he said. "My legs are killing me."

"What is the name of your village again?" Javor asked.

"Leleka," Radek said. "Stork." He gulped down water he had taken from the river, where it frothed white over a rock.

"Like the bird?"

Radek nodded.

"How much farther?"

"With these horses? Days."

"You said it was only two or three days' ride," Javor said.

"These horses are slow," Radek answered. "I hope you didn't pay much for them."

The going got even slower as the gorge narrowed and got steeper. They had to dismount to lead the horses along an uneven path high over the rushing water.

After nearly an hour of walking ahead of their horses, they crested a ridge where the thick forest suddenly ended.

Radek groaned when he saw the devastated, blackened land stretching for more than a mile in front of them. Heaps of ash choked the spaces between charred stumps, stirring in the wind that came up from the river below.

"Dragon," Radek whispered. "What else could have done this?"

"It wasn't like this when you passed here on your way to Constantinople?"

Radek could only shake his head. His eyes were wide, and his jaw hung open loosely.

"We'll have to find another way to go north," Javor said. "If that was caused by a dragon, we should not touch any of it."

He turned and led his horse back over the ridge, looking for a path along the crest to where they could skirt the edge of the devastation.

When the sun sank below the trees overhead, a frustrated Javor decided to make camp. While he put up their tent and started a fire,

Radek foraged. He returned with a pouch of berries and wild fruit as the horizon reddened.

They heated some of the ham Javor had bought, and ate it with the tough bread, washing it down with sour wine. "I hope your people in Leleka are better cooks than the people in Drobeta," Javor complained.

Radek made a visible effort to swallow his bread. "I think so. Better bread, anyway."

This time, Javor took the first watch, letting Radek sleep soon after the twilight faded completely. The night was warm, a gentle breeze coming down the gorge from the north, carrying odours of water, pine and memory.

*I'm closer to my home than I have been since I left it, eight years ago.*

Even after that time, the memory still hurt. *The feeling in his chest when Roslaw, the chief of his village, had told him to leave for the safety of the others. The rage when Mrost, who had tormented Javor his whole life, sneered and repeated the order to leave. The whirling confusion when Vorona, the wise woman, agreed. And the stabbing ache when Elli, the girl he had loved as long as he could remember, would not say "goodbye," or kiss him as he walked out of the village gate.*

*The only friend I had that day was Photius, the stranger.* He looked up at stars between the scattered clouds in the night sky. And now he's gone.

*So many people gone. My parents. Photius. Austinus, the man who brought me into the Order eight years ago. The Roman Emperor Maurice, murdered by Phocas.*

*My life is now completely different from how it started out. So why do I feel so much more at home tonight than I do in Constantinople?*

He made a decision.

At midnight, he woke Radek and stretched out on a bed of long pine needles, covering himself with a blanket and his cloak. His last thoughts before falling asleep were, *Radek probably won't stay awake.* But that's all right. He touched his amulet, reassuringly smooth and quiet.

*We're safe here. Hardly anyone lives in Dacia anymore.*

# Bilavod

Javor halted his horse at the edge of a clearing, looking at a steam that fell over a rock outcropping shaped like the end of a loaf of bread. It hit rocks at the base, frothed over miniature rapids and then wound back into the forest at the other end of the clearing.

Above the rocky outcropping, the top of the hill had been cleared and Javor could see the tops of a wooden palisade.

He recognized the village. Bilavod. *Which means my home village is only about three or four days' ride north.*

Radek reined in beside him. "We should turn back and go wide around this place."

Javor dismounted and stepped close to the little waterfall. *How could I forget this place?*

Radek stayed on his mount, his head turning back and forth as he peered into every shadow. "They say this place is haunted," he whined.

"Who says that?" Javor asked without turning around. He held his horse's reins in his right hand, his left resting on the pommel of the sword swinging at his hip.

"People," Radek answered. "They say a great battle was fought here. Demons from ... from Hell attacked the village and only a great warrior saved them. But he had to sell his soul to the Devil himself."

"That's nonsense," Javor said.

Without looking, Javor knew that Radek was crossing himself. "No, it's true. A host of demons attacked the village, and the only way they survived was because a travelling warrior sold his soul to the Devil. The warrior destroyed many of the demons, but even he could not defeat them all until an angel of the Lord came and drove the last of the demons away."

"And I'm telling you, that's nonsense." Javor pulled on the reins, coaxing his roan mare down the slope.

"What do you mean, nonsense? People say—"

"It's nonsense because I am that warrior. That was me." He turned to glare at Radek, who returned his gaze wide-eyed, clutching his own horse's reins.

"And it was no angel. It was a gryphon." He directed his horse up the slope. "Even if I wasn't there, I know the story makes no sense." He heard the sound of both horses' hooves, so didn't bother to check whether Radek was following.

"If the warrior sold his soul to the Devil, why would the Lord send an angel to help him? And if the demons came from Hell, why would the Devil help the warrior destroy them?"

"I—I don't know. But it's true. Everyone knows it," Radek stammered.

Javor looked at Radek when they reached the top of the hill. His wide eyes darted around, looking for dangers. He flinched when a hawk screeched, miles away. "Anyway, even if this place is haunted, it's the middle of the day," Javor said. "There are no spooks around now."

Javor's hand wrapped around the amulet hanging from his neck. It was still and cool. "Come on. I know these people." He stepped toward the uneven stockade made of small, rough-hewn trees that surrounded the *holody*, the stockade that protected the village of Bilavod.

"What people?" Radek said, his voice trembling. "Do you see people?"

Javor looked more closely at the stockade. There were gaps where trees had fallen inside or outside the structure. The cleared area around it was dotted with small trees and bushes. The grass between them was waist-high.

The gate he remembered was now only a wide gap. Inside, the steep-roofed huts had collapsed, grass and bushes growing up around and in them. Some looked scorched, while others were no more than piles of rotting logs.

"What happened here?" He stepped through the gap, unable to process the ruins.

"No one has lived here for years," Radek said. He did not step past the stockade, but held the reins of his and Javor's horses just outside the holody. "After the great battle, the warrior was taken to Hell by the Devil. And exactly one month after that, when the full moon rose over the village, the Devil himself led more demons to kill many of the villagers. The few survivors fled, never to return. Since then, only witches come here on the full moon to ... to consort with the demons."

Javor did not bother to argue. He touched the amulet, but it was still quiet. No danger.

He stopped at a pile of scorched logs. What had been one corner of a structure remained standing, blackened logs rose as high as Javor's chest. Had this once been the home of Mstys, the village headman?

He moved deeper into the ruined village. One hut still had four walls more or less standing, its roof collapsed inside.

*Was this the hut where Lalya and I made love?*

He moved on, stopping when his boot nearly hit something in the high grass. He pushed the grass aside and recognized a human skull.

He picked it up. Some of the spine dangled from the base.

*Where is the rest of the body? Probably eaten, the bones scattered by animals. He dropped the skull back into the grass.*

"No demons did this," he said, striding back to Radek at the gate. "This village was destroyed by evil men."

He mounted in one smooth motion, then waited as Radek struggled into his saddle.

"We should return south," Radek panted, urging his horse after Javor's.

"We're continuing north," said Javor.

"Why?"

"You are supposed to guide me to your village."

"I only went there two months ago to visit. I have not lived there for a year. They begged me to get help. I do not even know if they are still there."

"We have not yet found the dragon," Javor argued.

"Maybe it's gone away," Radek said. His voice still trembled, even as they went out of sight of the ruined village of Bilavod.

"Maybe. But our mission is to find it and kill it."

Radek moaned.

Javor set a quick pace north, but in the hilly terrain, the going was still slow. They took time to find fords across streams, and often had to dismount as their path took them through the dense forests.

*It is so good to be back in familiar territory. Forests, meadows, pastures, rivers. Clean smells. Clear air without smoke from thousands of chimneys.*

As the horses carried them under the shade of a great oak tree, he realized the greatest difference between his original home and his adopted city of Constantinople.

*Trees. There are hardly any trees in the city, other than in the gardens of rich men.*

*Even outside the city, the Romans have cleared the land to grow crops. Sometimes, the crops are not suited to the land, and the land looks barren.*

*The Romans are intent on conquering the Earth. They send their Legions everywhere. But even when they are in charge, they continue to force the Earth to meet their desires.*

*It cannot end well.*

Radek's whining interrupted his reverie. "This whole land is haunted. Everyone says so."

"Quiet," Javor growled. "I have to think."

While they rode, Javor thought again about his instructions for this mission. "Find what is behind the rumours of a dragon north of the Danuvius, kill it if possible, and report back what you find," Malleus had said.

And Gracian had added the necessity of spreading Christianity among the Sklavenes.

A new kind of conquest.

Malleus' final words about the mission had struck Javor as strange. "The underworld is erupting beyond the reach of God's people. We must learn what the objectives are if we are going to preserve Christian civilization."

Malleus had never been over-concerned about the future of Christianity before, being a secret Gnostic. Maybe that comment was solely for Gracian's benefit.

*But is he trying to tell me something else?*

*I just wish people would say what they mean.*

# Leleka

Radek's village looked so much like Javor's home in Nastaciu, it hurt. The same fields planted with grain and beans, the same pastures with goats and cattle grazing. The same ring-shaped wooden palisade around the crest of a low hill, the same thatched roofs rising from the ground, covering a home dug into the earth.

A man standing watch at the palisade's gate recognized Radek and stared at Javor. They dismounted and waited until the watchman told a dirty child to run and fetch the village headman.

Voislav's face was not old, but his hair and beard were grey. He had wide shoulders and huge hands. He wore a light coloured, knee-length tunic with a pattern embroidered around the bottom and sleeve cuffs, tied off with a wide embroidered sash, breeches and high leather boots. A large knife was tucked into the sash.

"Radek! It is so good to see you. You were away so long, we feared the worst." He embraced Radek and kissed him on both cheeks, then kissed Javor when Radek introduced him. "He comes from Constantinople to help us with our ... problem," Radek said.

Voislav led Javor and Radek to a long hut, dug into the ground to about Javor's waist level. Over it was a high wooden roof — a common house in the centre of the village. He called for ale and bread, and two thin young women wearing long whitish dresses and colourful aprons hustled to set plates and cups on a table at the mouth of the hall.

Javor followed Voislav's lead and sat on a rough little stool beside the table. Outside the hall, the village bustled as children and women of a range of ages carried baskets, jugs of water or wine, various bundles and babies. Men worked at tasks in front of their huts, or carried bundles in and out of the gate of the holody. Babies cried, children ran past, dogs barked. Javor saw a cat sleeping in a sunny spot near the door to the common house.

"One man is all that Rome has sent to rid us of a dragon?" Voislav said, his voice low and gruff.

"You're not actually within the Empire's borders," Javor answered. He took a long draught of ale. *Pretty good.* Then he tried the bread. *So much better than in Drobeta. Yes, it's like home.* "The limes, the border of the Roman Empire, is along the Danuvius."

"Drobeta is north of the river," Radek protested.

"It's still considered part of Rome," said Javor, chewing another bite of bread. "This is good, but do you have anything else to eat? I'm starving."

"Of course, of course." Voislav waved his hand at the girls. "Luda! Zlata!

The girls ran off.

"But you did not answer my question." Hands on his knees, Voislav leaned toward Javor to look intently into his eyes. "How does one man hope to rid us of a dragon? Why not bring a contingent of soldiers? What do you call it—a legion?"

"A legion is twelve thousand men," Javor said. "Do you think this village could feed that many?"

Voislav frowned. "Well, surely we could support more than one."

Javor finished the bread. "I don't need anyone else. I've killed a dragon before, and all the other men who were with me died. All but four, and only one of them did any good. I've killed plenty of other monsters, all by myself. When it comes to monsters, the more men you send, the more will die."

Voislav nodded, then glanced at the two young girls who brought more bread, a jug of ale, fruit, and some thinly sliced meat. Radek dug in, shoving meat and bread into his mouth before gulping ale.

Javor waited for one of the young women to refill his mug of ale. She was small and delicate looking, with her light brown hair tied up high on top of her head. He saw Radek smile at her as he chewed, and she smiled briefly in return before looking down at the ground.

*She reminds me of Elli,* Javor thought. He picked up a slice of meat. Cold chicken. *It's good.* He washed it down with ale.

"What is your plan, young warrior?" Voislav asked.

Javor had to chew for a few moments before he could answer. "I don't know, yet. I need to learn as much as I can before I run after something as dangerous as a dragon. What can you tell me?"

Voislav leaned back, his hands on his knees again, and looked up at the clear blue sky. "The demon first came at the end of the winter, after the equinox. It began by stealing sheep and cattle. We thought it was wolves or a bear, or perhaps Avar raiders.

"Then one of the shepherd boys, Dusan, came running into the village early in the morning, screaming about a dragon stealing two lambs. Of course, no one believed him. He came running in the next morning, again, and still no one believed him. We thought he was a fanciful young boy, that he had seen a large wolf. So that night, he took a friend to watch the flocks with him.

"The next morning, the friend ran back to the village, screaming. 'A dragon, a dragon!'" Voislav's voice rose, his hands waving in the air as if the sound of his voice pushed them aloft. "A dragon took three ewes."

Radek coughed. He looked down, his head shaking. "What about Dusan?" Javor asked.

"Dusan was my cousin," Radek muttered. His cheek shone with tears.

"Dusan was gone," Voislav croaked. "We did not believe him."

"The monster ate him whole," Radek whispered. "That's what Yasen told us."

"Yasen? Where is Yasen now? Can I talk to him?" Javor asked. He felt the amulet tremble a little at his words.

Voislav's eyes were closed tight, his face tilted toward the sky. "He is gone, too. The dragon took four young people, three more boys, and a young woman heavy with child. It also took half of our sheep. We asked the other villages around us, and they have been afflicted as well, but have not lost as many as we have." He took a deep breath, and Javor saw his eyes shine with tears.

"Where did this happen? Was it always in the same place?"

Voislav took a deep, shuddering breath. "Our pastures are north of here."

"Have you moved the herds?"

Voislav fixed his eyes on Javor. "Of course. That was the first thing we tried. The beast found the herds after two days. Then it not only killed the two young men watching the flocks by night, it tore them to pieces, leaving their mutilated bodies for us to find."

Javor realized he had eaten all the bread that was in front of him. He tossed back the rest of the ale and watched Radek pour more from the jug into all three mugs. "Take me to the pasture," he said.

"Tomorrow, at first light. I promise," Voislav said. "Tonight, we will celebrate the return of our Radek, here." He turned to the younger man. "You must tell us all about your journey. Did you really go all the way to Constantinople?"

"I did. It was a long journey. I had no idea that anything in the world could be so far away."

Javor laughed at that, thinking of the places he had travelled to beyond Constantinople, and the countries he had learned of: Persia, Egypt, Axum, and the most distant of all, the country of Qin, home to people called the Seres.

But Radek continued, describing climbing hills and then mountains, following rivers, working to pay for passage on a river boat. He spoke of strange foods and progressively more bizarre people and customs as other villagers drew around to listen. Occasionally they would ask a question, but each time Voislav would shush them with a glare.

Radek reached his climax with, "And in the morning light, I saw the greatest thing I have ever seen in my life. Great walls of stone, so high I could not see the faces of the men who walked on top of it."

The sun was getting low. Voislav barked orders and soon the common wooden table was covered with jugs of wine and ale, and bowls of bread, fruit, mushrooms, even some smoked fish and meat.

Javor dug in enthusiastically, and nearly choked when Voislav turned to him and said, "Well, young man, you must tell us about yourself."

At once, dozens of eyes were fixed on Javor, and there was no sound but the calls of evening birds.

Voislav continued. "You must have some amazing stories to tell us, a mighty warrior like yourself from Constantinople."

He took a deep swallow of ale, Malleus' warnings against revealing the secrets of the Order echoing in his mind. "Actually, I come from a place much closer to this than to Constantinople." The *ooohs* he heard relaxed his shoulders a little. He took another bite of a honey-flavoured bread. "It was a village very much like this one, some days travel north of here." His next statement surprised everyone, including him. "I would like to take the opportunity to travel there again."

"You came from around here? You're Sklavenik?" someone asked.

"Yes. How did you think I learned to speak the language so well?"

"You have a strange accent," Voislav said. After a pause, he laughed and slapped Javor hard on the back. "Don't worry about it! Many people speak strangely. Bogdan here speaks as if he has uncooked grain in his mouth." A dark-haired man down the table laughed and looked down.

"Tell us about Constantinople," someone else said.

Javor took another deep swallow of ale, and did his best to describe its cathedrals, its wide streets, the Hippodrome, the enormous cisterns and fountains. He described the great harbours that surrounded two sides of the triangular city, and the great chain that guarded the entrance to the Golden Horn.

When he described the ships that came from lands even farther east, to the end of the Euxine Sea, he could tell that people thought he was making up stories. Some began to argue among themselves about the likelihood of being able to go so far in any direction without finding the end of the world.

Javor relaxed. He had talked more than he liked.

The last red light of the sunset limned the horizon when Radek led Javor and Voislav out of the centre of the crowd. Under the firelight's shadow, Javor leaned close to speak low. "There's something I did not tell you, Voislav. As we came back, we passed through the old abandoned village east of here."

"The place where the stream falls and turns into a rapids?" Voislav asked, his voice also low.

"Bilavod," said Javor, and realized his voice was too loud. *Better slow down with this ale.*

Voislav and Radek nodded. Both of their eyes were wide. "And what did you see there?"

"I saw the ruins of an abandoned village. Oh yes, and a single human skull."

Radek shivered. Voislav's face was grave. "Bilavod is haunted. By demons, people say. That is why they left, never to return."

Javor shrugged. "I don't believe in haunting." He drained his mug of ale.

Voislav fixed an intense look on Javor's eyes. "You don't believe in haunting, yet you came all this way to dispatch a dragon?"

"I've seen dragons before," he replied, fascinating by the flickering firelight dancing on the faces before him. "I've seen and killed monsters. Witches. People—things that change from birds into something that looks like a woman. I've seen demons and monsters tear the limbs off strong men. I've seen sorcerers make fire out of nothing.

"But I have never seen or heard a ghost. I have seen many people die, men, women and children, and not one of them has ever come back."

# The hunt

The next morning, Javor rode the horse he had purchased in Drobeta north out of the village of Leleka. It was slow, and old, but he was beginning to feel attached to it. It was gentle and forgiving, even if it did stop to eat grass or flowers whenever it could. With the summer sun warm on his shoulders, he patted the matted, short yet somehow tangled fur on its shoulder. "Good horse," he said. The horse snorted in response and trudged along the path.

Behind him, Radek groused about continuing to travel. "I went all the way to Constantinople. I don't see why I have to come on this journey and risk my neck."

"Quiet, Radek," Voislav said, riding behind Radek.

Flowers and grass rose above the horses' knees, tickling Javor's ankles where they got under the hem of his trousers. He pulled the tunic away from his chest to try to cool himself. It did no good.

He wore a helmet, but he was glad he had left his mail coat and greaves in the packs slung over the horse behind him. They would have been too hot and would not have offered much protection against a dragon, anyway.

*That's what Preyatel is for.* He touched the amulet, but it was quiet and cool. He rubbed his thumb around its familiar, irregular edge.

He had a spear and a small shield strapped to the saddle, a long sword hanging on his back and, of course, his great-grandfather's dagger in a sheath at his hip.

Voislav dressed in typical Sklavenik warrior fashion with trousers, a light tunic tied at his waist, and stout, low boots on his feet. He wore no armour other than a steel helmet, but he carried two spears, a short sword and a hand-axe. A large shield, painted blue and yellow, bounced lightly against the horse's side.

Radek also carried an axe and a shield, but it was obvious he wasn't happy about the need for them. *He won't survive this outing if we do encounter a dragon. Or any danger.*

*On the other hand, he did make it all the way to Constantinople on his own. That's a dangerous journey.*

They rode along the edges of fields planted with grain and other crops before climbing a shallow slope. On the far side of the ridge, Javor saw wide meadows dotted with white sheep and brown cattle. "You have a wealthy village, Voislav," Javor said. "My people had not even a quarter of the livestock that you do."

"That's thanks to the strength of our warriors, defending our fields and our flocks against other villages, and against Avars who are always trying to steal them. We held our own. But we could not against the dragon. That devil has already taken close to a fifth of our herds."

Voislav led the way down the slope until they reached a boy who stood watching over the herds, a long walking stick in one hand. "Good morrow, Chestibor," Voislav said from his horse. "Any sign of the monster?"

"Not today, Chief. Everything is quiet," said the brown-haired boy of about 13 years. He was short and thin, but there was a wisp of fuzz on his upper lip. A little way along the slope was another boy, also thin but with lighter coloured hair, also holding a walking stick taller than himself. When he saw the three mounted men, he trotted toward them.

"Good. But at the first sign of the beast, or any other trouble, you and Drazen hide as best you can, and get back home. People are more important than a few cattle or sheep.

The other boy, Drazen, reached them. Javor was struck by the boy's beauty. He had light brown, almost blond hair, big green eyes and skin so smooth it looked liquid. His features were fine, almost feminine, but there was an incipient strength in his jaw and in the width of his shoulders.

"Who is this, then?" Drazen asked.

Voislav turned in his saddle. "This is Javor, a mighty warrior from Constantinople, skilled in dispatching dragons."

*Dispatching dragons? Oh, no.*

Chestibor squinted up at Javor. "Constantinople? Are you a Christian then?"

Javor nodded. "Yes. A Christian." *Gnosis is too complicated to explain this morning.*

"Where's your cross? I thought all Christians wore crosses around their necks."

Javor's hand rose involuntarily to his chest. He could feel Preyatel under his tunic. "I don't."

"So are you really a Christian, then?"

"His religion is not the reason he is here," Voislav interjected. "He is here to rid us of the dragon."

Chestibor squinted at Javor a little longer, as if trying to impress him on his memory. Drazen looked at him, too, quietly, without squinting. He seemed alert, loose, ready for anything.

"How will you do that?" Chestibor asked. "Get rid of a dragon?"

"I will kill it," Javor answered.

"Just you? By yourself?"

"Just me."

Chestibor looked at Voislav, then at Radek, and back to Javor. "That sounds good to me. I have no desire to get closer to the beast than I am now."

"It's safer for all of us," Javor agreed.

Two evenings later, Javor sat on a fallen log at the edge of the pasture.

Voislav slept on a bed of soft boughs under the trees behind him, beside the dim embers of the evening cookfire. Radek lay slumped against a tree, his chin on his chest. The two boys had long since driven the flocks to their home enclosures, near the village.

Javor did not feel bored. He looked for new constellations among the stars. *I don't see a bull, nor a bear. But that group of stars looks like a fish. Is there a fish constellation?*

Lower, the spruce forests on the slopes made a ragged black margin to the sky. A light breeze ruffled the leaves over his head, bringing the scent of pine and a hint of rain to come.

*No rain tomorrow, though. Maybe the day after.*

*Tomorrow. Time to move on. We haven't seen a sign of the dragon, seen a sign of it in two days, and we are well past the pastures of Leleka.*

*We'll leave at first light, move on.*

He sniffed at the air, as if he could smell the dragon. *Maybe I should get a dog. No, the dog would just get killed by some of the things I hunt.*

Javor closed his eyes and relaxed as much as he could while sitting on the uneven log. He pushed his thoughts and his senses inward, deep. *Preyatel,* he thought. *What do you know? Do you sense the dragon?*

*So far,* he realized, *the amulet has not helped me detect anything. It has protected me, hidden me from enemies' view, and warned me when they're getting closer.*

He brushed fingertips across the uneven surface of the amulet, but it was cool and quiet. *Which means the dragon is nowhere near.*

*We're definitely moving on in the morning.*

He turned toward the fire and lay down on the bed that Radek had made him out of pine boughs and straw. Javor settled his great-grandfather's sheathed dagger where he could grasp it quickly, pulled his cloak over himself, took one last look to make sure the fire was dying, and closed his eyes.

*Wake me if you sense anything,* he told his amulet. Confident, he fell asleep immediately.

The next morning's eastern wind pushed white clouds across the high sky. The scent of rain was stronger, the temperature cooler as Javor, Voislav and Radek walked along the edge of a forest, leading their horses.

"Why are we going farther north? And why aren't we riding?" Radek whined.

"Because the dragon hunter thinks we'll find the beast to the north," Voislav growled back. "He knows better than we do, and we're going to take his advice."

"But why are we walking? Why can't we ride?"

"I told you. We're resting the horses so they're fresher in case we need them to run fast and far later. Now shut up and let Sir Javor concentrate."

Javor barely noticed that the other two were talking. His eyes swept the view to the north: the thick forest that rose gently to the hills before them, the puffy clouds that glided past the crests, the hawks soaring over the fields to their left.

*The dragon has retreated from us. Did it sense me coming? That is, us—me, Preyatel and my dagger. How could it? Preyatel makes me invisible to supernatural creatures.*

*To their supernatural senses, that is. Maybe it saw me? But then, how would it know I was any different from anyone else here?*

*Another mystery.*

By the end of the day, the wind had died away, leaving a breathless, humid summer day. The clouds had become lower, as if holding the heat close to the ground. The little party halted under a stand of pines whose lower branches had died and broken away, leaving a shady space high enough even for the horses.

Radek went to fill the water skins. Voislav took his bow and returned in an hour with a brace of rabbits. As the sunlight slanted under the branches, he prepared a camp meal.

Radek fed the horses. "We're going to have to go back soon," he grumbled. "We don't have much food left. Two more days at the most."

"My home is a week's walk north of here, and a little east. On a horse, maybe three days at most," Javor replied. He turned to the others.

"Horses can eat grass. There's plenty of that here."

"Horses have to eat a lot of grass for most of the day if they don't have food like oats," Radek countered.

"Very well. In the morning, take enough for your horses for one day and return to Leleka without me. I'll continue north."

Voislav frowned. "Why?"

"It occurs to me that the dragon may have circled around us. Without your knowing, it may be savaging your village at this moment."

Voislav's face went white. "Oh, no ... do you think ..."

Javor regretted his words instantly. "I don't know, Voislav. But we've been away from your village for three days, now. We have no way of knowing. In the morning, the two of you will go back. If you need me, send Radek back. I will leave a trail easy enough to follow. Besides, you know already how he can find me. He found me in Constantinople, remember?"

Voislav was looking south, as if he could see his village burning. "Yes, yes," he muttered.

"How will I know which way you've gone?" Radek whined.

"Start at this spot. I will leave markers each time I change direction."

They ate without speaking again. Javor stretched out on a soft spot, and fell asleep quickly, trusting his amulet to warn him of danger.

# Dragon

Without Voislav and Radek, Javor covered ground faster, even though he walked beside the horse to give it plenty of rest.

In the mid-morning, as he emerged from a stand of trees onto a sunny, flowering meadow, he felt his amulet vibrate slightly. Twenty paces away, the land rose to a low ridge. He could see the tops of trees in the distance behind it. Above them, to the north, a hawk soared.

The horse whinnied and shied away as they approached the ridge. Frowning, Javor tugged on the reins. No use. He let go, and the horse took a few steps backward, eyes wide and ears swiveling back and forth.

He stepped to the crest to see another scene of devastation.

The meadow on the far side of the ridge was blackened like the slope. Twisted remnants of shrubs and small trees stood amidst crumbling ash. In the middle of it stood something that Javor had to study for a long time, until he realized it was the bones of a large animal—maybe a bull or a bear.

*The dragon was here. Does it poison an area every time it eats, or is it defending itself against attack?*

*I wonder if it's Sarbox. It's been seven years since I saw him—her? He—she?—It could have returned from the mountains to the west if its wing healed.*

He turned back, picked up the reins from the ground and led the horse along the edge of the blasted area. They wandered eastward, vaguely back toward the village of Leleka.

Preyatel trembled again. Javor looked up. There was the hawk again, now closer, soaring eastward. *Is it following me?*

He returned to the campsite where he had left Voislav and Radek in late afternoon to find someone he did not expect. Drazen, the handsome boy shepherd, was putting down two leather sacks beside the remains of the campfire. He held the reins of a small grey mare in one hand. The horse snorted when it saw Javor's.

"What are you doing here?" Javor asked. "Where is Radek?"

Drazen looked up into Javor's eyes, and Javor noticed two long, angry red scratches down the left side of his neck that led to ragged tears in his tunic. There was a bruise on his arm and dark half-circles under his eyes. "Radek is dead."

Javor felt a chill in his core. "What happened?"

"The dragon attacked the village when he and Voislav returned this morning. It smashed down our wall like grass and stomped on women and little children. It seemed to want to get to Radek. It chased him. It ... caught him." Drazen closed his eyes and shuddered. "It cut him in two with its claw."

Memories of a dragon claw piercing through a legionnaire and his armour flashed through Javor's mind. "And Voislav? What happened to him?"

Drazen took a deep breath, letting it out in a long shudder. "Voislav tried to drive it off. He attacked it with his sword, but it broke on the beast's hide."

"Is Voislav alive?" Javor's voice was frantic.

Drazen sighed and sat on the ground. He stared at his hands. "He was when I left the village, but I fear he will not live long. The beast spat on him. It burned his arm and his side. Voislav fell. He has not been able to walk since. We laid him on his bed and some of the women tended him."

Dry-mouthed, Javor asked "What happened to the dragon?"

Drazen's hands covered his face. "It took two children. Two little girls. It ate them, almost in one bite. Then it jumped into the air and flew away."

"How did you get those scratches?" Javor pointed to his face. "And those bruises?"

Drazen's hands fell. He looked up at Javor as if he were begging for something, but Javor could not guess what. "I tried to save one of the girls. The beast—the monster—brushed me away like a fly." Tears escaped his eyes. "I could do nothing. The monster has killed my whole family. I have no one left."

Javor crouched beside Drazen. He hesitated before putting a hand on the young man's shoulder. "I am sorry. I should have been there. It's my task to destroy this beast." He rose again. "Come. I will accompany you."

"No!" Drazen shouted, springing to his feet. "Voislav said to tell you not to come back, not until you have killed the dragon. He thinks somehow, it came looking for you. It was looking for Radek. And now, it will seek you."

"It won't be able to find me," Javor said. Before the boy could argue, he continued "I have ... something that prevents dragons and other monsters from finding me. Unless they see me. I will take you back to Leleka."

"No. I am going to help you kill this monster."

Javor shook his head. "There is nothing that you can do. I have—" He hesitated, unwilling to reveal too much. Malleus had warned him against telling others of his amulet and dagger. "...experience in dealing with these creatures. I have killed a dragon before."

Awe spread across Drazen's face, quickly replaced with stubborn determination. "Did you do it alone?"

"No," Javor admitted. He thought of the fearless Anthony, the boxer, and of Photius. Then he thought of Photius' horrifying, agonizing death. "I was with fifty experienced Roman legionnaires. Battle-hardened men. Who had armour and weapons. What do you have?"

Drazen picked up a hunting spear that Javor had not noticed before. "I know how to use it. And the bow," he said, pointing to a weapon hanging from his horse's saddle. "And this," he added, lifting a small hand-axe that hung from a strap on his belt.

Javor looked at him, at the ragged, torn tunic, the threadbare breeches on his thin legs. Javor compared his own sturdy, Legion-issued boots to the shoes on Drazen's feet. They were nothing more than flaps of cowhide, tied to his feet with strips of more cowhide.

*If he confronts a dragon with me, he will die. But if he returns to the village, he will probably die, as well.*

*And everyone dies eventually.*

"I brought food," Drazen said, pointing to the sacks he had put down. "Voislav told me to bring food for you, and me, and the horses. I took what I could and left as fast as I could."

Javor sighed. "Fine. Stay. You can make yourself useful by making a meal. And feeding the horses. I'm starving."

Drazen set to work. "I see you came from the north. Did you see the place the dragon burned?" He nodded in the direction Javor had ridden from.

"I saw it. It was poisoned by the dragon. You shouldn't touch anything there." He began to take the saddle and bridle off his horse.

"None of us go near it." Drazen answered. "There are other places like it, too."

Drazen started a fire faster than anyone Javor had ever seen, and made a surprisingly good meal out of leftovers and preserved food from Leleka. He fed the horses, too, and volunteered to keep first watch. Javor stretched out again on the bed of pine boughs, touching Preyatel. It was quiet. Crickets chirped, owls hooted. One of the horses snorted, contented and safe.

Javor woke to the smell of roasting rabbit and sat up fast. The sun was already above the trees, and the sky was a deep blue with high, wispy clouds. "Why didn't you wake me at midnight?"

Drazen was bent over a small cooking fire, poking at meat with a stick. "Sorry. I fell asleep and woke just before dawn. I got some rabbits, though."

Javor reached for his amulet, but it was quiet and cool, even though it had been lying on his chest all night. *That means there is no sign of the dragon, nor any other danger.*

Javor's stomach growled as Drazen pulled a rabbit off the improvised spit over the fire. He handed Javor a large leaf piled with roasted rabbit meat.

He had never tasted rabbit so good before. Drazen had flavoured it with herbs he had found, creating a unique sensation in the mouth. "You're a good cook, Drazen."

"Thank you." Drazen put his cooking things away. "Now, do we find the dragon?"

Javor finished the last bite. He sighed and fixed a hard look at Drazen's eyes. "I have a plan. But it's dangerous."

Drazen returned his look without expression. "Tell me."

"Pack everything up and load the horses. We are going to draw the dragon to us." He put his armour on.

An hour later, they reached the dragon-blighted valley. Javor dismounted. "Take the horses under the trees over there," he instructed, pointing down the slope. "Don't come out until I call you."

"What will you say?"

"I'll just call your name. Or I'll say 'help,' or something. You'll know." Then Javor pulled the amulet from under his tunic and hung it around Drazen's neck. Somewhere, just as Javor expected, an owl hooted. In the morning sun.

"Keep this on, and stay close to the horses. Very close. Make sure you can touch them all the time. But when I call you, throw the amulet to me."

"Amulet? That's what you call this ... necklace?"

Javor closed his eyes. "That's not what I call it. I call it 'Preyatel.'"

"'Friend'?"

"Just throw it when I call to you. Then run away as fast as you can.

Do not think you can help me after that. If you do, you will die. Horribly. And don't miss your throw. Or I will die, and then you will, for certain."

Javor stalked around the perimeter of the natural bowl that had been poisoned by the dragon's spit, loosening his great-grandfather's dagger in its sheath by his side.

*I hope this works. I hope that Drazen survives. And that I do.*

Javor stopped at a hundred paces. He turned but could not see Drazen or the horses.

He looked at the clear blue sky. To the north, a hawk soared, another in the west.

A peaceful morning. Birds chirped. Bugs buzzed. Again, an owl hooted.

*That's the sign. The dagger and the amulet are separate.*

He scanned the sky again. Nothing, other than two hawks spiraling higher. He sat cross-legged on the ground in the shade of a poplar tree, scanning the sky.

Hours dragged. From time to time, Javor rose, paced to the edge of the poisoned bowl, drew his dagger, re-sheathed it, walked back to the tree. He looked back toward the campsite, but never saw Drazen nor the horses.

By noon, his eyes and neck ached from looking up at the sky.

He sat under the poplar again, slumping against the trunk. His eyelids drooped. He heard birds sing.

To one side, a hawk screeched. Javor's eyes closed as his breathing slowed. The hawk screeched again, closer, and then a third time.

The fourth scream forced his eyes open. The hawk screamed again, and Javor looked up, wondering if it were in the branches above him.

Something darkened the brilliant summer sky.

The hawk screeched once more and Javor jumped as a reddish-brown shape swept past him. He spun, drawing the dagger, to see the hawk flapping its wings, climbing back into the sky.

He spun back and saw the dragon, more hideous than any he had seen before, and larger than any but one.

It stood on four legs, its neck arched like an angry snake. Its back was higher than the second-storey balcony on Javor's house in Constantinople, and the black leather of its outstretched wings blocked out the sky. It had a long neck, covered like the rest of its body in shiny, greenish-grey scales that each refracted the sunlight in shimmering rainbows. Its impossibly long, snake-like tail undulated behind it as if it had a life of its own. All four of its limbs terminated in a purple claw longer than Javor's forearm, thick and sharp.

Its face was broad, more like a man's than a snake's, but lopsided with a light-grey bulge behind the left eye. Four purple-red tongues flicked out between loose, wet-looking lips, then back in. It hissed, red eyes fixed on Javor's great-grandfather's dagger.

It extended its neck, the head coming closer to Javor. Its gaze shifted to his face. Javor looked into the eyes. He saw swirling patterns. His mother.

He pushed the scene out of his mind and waved the dagger.

Javor thought, *Bring me your young. They are so tender.*

*No. I did not think that.* He tore his eyes from the dragon's and threatened it with the dagger. "You want this?"

The dragon hissed as it drew its head back. Four tongues dashed out and in again. It opened its uneven mouth, revealing three uneven rows of triangular yellow teeth.

Its breath smelled like rotting death.

Retching, Javor sprang forward. The dagger rotated of its own volition in his palm to an underhand grip. He swept it down with every bit of strength in his arm.

The black blade pierced the iridescent scales between the dragon's front legs up to the fish-shaped hilt. He yanked it back, but the handle slipped from his hand. The blade stayed embedded in the monster's body.

The shrieking roar from its wide-open maw drove Javor to the ground. The monster collapsed to the grassy ground, twisting and writhing. Javor rolled to dodge a purple claw and leaped to his feet.

Javor knew his plan had a huge flaw, and now he felt a deeper fear than he had known for years. It was a chill that spread from his gut to his genitals, then through his limbs. He felt his heart hammering in his throat.

The dragon regained control of its movements. It stilled, then rose slowly to stand on four legs. Its neck rose, towering over Javor.

"Wait!" Javor called, looking the dragon in the eye again, even though he knew the risk that carried. "Why are you doing this? Why kill people?"

A hot wave seared through his mind. Anger. Hatred.

"Tell me!" he called. "Why do you hate us?"

A foreleg reached for him.

No use. Javor leaped forward again, closing on the dragon. He grabbed the hilt of his great-grandfather's dagger and wrenched it out, leaping away from the spurt of black, corrosive blood he knew would follow.

The dragon's roar deafened him, but Javor found his feet and ran toward the tree line in a ringing silence. He felt the dragon's tread behind him, shaking the ground. He smelled it closing, felt the heat. He saw liquid strike the ground beside him. The grass and flowers turned black and shriveled as he ran past.

Javor felt liquid splatter over the armour on his back. He fumbled to untie the straps on his armour as he ran.

*Why are my fingers so clumsy?*

Something golden flashed past him. Javor looked over his shoulder to see it fly into the dragon's face. A piercing shriek came from it, and huge, cat-like claws raked across the dragon's face.

For a moment he thought it was the hawk again, grown to a monstrous size, but then the wings spread and banked. When it circled past him again for another attack, Javor recognized the golden feathers, the whiplike tail, the eagle beak and the wildcat claws. "The gryphon," he whispered.

He had seen a gryphon once before, eight years earlier, near this very spot. Then, it had helped him in another fight, against mysterious mounted raiders who extorted food from villages, stole young women and killed men. Then, the gryphon had fended off Javor's enemies long enough for him to prepare his defence.

He realized this gryphon was doing the same thing again.

He managed to untie the armour and it dropped, dissolving into the ground. He turned and ran toward the trees again. "Drazen! The amulet!"

The beautiful young man appeared at the edge of the trees, his right arm whipping across his body. Javor caught the amulet in an outstretched hand as the dragon closed on him, double-toothed maw wide. It swept past him, knocking Javor to the ground, and crashed into the trees.

Javor leaped to his feet, finding the dagger in his hand again. Putting the amulet's chain over his head, he looked around. The gryphon was gone.

The dragon extricated itself from a stand of fir trees, raising its neck to hiss at Drazen. The boy held his hunting spear, aimed at the dragon's neck.

"Drazen!" Javor screamed. "Get back!"

But it was too late. Drazen thrust his spear into the monster's wide-open maw, aiming for the brain. As the spear tip penetrated, the beast coughed, enveloping Drazen in a dark grey cloud.

Javor struck down, the dagger piercing the dragon's long neck. With two hands, he forced the blade through sinew and scale. In a last effort, the beast sank long teeth into Drazen's chest. The boy's eyes locked with Javor's, but he did not cry out. Javor saw him clench his jaw and struggle to pull his spear from the monster's maw.

Javor pushed on the dagger. It cleaved through the iridescent scales and the red meat beneath. It stopped when it reached bone, and the dragon bit down harder. Still, Drazen did not cry out, but pushed his spear deeper.

The boy choked, and blood spilled down his chin, dripping onto his ruined chest. His eyes clouded. His hands released the spear and his arms went limp at the same moment that Javor's dagger cleaved through the beast's spine. The head, neck and Drazen's limp body crashed onto the ground, tangling in a gross, fleshy red heap.

Javor leaped away from the corrosive black blood, then carefully stepped close to Drazen. The dragon's grotesque maw still clung to his chest, hideous teeth piercing from both sides. But the boy's face was angelic in its peace and smooth perfection.

Javor pushed the eyes closed. *I cannot cry for you. I have no more tears for people who throw themselves into certain death.*

He looked at the dragon's great carcass. Beneath it, a spreading grey circle of grass and plants withered and died. A cloying stink rose from it, choking Javor.

He stepped back to wipe his blade on the ground, and the vegetation it touched blackened and died, too. He backed away, watching in sickened fascination as the dragon's carcass slowly collapsed in on itself, dissolving into dust and a noxious thick grey ooze that sank into the ground. Drazen's chest turned grey, the colour spreading like it had on the ground around the dragon, down the body, up to his head, across the shoulders and hips.

A black hole appeared in Drazen's chest, the edges crumbling like soil. Javor could not take his eyes away. He watched the dragon's head fall away as Drazen's torso dissolved, the boy's arms and legs fell away before they blackened and crumbled, too. His stomach heaved as Drazen's chin dropped off his head, and only then could Javor turn away to retch onto the ground.

He ran on shaky legs to find the horses. As he rode, he tried to think of what he could say to the people of Leleka. But he kept thinking of the gryphon, looking to the sky, hoping he would see it again.

# Return to Nastasciv

Javor decided not to return to Leleka. Instead, he headed north.

Finding Nastasciv, the village where he grew up, took Javor two more days than he thought it would. On the sixth day after he killed the dragon, he saw a familiar, round hill in the distance with the holody, or wooden stockade, around it and a stream flowing around its base.

Home.

He urged the horse into a canter up to the gate of the holody. It was only when he was halfway up the slope that he noticed no one in the fields, as they should have been during the summer. There was not a cow, pig or even a chicken outside the stockade wall.

But there was a new feature since he had been there last. A small watchtower made of rough-hewn logs, poked above the top of the wall to the right of the gate.

No sound came from inside the walls. Even the bees that normally buzzed among the wildflowers under the walls were silent.

As he approached the stockade, he saw a shadow move across a small, dark opening in the watchtower. *So someone is still here, after all.*

He dismounted and pounded on the rickety wooden gate. "Hey! It's me—Javor! I'm back!"

Nothing. No response. Behind him, at the edge of the forest, a bird twittered.

He pounded again. "Hey! I come from here! Javor!" he yelled up at the tower. "I left seven—no, eight years ago. You kicked me out. Now open up. I need to talk to you."

Still silence. Javor looked down the slope, empty of all except for small birds. High above the trees, he could just see a tiny hawk of some kind, soaring.

He took the horse's reins and walked all the way around the stockade. There was no other gate, but as he rounded the shoulder of the hill, he could see the low peaks of the huts of the village that lay outside the holody.

He froze. Every one of them was overgrown. Several had collapsed in on themselves.

*No one has lived there for years.*

He heard a commotion behind him, followed by a high-pitched shout. He whirled, staring at the holody. Then he strode back to the gate, leading his horse. "Open up!" he pounded. "I know you're in there. It's me. Javor. I won't hurt you. I need to talk to you. And you need to talk to me."

"Go away!" said a voice, thin and hoarse above him. Javor looked up to see the top of a head, ducking behind the stockade.

"I'm not going away until I talk to you. Where is Roslaw?"

A different voice responded, one familiar to Javor, a voice that raised revulsion and fear, and then anger. "Roslaw is dead. Go away, you freak." Javor recognized the voice. Mrost.

*That idiot Mrost is in charge?*

Javor's breath became harsh and ragged. He kicked the gate so hard, the horse backed away, showing the whites of its eyes. "Open up or I'll break this gate down," he shouted.

"For Perun's sake, let him in," said a third voice, another he recognized.

"No, Hrech. I am hetman now."

"You can be hetman of my arsehole. Step back from the gate, Mrost."

Javor heard scraping, grunts, then a slap, followed by the unmistakable sound of a fist driving into a belly, and finally a thump. Then the sound of wood scraping on wood, and slowly the heavy wooden gate slid to the side.

A second log palisade stood two paces inside the first one, with its own gate open to a space crowded with pitched, thatched roofs of more of the semi-sunken huts, and a group of people.

In front stood a young man Javor barely recognized, wearing the typical clothing of the Sklavenik people of the area: a tattered white tunic over dark trousers. His shoes were pieces of rough hide wrapped around his feet and secured with leather traces that wrapped around his thighs. A sheathed knife dangled from a strap attached to a sash at his waist.

Thick black hair and a thick black beard covered most of his face, but Javor could see his brown eyes widen and his lips, buried in a beard that extended down his neck, curve in delight. "Javor ... it is you." Javor stiffened, reaching for the sword at his side as the dark man lunged forward to wrap his arms around him.

"I don't believe it, I don't believe it," he said over and over, lifting Javor off the ground and swinging him slightly back and forth.

Javor looked down at the top of his old friend's head. "It's good to see you, too, Hrech," he said.

Hrech put him down and turned to the small crowd behind him. "It's Javor!" he announced. "I told you he wasn't dead. None of you believed me when I told you he was strong and smart. And here he is!"

Javor turned his attention to the rest of the people near the gate. A skinny, sallow man with thinning light brown hair was picking himself up off the ground, rubbing his head.

*That's Mrost.*

Two women in patterned aprons and white head scarves stood beside him. One began brushing the dust off his clothes, until he swatted her hands away.

More men and women came up from among the crowded huts, goggling and gaping. Javor recognized some of the faces, but could not always remember names. *Rodisa. Tomys. Bogud—he looks so much older.*

*Tekla, Roslaw's wife. Widow,* he corrected himself.

The sight of the village shocked him. Since the villagers had rebuilt their homes inside the palisade, the hilltop was crowded. The soft grass and wildflowers that Javor remembered were gone. The only green things were weeds struggling out of the hard-beaten earth along the second log wall. They doubled the wall, too. That makes the space inside even smaller, and doesn't really make them safer.

But most shocking was the state of the villagers themselves. They looked thin, pinched and covered in dust. Their eyes as they stared at Javor were filled with fear, not delight at the return of a long-gone son. They gathered around him, but other than Hrech, none came closer.

*They all look so much older after eight years. Do I look that much older, too?*

Finally, a small, grey-haired man limped forward. One eye was closed, and the lid drooped over the other. His tunic was grey and stained, without a sash at the waist, and his feet were bare. "Javor," he croaked, "Oh my boy, I thought you lost." He wrapped his arms around Javor, and his head barely reached the middle of Javor's chest.

Javor put his hands on the old man's shoulder and pushed back to take a more careful look. "Uncle Borys?"

"Yes, I am your Uncle Borys, nephew," the old man smiled. His open eye looked milky. "My last relative. I have lost everyone. I thought I was alone ... and now you have returned." He smiled toothlessly. *How old could he be?*

"Yes, I am back. For now."

"Where have you been, Javor? For eight years?" Hrech asked. He kept pacing back and forth between Javor and the villagers, occasionally pulling on someone's elbow to say "See? It's Javor!"

"Constantinople, mostly," Javor said, looking for familiar faces in the crowd. Peeking from behind their mothers, a few small children stared wide-eyed. *Where is Elli? Who did she marry? Did she marry?*

*Is she still alive?*

"Constantinople!" Hrech exclaimed. "Fantastic. You see? What did I tell you? Our Javor went to Constantinople." He turned to Javor again. "Did you ever see the emperor?"

"Several times," Javor answered, still scanning the crowd.

"Several times," Hrech guffawed.

Holding a hand at the small of his back, Mrost stepped up. "Next you'll tell us you met the emperor, too."

"Just once," Javor answered.

Mrost scoffed, then pointed vaguely at the crowd. "Someone close that gate before another warrior rides in here," he sneered.

"No one put you in charge, Mrost," Hrech repeated, but pushed the swinging gate closed. "Vojtek, Jaro, get some water and grain for this fine horse," he called as he led the animal away from the gate. Two young boys ran up and took the reins to guide the horse to a barn near the wall. "Mirna, bring some ale and something to eat."

"Of course," said a short, thin young woman with long dark hair, holding a naked baby on her hip. She smiled, revealing crossed front teeth. A memory flashed into Javor's mind: a young girl with crossed teeth laughing as she raced to catch flowers thrown during a spring ceremony. "It's good to see you again, Javor."

Javor needed a moment to remember her. "Mirna. Yes, it is."

Mirna laughed, shaking her head. "Oh, Javor. You haven't changed, even though your clothes have."

*What does she mean by that?*

Mirna took the baby in both hands as she bowed to enter one of the partially sunken houses.

Hrech pointed to a low bench beside the edge of the thatched roof where it sloped down to the ground. "Sit, sit. Rest. You've come a long way. How far is it to Constantinople from here?"

"At least a week's ride south until you find an old Roman highway, then several more days to the Danuvius River ..."

"What's a highway?" Hrech interrupted.

"Well, um, it's a kind of road, only very wide, paved with cut stones to make it smoother. Travel along it is quite fast."

"Oh," Hrech nodded. "So, it is a very long way. I thought so. Strange that it still has so much power, so far away. But what brings you back here? Why make such a long journey?"

"I am looking for something, and I wanted to talk to Vorona about it."

Hrech swallowed, closed his mouth and looked at the ground. "Vorona," he repeated after a long pause.

"What's wrong? Is she dead?"

"Dead? No, no ... at least, not that I know of. No. But ... well, her fertility ceremonies certainly were strong. So many babies were born after that summer. At least ten to young new mothers, and six lived more than a year."

Javor's mouth went dry. "What about Elli," he said, his voice a rasp. "Did she have a baby?"

Hrech smirked. "Yes." He held Javor's eye for a moment when Javor felt his pulse in his ears. Then he tilted his head back and laughed loud and hard, slapping his knee. "Oh, Javor, you should see your face. Don't worry," he clapped his hand on Javor's shoulder. "Yes, she's had three babies. Two are still alive. But they're not yours. She had her first baby ..." Hrech stood and leaned into the doorway of the hut. "Mirna, when did Elli have her first baby?"

"Four and a half years ago," came a feminine voice. "Little Slava will be five in the winter."

"How long is that bread going to take?" Hrech yelled, then sat down beside Javor again. "See? Elli's first baby cannot be yours."

Javor realized he had been holding his breath for a long time, and let it out. Hrech laughed. "Finally!" he announced as Mirna set a clay jug on the ground at Hrech's feet. "I thought you were brewing that ale. Now, where is—ah, bread. Good."

"You're welcome," Mirna said, then took the baby back inside the hut.

Hrech held up the jug to Javor. "You need it more than I do, old friend."

Javor took a long drink. He found his voice. "Elli. So she has children." He took another drink. "Who is she with?" *Please, not Mrost.*

"Vlad." Hrech took the jug and tilted it back.

"Vlad? Isn't he, what, two years younger than Ellie?"

Hrech shrugged as he wiped his mouth with the back of his hand. "Maybe. He's a pushy little guy. But tell me about yourself. Any babies for you?"

"One so far," Javor said. "And one on the way." He realized he was smiling as Mirna returned with a loaf of bread with butter. Hrech tore off a big chunk, dipped it into the butter and took a big bite.

"That's for our guest," Mirna warned.

*Does she ever put that baby down?*

Hrech offered the loaf to Javor, who tore off a chunk, sank it into the butter and took a big bite. He took another swallow of ale as Hrech tried to lick butter out of his own beard. "So where can I find Vorona?"

"Mirna!" Hrech shouted. "More ale!"

Mirna came to the door, glaring at Hrech, her lips a thin line. "We're out of ale," Hrech said, holding up the jug.

"Then get more," she said.

"I'm with our guest," Hrech responded, holding the jug higher.

Mirna shook her head, tossed a glare at Javor, took the jug and stomped off again.

"So ... you and Mirna?" Javor asked.

Hrech chuckled. "Yes. Hard to believe, eh? But I knocked her up at the fertility ceremony the year after you left, so I had to marry her."

Javor kept his mouth shut as Mirna brought another jugful of ale and dropped it at Hrech's feet, beer sloshing over the rim. He watched her hips sway angrily into the hut again. "She's too good-looking for you," he said.

Hrech tossed a healthy measure of ale into his throat, then laughed. "For my face, sure. But she didn't argue with my cock!"

The two friends laughed, and for a moment, Javor was a teenager again, sitting on a log beside his old friend, summer breeze moving through his hair. A bee buzzed by, birds tweeted in the trees. Somewhere, a rooster crowed. "It's good to see you again, Hrech."

Hrech stood. "Come on, I'll show you around. We've made a lot of changes since you left."

Javor linked arms with his old friend—his only childhood friend—and let him lead the way around the village. Hrech pointed to various houses, naming their occupants. "After you left, things were quiet for a few months. No more raiders, no more monsters, neither. And we had the best harvest in years, too.

"But we heard about other villages that were burned down by Avars. And right after the harvest, just when we had put up food and fuel for the season, a troop of about twenty of the bastards came in and took almost half of it. They hung around, too, for months, taking chickens or pigs whenever they wanted. They raped girls and even the older women. Grat got knocked up by one."

Javor stopped in his tracks. "Grat? Is she all right?"

Hrech looked up at Javor for a long moment. "She's well enough, now. Has three little brats. The oldest is the Avar's, we figure. Ugly little thing. Not that her other kids are much prettier. But you know, Javor, I am always surprised how much you cared about her. She was awful to you all the time. Mean little bitch."

"I don't care about her," Javor protested. "I just don't want anything bad to happen to her, that's all."

Hrech shook his head, then clapped his hand on Javor's shoulder. "That's you, Javor. You were always different from everybody else."

"So, Grat ... is she with Mrost now?"

Hrech snorted. "Nah. That prick wouldn't go near her once the Avars had her. She's with Little Borys now." Javor remembered a small, quiet boy, a few years younger than himself. The villagers had called him "Little Borys," so-called to distinguish him from Javor's uncle Borys, who was not his namesake's father.

Hrech led Javor to a hut that appeared newer and larger than most in the village. The beams and supports were thicker, the top of the roof higher.

Hrech leaned into the open door and banged on the frame. "Hey Elli! Come out. I have a special surprise for you."

Javor heard shuffling from inside the hut, and then scampering bare feet. A little girl of four or five burst out into the sunshine. "Where? Where is the surprise?" she demanded, looking up at Hrech and bouncing on her toes.

A woman emerged from the hut, with long, limp brown hair and large eyes. She did not look the same as she had eight years earlier, but Javor would always know the girl he had first loved. The first girl he had ever had sex with.

*Elli.*

She came out of the hut, glaring at Hrech, but before she could say a word, she saw Javor. She straightened, eyes widening.

"Hrech, Hrech. Where is the surprise?" the little girl repeated.

"Hush, Slava," Elli said, then turned to Javor again. "You're back?"

"Hello, Elli," he said. "It's good to see you again."

"What are you doing here?"

"Javor has come from Constantinople, on a mission from the emperor," Hrech piped up. "Sorry, Augustus is what they call him, right?"

"My mission is over. But I wanted to visit," Javor said. *Why did I come? What was I thinking?*

"Why? Are you bringing more trouble?" Elli demanded.

"What do you mean?"

"Hrech, where is the surprise?" little Slava demanded again.

"Hush, Slava," Elli said again. "This man is the surprise."

Slava looked up at him, pouting. Then she gasped and hid behind her mother's legs. "Mama, he's so big. I'm scared."

Hrech laughed and tousled the little girl's hair. "There is no reason to be afraid, little girl. Javor isn't so bad."

"Mama said he was bringing trouble," she whined.

Javor stepped back and took a good luck at mother and daughter. The little girl was tiny, scrawny, with reddish blotches on her pale skin.

Her dark hair was thin and her brown eyes small. *She looks like her father,* Javor realized.

Elli, though, was the girl he remembered. *No, not the girl. Now a woman.* She was still as thin as he remembered, but her hips were much wider than they had been the last time he had held them. She still wore her hair long and loose, but it hung limp. When she spoke, he could see she had lost more than one tooth, and there were lines on the face that he remembered as being soft and smooth as the surface of a pond on a windless day.

*Do I look that much older?*

"Well, what do you want?" Elli demanded again.

Javor could think of nothing to say, so just as he had when they had been children, Hrech spoke for him. "He just wanted to visit his old home, to see everyone. There's no trouble to be afraid of."

"Really?" Elli snapped. "You don't remember, eight years ago? When the Avars first came? First, that old Greek man came, looking for Javor and that witch, Vorona. Then came the raiders. Then that ... that ..." She looked down at her daughter. "Go, Slava. Go and play."

"But, Mama," the girl whined.

"Go on! Go find your father. He is probably with your Uncle Ihor. Go."

Reluctantly, the girl walked away, disappearing among the scattered dugout huts.

"Do you remember, Elli, how we loved each other then?" Javor asked. "Do you remember that night in the clearing, the night of the full moon, before the solstice?" He could still remember that night, Vorona's drum, the moon above the treetops, shining on Elli's naked skin. He could still remember her scent mingled with pine needles and wet grass.

"I never loved you," Elli interrupted him. "You were always following me like a lost puppy. You used me when that witch put a spell on us. That's all it was."

"And the next night, I saved you," Javor reminded her. "Hrech and I followed the Avars who had taken you, and we brought you and Grat back home."

Elli glared at him. "It was your bad luck that brought the Avars. It was you and your family that brought the monster that killed them. It wanted them, Javor. It wanted *you*. The rest of us just got in the way, but how many died? How many were maimed? It was that same bad luck that brought the Avars to our village in the first place."

Once more, Hrech stepped in. "Come on, Javor. I want to show you some more of the village."

Javor turned and never saw Elli again.

Hrech led Javor to the gate. "After the Avars left in the spring, I convinced Roslaw that we should all live inside the holody. People grumbled about it, and it took two summers to rebuild all the houses inside, but we did it. Some families use the houses that are still standing when there's no sign of strangers around, but I don't let them stay out here for very long."

"So you're the hetman now," Javor said.

Hrech scoffed. "No, no. I'm no hetman, you know that."

"It's not Mrost, is it? He said he was hetman."

"Gods, no! We don't really have a hetman anymore. We get together to make good decisions. Mrost makes a lot of noise, so he likes to say he's in charge, but we all know he's nothing but a blowhard. He used to be a bully, but he's no bigger than anyone else his age anymore. The only people he pushes around anymore are his poor wife and their one baby."

"Who's his poor wife?"

"Remember Young Slava?"

"Grat's sister? The really small one?"

Hrech nodded. "He took her as wife just to spite Grat. Made them both miserable." To end that conversation, Hrech pulled Javor to the inner log wall. "I convinced Roslaw to double the palisade. Poor old man, he didn't live to see it complete."

"Roslaw. He was a good man."

Hrech peered at Javor again. "He kicked you out of the village, Javor. Remember?"

Javor closed his eyes, but that did not prevent him from seeing Roslaw's freshly scarred face on that summer day, eight years earlier. Neither did his eyelids keep out the pain he felt. "I haven't forgotten, Hrech. But ... well, my life is so much better now."

"So why are you back?"

Javor sighed and opened his eyes. He scanned the village, then looked out the gate. "I have a mission."

"For the emperor?"

"He's called the Augustus. But he did not give me this mission."

"Then who?"

"I am part of ... a religious order." *This is much too complicated to explain in an afternoon.*

Hrech nodded. "Ah, the Church. I might have known. You know, another missionary came by here a year ago, talking about one god. He left when the weather started to get cold again. So you're a Christian now?"

"No," Javor answered.

"Yet, you live in Constantinople. Well, you always had your own way of thinking, Javor."

They went back to Hrech's hut. "How did Roslaw die?" Javor asked.

"He just got sick. For a fortnight, he got weaker and weaker. Couldn't keep any food in him. Vorona tended him day and night, but couldn't help. When he finally went, it was a relief."

"Vorona. You still haven't told me where she is."

Hrech looked at the ground again.

"Tell me if she's dead. I understand."

"I don't know. After Roslaw died, she left. I never saw her like that. She looked crushed. Completely defeated. She tried so hard to help Roslaw, but it was no use. And then, Vorona hardly came out of her home. You know, she never left her place down by the river. Even when the Avars overwintered here, they never bothered her. They were afraid of her. Never laid a hand on her. But she couldn't stop them, either. I guess her magic just wasn't strong enough."

"Where is she, Hrech?"

"I told you, I don't know. She left a month after Roslaw passed. She took her things from her house, and no one has seen or heard of her since. Except for one time: a boy from a village to the south, some place called Bilavod, came here with a message."

"Bilavod! I know it."

Hrech nodded toward his semi-sunken house again. "We heard about you there," he said as he led Javor back to the bench. He picked up the jug and pointed at the bench to tell his friend to sit. "I'll get more ale." He disappeared into his little house, and Javor could hear low voices inside arguing, but could not make out the words. When Hrech emerged again, he was scowling, but carried a full jug. He took a deep draught, then passed it to Javor.

Javor drank. The air was hot, and the ale cool. He passed the jug back to Hrech. "What did you hear about Bilavod?"

Hrech took another drink, then put the half-empty jug on the ground between his feet. "We don't get a lot of visitors. That old man who took you away was a real shock. Every so often, a trader comes looking to exchange furs for honey or wax, but we're a poor village. We've never had anyone who's as good a beekeeper as your father, Javor."

"Tell me what the boy from Bilavod said."

"He said that a great warrior and a sorcerer defended them against an Avar attack. They lost a lot of people, but the warrior trained them to fight. He was a young giant, the boy told us, with long yellow hair and eyes blue as a summer sky. I think he was in love with you, Javor."

Javor felt his face get hot.

"Anyway, the boy said that a wise woman with long black hair came to them and stayed for a few days. She was able to heal some sick people and relieved some people with sores and wounds. But she told them to leave their homes, to move west and south away from the Avars. And she sent us a message, too."

"What was it?"

"She told us not to leave. We have to stay here, to stay strong and defend. And one day, our answers will come to us."

"A prophecy?"

Hrech shrugged. "I never thought of it that way, but I suppose so."

"Answers to what?"

"I don't know. But we finished the inner palisade and built the watchtowers in between the two walls. And since then, things have been quiet, like I said. No more raiders, no Avars, no monsters."

# The house of the wise woman

The reception he received that night in Nastaciu was not like the one he had in Leleka. There was no feast, no pouring of jugs of ale—although he and Hrech certainly drank enough. No village begging him for tales of Constantinople and his adventures.

At sunset, he took a piece of bread and wandered outside the stockade. He walked through the ruins of the old village, wondering as he had in Bilavod, whether he could remember which hut had belonged to which person in his life.

He rounded the hill. From its collapsed front, he recognized the little half-sunken hut he had grown up in. Tears filled his eyes as he remembered his father lying in front of it, and he had to turn away instead of looking into where he had found his mother's broken body inside.

He kept walking and found himself down by the stream, looking at an empty, but somehow still intact hut built of logs and thatch, raised above ground level to protect against flooding. He pulled the door open. It was hard to see much in the failing light, but the shelves on the walls appeared empty, the floor swept clean.

When Vorona left, she appeared to have taken everything with her. Or given it away.

He jumped when a dog howled. He turned to the door of Vorona's hut and saw night had covered the hut. *How long have I been in here?*

The full moon shone on the stream's calm surface. *I didn't know the moon would be full tonight. What is happening to me?*

A dog howled again. Javor turned toward the sound and saw a stand of trees he did not recognize. Something glowed yellow and orange in its midst. He stepped toward it. He heard music, similar to the chants he had heard in the churches in Constantinople, but so quiet it was either very far away, or in his imagination. The high-pitched sound keened, whined, whistled in his mind. He shook his head, but the sound remained at the lowest edge of perception.

He pushed boughs out of his way until he saw what stood at the centre of the yellow and orange glow. A woman wearing a loose, hooded white robe stood in a small clearing, holding in one hand a lantern that gave far too much light for its size. A large black dog sat at her feet, watching Javor step into the clearing.

*Vorona?*

She lifted the lantern higher, and Javor realized she was probably less than twenty years old. Not Vorona. Her skin was flawless, her eyes wide and dark. Except for a fuller mouth, she reminded him of Elli, as she looked when he was in love with her, years earlier.

Javor, he heard, but the woman's mouth had not moved.

*It's like talking with a dragon.* "Who are you?"

YOU KNOW WHO WE ARE.

"No, I do not. You look like Elli. How do you know me?"

WE ARE HERE TO WARN YOU. Her appearance shifted, quickly but smoothly. Her hair suddenly was braided and coiled over her head. Her face seemed wider, somehow, her features more distinct. She looks older, Javor realized. And she no longer resembled Elli, but rather like Aunt Tiana in Constantinople.

YOU ARE UNDOING THE BALANCE.

At her feet, the dog lay down on its stomach, its eyes fixed on Javor.

"What balance?"

YOU HAVE KILLED SOME OF THE DEEP POWER OF THE WORLD. YOU ARE TILTING THE BALANCE TOWARD THE CELESTIAL.

"Was the dragon ... sacred to you?"

IT WAS SACRED TO ALL LIFE IN THIS WORLD, JAVOR. ITS DEATH WEAKENS THE EARTH.

"But it was killing people."

YOU HAVE ENDED MANY SACRED LIVES. IF YOU CONTINUE ON THIS PATH, THE EARTH WILL BE GRAVELY WEAKENED. AS WILL HUMANITY'S FUTURE. YOU ARE CHANGING THE WORLD IN WAYS YOU WILL NOT LIKE.

"Are you saying that monsters are necessary for humanity to survive?"

YOU HAVE BEEN GIVEN PRECIOUS GIFTS. THEY PROTECT YOU FROM HARM AND EMPOWER YOU TO ACCOMPLISH GREAT DEEDS.

Javor touched the amulet under his tunic. "They don't seem to help anyone around me."

IT IS YOUR ACTIONS THAT RESULT IN THE DEATH OF OTHER PEOPLE. YOU WERE CHOSEN TO RECEIVE THOSE GIFTS, BUT YOU HAVE JOINED THE WAR ON THE WRONG SIDE.

"What war?"

She changed again. Her hair was now grey. Deep lines defined her cheeks, and skin sagged under her chin. The hand holding the lantern was thin, bones and veins distinct under withered skin. Recognition jolted Javor: she looked exactly like Sophia, the woman in Constantia who had directed him to the Order in Chalkoprateia eight years earlier, before she was killed by archons.

I AM HERE TO ASK YOU TO SEEK FOR TRUTH, JAVOR. NOT EVERYONE YOU TRUST DESERVES IT.

"Who should I mistrust?"

RETURN TO THE CITY OF CONSTANTINE AND SEEK KNOWLEDGE.

"What knowledge?"

THE BONES OF THE EARTH AND THE POWER OF THE SKY.

The dog rose to its feet again and looked up at the goddess. She lowered the lantern and its light faded.

"I don't understand," Javor protested. He pulled the amulet out, holding it toward her, his other hand on the hilt of his dagger. "Aren't these the bones of the earth?"

YOU CARRY THEM, BUT YOU DO NOT KNOW THEM.

"Then tell me."

YOU MUST SEEK THE KNOWLEDGE FROM THE BONES THEMSELVES. THERE ARE HUMANS WHO CAN GUIDE YOU, BUT YOU MUST TAKE GREATER CARE IN WHOM YOU TRUST.

The dog lifted its head and howled again. The lantern's light died. Javor reached for the woman, touching only air. "Wait. Who can't I trust?"

There was no answer.

Two weeks later, Javor was back at his home in Constantinople. A smiling Calanthe greeted him in the atrium, holding a fat baby boy. "His name is Adam," she said.

Javor pulled the soft, pink baby close, marveling at the blue eyes and the hint of fine blond hair on his head. "He looks just like his father," Calanthe said.

Javor did not even wonder why his wife's parents were not at his house this time. He breathed in the smell from the top of his new baby's head, and then kissed his wife.

"We missed you, Javor," Calanthe said.

"I ... I missed you, too," he replied as Andrina, now two years old, ran into the atrium and wrapped her arms around his legs. He bent to kiss her head, then picked her up and squeezed her until she squirmed and giggled.

"You have grown since I left," he said.

"It has been over a month. Nearly two," said Calanthe.

He looked at his wife. "You have grown, too. You look fatter."

"Javor!" Calanthe's face reddened. "How could you say that?" She retreated into her bedchamber, leaving a bewildered Javor holding his daughter.

"Let's play, Papa," Andrina said.

Javor put his daughter on the tiled floor, stripped his clothes and sank into the cool water of the impluvium, the rainwater basin in the middle of the open atrium. He knew Calanthe would not like that.

She is mad at me already, so what difference will it make? He turned, seized Andrina and dunked her into the water. She jumped up, splashing and laughing.

Javor felt the tension of the mission and the return fall away from his body.

The day after his return, he had the servants help Tiana into a carriage, and they rode to the Abbey of the St. Mary of Chalkoprateia. Javor brought Tiana to Malleus, the head of the Order, in the secret rooms, and insisted on going to the library.

Javor was determined to find whom he could trust.

# Father, mother, daughter, son

*Year 604 Christian Era*

A hot summer day. The sun streamed straight down through the open roof above the atrium. Javor pulled off all his clothes save for a cloth around his waist.

He knew Calanthe would not approve, but he did not care. He picked up Andrina, now three, pulled off her clothes and held her close to his chest. He savoured the feeling of bare skin on skin and did not let himself feel Christian guilt over it.

Calanthe lay on a couch in the shadow of the overhanging roof. On a small table at her elbow stood a plate of honey-drenched dumplings and a jug of wine. A cup was in one hand, and she licked honey from the fingers of the other. Year-old Adam cuddled against her on the couch, playing with his toes.

Javor pressed his daughter close and stepped into the impluvium, the depression in the centre of the atrium's tiled floor and sank into the water, the remnants of the rainfall from two nights earlier. Sitting, the water reached only to his waist, so he slid back, submerging his head and his daughter.

She laughed when they came up, so he sank in again.

It felt so good to break the heat of the Constantinopolitan summer. Andrina loved it, too, splashing as he set her on the bottom of the pool.

"Javor," Calanthe protested. "What are we supposed to use for cooking, now?" Her double chins wobbled. She took a deep drink of wine.

"What is wrong?" But he knew she did not approve of his bathing in the impluvium. Bathing was something one did at the public baths.

Andrina laughed. "I like the water, Mama!" She splashed water at her mother.

"You see, Calanthe? There is nothing wrong. We are all enjoying ourselves, cooling off in the fine water. Come, take off your clothes and join us?"

Calanthe's eyes widened. "Not in front of the children, Javor!" She rose, unsteady, and took one more gulp of wine. "Now I am all wet. I will have to change my gown."

She left the atrium. Javor and Andrina continued to play in the water.

# Interlude 4

# A Conspiracy

*Summer 605 Christian Era*

Night in the city was quieter than the daytime, but still noisy. Shouting from the taverns. Thin, false laughter from the brothels. Horses' hooves on cobblestone and the calls of the night watch on the city walls that faced the Golden Horn.

Nighttime was smellier than the daytime, though. Leon, born in the city, did not notice it for longer than it took him to walk the length of the alley to where it met the street. Hand on the hilt of his sword, he peered up and down the narrow avenue, trying to penetrate the deep shadows between the few lanterns hanging over gloomy doorways.

He jumped, half-drawing his sword at a sentry's challenge, then sighed as it was answered from somewhere above. The night watch on the wall.

He thought for a moment of Dmitrios, his commanding officer. He would say Leon was disobeying orders, that he was disloyal to the Excubitors.

He shrugged off the feeling. I am loyal to the Empire.

He signaled to the door. Four cloaked, hooded figures stepped into the alley and hurried to Leon's side. He pointed in the direction where the street sloped upward.

The leading figure, the tallest, nodded. Leon led the way up the slope, feeling the absence of his helmet and armour. *Wearing it outside quarters when I am not on duty would have raised too many questions.*

The back of his neck tingling, he led the four behind him through the darkest shadows. They skirted the plaza in front of the biggest cathedral in the world and the guards on its steps. At the end of another dank alley, Leon stopped at a door and tapped once, softly.

The door cracked open, revealing only more darkness. To a deeper shadow, Leon whispered "Anastasia."

The door opened wide without sound. "Come quickly," the shadow whispered.

Leon pressed up against the wall to allow the four behind him to enter the cathedral's side door. At the threshold, the tallest paused. "Who is this?"

"This is Brother Michael," Leon whispered back.

"Please stay quiet," the monk urged. "The Patriarch must know nothing about this, nor Father Bardas."

The five filed into a narrow hallway. Brother Michael uncovered a candle, then shut the door and slid a wooden bolt into a lock. Finger over his lips, he led the party along what the flickering candlelight showed was a tunnel of rough stone with a barrel-shaped ceiling. The air inside was chilly and smelled damp. Leon kept his hand on his sword as he brought up the rear.

Brother Michael paused briefly to indicate the foot of a staircase, then crossed himself, raised the candle high and climbed. At the top, he pulled open a door that was markedly more ornate than the one that gave onto the alley. Yellow candlelight from the space beyond seemed bright in comparison to the monk's single taper.

Brother Michael held the door wide and gestured the others into the cathedral. Leon stepped onto smooth marble tile that reflected hundreds, thousands of candles.

No matter how many times he had come to this, the largest cathedral in the world, Leon always caught his breath at the sight of the soaring pillars, the gleaming marble, the mosaic portrayals of angels and saints and emperors. Leon could not prevent his eyes from scanning up. Though it was now dark, he knew that daylight through the windows ringing the immense centre dome made it look like it floated high above the congregants, as if suspended from Heaven.

"This way," Brother Michael said softly, but no longer whispering. He led them across the floor toward one of the *exedrae*, the semi-circular, half-domed spaces along both sides of the nave of the great cathedral. High in the wall, a window looked out only onto the darkness of the city at night. Below it was another mosaic depicting Mary, Mary Magdalene and Martha at the Tomb, surmounted by a gold and porphyry crucifix larger than Leon himself. On each side of the mosaic, wooden benches curved along the walls.

Four men stood in the space, staring at Brother Michael and his party as they approached. Michael halted just inside the exedra. "Thank you for coming this night," he said in a low voice.

"Why have you called us here?" asked a short, thin man with thick, curly hair and beard. Leon recognized him as Petros, the Demarch of the Blue Faction. He wore a long, dark tunica whose colour Leon could not be sure of in the dim candlelight. Over it was a light coloured cloak, fastened at the right shoulder by a complicated brooch that glittered with reflected flames. A leather pouch hung from his belt at his right hip, and he wore the fashionable toeless boots on his feet.

"We know why," growled a taller, stout bald man who stepped forward, frowning. His greying beard extended below his neck. He wore a simple grey tunica, belted with a green sash embroidered with a white cross. His feet were bare. "We're here to talk about the emperor."

The words sent a shock through Leon. And judging from the looks on their faces, through most of the others in the room, as well.

"Guard your tongue," another man hissed as he stepped between the two men. "What we are here to discuss is ... very dangerous." He was middle-aged, bald like the man in the grey tunic, but his clothes were rich: a brocaded, long tunic covered with a long cloak, decorated with a complex tablion, or square-pattern. Pale hose covered his legs, fine new leather shoes his feet. Even Leon could see the gold brooch at his shoulder was precious.

Leon loosened his sword in its scabbard. Just in case.

The man in grey glared at the rich man. "Who are you?"

The rich man straightened his back and looked the man in grey in the eye. "Flavius Clementinus, Senator of Rome." He turned slightly to indicate another richly dressed man, this one with greying dark hair. A sword hung at his hip. "This is Senator Flavius Maximinius. And I take it you are Probus, Demarch of the Green faction."

The man in grey grunted.

"You are correct in your assessment of our purpose tonight," Clementinus said. "The current holder of the office is a man of low birth, little breeding and meagre accomplishment. He is an embarrassment to the Empire and an affront to God. He is nothing but a usurper. Despite his claims, he was never asked to be *Autokrator*," using the Old Greek word. "He was sent only as a representative of the Legions."

"You tried deposing him three years ago," Probus said flatly. "We supported Germanus for emperor. And we were cut to pieces. The previous Demarch of the Greens was hanged and disemboweled for his trouble, and his family thrown into the sea."

"The Greens acclaimed him," Petros interrupted. "The Blues were far less enthusiastic about deposing Maurice."

"I remember seeing you cheering as the Legions of the Danuvius entered the city," Probus retorted. "I remember a lot of Blue banners flying high that day."

"None of the Blues cheered as the bodies of the emperor's sons were thrown into the Propontis," Petros said.

"None of the Greens celebrated when the heads of Maurice and his sons were put on pikes in the Hippodrome either," said Probus. "Maurice was not the first emperor of Rome to be murdered by the next to hold the post."

"Before anyone says ... that word again, I remind you, I—I implore you to be circumspect in your speech," said Brother Michael.

"'Circumspect'?" Probus asked.

"Cautious," said Clementinus. "That is wise, but we are safe here in the Hagia Sophia."

"If you want to be cautious, then maybe those people over there should show their faces." Probus pointed his beard toward the figures huddled behind Leon.

But another man, tall and straight, stepped into the light. He was younger than the senators, Leon thought, perhaps only a little older than himself. From under his cloak, he drew a leather bag, bulging as big as two of Leon's fists, and dropped it on the floor in the midst of the gathering.

"I am Flavius Paulus, representing General Germanus Patricius. He sends this deposit and promises enough gold to pay the Armenian Guard in Constantinople. And more to bring enough of the Praetorian Guard to our side."

"And which side would that be?" Probus asked from his couch.

"The side of the true heir to the throne, the Caesar Theodosius, eldest son of the legitimate Emperor Maurice. He is under the protection of General Narses."

"Theodosius is immaterial," Clementinus said. "Whether he is alive, as many believe, or dead, if people believe he is alive, they will support him. The point is to ... resolve the current situation."

"Gold is always helpful when you're planning to get rid of someone high-up," Probus said from the bench he occupied. "But I still don't know who is hiding behind the young guard over there.

The tall person behind Leon stepped into the light, throwing the hood behind the cloak to reveal a mass of rich, dark hair in complex braids over a high forehead. Even in the dim candlelight, the brown eyes that Leon knew so well flashed indignity. "My oldest son is not immaterial," said Constantina, the widow of Maurice and thus the true Augusta. "Maurice, my husband, made him Caesar and therefore the rightful heir. And I, for one, know he yet lives."

Behind her, the three other figures lowered their hoods, as well, revealing themselves as Constantina's three daughters, Anastasia, Theoctiste and Cleopatra.

Clementinus' jaw dropped. He took a step backward, blinking, before sinking onto one knee and bowing his head, his hand over his heart. "Empress! My apologies. I had no idea you would come tonight."

Maximinius, Paulus and Petros, the Demarch of the Blues, also sank to their knees. Probus remained slumped on the bench, glaring at the woman.

"My apologies as well, Empress. I should not have spoken about your son as I did," Maximinius said.

"There is no need to apologize, sirs. Please rise." Her voice was deep for a woman's. It was one of the reasons that Leon had loved her from the moment he became an Excubitor, one of the emperor's personal guards.

The kneeling men rose. "Well? Get up, fool," Maximinius snarled at Probus.

Probus scoffed. "You expect the Demarch of the Greens to grovel before the wife of the deposed Emperor Maurice?" Despite his words, he stood, pointing at the former empress. "Did you forget that Maurice cut the pay of the Legions on the Danuvius? Did you forget how he refused to ransom the legionnaires who were prisoners of the barbarian Avars? Did you forget how the savages cut their throats, to a man? The Greens do not forget. Not like rich men do. You only remember how much gold is in your purse."

Leon drew his sword and stepped between Probus and the empress. "Speak with respect to your betters."

"Or what? You'll stab me?" Probus scoffed. "In the Hagia Sophia? Before the Holy Crucifix? What kind of excubitor are you?"

"Does this mean we cannot expect the support of the Greens?" Clementinus asked.

"Support for what? For who? A dead boy for emperor? Why should we?"

"I heard the emperor's eldest son is in the custody of the Sassanid King," Petros said. Probus scoffed.

"Because Pho—the current occupant is not only an abomination, he is incompetent," Clementinus answered. "He has purged or blinded hundreds of men loyal to the true emperor. The Sassanids have invaded almost unopposed. The only other general who could have opposed them, Narses, has joined them. The Empire of Rome is faced with extinction."

"And all the man who now befouls the Great Palace will do is drink wine and fornicate with whores. Even in front of the poor woman whom he calls wife," added Petros.

"How would you know that?" Probus laughed. "When was the last time you were invited to an orgy in the Great Palace?"

Petros shrugged. "People talk."

"We agree, Phocas is intolerable," said the empress. "He was sent by the Legions of the west to represent their grievances to the emperor and seized the opportunity presented by the riots of your faction, Probus. Whatever your objections were to my husband, Phocas was never meant to be emperor. Need I remind you that the man on the throne not only commands the legions and the Roman people, he is also the pinnacle of the Church, Christ's representative on Earth? Is that ... degenerate, that debauch, the man to whom the Greens wish to continue to genuflect toward on Easter Sunday?"

Clementinus stepped forward. "My faction of the Senate will also contribute to the effort, equal to the gold provided by Germanus."

"As will my faction," Maximinius seconded.

Clementinus turned to Probus. "What about the demes?"

Probus hefted a bag of gold. "This is very persuasive."

"Put it down," Paulus, the representative of General Germanus said. "I will see the coins are distributed among your faction." He took the bag from the Demarch of the Greens, and holding it in one hand as if it were filled with leaves, he pulled four gold *solidi*. "Show this to your people as a gesture that we are serious."

Smirking, Probus dropped the coins into a hidden pouch in his tunic.

"It would seem the Greens are decided," Clementinus said. "What about the Blues?"

Petros looked at Probus, then at the empress and finally at the second bag of gold on the floor. He opened his mouth, his eyes darting from face to face. He swallowed. "I will have to confer with the others," he said with a wavering voice.

"What others?" Clementinus demanded.

"I—I cannot speak for all the Blues—"

"You are the Demarch," Probus hooted. "That means you do speak for the Blues."

Paulus' hand was on the hilt of his sword. "Decide, Demarch."

Clementinus had noticeably more trouble lifting the bag of gold from the floor than Paulus had. He opened it, drew out four coins and held them out to Petros. "Convince the faction."

Petros took the solidi with shaking hands. "Then we are agreed. The Blues will be ready."

"You will know the signal," said Clementinus. He bowed to the empress, and silently left.

Maximinius bowed and followed. Probus made an exaggerated bow to the empress and her daughters and walked away, his bare feet slapping on the marble tiles.

Petros bowed, but before he could leave, Paulus stepped in front of him. "If you fail, I will find you," he said.

Shaking, Petros ran from the church.

Leon let out a long, slow breath. He looked at his beloved empress, who nodded. As quietly as they could, the little group followed Brother Michael back through the tunnel to the outside, and then through the dark, smelly streets to the old, private home that was the prison to what remained of the imperial family.

# Uprising

*Summer 605 Christian Era*

Leon was ready when the signal came, in full armour outside the door of the empress's apartments. But he did not need any special code or message. The noise of the rioting Greens was plenty.

He stepped onto the balcony, wary of rocks or anything else that could be thrown by the horde stampeding through the streets toward the Hagia Sophia. The sinking sun turned the clouds pink, and an orange glow to the north betrayed a fire somewhere. Probably a rubbish heap, he thought.

Leon guessed the noise came from the Ox Forum, but then he heard another tumult. A crowd of men stampeded into the wide street below the balcony, shouting, some carrying torches even though the sun was still above the city walls. They surged like a river, never ending, in the direction of the Hippodrome and the Great Palace.

"It has begun." Leon jumped at the voice behind him, his hand going to his sword.

"Majesty!" Leon reached toward the Empress Constantina, who had entered the room without his hearing. He stopped himself before his hand reached her arm, remembering his place. "You should not come close to the balcony. Please."

The empress ignored his plea and stepped toward the window to see the continuing tumult. "What are they chanting?"

Leon listened. The words were hard to make out amid all the other noise. He heard bugle calls from the city guards and knew that his regimental commander would be looking for him soon.

"'Out the usurper,' empress," he said. "They're calling to remove Phocas from the throne."

Constantina moved a little closer to the window, but did not step onto the balcony. She showed no expression as she watched the rioters stream past. "Is everything else ready?"

"I am ready, for my part, my empress." Leon looked more carefully at the crowd. They had slowed to a fast walking pace as their numbers filled the street. "But I cannot speak for anyone else. And it would appear that the men below are only from the Green faction."

"Perhaps the Blues are in another part of the city?"

Leon wanted to believe that. "I pray they are, Majesty." Something inside told him that the Blues had betrayed their cause.

The city guard and the excubitors, the emperor's bodyguard, did not take long to respond. Leon retreated from the balcony when he saw armoured men appear on a side street, four abreast. Their helmets shining golden in the late sunlight, they struck at the men running past them.

The chants turned to screams of pain. The rioters fell, knocking down their comrades around them. The excubitors stepped over the bodies to club more men as they ran.

Some of the crowd turned to run back the way they had come, but were blocked by more Greens who were still coming, unaware of the opposition.

Men on the ground tried to crawl away but were clubbed again and again as more soldiers entered the street. Leon could see another group coming from the direction of the Hippodrome.

He turned to the empress again. "We must go inside now, your Majesty. You must be ready to move as soon as the next signal comes."

"I am ready. As are my daughters."

Leon nodded. He tightened his chin strap and loosened the sword in his belt, then led the four women down to the street level. They paused behind the colonnades, watching the roiling crowds in front of them. The noise was nearly deafening, the yells of the soldiers, the screams of wounded men, the stamping of feet and the pounding of drums in the rear ranks. The excubitors advanced steadily, beating the lightly armed Greens to the ground or thrusting spears through their bodies.

"Leon." The Empress startled him by touching his arm. He flinched away, alarmed at the prospect of having touched royalty. "Your greave is tapping on the column."

Leon's heart sank as he realized his knee was shaking. "Apologies, empress. I ... I am anxious to ... to move you to safety." His face heated at the lie.

She smiled at him gently, but her eyes were on the uneven battle beyond the colonnade. Leon bowed quickly, then turned and led them along the colonnade to a narrow alley. Crossing it to another colonnade would expose them to the thick of the fighting, but it was the most direct way to the Hagia Sophia.

Leon stepped down into the alley, holding a hand up to tell the empress and her daughters to wait. A man with a green scarf ran into the alley, long knife in one hand and confronted him. "Dog! Down with the usurper!"

Leon drew his sword. "I protect the rightful empress, fool."

The Green snarled and lunged. Leon parried the strike easily, then kicked the man back. He staggered, then grunted. Blood spurted from his mouth at the same moment a spear point emerged from his chest. It jerked back and Leon saw an Excubitor decurion, a commander of ten men, standing behind the dead man. "Do not waste time debating them, soldier. Do your duty."

"My duty is to take these noble women to safety," Leon replied.

The decurion's eyes widened as the empress stepped out of the shadow of the colonnade. His mouth opened and spurted blood before he could utter a word.

Leon yanked his sword out of the decurion's throat, stepping back as the Excubitor fell at his feet. “Come quickly,” he said, wiping the decurion’s blood from his face, and led the women down the alley.

The alley opened onto a broad avenue. A group of Greens bearing clubs stood to the right, the direction they would have to go to get to the Hagia Sophia. Leon led the women left, looking for a route around the men who were supporting the empress, but would take him for an enemy because of his excubitor’s armour.

They turned down another alley, taking them not closer to the cathedral but not farther, either. Leon saw an orange glow on the wall of a building, reflecting a fire somewhere. He looked at the women behind him. Empress Constantina’s face expressed calm determination. He could see Princess Anastasia trying to appear brave. Her arm was around her youngest sister, Princess Cleopatra. Behind her, Princess Theoctista pressed close to her sisters. Even in the dim light, Leon could see her trembling. Her wide eyes darted in every direction, seeking threats.

They came to another avenue—all the streets leading to the Hagia Sophia were broad avenues. Leon suppressed the urge to run, to avoid the attention of the trio of excubitors guarding an intersection.

They stole through the shadows of the church of St. Mary of Chalkoprateia, only a score of paces from the great cathedral. They could not help but dash across the last street, the avenue that would lead them to the Great Palace and the Hippodrome. But they ran alongside the cathedral, into the shadows to the side door. Brother Michael opened it again at Leon’s coded knock, and led them again to the chapel without saying a word.

Candles provided the only light, leaving deep shadows in the farthest corners. One exedra, the recess along the side of the cathedral, shone a little more brightly with a few extra votive candles. Clementinus, the senator and Paulus, Germanus’ representative, paced across the exedra. They paused and bowed when they saw the empress.

“My lords. What is the situation?”

“I fear not as planned,” Clementinus said. “The Blue deme has not joined in the uprising. As a result, our forces are less than half of what they could have been."

"A corps waits a signal at Sycae," Paulus said.

"I fear it may never come," Clementinus said. "We do not have sufficient numbers to take the Hagia Sophia nor hold it until aid comes."

"The people will rise to depose this monstrous usurper and restore the rightful emperor," the empress said calmly. "Where can we see what is happening outside?"

Footsteps slapped across the marble floor and Probus, the Demarch of the Greens, emerged breathless from the shadows. He dropped to his knees in front of Constantina. "I am sorry, my empress," he panted. "The uprising has failed. The Excubitors and the city guards have wiped out the Greens. The Blues betrayed us."

Probus' answer was preempted by the noise of the great front doors of the cathedral crashing open and the sound of thick soles slapping on the marble tiles. Excubitors in full armour stormed in, lances lowered. They halted in a semi-circle in front of the exedra, the points of their lances almost touching Leon's armoured chest.

A decurion strode up in the middle of the semi-circle. Leon recognized him: Gibbus, head of the guard this night. Behind him, two more Excubitors in full armour dragged a bloody man between them. Leon felt cold as he recognized Senator Flavius Maximinius, his hair matted, bruises already rising on his face, blood dripping from his nose.

"Put down your sword, Excubitor," Gibbus said.

Leon obeyed and crossed himself.

Brother Michael stepped to Leon's shoulder. "How dare you bring armoured men into the house of God?" he demanded. "It is an affront to—"

"Shut up, brother," Gibbus said. "All conspirators are under arrest and to be brought to the judgment of the Emperor Phocas." More excubitors stepped into the exedra and seized each man by the arms.

But all Constantina needed to do was give the men a sharp look, and they did not touch her or her daughters. Gibbus bowed a little and stood aside to allow the women to follow the senators, Demarchs and

Brother Michael to the foot of the staircase that led to the emperor's private entrance.

Gibbus stopped the Excubitors who were holding Leon. "Not him. Take him to the yard and behead him."

# The intercession of the Patriarch

Constantina only had to turn and look at her daughters once. Each one straightened their back, lifted their chin and wiped fear from their expression. Another well-placed glare and the Excubitors around them took a half-step away, raising their pikes to erect position.

In step, the widow and daughters of the former emperor followed the Captain of the Excubitors up the stairs to the portal that led from the cathedral to the Great Palace—the portal that had once been reserved for her exclusive use. Behind her, the troop followed. Two men with drawn swords drove Clementinus the Senator ahead of them. Two others still dragged the limp Senator Maximinius.

Constantina focused on Captain Gibbus' broad back beneath the swaying scarlet cape. She remembered when the young man had been elevated to an officer and had knelt in obeisance before Emperor Maurice.

She pushed down the thought of that emperor as her husband, the man she had lived with for decades, who had given her eight children.

No. I will not give in to grief tonight. She squared her shoulders, lifted her chin higher and strode after the Excubitor Captain.

The usurper was pacing along the gallery in front of the portal. He wore a purple cape over his nightclothes and purple slippers on his feet. He had also donned the Imperial crown, although it was crooked on his head. *Pretentious fool,* Constantina thought. *Usurper.*

*Murderer.*

Phocas turned to Constantina as Gibbus saluted. "My emperor, I have the conspirators. The excubitors who aided them are being executed at this moment."

Phocas' face was bright red, which made the scar on his cheek stand out despite the beard he wore to hide it. He was gritting his teeth so tightly that the tendons in his neck stood out clearly in the dim light of the torches. For a long moment, his eyes darted from Constantina to her daughters, to the men with them. Constantina counted four breaths before the usurper could open his mouth, and another before any sound came out.

When it came, it was a piercing shriek that made Cleopatra, her youngest surviving child, cry out and cover her ears. "Traitors! I should have killed you with your husband!"

Constantina's anger flared in her belly. She forced her voice to remain steady. "You are the traitor, Centurion. A low-born snake who turned on his emperor, the representative of our Lord Jesus Christ on Earth. A butcher. It is my duty to—"

Phocas shrieked again wordlessly. He ran to Gibbus and wrenched the sword from his scabbard, raising it over Constantina's head.

A shock went through Constantina's whole body. She felt cold but willed her knees still and her eyes fixed, not on the sword but on Phocas' horrible face.

All of her daughters as well as the four men cried out, but one word penetrated the din. "Hold!"

Everyone turned to the entrance as the head of the Church, the Patriarch Cyriacus, burst past the guards at the door. He wore only a plain robe over his night clothes and his feet were bare. "Majesty, no! Do not dare spill blood in the House of our Lord. Remember your vows." He ran between Constantina and Phocas, putting his own body in the way of the sword. His long beard shook as his jaw trembled, and sweat beaded his bald head. "Remember, too, that she is still Augusta of the

Romans. Killing her would be a grave sin. A cardinal sin."

Constantina could smell a strange odour from the man and realized it was fear—pure animal fear.

"She is a foul traitor and a danger to me. And the Empire," Phocas snarled, but he lowered the sword to his side.

"A danger to the Basileus of Rome, to a soldier such as yourself? She is only a woman, after all," Cyriacus scoffed, but his hands trembled. "A woman grieving for her husband and her sons, sons you killed in front of her."

Phocas vented his fury at the Patriarch. "I killed them for the same reason I will kill her and her daughters. They are the spawn of Maurice and an excuse for every dog who wishes to take my place on the throne." He raised the sword again.

"Emperor, no!" Cyriacus cried out. "You cannot spill blood in the House of God. Not in the Cathedral of the Holy Wisdom!"

"Then what would you have me do with them? They have lived in your care for a year, hatching plots against me."

"I will remove them from the cathedral and install them in a private home where they will be guarded, removed from all society so they cannot plot again."

Phocas glared at the Patriarch, grinding his teeth. The tip of the sword in his hand bobbed up and down.

"Remember, too, my emperor, that Constantina is still Augusta until the day she dies, and that she and her daughters are still loved by many in this city. Killing her this night could unite the demes, and incite a riot far worse than the one your men have only just put down."

"Do you seek to threaten me, priest?"

"No, no, no, no, of course not, Majesty. I seek to protect you. Of course, you have nothing to fear from me or the people of Constantinople. You are too powerful. But think of the lives lost and the expense of quelling the riot already this night. An expense that could be spent on so many other things to the glory of the Empire and your reign." Cyriacus took a deep breath and chanced a quick look at Constantina; she maintained her composure, but her heart was racing. She met Phocas' eyes and kept all expression from her face. From the corner of her eye, she could see her daughters huddled together, could hear their quiet sobs.

"All right," Phocas growled. "Take them away. But if I hear one more word about them, I'll kill them myself, no matter what you say." Phocas turned to the men of the conspiracy, surrounded by excubitors. "Flavius Clementinus. I knew you senators would turn on me eventually. And who are these other rats?"

Gibbus nodded and the excubitors dragged three men forward. "These are Petros, Demarch of the Blues, Probus, Demarch of the Greens, and Brother Michael, a monk of the Cathedral."

"The Greens. Of course they're against me. I should have every man of the Greens blinded." He turned to the Patriarch one more time. "I vowed not to interfere with the Church, priest. So I will not spill blood in it." To Gibbus, he said, "Bring them all to the front of the cathedral." He turned and stomped down the stairs, four excubitors scrambling to provide a bodyguard around him.

Gibbus nodded and the other excubitors dragged the men after the usurper. He then indicated the way to Constantina. She put her hand on her youngest daughter's shoulder and led the three of them down the stairs, Gibbus and one other Excubitor bringing up the rear.

Outside, a new moon barely penetrated the smoke over the city. Torches burned a sullen orange-red on the stands down the stairs of the cathedral. Constantina could not help stopping on the bottom step as the excubitors lined the prisoners up in front of the usurper, who still held Gibbus' naked sword.

The two excubitors dragging Maximinius dropped him and he fell to his knees, swaying slightly. He struggled to raise his head to look at the usurper.

Phocas stepped up to Clementinus, sword raised. "I have hated you since I came to Constantinople to bring the complaints of the Legions to that fool, Maurice," he said. "Always sneering at the common soldier who dared to question imperial authority."

Constantina pulled her daughters' eyes toward her body as Phocas pushed the tip of the sword slowly into the senator's belly. Clementinus' eyes went wide. He opened his mouth as if to say something, but only blood, black in the low light, bubbled out. When Phocas withdrew the sword, Clementinus fell to his knees, his hands uselessly clutching his stomach. Blood flowed like wine from a jug. He would die, Constantina knew, slowly.

Cyriacus, the Patriarch knelt over Clementinus, praying quickly and making the sign of the Cross over and over. The Senator held his eye for a second before coughing up more blood.

The next man was Probus, Demarch of the Green faction. Phocas told the excubitors to push him to his knees and hold his head still. Then he deftly flicked one of the man's eyes out of its socket with the tip of the sword. Probus shrieked and struggled but could not break out of the grip of his guards. Blood streamed down one side of his face. "I told you I would blind you Greens," Phocas said.

Constanina felt her stomach heave and tasted a hot bitterness at the back of her throat.

Do not give the monster the satisfaction, she thought, pushing the bile back down and pulling her daughters closer. Cleopatra whimpered continually.

Phocas stepped to the next man in line, Brother Michael, whose eyes were closed as his lips trembled with rapid prayer. "Open your eyes, monk. Your emperor commands it," Phocas said.

"No, your Majesty," Patriarch Cyriacus said, rising from Clementinus' twitching body.

Michael opened his eyes wide in fear. "Look at me," Phocas commanded. At his nod, the excubitor behind Michael pushed him to his knees and forced his head back so he had to look at his tormentor.

"I beg you, Your Majesty, spare a man of God," Cyriacus cried.

"Always praying, eh, monk? I've got a better use for your mouth." Phocas pushed the sword into Michael's mouth. Constantina's arms began to shake as she watched the usurper push the blade deeper, until it burst in a spray of blood from the back of the monk's head and he fell to the side.

Next was the Demarch of the Blues, Petros. Phocas raised the sword to his throat, leering. "Please, your Majesty, I had nothing to do with this. I argued against the conspiracy," Petros protested.

"Is that true?" Phocas asked in a mocking tone.

Petros' head bobbed up and down. "Yes. They called me here, and I came, but I told them they were being fools. I told them we Blues had deposed Emperor Maurice—"

"I deposed Maurice," Phocas said. The tip of the sword drew a blood line along Petros' throat.

"The Blues are loyal to you, Majesty," Petros said, his voice shaking as much as his arms. His whole body shook.

"Is that so?" Phocas stepped behind the Demarch of the Blues, keeping the sword at his neck. "Give him your dagger," he said to the Excubitor behind Probus. The guard complied. Petros craned his neck to look at the usurper as his hand closed around the handle of the long knife.

Phocas nicked Probus' neck again. "If you are loyal, kill this traitor," he said, pushing Petros toward the remaining conspirator, the limp Maximinius. "Show me you are true."

"Please, I've never killed anyone," Petros whimpered. Tears streamed down his face.

*I am responsible for this horror,* a tiny voice within Constantina said. *I brought these men together to die.*

"Kill him!" Phocas screamed.

*They are dying for their Augusta,* Clementina answered the inner voice. *They are doing their duty to the Empire.*

Petros looked at Maximinius with wide, pleading eyes. The senator shook, too, barely conscious, slumped on his knees. Blood dripped from his cheeks and fluid ran out of his nose. A puddle formed at his feet.

"Now!" Phocas shrieked again.

Petros took a deep breath, drew his arm back, and thrust it toward

Maxiuminius' chest at the exact moment the senator toppled into his own piss. Instead of penetrating his heart, the blade slid along the man's bald head, opening up a deep wound. Maximinius moaned. Constantina watched the blood pool on the ground.

Petros looked at Phocas, who pointed at Maximinius with the sword. The Demarch swallowed and knelt to put the dagger under the senator's chin. He sliced, opening up his throat. Spurting blood drenched his arms and face and he fell back onto his rump.

The Excubitor retrieved his dagger from Petros' hand and wiped the blood on a relatively clean part of Clementinus' cloak. At a nod from the usurper, he pulled Probus to his feet and dragged him before Phocas.

"Good. Now you have killed someone. This conspiracy is dead." He nodded toward Probus, who stood holding his hand over the ruined side of his face. "Take this fool to the other Greens and show them what happens to any who dare oppose the emperor."

Petros looked as though he could not believe his ears. He looked at Gibbus, at the Patriarch, at Petros and at Constantina before daring to look at the emperor again. "Yes, your Majesty." He took Petros by the arm and helped him walk across the courtyard in front of the cathedral.

Phocas watched them stumble away until they were out of hearing. "You," he said to the Chief Excubitor. "What is your name?"

"Gibbus, Your Majesty."

"Good. Have some men follow those fools. Bring back as many Green men as they can by morning and blind them." He gave back the sword and strode back to the Great Palace, surrounded by his bodyguard.

Constantina watched the demarchs too, until they disappeared into the shadows of the night city.

*I will make certain that you die, too, Petros, Demarch of the Blues. And for every member of the Green faction blinded tonight, ten Blues will be maimed when I regain my throne.*

# Part 3

# Austinus

# Attack in Constantinople

*Year 605 Christian Era*

On a warm day for winter, Javor went to the market in the Forum of Arcadius, west of the Vlanga district where he lived. He told himself it was to watch people, to try to hear what they talked about, to catch rumours of the city, the Empire and the world beyond it. But a deep part of him hoped to find again the most unique person he had ever seen in Constantinople: Anbasa Wedem, a large man with dark brown skin who said he had come from a land called Axum.

On Javor's first day in the capital, Wedem had given him a free sample of a hot drink made from beans he had imported from his homeland, Axum, far to the south. It was dark and bitter, but invigorating, and Wedem called it "kaffee." Javor had not liked it, but found himself craving it from time to time, even seven years later. He had never seen the dark-skinned Anbasa Wedem again.

With the sun going down and a cool wind promising more snow, Javor craved another drink of hot kaffee. The days were short at this time of year, but the market still closed at sunset. Javor walked from one end of the market in the Forum of Arcadius to the other, then around the stalls, listening to vendors and shoppers haggling, to others ordering their children or slaves to pack unsold wares into crates and sacks.

As the sun dipped to the roofs of the colonnaded buildings around the market, Javor paused at the foot of the enormous column to the Emperor Arcadius in the centre of the market, pulling his cloak closer around his shoulders.

A man stopped beside him. "I wonder, Javor, why you come here so frequently, yet buy so rarely."

Javor turned to see the stout Gracian, Malleus' second-in-command, standing beside the column's pedestal. He wore a soft, dark-coloured cap and a heavy cloak against the winter's chill.

Javor felt annoyed, but not afraid or shocked. "Are you watching me?"

"My interest in you is benevolent, I assure you, young man. I am only hoping to ensure that you are safe from danger." Even Javor could see his smile was not genuine.

"I can protect myself. Ask Malleus about that."

"Malleus ... yes. About Malleus, Javor. You may be putting too much trust in him."

"What are you talking about?" Javor felt his face get hot, his pulse quicken. "Malleus saved my life more than once. I saved his life. Tell me something, Gracian: have you ever fought? Do you know how to use a sword?"

"Of course, I know how to use a sword," Gracian scoffed. "I am a patrician citizen of Rome. But I also know that the first time you encountered Malleus, he tried to kill you."

Javor felt a shock spear him from heart to gut. "That is not true. He was only testing me. He would not have killed me."

"He used a real sword, did he not? A sharp-edged sword?"

Javor did not know how to answer Gracian. *The sword was sharp. And Malleus was—still is—very fast.*

*But my dagger was sharp, too, and still is. And I am faster than Malleus.*

"My point, my boy, is that Malleus was fighting in the interests of the Order, not you. He still acts in the interests of the Order, above all else. Even the Empire. That is part of the problem."

"What problem?"

Gracian hesitated, looking over his shoulder into the deepening shadows of the evening city. Most of the shops had closed. A slave came out of a house to light an oil lamp over the gate, casting a weak yellow light. Somewhere, an owl hooted.

"It is getting late. Let us walk toward home as we talk, Javor," Gracian said.

"I agree. It will start to rain soon."

"What makes you say that?" Gracian looked up. "The sun is setting, but the sky is clear."

"I can always tell. The clouds are coming. The rain will begin before midnight. It is a strange storm, but it is coming."

They fell into step beside each other, turning off a wide avenue onto a narrower street that led downhill toward Javor's. While more slaves lit more lamps in front of the larger houses, the twilight was nearly gone, and the narrower street was almost completely dark.

"The problem, dear Javor," Gracian continued, stepping over a fresh-smelling pile of horse dung in the street, "is as I say, Malleus consistently puts the interests of the Order, its continuation, its integrity, ahead of everything, including the Empire. And the Order is a very powerful, wealthy institution. So you can see that it can be perceived as constituting a threat."

"A threat to who?" Javor heard fluttering and the hoot of an owl again. The idea that the bird was following them glimmered in the back of his mind, until he thought *I cannot remember hearing an owl in the city before.*

Gracian tilted his head toward Javor's so that he could hear as his voice dropped. "To the Empire, of course."

"What? But Malleus is loyal to Rome."

"Of course, of course," Gracian gushed, straightening and suddenly talking louder. "We all know Malleus' loyalty to the Empire and the emperor. However," his voice dropped, and he leaned close again, "since Emperor Maurice let thousands of legionnaires die by Avar blades, there is ... talk, shall we say, of dissatisfaction among people with power. A delegation of the Legions visited Maurice to voice their dissatisfaction and plead for their pay. So within the Great Palace, men in power are attentive to any sign of unrest. Some within those walls will not be so willing to take Malleus' loyalty for granted. In effect, by continuing to behave in his own way, Malleus is putting the safety of the Order, and all its members, in jeopardy."

Javor felt his chest tighten. His breathing sped up and the sounds of the city, settling for the night, seemed to get louder in his ears. And there was the fluttering noise of a large owl again. "I do not understand," was all he could think to say.

He felt the amulet vibrating against his chest under his shirt. *Danger.*

"The men in power close to the emperor are more alert to any perceived threats, Javor." Gracian's voice rose, and his hands moved to stress his argument as he grew more excited. "And if they see a powerful man and a powerful organization that puts its own interests ahead of the emperor's, then they will think that one day, those interests could clash. As Malleus' interests clashed with your own that day you first met. Just as Malleus attacked you, the might of the Empire itself may one day clash with—"

Gracian's argument broke off with a splash and a curse as he stepped into a deep puddle. He put a hand on Javor's shoulder to steady himself as he shook off his wet foot.

Javor tolerated Gracian's hand as he scanned the dark street. Preyatel, his amulet, continued to vibrate in warning, but he could see nothing that looked threatening. The nearest oil lamp was at least twenty paces away and only dim yellow light leaked from the shutters of the houses.

But Preyatel kept vibrating, clearly warning him. Javor reached under his dalmatica and loosened his great-grandfather's dagger in its sheath.

Gracian took off his shoe, shook it, shook his foot, put the shoe back on and shook his hands. "You see, Javor—"

A flutter, a scream, a shrieking laugh and something landed on Gracian's neck. He fell face-first to the street, screaming and clawing at his back. Preyatel shook against Javor's chest as the dagger leapt into his hand.

Gracian rocked back and forth on the ground, screaming, with what looked like an enormous owl biting the back of his neck. Javor kicked at the thing, horrified as it lengthened before his eyes. The feathers turned into leathery skin, wings into stick-like arms, the beak into teeth, and then a woman, unnaturally thin with wild black hair, was biting Gracian, nails like talons ripping at his face.

Javor's foot connected with the hag's side. He heard a crack and the hag rolled away. Naked, she sat on the wet, cobbled street, lifted her shaggy head and emitted another howling laugh that echoed off the brick buildings.

Javor had to hold his hands over his ears—not easy when holding a dagger. The mad laughter went on and on. Gracian, too, covered his ears and rolled onto his back. He pushed himself back along the cobblestones, tearing and soiling his dalmatica.

The thing on the stones rose to its feet without having to push itself up with its hands, and Javor recognized it. "Strigoi," he said through clenched teeth. It continued to laugh, on and on, making Javor's head ache. It raised its hands, no, its claws, opened its mouth wider than any human could, revealing two rows of teeth. The maddening laughter flowed out of that maw. Shriveled breasts dangled as the thing stepped closer to Gracian.

The stout man continued scooting backward along the filthy street. Even in the dark, Javor could see the elemental fear on his face. His jaw worked up and down, but if any sound came out, Javor could not hear it over the strigoi's screams.

It leaped at the pathetic man on the ground, and fast as he was, Javor could not jump in time to block it. The strigoi's claws pierced Gracian's clothes and Javor could hear his screams as the demon's teeth dug into his flesh.

The dagger plunged into its back. It reared up, its laughter turning to howls of pain and rage. It twisted, dragging the blade through its leathery flesh around its side, and rose to its feet beside Gracian. It quieted for a moment, looking down at the rent in its side. It put two clawed fingers into the wound and pulled the flaps of skin apart as if curious about what it would see inside. Then it looked at Javor and began its screaming laugh again.

Javor stepped forward and slashed his dagger, ending the laughter as the thing's head flew off its shoulders. The head landed upside down on the cobblestones behind Gracian, the jaws and eyes still wide open. The body stood still for a moment, arms raised, then collapsed into a hideous leathery heap.

Gracian stared at the head, his mouth flapping like a fish's. Drool dripped from his chin, but he made no sound. He stank of urine and shit.

Javor sheathed the dagger and helped the man to his feet. He pulled him to the corner of the street, where the light was a little brighter. The marks of the talons bled down one side of his face and the other side of his neck.

"Did the teeth get you?" Javor asked, pulling on the clothes to get a look.

"No, no, I do not think so," Gracian said, his voice a rasp. "It scratched me, I think." He raised a hand to the back of his neck, and it came away red and dripping. "Oh, no, it bit my neck."

"Come with me." Javor took Gracian's arm, like he had Tiana's many times, and walked as quickly as he dared down the street. "I'll take you to my home, where we can treat your wounds. That thing may not have been alone."

Gracian stared at the dismembered strigoi as they stepped past it. Javor was torn between the need to move quickly, to assess the full damage to Gracian and to get away from any other threats that may have hidden in the dark streets, and concern for Gracian. He was obviously hurt worse than he admitted. He stumbled repeatedly on the uneven street and the debris and garbage in it.

By the time they had traversed the quarter-mile to Javor's domus, Gracian could barely stand, let alone walk. Javor banged on the front door until it swung open to reveal Gaetan holding a small lantern. He stepped back, eyes wide when he saw Gracian slumping in Javor's arms.

"Help me get him inside."

Gaetan put the lantern down on the floor and grabbed Gracian around his thick waist just as he went completely limp. Javor and Gaetan hauled him down the entrance hall to the atrium where they deposited him on a couch. "Get water and cloths to clean him up," Javor told Gaetan. "And bring Aunt Tiana here. Move!"

Gaetan took the lantern and ran deeper into the house, leaving Javor and Gracian in darkness. "And bring some candles!" Javor shouted after him.

Kyriake appeared in her nightclothes, carrying a candle. She gasped when she saw Gracian bleeding on the couch, but efficiently lit the candles in the wall sconces.

Gaetan returned and set a bowl of water on the floor beside the couch. Kyriake began wiping the blood from Gracian's neck, who lay, eyes closed, his breathing fast and shallow.

Tiana came in slowly, panting. She touched Gracian's face, neck, and hands. "He has a fever," she said. "Get me more cloths." Kyriake ran to obey. "Get his clothes off."

Javor and Gaetan struggled to remove the limp Gracian's cloak, robe and then his tunic, leaving him in his undergarment. Gaetan gasped when he saw the long red wounds down Gracian's neck and the evil looking rents in his side. Kyriake wiped them gently, dipping the cloth into the bowl that was already dark with blood.

"What happened?" Tiana asked.

"Strigoi," said Javor. "Three of them attacked me and Photius in Dacia, seven years ago."

"I remember you told me about them," Tiana said, inspecting Gracian's wounds. "Fetch my healing herbs," she told Kyriake, taking over cleaning the wounds. Javor and Gaetan turned Gracian onto his front so that Tiana could dab at the ragged bite wound on his neck. Then she held the light on the bite wound on Gracian's side. "This is dangerous."

Kyriake returned with a wooden box. Tiana took out a tiny jar and shook drops of clear liquid onto the wound. She gently rubbed it into the torn flesh until it was absorbed. "Get clear, cool water. We need to cool his body. Carry him to a bed."

Javor took Gracian's shoulders, and Gaetan his legs, and they hefted the unconscious man to the guest bedroom. Kyriake brought in a fresh bowl of water and Tiana wiped sweat off Gracian's face, neck, and shoulders, moving down to wipe his chest. Javor took a second cloth and wiped his legs. "He is still hot. We must cool him, any way we can. Open the windows."

Javor and Tiana sat on either side of the bed, taking turns wiping cool water onto Gracian's head, face and chest, as a wind swept over the city from the north, whipping branches of trees and loose shutters. Tiana asked him again what had happened.

"He came to me as the sun was setting, in the market of Arcadius. He wanted to talk to me, he said. We started walking back here, and by the time we turned toward the Vlanga, it was fully dark. I thought I heard an owl at one point, and I remember thinking that was odd, because I had never heard an owl in the city before. Then I heard a screech and a huge owl landed on the back of Gracian's neck and knocked him down."

"An owl did that?" Tiana asked, but he could tell she did not think that.

"No, I told you: strigoi. Photius and I were attacked by three of them in Dacia. They're incredibly skinny, ugly women with sharp teeth, and they can transform into owls."

"You saw it?" Tiana said quietly, sipping wine.

"Yes. I saw the owl grow, its wings change to arms, its beak to a huge, wide mouth. I kicked it off of him, and it looked at me. It had—it had two rows of teeth, Tiana. I have never seen anything like it."

Kyriake and Gaetan bustled in and out of the bedroom, bringing fresh water and rags, more candles, wine for Javor and Tiana. They stayed quiet until they were alone again. Javor closed the windows as the room was very cold.

"Did the strigoi in Dacia have double teeth?" Tiana asked.

"I do not know. I do not think we ever got a good look at them. It was dark then, too."

"What did you do?"

"We ran and jumped into a river to get away. I think they do not like water—they ran along the bank instead of jumping in after us."

Tiana smiled a little. "I mean, what did you do tonight?"

"Oh. It started to laugh, like a mad woman, screaming so loud it hurt my ears. Then it jumped on Gracian again and bit him."

"How did you get him away?"

"I stabbed it with my dagger. You know the one." Tiana nodded. "It...it was the most horrible thing I have ever seen. And I have seen many horrors."

"I know."

"It twisted away, and that meant that my dagger cut right through it. I cut a huge slice in it, and it got up and looked at it. No blood came out. Nothing. It was like cutting into a piece of dried liver or something. It started laughing again. I thought I would go mad."

"So what did you do?"

"I cut off its head. That killed it."

The shutter over the window flew open, banging hard against the outside wall. The wind howled through the open window, fluttering the edges of the bedclothes and tossing Tiana's hair. Javor reached outside and struggled to pull the shutter against the wind before closing the latch.

Tiana was still focused on Gracian.

"Where did it bite him?"

"On the side, I think."

"What about the bite on the back of the neck?"

Javor thought for a moment. "I think that is where it first bit him, when it was still in the form of an owl."

Tiana nodded again. "That may be a saving grace. The strigoi are blood suckers, but they are also spreaders of disease. That is why Gracian has such a fever. I am afraid we may not be able to save him. And if he does die, Javor, we will have to decapitate and dismember him."

"Why?" Javor began to think of where they would do such a thing. Not in his house. "And what will we tell his family?"

"We will have to decapitate him, because he is likely to become another strigoi himself, and a great danger to the Order and the Empire."

"To the Order...strange." Javor loosened the dagger in its scabbard. "Gracian seemed very worried about the Order, too."

"What did he want to talk to you about?"

The wind shrieked around the corner of the domus. Somewhere, a dog began to bark wildly, adding to the cacophony of rattling roof tiles, cracking branches and debris scrabbling down the cobblestones ahead of the wind.

Javor had trouble saying: "He wanted to warn me against Malleus."

"Why?"

"He said that Malleus was putting the Order in danger, because he put its interests ahead of the Empire's."

"Thereby arousing suspicion in the emperor and those in Imperial positions of power."

"Ummm ... yes, that's right. That's what he said. He also said that I should not trust Malleus, because he always puts the Order first, and if my interests were ever different from the Order's, then he might ... I don't know. What would happen, Tiana? Would the Order turn against me?"

The shutters rattled again as another gust howled through the Vlanga. "Do you think the wind is from archons?" Javor asked.

"Possibly," Tiana answered, sipping her wine. "You encountered a minor archon in the form of the strigoi. It is many, many emanations away from the Demiurge, to be sure, but it was not likely alone. On the other hand, Javor, it could just be a storm off the sea. Constantinople has been known to have windstorms in the past." She smiled a little. "As for your first question, Javor, remember that you are not the Order. You have deliberately set yourself apart from the Order by living here, instead of in the abbey. And you married, in opposition to the celibate tendency of the other leaders."

"But you and Austinus were married." Javor could not understand why he felt so anxious at the thought of opposing the Order. He drained his wine and looked for more.

"And now, I live here with you. Austinus and I were anachronisms. Throwbacks to the early days of Christianity and Gnosticism," she answered, wiping Gracian's sweating face again. "Most of the senior people in the Order, both men and women, have adopted celibacy for religious leaders, as has the Western Church."

"But not the Eastern Church, right?"

"Indeed, no. But bishops cannot marry. And for all his disdain for Orthodox and Catholic Christians, Malleus also believes in celibacy for himself as well as for the senior men and women of the Order."

"Other than you, what women are leaders in the Order?"

Tiana nodded, her eyes drifting away from Javor. "You are right. It is a weakness of the Order to have so few women in authority. Austinus was not assiduous in including women in his major decisions, and Malleus seems not to value women's views at all."

Javor took his turn wiping Gracian's body. "Do you think I am in danger from the Order, Tiana?"

She took his hand between hers. "Not now. You are far too valuable as the Order's greatest warrior. But you need to be wary and cautious, Javor, for if the Order drifts closer to the Church and the Empire, its interests may diverge from yours far enough that they will not value you, anymore."

The wind grew until they heard a crash. Gaetan shouted for Honorius, the groomsman, to help him push the front door shut again. Kyriake came in with cakes and wine, but dropped them and ran screaming as the shutters blew in again, slamming against the window frame. Outside, debris flew ahead of the wind, hitting the corners of homes and shops, and continued their flights, spinning.

Gracian startled Javor and Tiana by moving for the first time in over an hour. His head whipped from side to side and he arched his back so his belly rose over the bed. His lips moved soundlessly, spit drooling out of the corners. He lurched to one side, then the other, rocking on his shoulders. His eyes opened wide and his arms rose. Choking noises came from his mouth. He lurched sideways again, and his flailing hand nearly hit Tiana on the nose. Both she and Javor stepped back, alarmed.

The choking noises became words in a language Javor had never heard. “What is he saying?”

“I don’t know. It’s nothing I have ever heard. Push his arms down, Javor, and hold him on the bed before he flings himself off!”

Javor grabbed Gracian’s wrists and struggled to push the man back down on the bed. Gracian’s eyes were open so wide, Javor could see white all around the pupils. But there was no recognition in those eyes. The man seemed to stare through him as he fought Javor’s attempt to push him down. Sweat poured down his face, dripping onto the bed, and more nonsense came from his mouth.

His leg came up, kneeing Javor in the side. Javor stumbled sideways, but managed to keep his grip on Gracian’s wrists, even though they were slick with sweat.

He heard rain begin, big, fat drops striking the roof and streets. Rain blew in the open window, splattering on his back as he struggled to restrain Gracian.

Tiana put both hands, crossed, against the sick man’s chest, leaned close to his head and whispered. Javor thought he heard “Api daix, ata kalag, tingiz, hus.” He had no idea what it meant, but Gracian’s body fell against the bed.

Javor let go of Gracian’s arms, and they fell onto his body, then slid off to hang limply off the sides of the bed.

“Is he sleeping?” Javor’s voice was hoarse.

“Yes. I recited an old, old sleeping spell, the kind we used to say to children.”

Javor shivered as the wind blasted in more raindrops. They stung when they hit the back of his neck. He closed and latched the shutters, then put a footstool on the sill to keep them closed. “This is not a natural storm. Not when it is blowing in the windows and doors.” From above, they could hear the roof tiles rattling under the onslaught of rain.

"Call for more cool water," Tiana said, wiping Gracian down again. Javor leaned out the bedroom door and bellowed for Kyriake. "And bring some wine, too!"

Javor looked at Tiana. Slumping on the foot of the bed, she seemed exhausted. Her face was drawn, her shoulders hunched. Her eyes were red, and still she wiped Gracian's face.

Javor took the cloth from her hand. It was nearly dry, and warm from hers and Gracian's body heat. "Hurry up with that damn water!" he called again. A moment later, Kyriake stepped into the bedroom, hesitating until she was certain the shutters were not open. They rattled as if to warn her as she put a fresh urn of water on the little table beside the bed, and she turned and ran.

"Where is the wine?" Javor called, then shook his head when there was no more sign of his servant. He dipped a cloth in the water—at least it was cool. He wiped the sweat off Gracian again, starting with his head, then his shoulders and chest. Tiana reached for another cloth, but Javor took it from her hand to stop her. "You should rest."

"It's nearly morning," she replied, her voice barely a whisper. The shutter rattled again, but the rain had changed from a continual rattle on the roof and shutters to a steady hiss. "If he lives until sunrise, I will rest then."

Gaetan came in then with another jug of wine and refilled their cups. "The horses are afraid, sire," he said.

"I am not surprised," Javor answered.

"Honorius is with them."

"Good. Make sure they have water and something to eat."

"No one is getting any sleep, sire."

"I expect not. How are my wife and daughter?"

"Martha is comforting the child, to no avail. She has not stopped crying for hours. And Lady Calanthe is at the door."

"Let her in, then!"

Calanthe pushed past Gaetan to wrap her arms around her husband.

"Are you all right?"

Javor stroked her long hair and held her close. "Yes, my dear. I am unhurt."

"But they said you were attacked." He felt her tears against his neck.

"Gracian was attacked. He was wounded. Aunt Tiana is doing what she can for him."

Calanthe drew back, sniffling. She looked at Tiana, who had taken the cloth from Javor to wipe Gracian's skin. "Tiana? Will he live?"

"I do not know. I am doing everything I know how to do," Tiana replied, her voice low and weak.

Calanthe reached across the bed and put her hand on Tiana's knee. "Aunt Tiana, I am glad you are here."

Javor turned to Gaetan. "If everyone is awake, have Michael and Kyriake start breakfast. It will be morning soon, and we will all eat soon after sunrise before services."

"Before services? But sire—"

"This has been a difficult night for all of us, Gaetan. There is no point suffering longer without something to eat, just because the Church wants us to be hungry through Mass."

"But sire, after a night like this, a Mass is what we need more. Michael is praying in the chapel now."

"He has prayed enough. Have him prepare a breakfast for us all. The servants, too. We will all eat together. If the rain stops, we will take it in the atrium. If not, in the hall."

Gaetan's face was an impassive mask. "Very good, sire." He bowed and backed out of the room.

I hate it when he does that.

Javor and Tiana remained in silence, alternately washing down Gracian as the night wore on. Slowly, the wind diminished. The rain eased. When he could see grey light between the shutter slats and around the frame, he took down the stool from the window and eased one shutter open.

A tree in the garden swayed in the breeze, but there was no garbage whipping down the street. Overhead, the sky was dark grey, clouds roiling close above the church spires. He could see puddles ruffling in the wind.

"The rain has stopped," he said.

Behind him, Tiana said, "Gracian's fever has broken. He is breathing normally, too." He turned to see her with one hand on Gracian's forehead, the other on his chest, over his heart. "He has ceased sweating, as well. He may survive this."

Javor looked out the window again. Above the roofs to the west, he could see a patch of blue sky.

"It is time to take him home."

# Treating Gracian

In mid-morning, Javor sat in front of his wagon beside Honorius as they drove through the crowded streets of the Vlanga toward the Chalkoprateia, near the Imperial Palace.

Gracian lay on a pile of featherbeds and pillows in the back, covered with a fur blanket. In the chill of the winter morning following the insane storm of the night before, and despite the fever he had had, Gracian said he felt cold as an exhausted Michael and Kyriake brought him bread and heavy red wine prescribed by Tiana.

Gaetan brought him one of Javor's tunics and a heavy, warm cloak. Kyriake and Honorius arranged two feather-stuffed blankets and down pillows in the back of the wagon, and after Gracian had climbed in, covered him with a fur blanket.

The horses' hooves splashed in puddles. Honorius yelled at the pedestrians to make way. Low, dark grey clouds fled eastward from blue skies clearing in the west.

*It is cold today,* Javor thought, looking at the right-hand horse's mane swinging in the rhythm of its pace on the cobblestone street. He pulled his dalmatica closer around his neck.

*Did last night really happen? Was it a nightmare? It does not seem real, now, with the sun breaking through the clouds, with the sounds and the smells of the market all around, the feeling of Honorius' arm brushing against my shoulder, the hard bench under my butt.*

But it was as real as the memory of the gigantic snake in Paphlagonia, as real as the King of the Mountain six years earlier, as real as the bones of the earth.

*These unbelievable things keep happening to me. Why?*

But he knew the answer. The powers of earth and sky had given him gifts, abilities, knowledge.

*So they can use me as a weapon in their own struggles.*

*But which side is using me?*

*Which side do I want to use me?*

*Why do I have to be used?*

His reverie ended as Honorius reined in before a heavy wooden gate with black iron brackets. "Good morrow, Abbey!" he called. "My master Javor Sklavenius requests entry!"

A monk peeked through a small door set in the centre of the gate, saw Javor and disappeared again. Seconds later, the gate swung open, the hinges screeching. Honorius flipped the reins and Gracian groaned as the wagon lurched over the bump between the street and the courtyard of the Abbey of the Chalkoprateia.

Seven years earlier, Javor had entered the Abbey through a small, battered door set in an eroding, grey plastered wall in the back of the building, across a small square from the modest Church of St. Mary of Chalkoprateia—the copper market.

The Abbey's front entrance was only a little more impressive than the back door. At least it looked sturdy and in good repair. But the courtyard was barely large enough to accommodate Javor's horses and wagons, a few people, and access to the Abbey's own barn, stable and paths to the living quarters and chapel. A wall separated the Abbey from the convent that shared the Abbey's name.

It also shared the lie. It appeared to be a typical Orthodox Church, monastery and convent, but it was really a front for the Gnostic organization that called itself, simply, The Order.

Cometus, Malleus' advisor, hurried to the wagon as a young monk helped Javor get down. "Good morning, Javor. What brings—" He stopped in mid-stride when he saw the man in the back of the wagon. "My lord Gracian! Are you unwell?" He directed two monks to help the man stand up and get down from the wagon.

"I am as well as can be expected, thanks to our friend and his...aunt." Gracian's voice was still frail, his face pale, his steps weak and unsteady.

"What happened?" Cometus asked, his eyes wide.

"Let's go inside. I need to speak with Malleus."

Cometus sent a young monk to alert the head of the Abbey, then took Gracian to the Abbey's infirmary.

Javor ignored the novice who offered to guide him to Malleus' private study. The monk who had run ahead was stepping out of the door when Javor reached it. "He is ready for you, sir," the boy said. Javor ignored him, too, and stepped inside.

Malleus stood in the middle of the small room, wearing clothes similar to what he had the first time Javor had seen him: dark trousers like an Avar, soft black boots, a plain shirt with an open collar and an intense expression on his face. He finished buckling a sword belt and looked up at Javor.

"What happened to Gracian?" There was no greeting this time, no kiss on the cheek.

"He was attacked, bitten by a strigoi last night." Malleus only looked more confused. "A strigoi is a blood-sucking shape-shifter. Photius and I were attacked by a group of them in Dacia, seven years ago. Before I came here."

"Where did this happen?"

"Yesterday, after sunset. Gracian found me as I was walking home from the market. I heard what I thought was an owl following us, and then it landed on Gracian and bit him. I killed it and Aunt Tiana treated Gracian."

"Where is he now?"

"Cometus took him to the infirmary. He is weak, but well."

Malleus' gaze became, if anything, even more intense. Javor felt like Malleus' eyes were stabbing into his head. "Why was he in the market?"

*What can I tell him?* "He wanted to tell me something." Malleus did not need to say, "What." His eyes said it. "He wanted to warn me about a threat to the Empire and the Order."

"What kind of threat?"

Javor wanted to tell Malleus, a man he had known for years, whose life he had saved and who had saved his, about Gracian's suspicions and warning. But Preyatal vibrated a short buzz, and he said, "I don't know. Before he could say anything, really, the strigoi attacked." *Am I siding with Gracian against Malleus now?*

Javor turned and looked out the window of Malleus' second-storey study, over the Abbey's courtyard. Thoughts and feelings swirled around his mind. "Are my interests different from the Order's, Malleus?"

Malleus looked puzzled. "Why would you ask that, my friend?"

Javor searched for the words that would not alarm the head of the Order, nor incriminate Gracian. "Someone told me that my interests are not the same as yours. Is that true?"

"Well, obviously, in some small respects..." Malleus was searching for words, too. "You do not live according to the Order's Code. You married and live apart. So you have made yourself distinct in some ways from the Order. You have made clear that your interests are different from ours, Javor.

"But on the other hand, the Order's interests are those of all civilized men. We are here to protect Rome against the chaotic forces that seem bent on wiping humanity off the earth. As a citizen of the Imperium, then, your interests are entirely congruent with the Order's."

"I'm a citizen? I was born beyond the Imperium's borders."

Malleus smiled and clapped a hand on Javor's shoulder. "My boy, that was the first thing I took care of when we returned from the Alps five years ago. I spoke to the emperor himself—yes, the Emperor Maurice, bless his soul—and he declared you a full citizen of the Empire, with all the rights and responsibilities that implies."

Javor felt as if the room was spinning around him. "A citizen...I did not know, Malleus."

Malleus pulled Javor close for a hug and a kiss on each cheek. Javor's back stiffened, his arms rigid by his side. "You are right, Javor. I should have told you," Malleus said. "It means your children are also Roman citizens."

Malleus released Javor and stepped back. He went to the map table and looked at the map of the Empire and the lands surrounding it. "The chaotic forces have co-opted the chthonic archons, Javor. The common people, even the educated nobility, insistent as they are on orthodox Christianity, do not appreciate this. They turn their eyes from this fact.

"The Earth has decided humanity is its enemy. A parasite to be disposed of," Malleus continued. "We see it in many places. The eruptions of the underworld, far to the east. Mount Aetna in the west. Vesuvius. All around the world, we can see the Earth bearing down on the civilizations, the crowning achievements of Man."

This information, combined with the news of his Roman citizenship, sent Javor's mind whirling. "If the Earth itself has turned on us, what hope do we have?"

Malleus could not look at him. "There is always hope, Javor, for those who have attained gnosis. Our only hope is the celestial archons.

"There is a war, my friend, among the archons. They have divided: celestial against chthonic. Sky versus Earth. And as we can see with this attack on Gracian, we can see that the chthonic forces will stop at nothing.

"You sought to remove yourself from the Order. You married, had a child, looking for the life your family had. But you cannot hide from this, Javor. This war is inescapable for every man and woman in the world.

"I know about your amulet, Javor," Malleus continued. "I know you call it 'Preyatel,' your 'good friend' in your barbaric language." He held up a hand, palm out. "Do not take offence, my friend. You know I love you. I use the term academically. My point is this: you have sought to escape this war among the gods.

"There is no escape. The archons have brought it to you. Gracian was not the target of this 'strigoi,' this chthonic archon. You were. It is only because of your amulet that it was not able to see you until it was physically in your presence. Make no mistake, Javor, my dear friend. The chthonic archons have identified you as a key enemy.

"You cannot escape this war, Javor. It has come into this city, the centre of civilization. It has come to you."

# The second son

*Year 605 Christian Era*

Six months passed after the attack on Gracian. Six months with no more dreams that Javor could remember. Half a year of occasional visits to the Abbey with Tiana, where they would go to the secret library that even Gracian did not know about. Six months without finding Anbasa Wedem again, without finding more clues about the bones of the earth in the Order's collection of old, arcane writings.

Six months of regular visits to Calanthe's parents, or visits from them so they could dote on their grandchildren.

But it was not a half-year without any events. Two months in, Calanthe announced to her parents and husband that she was expecting another child.

Mauricius and Anna cheered, their faces so bright and happy, Javor thought they might crack. Calanthe, however, did not look as happy. She smiled with her mother, but even Javor could see that there were other emotions mixed with the hope and happiness. Fear?

*Is she afraid of another birth? Of being tired again?*

*Or of something else?*

At the end of the months of waiting, Javor paced outside Calanthe's bedroom in her parents' home again as Mauricius Macedonius lazed on a couch, a goblet of wine in one hand, playing backgammon with one of his slaves, an old man named Sotiris. Javor briefly wondered how his father-in-law could concentrate on a game while his daughter moaned and shrieked behind the doors.

Javor's head ached. He went to the window, pushed the shutters open and breathed in the night air. It smelled bad, too, but he needed to dispel some of the odour of melting wax, sweat and whatever was coming from under the bedroom door.

That door opened just enough for Anna, Javor's mother-in-law, to poke her head out. "It won't be long now," she said, eyes going from her husband to Javor and back. "Sotiris, will you bring us some more wine and cool water?"

"He is in the middle of a game with me, Anna," Mauricius grumbled.

"The birth of your new grandchild is more important than that silly game you love so much," Anna retorted. Sotiris rose, his knees cracking. He bowed to Anna and then to Mauricius and disappeared down the hallway.

"Why is it taking so long?" Javor demanded.

Anna rolled her eyes and disappeared back into the bedroom. The door closed with a thud.

Mauricius embraced Javor. "Cease worrying, my son. It will take as long as it takes. There is no sense in trying to hurry a baby. Nor a woman, for that matter."

"You told me that Andrina's birth took two hours. And that the next child would take less. And we have been here—" He glanced out the window, trying to guess what time it was. But the day had been cloudy, and the night sky was deep and black. "Well, most of a day now. Is it because the baby seems to be coming early?"

Mauricius shook his head. "There is no predicting these things." He held out a goblet. "Have some wine. Relax."

Javor leaned on the windowsill, peering into the deep blackness of the city street. "No, thank you. It is already giving me a headache."

Sotiris returned with two jugs, one of wine and the other, water. Another slave hurried behind him to open the door. They all jumped as a long wail erupted from Calanthe.

Javor pushed past the slaves. He saw Anna standing at the foot of Calanthe's bed, the reddish-yellow candlelight reflected in the tears on her cheeks. Martha, Calanthe's nurse, knelt beside the head of the bed, holding something in her arms, her head shaking.

Calanthe lay spread-eagled and naked on the bed, her thighs and torso covered in blood, her arms outstretched, her head thrashing from side to side. Her mouth stretched wide with a formless, continuous wail, and her eyes were squeezed shut. Her long dark hair lay matted and chaotic around her.

Javor could not breathe. He fell to his knees beside Martha, begging with his eyes to change the reality they saw.

Tears streamed down Martha's face. She held the blanket-wrapped bundle in her arms out to Javor, and he gathered it to his chest. He bent to kiss the tiny forehead and felt wetness on his own cheeks.

"I am so sorry," Martha whispered.

Javor could only look at the perfect little face below his eyes. The delicate curve of cheek, the traces of eyebrows, the stillness of the mouth. He moved the blanket to see the tiny hand, gently touched it with the tip of a finger. The hand did not move.

The tiny mouth did not move, nor seek milk nor air. The legs did not kick. No breath struggled into the little lungs.

Anna sat on the bed, pulling her daughter to her. Martha reached her arms around Javor and the baby and repeated, "I am sorry."

Javor pulled away from the nurse, drawing in a deep, shuddering breath. The blanket fell away from the baby's body. He kissed the forehead again, breathing in the smell of blood and sweat and newborn baby. He tried to ask what had happened, what had gone wrong, where his first son was, but there was no breath in his lungs, no moisture in his throat, no strength to utter a protest against a god that could take away an infant life before it had even started.

Mauricius knelt at Javor's side and pulled him close, offering his strength when there was nothing it could do. "I am sorry, Javor," and

Javor could hear the tears in his voice.

Somehow, Javor stood, the baby boy still in his arms. Eyes closed, he found the strength to whisper. "Austinus," he said, the name of the previous head of the Order, the man who had treated him like a son when he had arrived in Constantinople years earlier. "His name is Austinus."

# Interlude 5

# A Second Conspiracy

*Year 606 Christian Era*

Every torch and brazier in the throne room was lit, but Augusta Constantina shivered. She stood still and erect between two Excubitors. To her left, more guards held her three daughters, Anastasia, Theoctista and Cleopatra. The youngest was weeping.

Constantina kept her expression blank as she met the eyes of the usurper, Phocas.

He paced before her, his face twisted and even more florid than usual. His red hair seemed to have a life of its own as it bounced on his shoulders with every step.

"Who supports you?" he yelled.

"I need no one to support me. I am the Augusta. The people and Jesus Christ are enough to restore me to power, usurper."

"I am emperor now, bitch. Tell me who supports you and I will not kill your daughters."

"The Empire is not worth living in, under you."

Phocas looked at the former Augusta for a long moment. He nodded at his guards.

An Excubitor pushed her youngest daughter, Cleopatra, to kneel at the usurper's feet. Casually, Phocas took a sword from one of his guards. He kept his eyes locked on Constantina's as his right arm slashed.

The former Augusta could not suppress a gasp as her youngest daughter's head fell to the marble floor. She bit back her sob and forced herself not to look at the headless body.

"Bind her," Phocas said.

Constantina did not resist, but neither did she cooperate as the excubitors tied her wrists and ankles with thin, tight cords.

"My once loyal legions, even some of the excubitors, betray me," Phocas said, swinging the sword in circles as blood oozed from Cleopatra's neck and severed head. "Even the great Germanus, the general who defeated the Avars and humiliated the Gepids, the man who put his own family in harm's way for the sake of his emperor, turns against me. So you see, Augusta — or rather, former empress — I know all about your conspiracy."

Phocas knelt in front of Constantina and took her hand in his. "I was merciful two years ago," he continued, his voice taking on an oddly calm, sermonizing tone. "I listened to that fool of a Patriarch to let you and your daughters live, so long as you did not conspire against me. But you, former Augusta Constantina, did not honour your side of the contract."

He bent the fingers of her right hand back until they snapped. Constantina cried out and wrenched her bound hands from Phocas, and then swung them, clasped together, at his face. The shock of pain in her broken hand was even more satisfying when she saw blood trickle from the usurper's nose.

He wiped his nose with the back of his hand, looked at it and smiled. It was horrible. He stood and nodded at the Excubitors again. One, dressed in a simple black robe, knelt before Constantina. He bowed and kissed her broken hand. "I am sorry. I love you, Augusta."

He drew a small, long blade and severed the small finger of her left hand.

Constantina did not cry out.

Another woman did cry out, though. Constantina turned to see an Excubitor pull a woman by the hair in front of her. Constantina remained impassive as she recognized her maidservant, Petronia.

Phocas dropped a crumpled sheet of paper in front of Constantina. She felt a cold shock when she recognized the letter she had written to the great general, Germanus, and entrusted to Petronia. Constantina looked up from the paper on the ground, past the raging usurper to Petronia. Both eyes were swollen and black and one arm hung loose from her shoulder.

"Your servant was most ... forthcoming," Phocas said, pacing.

Constantina's eyes met Petronia's for a brief moment, before the maidservant looked down. Constantina's vision blurred then as her ruined hand throbbed in pain.

Phocas stepped between the two tortured women. "Petronia told me about you and Germanus. The great general, the man who vanquished the barbarians. The man whose name strikes fear into the hearts of the heathens. Yes, Augusta, widow of Maurice, I know all of your plans." Blood was still trickling out of his nose, and he smeared it into his beard.

"Who, Constantina? Who else in the Senate is conspiring against me?"

Constantina said nothing.

"Save your daughters."

Constantina did not dare to look at her surviving daughters.

The man in the black robe drew the tip of his blade up Constantina's leg, leaving a fine trail of blood. At Phocas' nod, he severed her little toe.

"Tell me, Constantina," Phocas said.

"Tell him," the man in black whispered in her ear. "Please, Augusta."

Constantina bit the inside of her cheek.

"You could save so many people," Phocas said. "You could prevent useless violence. You could preserve the Empire. Keep the barbarians at bay. But you and Maurice never cared about that, did you? Very well," he said, picking up the sword again. He pushed it slowly into Petronia's belly. The maid screamed for only a moment before Phocas cut her lungs open.

"Well?" Phocas said. Blood spread over the floor, pooling around his feet. "You, and Germanus, and who else?"

Constantina bit her cheek again.

The man in black wept as he removed another finger.

Constantina's vision blurred, but she remained silent.

Phocas knelt before her again and took her ruined hand. He held it to his mouth and sucked blood from her wounds, smacking his lips. "The blood of the imperials," he said.

He stood and nodded again. An excubitor pulled her surviving daughters before her. Theoctista, the younger, whimpered. Her sister, Anastasia, wept quietly. Befitting an emperor's daughter.

Phocas grabbed Theoctista's fair hair in his left hand and pulled down so that the girl was bent at the waist. "Hold her," he ordered, and an Excubitor took over holding the girl's hair. She screamed and struggled in a futile effort.

Phocas severed the head of another of the Imperial daughters. The body dropped to the floor, spurting blood over Constantina's face.

Anastasia screamed. Then, Augusta's body heaved and bitter bile filled her mouth, streaming over her chin.

"Flavius Comentus," Anastasia cried. "And Ionnes Nikus."

Constantina had to close her eyes. Her stomach heaved again, but there was nothing to bring up.

"I knew it," Phocas said. "Did you hear that, Constantina? Your daughter has come to her senses, at last. She is trying to save herself, and you." He turned to the young woman. "Smart. I wonder why your fool of a father never married you off. You would have made a good alliance. You have wisdom, for a woman. And as I promised, I will be merciful." A third time, his powerful right arm swung. Anastasia's dark head and her body hit the ground at the same time.

"Arrest Nikus and Comentus," Phocas ordered. Constantina heard footsteps as a group of excubitors hastened to obey the usurper. One of them slipped in the blood that flowed across the floor, falling on his butt. No one laughed as his fellows helped him back up.

At Phocas' orders, the torturer tied Constantina's hands behind her back, He bound her arms at the elbows, bringing pain to her upper arms and shoulders and across her chest.

Phocas tore the remains of her gown off and dropped it into the puddles of blood. "You, Germanus, Nikus, Comentus. And I already knew about Aspar. That old man Heraclius has also declared against me in Africa. I should just have the entire Senate killed and replace them with loyal legionnaires. To hell with the Senate. I am the only one to hold the Empire together."

Constantina trembled. Somehow she found the strength to say, "The Sassanids have occupied most of Asia Minor under you."

Phocas grabbed the torturer's knife and slit open Constantina's belly. She watched her entrails spill out. She coughed and blood spilled out of her mouth.

Phocas screamed one more time and severed her head.

# Part 4

# Charita

*Year 609 Christian Era*

# Tell us a story

"Tell us a story, Papa." Eight-year-old Andrina sat on the floor in front of her father's feet, blinking her dark eyes up at him.

Adam, five, dropped his ball and ran up, jumping onto Javor's lap. "Yes, Papa, tell us a story!" He pulled at the fine chain around his father's neck.

Javor looked from his son to his daughter to Tiana, who sat on another couch, reveling in the sunlight through the atrium. She smiled and nodded.

Javor pried Adam's fingers from the chain before the child could pull the amulet from under his tunic. "What kind of story do you want me to tell you?"

"Tell us about when you were little," Andrina said. She turned on her bottom to lean against her father's legs, gazing up at him upside down. "Tell us about the place you came from."

"Didn't you come from Constinopy, Papa?" Adam asked, playing with a tassel hanging from the cushion Javor sat on.

Javor looked at Tiana for support, but her eyes were closed. She had turned her face up to the warmth of the morning sun. A tiny smile played at the corners of her mouth.

Javor sighed again. "No, Adam, I was not born in Con-stan-tin-o-ple. I come from a land far to the north."

Adam frowned at him, dropping the tassel. "Where is north?"

Javor pointed vaguely toward the wall. "That way. Many days, many weeks' journey from here."

"Tell us. How you came to Cons...Constinoppo, " Adam demanded.

"Con-stan-tin-o-ple," Javor repeated. *My Greek is not that bad.* "I walked here."

"How long did it take you?"

"About a month." He picked Adam up off his lap and set him on the floor beside his sister. "Now be quiet, and I will tell you about my journey to the Queen of Cities."

"Where?" Adam demanded.

"It's what people call Constantinople. Now, hush and listen." He adjusted his posture on the couch. "It was summertime. I travelled with a wise man who had come from Constantinople, named Photius. We left my little village, which was called Nastaciu, and we walked south across the country for many days."

He did not allow himself to think about what had led up to his leaving the only home he had ever known. The shunning by his people. The attack by the Avar horsemen. How they had stolen Elli, the girl he had loved. How he had gone after them, and how he had found the horsemen's dismembered bodies. And what he had found when he had brought Elli back to the village ...

Nor the fear on the face of the headman of the village the day he had left, nor the look in Elli's eyes.

He took another deep breath. "We walked southward and had many adventures," he continued. "We came to a village beside a fast stream, where it fell over a rock. Because of that, the people called their village 'Bilavod,' which means 'white water.' That poor village had been attacked by barbarian raiders." He pushed his emotion down somewhere he did not allow himself to think about. "But Photius and I helped the villagers fight the barbarians."

"Tell us how you fought the barbarians!" Adam exclaimed, jumping to his feet and clapping.

Javor pushed down the memory of the young men of Bilavod, killed in the first moments of the fight. "They attacked the village without warning some days before Photius and I arrived and killed some of the people. Photius was a healer, and he helped a man with a terrible wound to his chest, and another who had lost an eye ..."

"How did he lose his eye?" Adam asked, now kneeling and attentive.

Javor smiled at the innocence of the question. "He did not leave it behind somewhere, like you leave a toy. One of the barbarians cut it with a blade." Adam and Andrina's eyes grew even larger at that, and they shrank back away from him a little. "But old Photius made him feel better," Javor said quickly. He moved on with the story. "Two or three nights later, Photius cast a magic spell to make our weapons stronger. So that they could defeat anything the barbarians had."

"A magic spell, Papa?" Andrina said. She sounded doubtful.

"Yes, my dear. At night, under the thinnest sliver of a new moon. Photius said it looked like the horns of a bull." Andrina looked even more doubtful at that, but she stayed quiet.

"The next morning was cloudy and dark, but hot. Stuffy, like Constantinople gets in August. And then I saw them coming in the distance. Everyone ran inside the village and closed the palisade—"

"What is a 'palisade?'" Adam asked, his eyes fixed on his father.

"A wall around the village, made of logs. Now listen. The raiders set fire to the palisade, and while we were trying to douse the flames, they smashed down the gate. Then they were inside, with their horses, hitting and cutting people, setting fires everywhere."

"What did you do, Papa?" Andrina asked, leaning closer on her knees. Adam was now lying on his side, looking at his fingers tracing along the floor tiles.

"I fought against the barbarians."

Adam sat up again at that. "Did you use a sword, Papa?"

"Yes. I did. I killed ... three, no four with my long sword —"

"You killed them?" Andrina cried, cringing back.

"Yah!" Adam jumped to his feet again. "Kill those barbarians!"

"Yes, I killed them. I had to. They were about to kill me and many other innocent people. Finally, when they saw that the people of Bilavod were fighting back, they ran away."

"Just like Ionnes. He runs as soon as you fight back," Adam said.

"Who is Ionnes?"

"He lives down the street. He likes to hit other children with his fists," Andrina said.

"Does he hit you?"

"He only hit me once," said Adam, shrugging. "Then Andrina kicked him hard and he ran away. Now he runs away whenever he sees us."

"Whenever he sees me, you mean," Andrina corrected.

Javor felt suffused with a deep pride in his daughter. He pulled her into his lap and held her tight for a long moment, until she began to squirm. "Papa." Her voice was muffled in his tunic.

"Very good, my daughter," he said softly, and then put her down again.

"What happened after that, Papa?" Adam demanded.

"Photius shot arrows after the retreating barbarians, killing two as they ran into the forest. They came back at sunset. There were even more of them. But Photius had prepared for them. He had made arrows that burst into flame when they struck their targets. And he had filled pots outside the stockade with a special powder that also burst into flame. Many of the barbarians caught fire, and the rest ran away in fear. And this time, they did not come back."

*That is not true. They attacked another village and drove the survivors to Bilavod. Two days later, they lured the young men of the village out and killed them all. They would have killed me, too, but Photius' magic saved me. That, and Preyatel.*

The amulet trembled under his tunic.

*Do not worry, my friend. My Preyatel. I will not reveal your presence. Not yet. Not until they are old enough to understand the importance of preserving your secret.*

"You are a hero, Papa," Andrina said solemnly.

"What? No, no. I am no hero. I am just a man."

"Yes you are. You are a real hero. Like Heracles or Theseus. You saved those people."

*So many died.* "I only did what I could do. And I was not alone. Without Photius, I ... I could have done nothing. I would not even have come to Bilavod. Nor to Constantinople."

"Where is Photius now?" Andrina asked.

Javor had to look away. His gaze lingered on a crack in the wall. "He died."

Andrina and Adam nodded. They had seen many deaths in Constantinople.

"Tell us another story, Papa," Adam demanded, pulling on Javor's tunic.

"Well, I don't know. What kind of story?"

"Tell us what it was like where you came from," said Andrina, squirming against her father's shins.

Javor reached down and tousled her dark hair. "Very...green. Beautiful. Hot summers, cold winters. Sometimes, there was so much snow in the winter, we had to dig through it to get out of our houses."

"Really, Papa?" Adam asked.

Javor surprised himself by chuckling. "Yes. Now, our houses then were not grand like this one. You children are very lucky to live in a house like this. No, when I was your age, we were all living in a house smaller than this room. The house was dug halfway down into the ground, and the door was low, so the snow often would block the whole thing."

"Why was the door so low?" Andrina asked. Her elfin face contorted in confusion.

Javor shrugged. "That was just the way everybody built houses there. Everybody had to bend down to get through it. Even my mother, who was very small."

"Small?" Adam questioned. "But you're so big. Is your papa big, too?"

"No, not as big as me, anyway. He was ... thin. Not small, but strong."

"As strong as you, Papa?" Andrina asked.

"I ... do not think so, daughter."

"Do your Mama and Papa still live in that funny house underground, Papa? Can we go see it?"

Javor's breath caught in his throat. His eyelids became heavy and wet. He turned his face away so his children would not see his tears. "No." His voice was a rasp on wood. "No, we cannot."

"Why not?" Adam asked, and started to climb up to Javor's shoulders.

He took a deep breath and closed his eyes to keep the tears from falling out. "Because they died," he croaked. "They have passed on." His head slumped down, too heavy for his shoulders.

*How do I tell them?*

*How do I tell them that a horror from Hell tore their home apart, broke their bones and killed them? How do I tell them it was my fault for separating the dagger from the amulet, breaking the spell that hid them from the monster's senses?*

*How do I tell them about the horrors that threaten their lives, the lives of all people? The forces of the Earth that want to destroy civilization before we destroy the Earth?*

Andrina pushed her brother off Javor's shoulders and wrapped her arms around Javor's neck. He jerked erect, surprised at the strength in her arms.

"Don't be sad, Papa. They're in heaven, now."

Javor let himself breathe in her scent, clean and sweet, and rocked her gently for a long time until he heard Gaetan clear his throat.

The head servant handed Javor a folded paper. "Sir, a messenger arrived."

It was a summons from the Order. Malleus' name was at the bottom, but Javor recognized the handwriting as Gracian's. He crumpled the paper, which was wet from his hand, and stepped out of the impluvium. Then he thought again, stepped back into the pool and lifted his children to the side. Before he could call, Martha appeared, Lydia behind her. "Lunch time," Martha announced.

Martha bustled Lydia and the children to the back of the house and Javor went to dress.

# Celestial Warrior

*Year 609 Christian Era*

Malleus sat on a couch in his study at the Abbey. Javor noted that he was not in the Order's council room. Neither of his usual advisors, Zeno nor Cometus was present. Gracias stood beside Malleus' chair. A young monk with a long, thin face, a sharp tonsure and stiff-looking habit, and a shorter monk with a sword belted around his habit stood on either side of the door.

"Hail, Javor!" Gracias boomed, smiling broadly. Malleus nodded and smiled a little, but even Javor could see he was glum.

The two monks said nothing, but their eyes did not leave Javor.

"Hello. Why did you summon me?" Javor asked. The room was uncomfortably warm. Sunlight shone through an open window, heating the floor tiles. Javor looked for a jug of wine, but other than a table covered in scrolls and papers and a shelf of books, the room was empty.

Gracian strode up and clasped Javor's shoulders. "My boy, it is always good to see you. I have not forgotten how you saved me from that devil that night."

Javor looked around the room again, but there was not even a place to sit. "Do you have any wine? It is a hot day."

Malleus nodded at the shorter monk, who disappeared down the hallway.

"Is your family well, Javor?" Malleus asked. His voice sounded strained, low. *Sad,* Javor thought.

"Yes, Andrina and Adam are well. They seem to grow every day. Calanthe is well, too."

Malleus smiled at that, but his eyes were still sad.

Gracian took control of the conversation again.

"Javor, we have a new mission for you. We have reports of a chthonic devil plaguing one of the most important cities in the Empire, and in Christendom: Antioch, the cradle of the Christian faith."

That description sparked several questions in Javor's mind, but he let them go to focus on one. "A chthonic demon?"

"The villagers around the city have reported a monster is eating their livestock—sheep and goats, mostly, but also some of their children."

"A monster is eating sheep and goats? What I have found when villagers complain about a monster is that wolves or lions are eating their livestock," Javor said.

"Children, Javor," Gracian repeated. "They have lost children to this hellion."

"I have heard stories like that before, as well," Javor answered. "And I have never found anyone who lost their own child to a monster. Or demon, or whatever. It is always someone else's child, or a child from the next village. Not once in missions like this have I found a mother weeping over her own child killed by a demon or a monster."

Malleus stood. "Javor, we have more than one source of information. We have corroboration about not only this, but several instances. Chthonic forces are on the move. Not only in Antioch. Not only in Sklavenia. In Persia. In Africa. Javor, we need to at least have someone confirm these rumours. We need more facts from an eyewitness. And that eyewitness will need to be able to defend himself. He will need experience in dealing with the supernatural. Who better than you in those regards, Javor? Who?"

Javor closed his eyes and sighed.

"Find out, Javor," Malleus continued. "Find out what is happening in the hills above Antioch. And deal with it, if necessary. But protect yourself. Your children need you. And we need you. Rome needs you."

"Calanthe will not like it. I hate to go when the baby is so close."

"And her Church needs you, too," Gracian added. "We are under threat from the forces of Hell, itself."

Javor did not know what to say to that.

"When you get to Antioch, go first to the Chalcedonian Bishop of the city, Anastasius." Gracian handed him a scroll. "That is a letter of introduction, countersigned by Patriarch Cyriacus of Constantinope. It will ensure that he provides you with as much aid as you need.

"However, beware of the Monophysite Bishop Athanasius. He calls himself the 'Patriarch of Antioch,' but he leads a schismatic sect. In essence, a heretic, who holds himself independent of the true Patriarch in Constantinople, and even of the See of Rome."

"Anastasius and Athanasius?" Javor asked. "One is our friend, the other an enemy?"

"Athanasius is a monophysite," Malleus explained.

"A heretic," Gracian said, nodding.

"But still a Christian?"

"A false Christian, perverting the True Faith," Gracian answered.

"You said the Church and Empire are facing destruction from Hell, and you are willing to fight other Christians because of a minor disagreement over the nature of God?" Javor exclaimed. "Most people do not even understand the difference. Jesus Christ is half human and half divine, versus completely human and completely divine? Can anyone really explain that?"

Gracian's face flushed red. His nostrils flared and his eyes narrowed.

Malleus put his hand on Javor's arm. "These may seem to be abstract distinctions, Javor, but they are important."

"One is the true doctrine of the Church, defined in ecumenical councils," Gracian snarled. "To twist doctrine is to mislead the faithful into damnation, further weakening the true Church. And the true Church is indivisible from the Empire."

"The point, Javor, is that Anastasius is our ally and is preparing to help you in this mission," Malleus explained. "When you arrive in Antioch, go directly to Bishop Anastasius, not Athanasius."

"Those names are very similar," Javor protested.

"To ensure that you do not confuse the two," Gracian said with a tone of exaggerated pedantry, "Anastasius will have further advice for you in a sealed scroll that we have already dispatched by our fastest courier."

"More advice? Why not just tell me now?"

Gracian stepped back and tilted his nose up. "That will be clear when you get there."

Javor started to open the scroll, but Gracian put a hand on it to stop him. "Do not open it yourself. It is vital that its recipient be the one to break the seal, to ensure its authenticity."

Javor nodded and turned to leave.

"Wait," Gracian said. "One more thing before you make preparations to leave for Antioch. We have prepared a special ceremony for you, Javor."

"A ceremony?" Another ceremony? Has Gracian become a Gnostic now?

A look at Malleus told Javor that was not the case.

Gracian led the way to a chapel in the Abbey. Not the main chapel, where the monks and, at different times, the nuns would gather, but not the secret areas, either, where the Gnostics held their secret worships of the Pleroma, Christos and Sophia. It was just a small chapel, with an altar and a crucifix hanging over a tabernacle behind it. A monk was lighting candles as they entered. Javor noticed that the two monks from the meeting followed them and took up positions on either side of the door.

Fools, if they think they can stop me from leaving when I want to.

Gracian went behind the altar and began praying. Javor recognized the minor mass. *Great. Now I have to stay here for at least an hour.*

But the ceremony moved more quickly. When Javor was expecting the Kyrie, the prayer shifted to something he had never heard before.

Gracian came around the altar and approached Javor, bearing a golden bowl. He dipped his hands in it, and Javor realized it was myrrh.

Gracian traced a cross on Javor's forehead, then on his throat, and finally on the backs of his hands, muttering too low for Javor to understand. He genuflected, rose again and returned behind the altar. He turned his back to Javor.

Then came a Eucharist. Gracian approached Javor again with a golden goblet in one hand and a piece of dry bread in the other. In front of Javor, he dipped the bread in the sweet wine in the cup. "Kneel, Javor," he said.

Javor looked at Malleus, who nodded. Sighing, Javor knelt before Gracian. Muttering in a language that Javor did not understand, he held the wine-soaked bread before Javor's mouth. He took it. *Lousy wine,* he thought.

Gracian placed the goblet on the altar, then turned to Javor again. "Rise, Sir Javor, with the grace of our Lord Jesus Christ as the Celestial Warrior!" He made the sign of the cross again.

Javor rose. Malleus approached and kissed him on both cheeks. "Thank you, Javor, for protecting us."

"I am only one man."

Malleus smiled. "An extraordinary man. We both know that."

Gracian clapped him on the shoulder. Javor felt the amulet stir. "We are depending on you, Javor. All Rome looks to you now for salvation."

Javor did not know what to say. Preyatel sent him a mild warning, but against what, he could not tell.

# A slow and difficult journey

Javor realized he enjoyed sailing. The feeling of the wind in his hair, the smell of salt and fish and wet wood, the sound of the water gurgling under the hull, even the rush of the oars pulling, were somehow thrilling and comforting at the same time.

The sun warmed the back of his neck, even though the wind chilled his shoulders. He watched as the second mate tightened a rope—a "sheet," he remembered the men calling it—and then the captain adjusting the tiller.

Javor closed his eyes and savoured the feeling of the wind on his face. Such a relief from the oppressive heat of Constantinople. When he opened his eyes again, they fell on the men rowing the galley.

Slaves. The men who make this boat get to where I want it to, where I need it to, are slaves.

Which makes me as much of a slave master as my father-in-law.

Mauricius Macedonius, his father-in-law, would not be happy to learn that Javor had commandeered his swiftest ship for the transit to Antioch.

Calanthe had been even more unhappy than Javor had anticipated, weeping when he told her he was leaving, screaming at him when he would not tell her where he was going. She shoved him out of her bedchamber and slammed the door.

Javor's mind went to the next, sunny morning on the wharf on the harbour in Constantinople. He had come to the port when the sun was still low in the east and found the ship when they had begun loading the cargo that his father-in-law had commissioned.

"Take me to Antioch," Javor had said to the man on the wharf, watching the loading. A head shorter than Javor, with a head of thick, black hair and a stiff, black beard, he had turned toward the ship and barked out a few words that Javor did not understand.

Another man approached, wearing a heavy cloak and a thick woolen hat. His beard was peppered white and his face was weathered. He exchanged a few words with the man Javor had spoken to, then turned to Javor.

"What do you want?"

"Are you the commander of this ship?"

"I am Captain Herius Cyprianos. Now what do you want? We are busy."

"To go to Antioch," Javor had replied.

"We are bound for Tripolis in the Levant," the Captain had replied.

"My father-in-law is the owner of this ship," Javor said.

"I know who you are," the Captain retorted. "But we have a cargo to take to Tripolis."

"Antioch is not far out of your way," Javor said. "You will probably have to overnight there, anyway."

"I do not need to sail to any place I do not want to," the captain said.

Javor threw him a small, heavy sack. The captain caught it and hefted it. "Sailing to Antioch is not possible," he said, opening the sack to look at the silver coins inside. "It's miles from the coast and the river is too shallow. The closest I can get is Saint Symeon, the port on the coast. You are on your own after that."

Javor nodded. "Do not tell my father-in-law," Javor said.

The captain winked and returned to supervising the men loading the bales.

Eight days later, Javor was not so enthusiastic about sailing. He had easily become used to the rolling motion of the sailing ship as it moved away from the coasts to the open seas. Captain Cyprianos preferred sailing well away from the coast, to the point where it was a barely visible line at the horizon. "Sailing is faster this way," he growled, one of the few times he said a word to Javor. The rest of the time, he restricted his words to growling orders at his first mate, Leander, or another crewman.

After a week of living on the rear deck of the ship, and spending his nights in a cramped cabin below the deck, where he could not even stand up straight, Javor was looking forward to getting off the ship and standing on a surface that did not move under his feet.

The ship had stopped in ports along the Sea of Marmara, along the coast of Anatolia and in Cyprus. Sailing into the port of Paphos on Cyprus, the Captain's hometown, was the only time that Javor saw the captain not scowl at every word said to him.

But the stop was short. The ship took on fresh water and some food, and at sunrise on the day after they arrived, they set off again.

And that was when the captain began cursing the winds and the waters.

"What is this? The currents do not flow against us at this time of year," he groused, struggling with the tiller and barking at the crew.

"And the winds—where are the western winds? We have always had easy sailing from Cyprus at this time of year." He cursed and spat over the ship's rail.

Javor watched the clouds gather, thicker and darker every day, ahead.

"Storms over the Levant?" Leander asked. "At this time of year?"

The wind grew stronger by the hour, straight out of the east, blowing the ship away from the coast that Javor wanted to reach. The captain turned toward the south for most of the afternoon, the wind blowing across the ship's deck, before trying to tack northward again.

To little avail. As the sun got lower, Cyprianos uttered a string of curses and pushed the tiller over. The ship sailed southeast, Javor gazing up the coast toward his goal.

“The gods do not want you to reach Antioch,” Leander said.

That pricked Javor’s curiosity. “The gods? Not one god?” Preyatel was still and calm.

Leander’s eyes widened. “A figure of speech,” he said and turned away quickly.

Javor watched his back as he started pulling on a rope. *Why bother him? Sometimes I wonder about the things that I do.*

As the sun touched the horizon, Cyprianos steered the ship into a narrow bay. The shore, as far as Javor could see, was empty. Green fields came down to a narrow, stoney beach. With the last of the light, the captain found a calm area where the surface of the water rippled only a little. Men pulled on ropes, furled the sail and dropped the anchor over the side with a heavy splash.

Leander supervised a shipboard supper of fish and dry bread. Cyprianos emerged from his cabin and returned Javor’s purse, although it was notably lighter.

“It’s half your money,” he growled, looking over the rail toward the dark smudge that was all they could see of the shore. “You are not where you contracted me to take you. And a fine gentleman like yourself will need to hire a wagon or buy a horse to get to Antioch from here. I reckon it’s about ten or twelve miles from here to the Orontes River, and then upriver from there to the city gates.”

“Then why not give me back all my money?”

Captain Cyprianos fixed his little eyes on Javor, squinting upward in the dark. “I will need to distribute the rest among my crew. I do not need word to spread that Captain Herius Cyprianos failed to reach a port of call.”

“Can we not just try again tomorrow?”

The captain nodded upwind. “This wind is not going to stop tomorrow.”

“How do you know?”

“I have been sailing these coasts from Constantinople to Alexandria for twenty years, boy. Do not tell me my business. Now come. If you can keep your mouth shut, you can share a meal with us."

The next morning, Javor stood on the damp shore, watching Mauricius' fastest ship sail south, nearly flying ahead of the wind from the northeast.

He turned away from the boat, into the wind. The captain had landed him the night before on a steep, sandy beach. Rough waves chased him up the sand, as if trying to claw the land back below the surface before receding again with a bubbling hiss.

To his left, north, a rocky outcrop into the sea had provided the protection from waves and wind for the night. On his right, the beach ended with cliffs twice his height, topped with low bushes.

He strode up the sloping beach, directly into the wind. Above the highest reaches of the tides, grey-green bushes clung to the sand against the wind.

At the crest of the slope, he was even with the tops of the rocky outcrop to his left. To his right, the land continued to rise to a mountain in the south. But ahead, to the north and northwest, the land continued more or less level for a quarter-mile before falling again.

Javor zigzagged down a steeper slope on the north side of the hill to a broad beach that stretched, straight as a knife-edge to the north, farther than he could see. To the left, eastward, the land rose smoothly to the foot of steeper hills. Far to the north, he could see low mountains. His study of maps in Constantinople told him that somewhere between where he was and the feet of those mountains was the Orontes River, which would lead him to Antioch.

He set off along the beach, choosing the part where the wet sand was firm under his boots. Before long, he reached a tiny fishing village, really only a collection of crude huts clustered at the point where a tiny creek leaked out from the grassy plain on the right, onto the sandy beach.

He approached a group of men repairing a small boat. A boy of about ten stood, holding a net, watching him. The men ignored him until he was ten paces away. Then the oldest, with a grey beard and bald head, growled at him in accented Greek. "What do you want?"

Javor stopped. He noticed they had knives and long, sturdy-looking poles. "A boat to take me to Antioch," he answered.

The other men squinted at him as the oldest one stood slowly. "Antioch is a long way."

"I can pay," Javor said, resting his hand on the hilt of his sword.

One of the other men rose and spat onto the sand. "How much?"

"It is going to be a bitch going upriver in this wind, Timoteo," said the older man.

Timoteo shrugged. "How much will you pay?" he repeated.

"Two nummi," Javor said, enough to buy two big jugs of good wine.

"Six nummi," Timoteo said.

"What? That is ridiculous."

"It will take two of us to row upriver, and upwind as well. The mouth of the Orontes is a mile up the beach, and we will want to be back before nightfall. Plus, we will need to buy food somewhere. So six nummi. Three each."

Javor calculated the number of coins in his purse. Sighing, he nodded. "Very well. Six nummi." He handed three of the tiny bronze coins to Timoteo. "The rest when we reach the city."

Timoteo nodded toward the beach. "My boat is down there. Come on, Marco." He strode toward the water. Another young man with a thick tangle of curly black hair followed, and Javor followed them to a long rowboat.

Javor settled onto a bench across the width of the boat, watching as Timoteo and Marco rowed. The moment their oars dipped into the water, the wind strengthened, rippling through Javor's blond hair.

The small boat pitched and rocked over waves that grew higher and rougher every minute. They pushed the boat back. When Javor looked at the shore, he could see that they barely made any progress.

Two hours of hard rowing later, they had not made more than half a mile. Javor took over rowing from Marco for a time to give the young man a rest. Then Marco took Timoteo's oar in turn.

The sun reached noon before a town came into view. "Saint Symeon,"

Timoteo panted as he took an oar from Javor. "It is the port of Antioch. The Orontes River flows through it to the Levantine Sea here."

But it took at least another hour of rowing, Javor taking his turn at the oars before they turned toward the mouth of the Orontes. "This is it," Timoteo announced as he directed the vessel toward a broad beach south of the river's mouth. "This is as far as we go."

"But you agreed to take me to Antioch," Javor protested.

"There is no way we can get to Antioch in this weather," Timoteo said, panting. "The wind is shifting again. It is coming straight down the river." He looked over his shoulder at the river's mouth, where white-capped breakers rolled out to crash into the sea's own frothing waves.

Javor could see low wooden buildings lining both banks of the river. A short distance upstream from the mouth, a variety of boats and ships bounced and rocked against docks.

"The river is very high, too," Marco said.

"It was not this high three days ago, when I last was here," said Timoteo. "For some reason, it is in flood. Which means the current is even stronger than normal. So, rich man, this is as far as we go."

The rowboat's hull grated against the sandy beach. Marco jumped out and pulled the vessel up the beach.

"I paid you to take me to Antioch," Javor repeated.

"You only gave us half the agreed-on price. You can keep the rest. Me and Marco are spent. The only good thing is that this wind will likely blow us all the way home. If it does not capsize us."

For the second time in a day, Javor climbed out of a small boat and splashed his way onto a beach. This time, however, he did not waste time watching the two Levantines row away.

Instead, he walked into the town, to the crowded wharf along the surging river. Fighting his nature, he spoke to weathered, browned men until he found someone willing to take him upriver to Antioch in a slightly larger boat than Timoteo's. This one was outfitted with a single mast and sail, in addition to two oars.

But as soon as the owner had directed his two-man crew to loosen a rope, a powerful gust ripped through the town, tearing breath from people's lungs. Waves frothed white on the river. The rope wrenched from the owner's hand and the boat, loose at the stern, slipped downwind to crash into its neighbour. Javor heard a splintering crash. A piece of iron stuck through the boat's hull, river water gushing in.

The owner cursed and his crew rushed to minimize the damage.

Javor tucked his purse away and turned without another word.

He found a stable and asked about hiring a carriage to take him to Antioch, some twelve miles upriver. The owner was a short, fat man who chewed on something continually. He mumbled something, disappeared into a dark barn, and emerged some minutes later, leading a horse pulling a battered-looking, two-seat cart.

Javor threw his pack into the back, behind the seats. Then he heard a loud crack. The stable owner cursed and bent down. "Damn it! The axel is broken. Now how in Christ's name did that happen?"

Javor sighed. "Never mind the cart, then. How much for the horse? Just to take me to Antioch. I can return it on my way back."

Javor instantly regretted the question. The horse was old, small and thin. Its back sagged and it looked at Javor with sad eyes, as if to say, "Is there no one smaller than you to carry?"

The fat man straightened and scratched his prominent belly. "Ten nummi," he said. "I will return five when you bring her home."

It was a steep price, but Javor knew he had no choice. *I am going to demand that Gracian pay back some of the costs of this mission,* he thought. "All right," he said. "But that includes the saddle."

The fat man scowled, but agreed. He started back to the barn, and Javor reached to pat the horse's neck. As soon as his fingers touched the short fur, the horse shied away, neighing and snorting.

The fat man returned with a worn saddle. He put it on the ground when he saw his horse's behaviour. "What's wrong, Dolly? I do not understand, sir. She is always such a sweetie. She likes everyone." He patted the horse's shoulder.

Javor reached toward the horse again. Dolly snorted and stepped back, her hindquarters pushing on the cart it was still strapped to. Dolly tossed her head. When Javor stepped closer, she stepped away and screamed. She rose onto her hind feet, crashing down farther away from Javor. She gave him one more look, then broke into a run, dragging the cart behind her. Javor managed to snag his pack from the back as it went past him.

The fat owner cursed again and chased after her.

"I will walk," Javor grumbled.

But as soon as he stepped out of the stable, the wind tore at his head, nearly pulling his cloak from his shoulders. Hoisting his pack onto his back, he began to walk upriver.

Directly into the wind.

He pushed upwind, squinting against dust and sand that stung his face and eyes. "Stupid horse," he mumbled.

The wind felt like a hand pushing against his chest. By the time he reached the eastern edge of the town, the sun was orange, shining onto his back. He saw an inn with a lantern shining over the door, swinging wildly in the wind. He pushed his way inside, into a common room where a dozen men and one woman sat at tables, eating.

A thin woman in an apron approached and looked at him, but said nothing.

Javor coughed out dust. "How far is it to Antioch?"

"Close to fifteen miles," she said in a voice as coarse and rough as Javor's lungs felt.

Javor sighed. "Do you have a room for the night?"

"Two nummi," said the woman. "Another for supper. You have arrived just in time for the last serving." She led him to a table, and he sank onto a stool. *I just realized how tired I am. I never thought, before, that wind could make you tired.*

The food was bland, the wine sour, and the room cramped, but clean. Javor dumped his pack on the floor and pulled off only his boots before stretching out on the thin cot and fell into an immediate, deep and dreamless sleep.

Javor woke at sunrise, pulled on his boots and slung his pack on his back. He followed a heavenly aroma. In the kitchen, he found a man in an apron, pulling fresh loaves from a brick oven. The man had surprisingly large, dark and shining eyes that looked wet to Javor. "Breakfast is not ready yet," he said in an accent Javor had never heard before.

"I am in a hurry," Javor answered. He picked up a fresh loaf, then dropped it back on the wooden counter because it was too hot.

"Bread does not care whether you are in a hurry," said the baker.

Javor let the loaves cool and went to one of the wine barrels, from which he filled his own wineskin. The baker ignored him, taking bread from the oven using long tongs, and arranging the loaves on the counter.

Wineskin bulging, Javor picked up two loaves which were now cool enough to touch, wrapped them in a cloth, and put them in his pack. Then he picked up a third loaf and turned to leave.

"How much bread do you plan to eat?" the baker asked.

Javor shrugged. "I think it will be a long day." He fished another bronze coin out of his purse and put it on the counter. The baker glared at him and turned away.

Javor shrugged again, and left.

Out on the road, the wind still blew hard from the northeast, the way to Antioch. Javor took a bite of his bread and washed it down with a swallow of wine. He kept on eating as he walked up the road that followed the river for about a half-mile until it left the bank at a great bend in the water course. From there, the road was shaded by rows of tall trees on either side. Beyond them, farmers' fields stretched.

It was not long before he began to regret his strategy of eating breakfast while walking. The wind blew more and more dust into his face and his food, knocking down leaves from branches that overhung the road. Within a few bites he was chewing on grit.

He drank more wine, shoved the rest of the loaf into his pack, bent his shoulders into the wind and moved on.

A man and boy pushing a two-wheeled cart came toward him. The cart was piled with vegetables and fruit, and Javor moved aside to let them pass. *Must be market day.* Sure enough, behind them came a small flock of sheep, followed by a shepherd with a long staff. He stepped to the side of the old Roman road to let them pass. Preyatel, his amulet, vibrated against his skin under his shirt. As he stepped on the edge of the flagstone, he felt it crumble under his foot. He pitched forward, striking his knee on the packed sand on the side of the road.

He cursed and rose unsteadily. His knee throbbed.

The sheep moved past. The shepherd stared at him for a moment, then turned away. Gritting his teeth, Javor moved on, into the wind.

The sky in the east burned red and orange even as the sun rose higher. Dark grey clouds scudded below higher, brighter ones, racing over his head.

Next came a herd of cattle, driven by two boys and followed by, Javor assumed, their father. He limped past them, stumbling on the uneven ground beside the Roman road.

After some time, the pain in his knee diminished. The wind, however, did not let up. Instead, it seemed to grow stronger. Clouds of dust blew into his face again and again. Gusts made his feet slip, his boot soles grating against the flat stone of the road.

He knew he was moving very slowly. It was the wind, hot and dry. While the clouds only drew lower and closer through the day, there was no hint of rain.

He swallowed more wine, but it did not alleviate his thirst. By the time he judged the cloud-shrouded sun to be at about noon, he was covered in dust caked to his skin by his own sweat, his throat ached with thirst, his wineskin was empty, and he did not dare try to take more bread out of his pack.

Squinting into the gloomy wind, he made out a shadow ahead that looked a little more solid than the clouds of dust. As he neared, he could see it was another roadside inn. He stumbled in, pushing the door shut against the wind. Its pitch rose to a whine and then a whistle as the door closed.

He turned to see a teenaged boy with a bucket of water in one hand

and a cloth in the other. Before Javor could react, the boy reached up and wiped the cloth across his face.

Javor flinched, his pack hitting the door behind him. "Do not fear," the boy said. He had thick, dark, curly hair and huge dark eyes that reflected the candles in the wall sconces. "On days like this, when the winds bring the dust from the northern valley, we always offer visitors a clean rinse."

Javor stared at the boy. For years, no one outside his own family, or Malleus, had dared touch him without asking first. The boy reached up again and gently sponged dust from his cheeks, nose and chin. Then he reached for Javor's hands and washed them.

Even in the dim light, Javor could see that the water in the bucket was now dirty. "Thank you," he managed to say.

The boy seemed small for his age, which Javor guessed to be about 16, and very thin. There was a beauty in his face and grace in the way he moved as he showed Javor to a seat. "Traveler, what can we do for you today?" he asked in a soft and musical voice.

"Wine," Javor rasped. In seconds, a clay cup was in his hands and the boy poured from a jug. The wine tasted far better than what he had taken from the inn in Saint Symeon. *Maybe that is because I am so thirsty.* He drained the cup and the boy filled it again.

"How much farther to Antioch?" he asked.

"Seven miles."

*Halfway. In a full morning, at least five hours, I have only managed to walk seven miles. I should have come more than twice that far. I should be well within Antioch by now.*

Javor looked around. "There is no one here." The common room was empty save for him and the boy. Wind howled around the corners outside and whistled through spaces between the wallboards.

"On days like this, people do not travel much," the boy answered.

"Are there many days like this, here?"

"Almost never. But most people have wisdom enough not to travel when the wind carries the dust for miles." The boy smiled. "Would you like something to eat? We have cheese, bread, and some fish from the river."

Javor's stomach growled, the sound louder than the wind outside. "I suppose so. Please." He shrugged his pack off and stretched out his long legs.

The boy bustled from a back room, carrying plates and more wine. Taking a bite of fresh fish, Javor asked, "Are you here alone?"

"No, my sister is cooking in the kitchen."

"And there is no one else?"

The boy looked down, long eyelashes fluttering. "No, not for two years, now. Not since the plague."

"There was plague here?"

"For a short time. But please, worry not. It has gone these past two years."

"But it killed your parents?"

The boy nodded once, eyes on the floor. "Yes. And my brothers and sisters, too. There were six of us. Now there are only my sister and me. We have kept our father's inn since those days."

"I am sorry." Javor finished the cheese. "What is your name?"

"Stylian," said the boy.

Javor tossed down the last of the wine. "Thank you, Stylian. That was the best meal I have had in a long time. But now I must go."

"Oh, no, sir. You must not travel during the windstorms. It is not safe!"

As if to stress his point, a whistling gust shook the walls of the inn, followed by a groan and a crash. Javor and Stylian looked at each other, and then Javor tore open the door. Stylian made an inarticulate protest and followed Javor into the windstorm.

Just beyond the lonely inn, a great tree lay across the road, limbs and crown filling the full space between the rows of swaying trees that still stood, their branches sweeping back and forth like agitated snakes.

"You see, sire, you cannot travel to Antioch. The road is blocked."

"I can just walk around it."

"If one tree fell, do you not think that another could, too? They are very old. Or a big branch could fall on your head. Please, sir, stay the night. We will not charge you full price. Plus, my sister is making her honey cake for dessert."

The wind howled louder, lashing both of them with dust. They watched broken branches flee from the gusts, skittering down the road.

Javor sighed. "All right," he said finally. "I will stay the night. Wake me early. I must get to Antioch."

Stylian smiled, his grin a flash of light in the gloomy day. Javor followed him to a dim, but surprisingly comfortable room with a thick bed, a table with a bowl and ewer and a stand of five candles. The boy lit them all, took the ewer and ran down the corridor.

Javor put his pack on the floor and was pulling off his boots when Stylian returned with the ewer filled with water, a bundle of blankets tucked under his arm. He dropped the blankets on the bed and poured steaming water into the bowl. "I will call you for supper," he said, and closed the door.

Javor stripped to wash the dirt and dust of the road off. By the time he was done, the water in the bowl was a thick dark grey. He collapsed onto the bed and pulled a blanket over himself. Outside, the wind continued to howl. Something knocked rhythmically. An intermittent whistle came from somewhere near the ceiling.

*Something does not want me to get to Antioch. As a boy, I would have called it Stribog, the God of wind and strife. Now? An archon? An aeon?*

*Or probably, just the weather.*

*Strange, though. I cannot predict what the weather will be tomorrow. That has never happened before.*

# A night at the upriver inn

Knocking on the thin door startled Javor awake. Preyatel was quiet, though, so he knew he was in no danger.

"Sir? Mr. Javor? Supper is served," Stylian's voice came through the door.

The sound of the wind had diminished. The light leaking into the room around the shutters had changed to orange.

"Thank you, Stylian," Javor said, his voice rough from sleep. "I will come right away." He swung his feet to the floor and found his boots.

He thought about washing again, but dismissed the thought when he looked at the grey water in the bowl. He went to the common room, where he found Stylian pouring wine into a cup on a table. "Good evening, sir," he said.

"You can call me 'Javor.'"

"Thank you, Sir Javor."

"No 'sir.' Just 'Javor.'"

"And you may call me 'Stylian.'"

"I have been calling you Stylian."

"My sister, Miriam, has prepared a very special evening meal. Roast chicken with her own blend of herbs, along with a mixture of greens and beans, hummus, and a honey cake dessert. Miriam makes the best honey cake for miles around."

Stylian disappeared into the kitchen and returned with a platter and plates of food on a large tray. As he set out the food, he said, "If it is all right with you, sir—I mean, Javor, my sister and I would like to join you for the evening meal. We have no guests other than you tonight."

Javor said, "All right. It will be good to have company." Although he was not certain about that.

Stylian smiled. "Thank you." He leaned into the kitchen door and called.

A thin woman emerged, wearing a white apron over a thin yellow shift, her hair covered by a patterned scarf. "Javor, please meet my sister, Miriam."

Javor nodded.

She was smaller than her brother, and older. Still young, but more worn. Her hair, like her brother's, was dark and curly. She had large dark eyes and a bump in her nose. A dark birthmark shaped like a hook curved over her left cheek.

Miriam said very little through the meal, but Stylian kept up a stream of attempts of conversation. He asked about Constantinople and about the political situation.

"We hear that the Emperor Phocas has made many changes."

*Be careful, Javor.* "Yes. There are many different people in charge of different parts of the Empire and the army."

Stylian leaned closer. His voice dropped. "Is it true that he executed the Empress Constantina and her daughters?"

Javor suppressed a cough and swallowed a mouthful of wine. "Yes, that is true. He accused her of treason. There was a conspiracy to kill the emperor."

Stylian nodded. Javor changed the subject. "Do many people stop here on the road to Antioch?"

"To tell you the truth, custom has considerably decreased these past three years or so," Stylian said.

"It has been longer than that, brother," Miriam spoke up. "Even before our parents passed away, this was not a busy inn. Mother told father not to open an inn halfway between Antioch and the port."

"Sister, I do not think that our guest needs to hear this ongoing dispute between us," Stylian said.

Miriam focused on Javor. "My father's dream was to have an inn. But there were too many already in Antioch. Too much competition. So he thought of one here, halfway between the citadel of Antioch and the port of Saint Symeon. But it is not far enough to necessitate an overnight stop. As a result, this inn has never been prosperous. Our trade is usually people like you, who arrive here later than they anticipated."

"I am certain our guest does not wish to hear our troubles," Stylian interjected again.

"It seems a fine inn," Javor said, trying to be encouraging.

Miriam scoffed. "The building barely stands. I am surprised the windstorm today did not knock it down utterly."

Stylian rose to gather the empty dishes. "Miriam, please bring in your wonderful honey cake. I have told our guest all about it."

Miriam glared at her brother, lips pressed tight together. "Very well." She rose, curtseyed and went to the kitchen. She returned with what looked like a dark brown loaf, dripping with honey. She cut pieces for Javor, her brother and herself.

"You are right," Javor said to Stylian. "This is wonderful. This is the best honey cake I have ever had. And that's even compared to my mother-in-law's."

"Not your mother's?" Miriam asked, a smirk on her face.

A pang went through Javor. "Yes, better than hers. Although I have not eaten hers in many years." His voice dropped. "She ... passed away, too, more than eight years ago."

"I am sorry," said Stylian.

"How did she die?" Miriam asked, and Javor felt another pang.

"She was murdered," he whispered. He was surprised to see a tear splash onto the table.

A hand touched his shoulder. "I am very sorry, my friend," said a low voice, but Javor could not tell whether it was Stylian or Miriam.

Javor finished the cake and found himself in his room, with no memory of walking there. Someone, probably Stylian, had tidied it since he had left, and lit the candles. He undressed and extinguished them, then fell into the soft bed.

He had no idea how many hours later he woke when he felt a body pressing against him. Opening his eyes to a single candle on the table, he saw a nude female figure outlined in the dark.

"Who—"

"Do not fear." A finger touched his lips and he recognized Miriam's voice. He felt the warmth of naked skin against his own as she slipped under the blankets. He hissed an intake of breath as he felt her lips against his throat. Kisses trailed up his jaw to his mouth as fingertips traced down his chest.

"Miriam," he managed to say between kisses, his voice hoarse. "I am married."

"Your wife is a thousand miles away," she said, cupping her hand around his testicles.

Javor groaned. "Miriam, you are a maiden. A virgin."

She scoffed. "I am no child. Would a child know how to do this?" In one motion, she took him into her mouth, and Javor could not think anymore.

She came up to kiss his face some time later. "You are a beautiful man. Love me. The only one who loves me is my brother, and he loves me as a brother should. Love me as a lover." She straddled him and sank her heat onto his.

Javor surrendered.

Later, she lay beside him, stroking her fingertips up and down his naked chest. She kissed his nipple and asked, "Was that so terrible for you, Sklavene?"

Javor's breath caught in his throat. "How did you know?"

She scoffed. "I did not, until now. You could have been Sarmatian, or one of those fabled barbarians from the far north. But I guessed you were Sklavene because of your accent."

"It was not terrible," Javor admitted. "But are you not concerned about the morality? The Church says—"

Miriam scoffed again. "You do not believe the Church any more than I do."

Javor did not know what to say.

"I know you, Javor the Sklavene. I know you are not an Orthodox Christian. You are a Gnostic."

Javor could not breathe.

Miriam chuckled. "Do not fear, lover. Your secret is safe with me. Not even my brother knows my beliefs. He is a dear, but he is not the sharpest blade in my belt."

"How—"

She picked up the amulet that rested his chest. "This, for one. A true Christian would only wear a cross or a crucifix. And little things, signals that only a woman would notice. Men can be beautiful and satisfying, but you are not as wise as women."

Javor thought for some time. Then he asked, "Do you...make love to all the beautiful men who stop at your inn?"

She laughed at that. "Would that happen more frequently. As I told you, Sklavene, we get very little trade here. We can barely afford to feed ourselves. Were it not for the chicken coop in back and the vegetable garden — both of which I tend, without help from my brother — we would have starved to death long ago.

"No, Javor, I do not seduce every handsome man who comes through here. But I have had my share of lovers."

"Do you not want a husband?"

She laughed, deep and throaty. "No man here will marry me. I am too old, now. And with this mark on my face?"

"What is wrong with the mark?"

"As long as I can remember, people called it the 'mark of Cain.' Making me untouchable. Undesirable. And certainly unmarriable. And then there is the fact that I am known not to be 'pure.'"

"Do people around here know that?"

She scoffed again. "My father took my virginity when I was seven. It was no secret."

Javor sat up a little. "Seven? But —"

"It was a long time ago," Miriam said, putting her finger on his lips again. "And he has paid for his transgression."

"How?"

She kissed him. "When my mother died of the plague, all his attention turned to me. It was intolerable. So ... I did not tolerate it."

"But Stylian said he died of plague."

He felt her shrug. "Stylian is so trusting. Our father died coughing up blood. Who can really know what caused it?" She kissed his chest. "Since then, I have taken only men I want to take." Her lips went to his throat, then began kissing lower.

Javor thought of a man bleeding from his mouth, but when Miriam's kisses reached lower than his waist, he stopped thinking.

# The gate

When Javor woke in the morning, Miriam was gone. He opened the shutter to see a clear, blue sky. A gentle breeze stirred the trees, but nothing like the previous two days.

As he washed and dressed, he wondered whether the archons or aeons had given up trying to prevent his reaching the city. *Or maybe they think I have given up.*

*No. I will not give up.*

He looked out the window again to make sure his thought did not stir the wind again.

Stylian was already bustling around the common room. Javor heard clattering from the kitchen and assumed Miriam was baking or cooking again.

"Thank you," he said, laying some coins on a table.

Stylian's face became darker and he looked down, then to the side. "This is too much, sir. Mr. Javor, I said I would not charge you full price."

"You provided what you promised: a room and excellent meals. It is only fair that I pay the full fare."

"At least, take some breakfast. My sister has made fresh loaves and the water has just boiled." He poured liquid from a jug into a clay cup. "And I just opened a fresh barrel of ale."

"All right." Javor drank some of the ale. "Are there any honey cakes left?"

Stylian grinned. "One or two." He went to the kitchen.

Javor sat and drank the rest of the ale. Stylian returned with loaves, butter and a steaming kettle and arranged them on the table, then left Javor to eat alone.

Javor ate until he was no longer hungry, then stored the remaining food in a pocket of his pack that was easy to access as he walked. He poured the ale into one of his wineskins, and filled another skin with water from the jug on the counter. He left another coin for payment, and left.

As he walked to the Roman road, though, Miriam came around the corner of the inn. "So that is how you leave? Without even saying goodbye?"

Javor stopped. "I—I did not know what to say—"

"Of course not," she interrupted him. "Men never do. Especially men like you."

"What...do you mean, like me?" *What does she know?*

She scoffed and waved his hand. "Go. Leave. Do not come back." She spat on the ground and went back through the kitchen door.

Javor looked at the door for a heartbeat. *What does she know?* he wondered again. *Whose side is she on?*

Finally, he hiked up his pack and joined the crowds on the road.

A group of men that Javor assumed were local peasants had hitched oxen to drag the fallen tree off the road. As Javor passed, he watched them untie the tree from the oxen. Other men brought axes and saws and began cutting the wood.

Without a windstorm blowing, there were people on the road. The weather was fine, the sky clear, the air warm, and a gentle breeze blew from the west.

His long legs made for a pace that passed most of the others on the road. No one looked at him, though he was a stranger. *Everyone on the road is a stranger,* he realized.

He looked around as he strode, now that he could see the landscape. On either side of the road, farmers' fields stretched. Men, women and children stepped in them, cutting or pulling or doing other tasks. The road still followed the Orontes River, which flowed from the northeast through a broad valley. About a mile or so to his left, hills rose to end the horizon. The same distance to the right, a row of mountains stretched north and south.

As he progressed, the road became busier. Men and women on foot, some carrying children, others bearing bundles or pushing carts, horses, the occasional oxcart or horse-drawn carriage.

Around noon, he could see the city in the distance. It seemed to be pushed up against the feet of the eastern mountains. Antioch, from Gracian's description.

He drank the rest of the ale and ate the last of Miriam's honey cakes. After a rest, he continued on.

The traffic got heavier, more crowded than Javor had seen, even on the big roads near Constantinople. When he neared the city, he realized that it was joined by two other big, paved roads, one coming from the northwest, the other curving from the east around the feet of one of the mountains.

He wiped sweat from his forehead as he stepped to the side of the road to let a large carriage, drawn by two black horses, rumble past him from behind. It slowed at the crossroad and took the right-hand branch, going east.

As Javor stepped forward, he felt his amulet tremble. He paused, amazed to see the paving stones on the road crack and crumble. They sank into the ground as a hole opened up, stretching from one side of the road to the other, wider than he was tall. A woman coming with a group from the other direction screamed as she stopped, swaying on the far edge.

A man beside Javor cursed. "Damn sinkhole."

People began walking around the hole. Men led horses pulling wagons slowly, careful not to let the wheels get close to the edge of the sinkhole.

Javor followed. With the obstruction of the sinkhole, the road was even more crowded with foot traffic.

As soon as Javor's foot touched the intersection, Preyatel trembled again and the sky became dark. The other people vanished in a thick, misty gloom, the horses and donkeys and oxen, too. Nighttime chill replaced the afternoon heat. Javor's skin tingled.

An arch stretched over the crossroads now, which had not been there a second before. Javor turned around to try to see beyond the mist. When he faced the city again, he saw her.

He had no doubt. Hekate, as a slender young girl with long, dark hair. She held a large keyring in her left hand. At her feet, again, the immense black dog sat, its eyes fixed on Javor.

YOU HAVE NOT HEEDED OUR WARNINGS, she said without moving her mouth.

"I have heeded you," he answered. "I have not raised a hand against anything that has not attacked me or my family, first."

YOUR MISSIONS ARE HARMFUL TO BOTH SIDES OF THE BALANCE. THEY WILL ALSO BE FUTILE IN THEMSELVES.

"The balance again. You mean Earth and Sky."

YOU CONTINUE TO FOLLOW MASTERS WHO LEAD YOU AWAY FROM YOUR DESTINED PATH. THEY SEEK TO USE YOU FOR THEIR GODS' PURPOSES. THEY SEEK TO USE THEIR GODS, CELESTIAL ARCHONS, FOR THEIR OWN MATERIAL WEALTH. FOR TEMPORAL LUXURY AND POWER OVER OTHER HUMANS. THEY ARE WILLFUL FOOLS. THEY BLIND THEMSELVES WITH FANTASIES OF HEAVENLY GLORY. THEY ABANDON THE MOTHER WHO BIRTHED THEM.

"Do you mean Moist Mother Earth?"

As she had in Javor's homeland, Hekate changed from a young girl to a mature, beautiful woman, hair curled in Roman style.

ONE OF YOUR WORDS FOR IT, YES. HUMANITY'S MOTHER. ONE SOURCE OF ALL LIFE.

"The Christians talk about their heavenly father. But you are on the side of the earthly mother."

BOTH ARE NEEDED FOR LIFE.

Hekate changed again, becoming the crone. Her hair hung limp. Lines creased her face, but she was still beautiful.

YOU HAVE TWO MISSIONS. THE FIRST IS TO DESTROY A HARMLESS CREATURE. AN EMANATION OF THE BONES OF THE EARTH, YES, BUT HUNDREDS OF GENERATIONS AWAY. A DUMB, HARMLESS BEAST.

"It has eaten children."

DO NOT BELIEVE EVERYTHING THE SKY-WORSHIPPERS TELL YOU. ON THIS MISSION, YOU WILL SEE AN OPENING. A CLUE TO THE DIRECTION OF DEEPER TRUTH.

"What does that mean?"

IT MEANS YOU MUST BE AWAKE AND AWARE OF EVERY DETAIL.

"You said two missions. As far as I know, I only have one: to destroy the beast that plagues Antioch."

YOU KNOW YOU WILL RECEIVE MORE INSTRUCTION FROM THE PRIEST OF THE CITY. THAT MISSION IS ONLY SPITEFUL. TO THE BALANCE, IT WILL MEAN NOTHING. TO HUMANITY, IT COULD BRING GREAT HARM.

She changed again, features flowing, hair becoming wavy. The lines on her face faded. Her back straightened, and Hekate was the maiden again.

The dog raised its head and howled. The light grew stronger as Hekate and her hound faded.

"Wait!" Javor stepped forward to keep the vision real, and collided with a bearded man pushing a cart across the intersection.

"Watch where you are going, you twit," the man snarled, bending to pick up vegetables that Javor had knocked from the cart.

The mist was gone, the sun high and bright in the blue sky. No dog, no maiden, no beauty, no crone. Ahead, a bridge over the Orontes River leading to a gate in a high, thick stone wall. Javor joined the crowd of people, horses and carts shuffling across.

His first stop was at an inn near the gate, where he paid too much for a jug of ale and a loaf of tasteless, dry bread. *I need to clear my head after a vision of a goddess,* he told himself.

# The Patriarch's mission

Getting around in Antioch was not easy. An important city in the Empire and one of the main centres of Christianity, it compressed a large population into a small area within high, strong walls.

As a result, the narrow streets were crowded with people and animals literally rubbing shoulders as they edged past one another.

The Patriarch's cathedral was in the centre of the city, next to the small and also crowded Forum, where vendors haggled loudly with customers, chickens squawked before their decapitation, donkeys brayed and children shrieked.

The Cathedral of Saint John Cassianus was nothing like the grand churches of Constantinople or cities in Anatolia. It was built of dark brick, darkened further by centuries of soot and city grime. And it was small, no bigger than a poor local chapel would be in a Constantinopolitan suburb. The insides were cramped and dark, smelling of candle wax and sweaty people.

The Bishop met him in his residence behind the cathedral. He was just as unimpressive: a short, fat man with an untidy beard that hung to the top of his bulging belly. As the Bishop, he wore a simple black robe that reached his ankles, and a smooth, round black cap. Three chains hung around his neck, each weighted with a big golden symbol: a cross in the middle, and two round amulets, each decorated with an icon, one of Christ, the other of the Virgin Mary.

Javor gave him the letter from Gracian. "Yes, Javor Sklavenius, of the Order of St. Mary of Chalkoprateia in the Copper Market in Constantinople," he said, not raising his eyes from the page. "I expected you some days ago."

"The weather was against me."

The priest nodded, still not looking at Javor. "We heard of the windstorm near the coast. Very well, young man." He opened a drawer in a small, ornate table and drew out another piece of paper, folded and sealed with wax. Javor recognized the seal that Gracian liked to use: a cross within the curve of a large Roman letter C.

"I understand you have been sent to rid us of a beast that has been plaguing the city."

"Speaking of plagues, was there a plague here recently? About two years ago?"

The Bishop's eyes narrowed. "No. We have been free of pestilences here since I became Bishop, ten years ago. Why do you ask?"

"Umm...I just want to verify the risk to myself before I go into the countryside."

The Bishop scoffed. "You need not worry, my boy. I will give you a blessing before you leave.

*I do not think that will make a difference.*

*But if there was no pestilence here, what killed Miriam's mother and father? Did she kill them both and convince her brother it was plague?*

He dismissed the thought. It would not change anything. He lifted the sealed letter. "This second mission —"

The Bishop raised his hand. "We will not discuss it here. Know that it was I who requested aid from the Patriarch of Constantinople, and devised both missions — the destruction of this demon from Hell, and ... the second. Patriarch Thomas was most gracious in accommodating me."

"I was given this mission by Mal — I mean, Father Gracian of the Order of St. Mary of Chalkoprateia."

The Bishop nodded. "Ah, yes. I know him. A most capable man. I am glad to hear that he has obtained the trust of the Patriarch."

Javor hesitated before breaking the seal and reading the instruction. *I wish I did not know this, now.* "Are there a lot of Jews in Antioch?" he asked.

"Unfortunately, yes. There is a large and active community. They are great debaters on matters of theology and doctrine. Together with the Monophysites, they lead many souls down wrong paths to damnation."

*He said he requested both missions. And now I see why he does not wish to discuss them.*

The next day, he followed a black-robed monk up the steep slopes above the city. After scrabbling over a ridge and then a scree of loose gravel, they arrived at a pasture, a field of grass between two ridges like rocky arms of the mountain above Antioch. Flowers competed for space with grass and crudely hacked stumps of trees.

Bleating goats pranced up. Javor bent to pat one, and it bit off a piece of his sleeve.

Javor cursed and wrenched his arm free. The monk laughed. Javor took a good look at him. He was a head shorter than Javor, like most men in Antioch, and his belly pushed out the front of his habit. His tonsured head shone with sweat in the summer sunlight.

"Is this the place?" Javor asked.

"This is the pasture where the devil last took livestock, yes."

The goat came closer, looking for another bite of sleeve. Javor pushed it away as gently as he could with his boot. "I guess it took a goat?"

"Yes. And last week, it took two sheep from another pasture."

"I heard it ate children."

The monk squinted. "Children? No, never a child. There was a farmer a month ago who claimed it came down to his farm and stole a piglet, but I think his neighbour stole it."

"No children, though?"

"None that I ever heard of."

"Does this ... theft always happen up here? On the mountain?"

"Ever since last summer, yes."

"This started last year?"

"Yes. There were old stories about people who saw a demon before, but it never harmed anyone. Not physically. Although there has always been much to tempt sinners in Antioch!"

Javor sighed. "Why did it start stealing livestock from here just last summer?"

The monk shrugged. "Well, there was no pasture here before that. The people of the town only cleared it the previous spring."

Javor sighed again. *They invade a predator's territory, and then wonder why it's eating their animals.*

The monk pointed. "That is the goat herder's hut."

Javor saw a low lean-to made of sticks. "Good. I want to talk to him."

"Well, he will not be in the hut."

"I used to tend flocks, too. I know he will be at a good vantage point to watch over his father's goats."

The monk led Javor across the meadow, to where cliffs climbed again. "Ho, lad!" he called.

From a ledge over Javor's head, a boy of about 12 years climbed down. He was thin, with dark hair and sun-browned skin. His big brown eyes were fixed on Javor and his weapons. "This is Sir Javor, and I am Brother Niceus from the Cathedral. Tell Sir Javor about the devil that is stealing the goats."

The boy continued to stare at Javor until the monk prodded him again. Then he said, in a small, timid voice, "It was a woman with eight legs."

"A woman?" Javor asked.

"Are you certain, boy?" the monk demanded.

The young goat herder recoiled from the monk. After a moment, he nodded. "Yes. I saw it. A woman, with dark brown skin and eight legs like snakes. She—it—moved very fast."

Javor crouched so that he was eye level with the boy. "What did it do?"

"It came down the mountain," the boy pointed up a slope that led to thick, short trees. "And it seized a nanny." The boy's eyes brimmed with tears, but he held them back. "She was my favourite," he whispered.

Javor straightened and looked up the slope the boy had pointed out. The trees were close together, but stunted at this elevation. Above them, the mountain rose to bare, grey rock. Plenty of places for a hunter to hide. "When did this happen?"

"Eight days ago," said the boy. "Just as the sun was setting. I was late to bring the goats down from the pasture. The sun had gone behind the hill," he pointed to a rocky outcropping to the west. "And the shadows were long. I was afraid that my papa would beat me. Then the monster came. It grabbed the goat and ran back up the mountain."

"Ran? I thought it had legs like snakes."

"Do not lie to us, boy," the monk snarled.

"I am not lying," the goat herder insisted. "It moved with its legs like...like...I do not know. Not like snakes, but...I do not know."

"How did it grab the goat?"

The boy took a deep breath. "With one of its legs. It curled around Lady. She bleated as it took her up the mountain." He looked down at the ground.

Javor nodded. "What is your name?"

"Simon," the boy murmured.

"Well, Simon, we will take care of this eight-legged beast for you.

The boy nodded.

Javor turned to the monk. "You can go back now."

"The Bishop said I should accompany you as a witness to the destruction of the devil," the monk protested.

"No. It is too dangerous."

"I am not afraid. The power of Christ will protect—"

"The last time men protected by Christ came with me, they died. Eight out of nine of them," Javor barked. "And each of them was armed." He pointed down the slope with his left hand, his right going to the hilt of his sword at his hip.

The monk swallowed. He opened his mouth as if to protest, but then caught Javor's eye. He turned to clamber back down the slope.

Javor strode up the meadow, leaving the boy to herd his goats. For a moment, he thought of his second mission, the one he was to complete when this one was done.

*Concentrate. One thing at a time.*

He found several openings in the line of trees and chose the one that looked most likely to be a trail large enough for a human-size creature to use. He paused, wondering, when a screech broke the peace. A golden eagle swept over his head, and settled at the base of a tree twenty paces away. It fixed an eye on him and screeched again.

Beside the eagle, a wide gap yawned between stunted trees. The ground beneath was worn, dead leaves flattened and shredded over packed mud, or lying lonely on bare rock.

Javor approached the bird. It screeched once more and flew off, disappearing from sight. So Javor stepped onto the path the eagle had shown him.

As soon as he went under the cover of the branches, he felt a chill on his face and hands. He backed out again from under the shadows, into the warmth of the mid-morning sun. Hanging his pack on a branch, he strapped on his breastplate and adjusted his sword-belt. Putting on his helmet, he stepped back into the cool under the trees, adjusting the chin-strap as he went on.

Not only was the path that much cooler than the open meadow, it was darker than Javor expected. He saw nothing except low bushes and gloom.

He followed the path as it wandered and twisted uphill, always going up. Soon, he came to a small clearing. On the other side were two paths. He picked the wider one, which curved downhill, but as soon as he set foot on it, he heard another screech. He looked up to see the golden eagle again, spiraling down on motionless wings.

He took the smaller path that led uphill. The bird stayed quiet.

The path got narrower and steeper. The boy said it was a woman with eight legs, so it must be at least the size of an adult woman. If I can get up this path, I think the creature could, too.

Like any game trail, it twisted and wandered, but mostly went uphill. Where it branched or crossed other paths, he chose the path that led more uphill. Occasionally he could see the sky above, and every time he looked, he saw the eagle overhead.

His amulet did not tremble or vibrate. The mountainside was quiet. Not even the buzz of insects, the trill of a bird nor wind in the branches broke the silence.

Gradually, the forest thinned out. The trees became shorter and thinner and more widely spaced, until they gave way to low bushes and coarse, brown grass clinging to the surface of unforgiving rock.

The eagle lit on a rock ahead of him, off the path, holding him in its gaze. Preyatel trembled. Just once, just slightly, but Javor knew its signals well. He scanned the slope, right hand on the handle of his great-grandfather's dagger. To his left, he could see the summit of the mountain. To his right, the thicker forest.

And ahead, a boulder taller than him leaned over the path. And something crouched in the shadow. Something grey and naked.

Javor stepped closer. Slowly, cautiously. He could feel his heart pounding, but his amulet was quiet. Cool.

Hand on the hilt of his dagger, he approached the boulder and bent to see the thing hiding under it.

The eagle screeched at the same moment that Preyatel trembled. Javor looked up to see the bird had not taken its eyes from him.

He crouched. The thing under the boulder was unlike anything he had ever seen before. Smaller than a woman, the size maybe of a child of eight or nine years. Or maybe that's because it's crouched down.

It was covered in smooth, grey skin, almost the same colour as the boulder it sheltered under. A cylindrical body, pressed against the rock, rose above a tangle of snake-like tentacles almost like an octopus' at the fish market, but larger and without the suckers.

At the top, the body bulged slightly to a head without a neck. And in the front, a beak under two of the largest, bluest and most expressive eyes that Javor had ever seen.

*Beautiful.*

Then he could see that the creature was trembling. Part of the body bulged and contracted as if it were panting.

He stepped back. The creature's eyes held his for a beat, then another. Then it moved, just a little to the side.

The eagle screeched and flapped its wings, but Javor ignored it. He watched the creature edge away from the boulder, up the slope to a dark spot.

The eagle flapped and flew the short distance to land a step from Javor's feet. It screeched again.

"What do you want?" he demanded. The eagle only screeched again.

"Are you the same bird I saw on the Danuvius? Why are you following me?" He stepped closer and it flew up to the top of the boulder. At the same moment, Preyatel trembled.

Javor walked around the boulder, going a step up the hill. There, the eagle on the boulder was eye level with him. "What is it you want? You led me to that poor ... thing, whatever it is. Is that what has been eating sheep and goats? You bring me all the way from Constantinople, away from my wife and family, to kill some weird ... land octopus?"

*That is the demon the people of Antioch have asked me to kill,* he thought.

*No. That was not a thought. That was a message.*

"What are you? An aeon?" he asked aloud.

*I am an archon. I have been sent to guide you on your missions.*

"Missions? So it was you on the Danuvius. And in Sklavenia."

*The creature you pursue is an emissary of the underworld.*

"You mean, it is chthonic. Whereas you are celestial." He watched the creature move across the rocky summit, fascinated by the motion of its tentacles.

Preyatel twitched once more. The eagle flapped once to glide in front of him.

*Your mission was to kill the echidna.*

"No. I will not do it. It is not anything supernatural, it's just a strange creature. Probably the last of its kind. I do not believe you anymore. You are not an eagle. You are just—"

As Hekate had, the eagle changed. Smoothly, instantly, it became a man with long grey hair and beard, and intense eyes. He wore a long, black robe trimmed with silver, a large ornate chain around his neck and jeweled rings on his fingers.

*Austinus.*

*You perceive me in a form that your mind can comprehend. Do you find me more credible now?*

"No. Now you mock a man I loved. The wisest man I ever knew." Javor stepped around the apparition and strode toward the creature. It paused and twisted to focus its eyes on him. Javor held his hands away from his body, palms toward the creature. "Go. Be free. But for your own good, best stay away from this pasture, right?"

The creature blinked, as if in acknowledgement, then turned and slithered off, disappearing into a crack or crevice that Javor could not see.

A hand fell on his shoulder. "Why did you do that?" a familiar voice demanded.

He turned. "You have taken the form of Gracian now? Do you think I will believe you in this form?" He went down the mountain. "Go to hell. Or wherever you came from."

He found the path he had taken to the summit, and when he glanced back, Gracian, pseudo-Austinus and the eagle had all vanished.

*To hell with the second mission, too. I am not a murderer.*

# Death of a Patriarch

The sun was at noon when Javor emerged from the cover of trees and back into the meadow. The first thing he noticed, though, was the black cloud rising over Antioch, below him.

He rushed down the hill to find the city gate closed and locked. No one responded when he shouted and banged on the heavy wooden gate.

Javor looked around, his eyes stopping on the guard tower and its door with black iron hinges.

He drew his great-grandfather's dagger, placed the blade at the top edge of the upper hinge and began drawing down. It was not easy—iron is a tough metal. But the blade made from the bones of dragons cleaved through.

Preyatel began to tremble as the iron hinge groaned in protest. The hinge snapped apart and the blade sprang free. Javor repeated the motion on the lower hinge, then swung the door open on the crude wooden latch. Ducking under the wooden bar across the doorway, he entered a deserted room with hooks along the walls.

He smelled smoke. Near the gates, the streets were deserted save for two guards, who were focused on action down the street and did not seem to notice Javor emerging from their guardhouse.

"What is wrong? Is there a fire in the city?" he asked the closer guard.

Both guards jumped back. They swung their spears toward him and adopted a fighting stance. "Who are you?" the older one demanded.

"I am Javor Sklavenius, here on a mission from the emperor," he answered. He tried to adopt a non-threatening posture, but was not sure it worked. "Is there a fire?" he repeated, and felt stupid. *Of course there is a fire. That is why there is smoke.*

"There is a riot," said the older guard. "The Jews have risen against the emperor." He spat on the ground. "They're killing Christians. The Bishop has barricaded his house."

"Why?"

The guard spat on the ground again. "Who the hell knows with Jews?"

"It's because the emperor demanded that all the Jews accept Jesus Christ as their Lord and Saviour," the other guard said. He looked young.

Javor sprang into a run toward the sound of tumult and the smell of smoke. He found a crowd of men in a square, all shouting and waving raised fists and torches. He recognized Jewish dress and headgear.

He touched the shoulder of an older man who seemed calmer than most. "Who is the leader?"

Preyatel shook, but it was too late.

The man gaped at him, eyes scanning up and down, taking in Javor's height, his long blond hair and the weapons hanging from his belt.

"Do not worry. I mean him no harm," Javor said as calmly as he could, although he had to shout over the tumult around them. "In fact, I am here to warn him."

The man said something Javor did not understand. In an instant, three young men seized his arms. When one tried to grasp the hilt of his sword, Javor shook free.

He resisted the urge to draw a weapon. "I mean no one here any harm." It was hard to concentrate as his amulet vibrated so hard, it grew warm. "I have an urgent message for..." He hesitated to reveal too much, but Preyatel buzzed loud enough for others to hear as one of the younger men moved behind him. "...for Benjamin of Tiberias."

Two young men grabbed his arms again. Javor felt something sharp pressing into his back. He decided not to resist. "Take me to him."

The older man still gaped at him. After a pause while Javor felt his heart beat in his throat, the man nodded, turned and began picking a path through the jumping, yelling crowd.

Javor felt the knife at his back press a little harder and wished he had been able to don a back plate. It will not be easy for him to press that knife through the leather, at least. The young men at his arms pulled him after the older man.

After several minutes of squeezing between shoulders, the little group arrived at the centre of the square. A man stood on the edge of the fountain, so that he was elevated a little over the rest. For Javor, this put his mouth at eye level.

The old man called up at the leader in a language that Javor did not understand. The leader glared down at them. "Well? What do you want?" He spoke Greek with a strong accent.

Javor wrenched his arms from the young men's grasp. One fell to the ground, and the other stepped away, alarm on his face.

Javor held his hands up, palms out. "I have a message to show you."

He reached into the small satchel that hung at his hip. The knife at his back pressed harder, so Javor took a small step away and turned. "There is no need for that. If I wanted to harm you, I would have done so by now. And you should know that you cannot harm me."

The young man with the knife gaped. He lowered the knife for a moment, then raised it quickly to Javor's chest, saying something in his own language.

"As you can see, I am wearing a breastplate," Javor explained, keeping his voice as calm as possible in the tumult.

The young man scowled.

Javor felt a hand on his shoulder and turned to see the leader using him to help step down from the fountain.

"Are you Benjamin of Tiberias?"

"What do you want, barbarian?" the man demanded, his voice hoarse.

Javor unfolded the paper from his satchel and handed it over, taking the opportunity to get a look at his quarry. Like most of the men of Antioch, he was more than a head shorter than Javor. A thick black beard circled his chin, thin moustaches drooping from his lip. He wore the same round hat as the other Jewish men in the square, and a long, multi-coloured, loose robe.

He only needed a few seconds to read the message. "Where did you get this?"

"It came from Constantinople, from someone close to the emperor, through the Bishop Anastasius."

"Anastasius is dead," Benjamin growled, crumpling the paper. "We killed him."

"We tied the bastard to a horse and dragged him through the streets," said the man with the knife.

Javor felt something inside him sink. "Why?"

"Centuries of offences, barbarian. But the final straw was the edict that we must all convert to Christianity."

"You must realize that the emperor will punish you for this," Javor said. "Especially one like Phocas."

Benjamin spat on the ground, and the other men around him copied the action. "Phocas be damned. The Sassanians are ready to finish Rome, once and for all.

"But tell me, barbarian," Benjamin continued. "Why did you show me this?"

"I am not a murderer," Javor said. "I have killed men, but only in self defence."

"Good for you. The execution of Anastasius was also in self defence of our people and our faith. But again, barbarian, why tell me this? If you did not wish to kill me, why not just tear up the paper and leave?"

"My name is Javor, and I am not a barbarian. I am a citizen of Rome. I wanted to warn you," Javor said. "If I just leave, the emperor will send someone else."

"I expect he will. But thank you, Sir Javor, for your warning. I suppose you expect some reward?"

"No. All I need are that paper back, and safe passage from the city. I will return to Constantinople now."

"I take it that you will return to the coast to take a ship?"

Javor hesitated before revealing more details about where he was going. "Yes," he said eventually.

Benjamin nodded at the old man who had conducted Javor to the fountain. "Lev, see to it that he finds a boat to take him down the river."

Lev scowled, then nodded. He led Javor to a gate, where young men in Jewish dress stood guard, their swords ready. At a word from Lev, they opened the smaller gate that led to the port on the river.

Javor found himself back at the seaport of Saint Simeon before the sunset, the favour of a strong current and a favourable wind.

# Unmasked

By the end of the first day's sailing back to Constantinople, Javor had his speech to Malleus and Gracian fully prepared. He spent most of the rest of the long journey back to Constantinople rehearsing it, pacing on the deck near the bow of the ship. After a few days, though, he noticed the looks he was getting from the crew when he exclaimed under his breath.

He resorted to rehearsing only in his mind, although that did not stop him from pacing the deck during the days. Nor did the strange looks from the crew end, nor their jokes behind his back.

After the first week, he stopped rehearsing and spent his time nursing his anger. He spoke to no one but his amulet, which hung quiet from his neck.

The ship pulled into the merchant's harbour in Constantinople as low, dark clouds shrouded the rising sun. A dull drizzle did nothing to dampen Javor's anger.

He rehearsed his speech again, but he would not go to Chalkoprateia first. His first stop was to his home. Adam raced to the front of the house when he heard his father's voice, and Javor gathered the six-year-old into his arms.

Andrina was right behind her brother, so Javor bent and strained to pick her up, as well. Both children were tall for their ages, with long legs and arms. Adam's hair was noticeably fairer than before Javor had left, only a month earlier. Javor also noticed that Andrina's black hair was much shorter than when he had left.

He kissed both children and set them down on the floor, stepping back to get a better look at them. "I swear, you both have grown since I left. Andrina, did you cut your hair yourself?"

"Yes, Papa," she nodded.

"Your mother could not have been happy about that."

"She was so cross!" Adam exclaimed.

"It was in the way when it was long," Andrina said. "I asked Mama to let Kyriake cut it, and she said 'no.' So I cut it myself."

"Where is your Mama?" Javor asked.

"Right here, husband," said a voice. Calanthe stood at the entrance to the central hall. Beside her, Aunt Tiana leaned on her cane.

If the children all looked taller and stronger than before, Calanthe looked even fatter. Her thick black hair was piled in an elaborate pattern on top of her head, held in place with sparkling combs and clips.

Aunt Tiana looked tired, with the lines on her face even more prominent than Javor remembered. She smiled weakly and Javor kissed her cheeks before throwing his arms around his wife.

"Not so tight, Javor," she protested. "And do not ruin my hair. I spent an hour on it." She pulled away from him to ask, "Why were you so long?"

"Contrary winds," Javor answered as he took his wife's hand and pulled her toward the bedchambers.

"Javor, stop," she protested.

Javor said nothing, but pushed her into her bedroom and closed the door. He ignored her protests and pushed her onto the bed with one hand, pulling off his tunic with the other.

"Javor, what has come over you? It is still morning, for heaven's sake."

By the time she had said that, Javor had kicked off his boots and dropped his trousers. Calanthe squealed, but not too loudly, as he pulled her gown off her shoulders and kissed her neck. Her breasts, heavy now after nursing children, filled his palms. She sighed and arched her back as he caressed her and kissed her nipples.

Her skin was just as soft as he remembered as her thighs rose around his. He looked down, marveling as he did every time at how much darker her skin was than his, even after he had spent a month on board a ship.

And then he did not think. He only felt.

Two hours later, after making love to his wife for a second time and a bath, he had Honorius drive him and Aunt Tiana to the Abbey of St. Mary of Chalkoprateia.

"The creature you encountered in Syria was an echidna, from your description," she said in her slow diction, recalling what Javor had told her when asking her to come to the Order with him. "Herodotus describes it as the offspring of Typhon, the great serpent defeated by Zeus, the god of the sky. In other words, the echidna was, to the ancients, a chthonic power, defeated by a celestial one.

"But I do not think the creature you encountered was supernatural, Javor." She patted his knee. "It was only an animal. A very rare, special creature, one I have not heard of in the world before. Perhaps a terrestrial relative of the octopus. Aristotle classified animals by their body shape, so perhaps we can classify this creature in that way.

"As for the eagle that confronted you. That was definitely an archon. The embodiment of a celestial emanation of the Demiurge."

"Why did it come to me?" Javor asked. "What does this mean?"

Tiana did not answer, instead looking down the straight road toward the harbour. Finally, she said, "I do not wish to pronounce any decisions yet, my boy. I must consult some writings in the Order's library, first.

"But I am also concerned about the mission you were assigned, Javor," she continued. "I have known Malleus a long time. I know that he can be violent. He is a skilled warrior. You know that. I saw your first encounter, where the two of you fought each other to a standstill. Neither outdoing the other."

Javor felt another shock. Fourteen years earlier, when Javor had first come to the capital and found the Order, Malleus had challenged him to a duel with swords, to defend the Order's secrecy. It was the closest fight that Javor had ever had. "You saw that?"

"Of course I did, Javor. At the time, I was a senior member of the inner Council of the Order. I was also Austinus' wife. There was nothing of import that I did not see."

"I...did not know you were there."

"As I recall, that was one day I dressed as a man. It made some things easier. But, to return to the matter of Malleus: I worry about him, Javor. He has changed, and not just because he bears great responsibility as the head of the Order. I think that he has been greatly troubled since Gracian became his second-in-command. He was forced upon the Order, you know, by the Church. That increased Malleus' burden, to keep the Gnostic nature of the Order secret, yet continuing our essential work."

"I have planned some choice words for him."

"Be careful, Javor. Malleus is your ally, even today."

When they arrived at the Abbey of St. Mary of Chalkoprateia, Javor helped Tiana to the Order's secret library and ordered the Gnostic monk in charge to bring her wine and make sure her every request was met.

Then he strode to the Order's main council room, his speech ready to spring from his lips. But the only man he recognized there was Gracian, sitting on Malleus' chair, reading a codex.

Preyatel trembled. *Why? What is the danger?*

*Gracian.*

*Do not be ridiculous. He is no threat. And he owes me his life.*

There were three other men, dressed as monks or priests, but none of the Gnostics that Javor knew. They all gaped at him as he threw a tattered, crumpled piece of paper at Gracian's feet.

"How dare you? How could you even try to order me to commit murder in the name of the Church?" Behind him, one of the priests gasped.

He hesitated. He had prepared his speech to deliver it to both Malleus and Gracian, together. "Where is Malleus? I demand to speak with him!"

Gracian closed the book and picked up the paper Javor had thrown. "Welcome home, Javor. It is gratifying to see you well after another dangerous mission. But I take it you were not successful in carrying it out?"

"You should have known I would not carry that out, Gracian. I am not a murderer."

"Murder was not the mission, Javor. You were to eliminate a demon that was afflicting the Christians of Antioch."

Javor leaned over Gracian and stabbed the paper in Gracian's hand with his finger. "I am talking about the mission you sent ahead of me, to the Patriarch. You asked me to kill the head of the Jews in Antioch."

"An enemy of all Christianity. An enemy of Christ. Did you forget that I anointed you as the Celestial Warrior? And that it is your God-given duty to defend—"

"To hell with your Celestial Warrior!" More gasps from behind him. Javor turned to see the three priests huddled together, staring at him with wide eyes and open mouths. "Who are these fools? Where are Zeno and Cometus? And where in hell is Malleus?"

He felt lost. This was not going anything like the way he had imagined over the weeks on the ship. There was no pleading from Gracian. Malleus was not stumbling over his defiance to Javor's righteous anger, then admitting his error. Instead, Gracian sat, comfortable and calm, and Malleus was absent. And then there was the audience of strangers behind him. "Where is the Order's senior council? What is going on here?"

"There is no need to shout, Javor," Gracian said, calm as ever. "Malleus is no longer head of the Order. He has become a threat to the sanctity of the church, the safety of God's people, and the rule of his appointed emperor."

"The emperor? Phocas, the usurper? We serve Phocas now? Where *is* Malleus?"

"He has been arrested and is being held in the Great Palace."

Javor felt as if the floor was slipping beneath his feet. "Arrested? For what reason?"

"Heresy and blasphemy."

It was as if the world faded. All Javor could see was Gracian's face. "I...I..." was all he could choke out.

"He was harbouring forbidden, Gnostic ideas, and worse, spreading them through the Abbey. When I learned of this, I had no choice but to report to the Patriarch and the emperor, and to order his arrest. I am sorry, Javor. I know you love him, but he is a threat to our immortal souls."

Javor had to step back. "A threat...no, no, Malleus is my oldest friend in Constantinople."

Gracian rose, at last, and put a hand on Javor's shoulder. "I am sorry, but it is for the best. We cannot let this corruption spread. Perhaps, with prayer, Malleus can be rehabilitated one day. He has done much good for the Church, after all."

Javor shrugged Gracian's hand off. "*You* arrested him. This was your plan all along." When he said it, he felt its truth. He felt more certain of it with every word that poured from his mouth. "You wormed your way into this Order. You made yourself second-in-command. I knew Malleus did not like it. I could tell something was wrong, every time you two were together. You planned this. You waited until you could send me away so that Malleus was undefended. And now you have imprisoned him!"

Preyatel trembled again. Javor turned to see the three priests coming closer. From the high main doors of the council room, two spear-carrying guards came closer. "Do not even think about it. Do you think you fools would have a chance to stop me?"

He turned back to Gracian. "I will not let you get away with this, Gracian. I will, somehow, release Malleus. And I will never carry out another mission for the Order, so long as you are in charge."

He turned and strode to the doors. The guards stepped back, holding their spears across their chest in a defensive posture. Javor ignored them and walked quickly to the secret library, where he was surprised to find Aunt Tiana sitting at a table, surrounded by codexes and scrolls. "Javor? Are you finished so soon?"

The librarian, a small, thin old monk with no hair on his wrinkled head, shuffled closer. "You seem troubled, young Javor."

"You had better get out of here, Arethas," Javor answered. "And take as many books as you can. Gracian has imprisoned Malleus."

Arethas nodded. "Yes. It is a purge. The emperor, being a usurper, must eliminate all traces of the old regime and replace them with his own supporters in every institution."

Javor felt his frustration rise. "I do not think you understand, Arethas. Gracian is not a Gnostic. He thinks Gnosticism is heresy and blasphemy. I think he has had Zeno and Cometus killed."

Arethas nodded again.

"Well, what are you waiting for? Do you want to join them?"

Arethas nodded. "Where would I go, young man? I am old. I have lived my life. My place is here, to defend and protect the wisdom of the ages."

"How are you going to defend anything against the armed guards? Gracian has soldiers with him, and they are no one I recognize. He has taken over, and he means to eliminate the Gnostics and anyone else he sees as a threat to Christianity or himself."

"You go, Javor. This Abbey has been my only home for more than six decades. I have nowhere else to go. No family. When I die, which surely will not be long now, one way or another, no one will miss me." He gathered scrolls and put them into a leather satchel. "But you are right about protecting the ancient writings. Take as many of these as you can."

Tiana shuffled over, her arms filled with books. "And these."

Arethas fetched two more satchels. Tiana and Javor joined him in filling them as quickly as they could, and then Javor and Tiana left. With three heavy bags hanging from his shoulders, Tiana leaning on his arm, Javor felt increasingly anxious as they walked to the entrance.

He scanned every branching corridor, inspected every monk they passed for weapons. But strangely, no one tried to stop them.

He breathed out in relief when he saw Honorius sitting on the buggy as they emerged from the Abbey. He threw the satchels of books into the back and lifted Tiana onto the bench. "Go home, as quickly as you can," he told Honorius. "Lock the gate and all the doors, and let no one out."

"Are you not coming, sir?" Honorius asked. He looked terrified.

"I will catch up to you, but there is something I have to do, first." He watched Honorius slap the reins and the carriage start to roll away from the Abbey. Then he turned and hurried across the square to the Convent of St. Mary in the Copper Market.

He paced in the little anteroom until the Abbess appeared. He sighed again in relief when he recognized Mother Helena. *Gracian has not pushed her out yet,* he thought. "Mother Helena, I know you want advance notice, but it is vital that I speak to Danisa, immediately."

Mother Helena had a kind face with large brown eyes, framed with little lines. "I am sorry, Javor, but I cannot bring her to you."

"Please, Mother. It is very important. Did you hear about Malleus?"

"Yes, of course, I know about Malleus' arrest. It was a shock. We have been praying for him daily. But your request is moot. Danisa is no longer here at the Convent."

"What? I thought the vows were for life."

Helena shook her head. "Danisa never took vows. She never accepted Jesus Christ. She has remained a pagan since you brought her to us. We only held her at *your* request. Did you know that she tried to escape three times in the first year, alone? Did you know she has repeatedly attempted to seduce young initiates into perversions of fleshly pleasures? Did you know she has sometimes succeeded?"

Javor had to sit down on a hard bench. "No...no, I did not know any of that. When...when did she leave? Why? How? Did she escape?"

Mother Helena put her hand on Javor's shoulder. This time, he did not shrink away. "Not at all. She was released on order of the Abbot."

Javor looked up at her. "Malleus or Gracian?"

Mother Helena closed her eyes and sighed. "It was Gracian. The same day that he arrested Malleus and took over the Order."

Javor thanked her and ran across the square. There was one more place he had to stop before he could return home. He prayed he would get there before Gracian's agents—or Phocas'.

One name repeated in his mind. *Darko.*

*Darko.*

*Darko.*

In the Abbey proper, the complex where monks lived, ate, prayed and mostly worked at drudgery, he found Brother Bartholomew, the senior monk in charge of the novices. He stood outside the chapel, watching the newest tonsured recruits file in for prayers.

"I have to speak to Darko," he panted.

"Calm, Brother Javor." Brother Bartholomew had always considered himself the most important in the Abbey after Malleus and Gracian. Now he must be number two. "The brothers are at sext."

"This is a matter of life and death. I need to speak to Darko *now.*"

Bartholomew fixed Javor with a stare he assumed was meant to intimidate him. "We never interrupt prayers, no matter what the situation. The Lord God will decide matters of life and death."

Javor took a deep breath to avoid punching Bartholomew in the face.

"But anyway, Sir Javor—"

"I am not 'sir,'" Javor muttered around a clenched jaw.

"—Darko is not here."

Javor blinked. "What? Where is he, then?"

"He left the Abbey."

"Him too? I thought vows were for life," he found himself saying for the second time in a few minutes.

Bartholomew's lips thinned. "They are. But Darko simply walked out the front gate one day and never returned. My belief, from speaking with some of his friends, is that he has joined the Legion."

*Darko a soldier? In the Legion? When the city is on the brink of another civil war?* "Please, Brother Bartholomew. Help me. Do you have any idea where he might be, now?"

Bartholomew glared. Even Javor could feel the hostility. Preyatel trembled once. "He has gone. He has betrayed his vows to the Church. I have not a care for a traitor."

"Please. He is in danger. He is not a fighter, and the city is on the brink of civil war. We could have legionnaires fighting against each other."

"Emperor Phocas is taking the long-awaited measures to cleanse Rome of centuries of corruption and the lingering stains of paganism," the monk stated.

*It is useless,* Javor realized. Without another word, he turned and ran out of the Abbey.

Dodging people, horses, oxen and carriages, he ran as hard as he could the mile-and-a-half from the Abbey to his home in the Vlanga district.

Gaetan and Honorius stood inside the half-open gate, slamming it shut as soon as Javor was inside. Javor knelt by the impluvium and splashed captured rainwater over his face, letting it trickle under his tunic to cool his skin. He was almost tempted to drink from it, until Gaetan shoved a cup of wine under his chin. "Thank you," he rasped.

"Lady Tiana is waiting for you in the tablinum," Gaetan said.

Javor nodded and rose. He kicked off his boots and dropped his cloak and hat into Gaetan's arms, and, gradually bringing his breathing under control, joined Aunt Tiana.

She sat at his desk, codices and scrolls spread out around her. "Thank the heavens and earth you are well, Javor. I did not know that Malleus had been supplanted, let alone arrested. It is so difficult for me to get out of the house and communicate with colleagues."

Javor slumped onto a couch and gulped more wine. "Did you learn anything?"

"I have not found anything related directly to your experiences in Syria. Or of your vision of the archons over Jerusalem and the far southern city, which I believe is Mecca in Arabia. But I fear it shows a new strategy among the celestial archons, a new belligerence."

"Belligerence?"

Tiana leaned close. "Javor, there has been a struggle between the celestial and chthonic forces in the world for a long time. But since the year without summer—long before you were born, during the reign of Justinian—I see a redoubled effort, greater struggle on both sides."

"What do you mean?"

"I mean, the Earth and the Sky are at war, Javor. And it appears the Sky is becoming more powerful."

# Books

*November 609 Christian Era*

Winter came early that year. Calanthe, swelling bigger in her pregnancy than she ever had before, kept Gaetan and Kyriake busy stoking the braziers and fireplaces until she complained when she felt too hot.

Javor and Tiana spent days and weeks poring over the scrolls and books they had rescued from the Gnostic library. But by the end of the fall, Tiana had exhausted their information.

"There are codices I know of still in the library. There is information in them I need to see."

"If you know what is in them, why do you need them again?"

"Details, Javor," she sighed. "It has been many years since I read those words, and they are in many different, ancient languages. I do not trust my memory to be exact, not since Kriemhild hit my head with a huge gemstone. And in these times, we need exactitude."

"Then we will save those books," Javor said.

After eating a hot meal, Javor and Tiana, heavily bundled, sat behind Honorius as he drove them to the Abbey of St. Mary of Chalkoprateia. Honorius stopped in front of the main dormitory building beside the chapel, and Javor was helping Tiana climb down from the carriage when they heard Gracian's voice boom out: "You are not welcome here."

Javor turned to see Gracian, in a heavy cloak and thick hat, standing at the top of the stairs, in front of the heavy oaken door. A small group of other tonsured monks, tattered robes blowing in the wind, stood behind him.

Fat snowflakes began to fall, sent into whirls by a gust of wind. Javor saw Tiana shiver and wrapped his arm around her shoulders.

"Go, heretics. Pagans." Gracian spat onto the freezing step in front of Javor's feet. "Go, and never come back again."

"What did we do, Gracian?" Javor asked.

"Do not bother, Javor," Tiana said. "There is no point."

"Be grateful that I do not have you arrested and burned as witches," Gracian snarled.

"Come, Javor. I want to return home," Tiana begged.

Javor lifted her into the carriage, climbed in and nodded at Honorius, but the faithful driver already had the carriage moving.

Back at his home, Javor stoked up the braziers. Gaetan rushed in to bring wine and food and extra charcoal.

"Leave us," Javor ordered.

Gaetan looked worried, but disappeared from the room.

"What do we do, now?" Javor asked.

"We must find a way to get those books, Javor. I am trying to recall the details, but there is information in them that we need."

Gaetan reappeared at the door to the tablinum. "What is it?" Javor snarled.

"My apologies, my lord, but there is a monk here to see you."

The monk shivered as Gaetan brought him into the domus. Tiana took a blanket from her shoulders and handed it to him. Gaetan stoked the fire again, then withdrew.

"I am Brother Isaac. You are Javor?" the monk asked around chattering teeth.

"Yes, as my servant said."

The monk looked at Tiana. "And Mother Tiana?"

"I was, once," she replied.

Javor gave the monk a cup of wine. He drank, and his shivering diminished. "Thank you. I came from St. Mary's after I saw Gracian send you away."

"Why?" Javor asked.

"I know who you are, Javor Sklavenius."

"Everyone knows who I am. I lived at the Abbey, years ago. I have come and gone since then, until today."

The monk finished the wine in the cup, then leaned forward. His voice dropped. "I know that you were initiated into the inner mysteries of gnosis," he whispered.

"We do not talk about that," Tiana said.

"I understand. Gracian does not know about us, not yet. But he suspects. He is purging anyone he suspects of gnostic knowledge or belief. Like Malleus."

"How did he supplant Malleus?" Javor asked.

"Gracian was appointed at the insistence of the previous Patriarch, Thomas. The Church insisted on an Orthodox representative. You know, because of the Monophysites."

"Yes," said Tiana. "The friction between the two sects has been increasing."

Javor remained confused.

"Gracian's role was to observe Malleus and report to the Patriarch anything that deviated from Orthodoxy. Especially Gnosticism. It is identified as heresy," Brother Isaac explained.

"We know," Tiana answered.

"It got worse after Thomas died and Phocas appointed Sergius as Patriarch. Gracian began to send written reports to the Patriarch weekly."

"Why?"

"Patriarch Sergius sees Gnostics as a threat to the unity of the Church, worse than the Monophysites. He is a Monophysite, himself—or was. He is looking for a new enemy."

"Why are you telling us this?" Tiana asked.

"Because Arethas, the librarian, is dead." Javor felt a chill down to his toes, despite the heat from the braziers. "You are the only remaining Gnostics who are free. The ancient knowledge must live on."

"Thank you," Javor said. He stood and called Gaetan to bring food.

"I have one more thing to tell you," said Brother Isaac. "Malleus is not in the Grand Palace. He is being held in the dungeon below the Abbey."

"What dungeon?" Javor demanded.

"There are dungeons," Tiana said. "They have not been used in over a century, but there are cells below ground, under the dormitory."

"One day, a group of soldiers arrived at the gate. They outnumbered the Order's guards by many times. With them was the Patriarch himself. They stormed into the Abbey. Gracian guided them to Malleus' study. The Patriarch announced Malleus' arrest. The head of the Order demanded to know what authority he had.

"Then one of the soldiers stepped forward and removed his helmet. And then I recognized him. The emperor. Or rather, the usurper, Phocas. He ordered his men to drag Malleus to his knees. And then—" Brother Isaac broke off.

"What?" Javor demanded.

"Phocas drew a blade and…he blinded Malleus. Right there, on the floor of his own study. Stabbed out both eyes."

They sat in horrified silence until Gaetan appeared with a tray of hot food. The monk grabbed everything he could. Javor watched him wolf it down.

Finally, Isaac stood. "I will meet you at the entrance to the dungeons at midnight and lead you to Malleus' cell," he said.

"I will tell you the way," Tiana said to Javor.

"Dress well," Javor said. "It will snow heavily after midnight."

At an hour before midnight, Javor stood outside the wall of St. Mary's Abbey. He pulled his cloak off, leaving it on the ground beside the wall. It would only get in the way.

A leap and a grab, then a pull brought him to the top of the wall. He dropped to the other side, landing in piled snow that absorbed the sound of his impact. With only the moon for light, he crept across the courtyard.

Unfamiliar shadows loomed from the middle of the space. He came closer.

It was a gibbet, with bodies hanging by their necks.

Gracian has hanged monks? Or was it the Patriarch, or Phocas? Even for Christians, that is extreme. He could not see their faces in the dark, and hurried to the back wall of the wing of the Abbey building that Tiana had described.

There, he found the false chimney where Tiana had said he would find the secret door.

"Secret door?" he had asked Tiana, hours earlier.

"We planned for an eventuality such as this," Tiana said. "Now pay attention, Javor. The door is hidden by physical means, not by any magic or hidden knowledge. It looks like the outside of a chimney. Press the third brick down from the top left corner where it narrows."

Javor shivered as he recalled Tiana's careful instructions. He pressed the brick.

Nothing happened.

He pressed again, harder. Still nothing, so he put both hands on the brick and put his full weight against it. He heard a grinding noise and felt a slight movement. He pressed more, and felt the brick give way, sliding a hands-breadth into the wall.

More scraping noises and the shadow that was all he could see of the outer surface of the chimney became darker. He reached forward to find only empty space where the chimney had been.

He bent as low as he could and stepped into the tunnel that Tiana had described to him. One hand on the wall, the other on the hilt of his dagger and his hair brushing the ceiling, he crept forward. The tunnel smelled of dampness and disuse, of age and threat.

Forty paces in, the tunnel turned to the right, just as Tiana had described. Another ten paces and he could stand up straight.

But he could see nothing. He groped in front of him until he felt a rough brick surface. He traced his fingertips upwards until he felt a long, thin piece of metal. He pulled it until he felt it stop, then wrenched it harder.

A click. He sensed a change in the darkness in front of him, and then felt air on his face. It smelled of burned wax and human sweat and decaying paper. He put his hand out and the surface in front of him gave way.

The dimness of the room in front of him seemed bright after the depth of the secret tunnel. He moved forward to a large, glazed window and looked at the courtyard between the Abbey and the Convent of St. Mary of Chalkoprateia. To the side, a yellow light glowed in a second-storey window.

Javor realized it was the quarters of the head of the Order.

Gracian.

He peered as hard as he could, but could not discern any details beyond the glass. *Strange. Gracian is there, probably afraid of Gnostics, completely unaware of the existence of this room and these books.*

He crept across the spacious room to the wooden cabinet that Tiana had described. He took out the key she had given him and followed her instructions: "Twice completely around to the left, once completely around to the right, then back a half-turn so the key is straight up."

The door popped open with a tiny sound. Javor opened the satchel over his shoulder and started loading codices and scrolls.

"Is that you, Javor?" The unexpected voice made him jump. *Where were you, Preyatel?*

He turned to see a slim shadow near the window. "Arethas?" *Brother Isaac said he was dead.*

"Yes, it is I. I am not dead. Not yet anyway."

"But—"

"I have been hiding this past week in the secret library. Gracian knows nothing about it. Malleus did not trust him from the very beginning."

"I am going to rescue Malleus," Javor said.

The old librarian limped forward and sat on a bench. "I wish you luck, my friend. You will need it." He paused, and Javor could see that the old man was panting.

He continued loading books into his satchel.

Arethas stood and shuffled to another cabinet. He pulled out a thick, heavy-looking codex and handed it to Javor. "This one will be especially valuable in your efforts."

"How do you know what my efforts will be?"

"It is obvious. We must act for the balance."

"Balance between what?"

"Between earth and sky. Dark and light."

"Good and evil?"

Javor heard an exhalation that might have been a laugh. "Those are human concepts, Javor. Have you not learned that, yet?"

Javor put the book into his satchel.

"Would you have any food, Javor? Any wine?"

"Uhh...no, sorry. I do not usually carry them with me. At least, not when I am in the city."

In the dim light, Javor could not be sure whether the old man smiled. "Ah, well. No matter. I am glad that you are taking these texts. To Tiana, I trust. She is best to have them. If Gracian does ever discover this place, at least those texts will be safe from the fanatics."

"Fanatics?"

"The Christians. They are becoming more strident, more insistent on the exclusivity of their interpretation of the universe." He sighed.

Preyatel trembled. Javor jumped at a loud bang from somewhere outside the library. Someone shouted.

"Farewell, young man," Arethas said.

They heard banging on the door to the secret library.

*We have been discovered.* "Come with me," Javor said on an impulse that surprised him.

The old man shook his head. "My work is done, Javor. I have preserved the knowledge handed down by our predecessors, knowledge that predates Rome, Mani, even Zoroaster. In the current circumstances,

I know these texts are in the right hands."

Javor heard a crash and a splintering noise. "They are getting in! Come with me. I know the way out."

The old man shuffled closer. "I would only slow you down, young man. But I can also slow down the soldiers at the door to aid your escape."

"But—"

Arethas rose and moved faster than Javor could believe to intercept two armed men who smashed their way through the door. "Go," he hissed over his shoulder, then said "Hold! What are you doing here?"

Javor dived into the tunnel and ran, one hand on the wall. He heard the unmistakable sound of a body hitting the tile floor. He saw the orange glow of fire over his shoulder.

Then he turned the corner and plunged into the impenetrable darkness of the tunnel he had entered through. The heavy satchel bounced against his side as he ran, crouched to an uncomfortable degree.

As Tiana had described, he turned right at a branch in the tunnel. Six paces in, he paused, feeling ahead with his foot for the stairs Tiana had described.

Soon, he emerged into a dim, damp and cold passage, lit by flickering wall sconces.

The dungeon.

He rushed ahead, listening for any noise, and stopped when he saw legs sticking out around a corner. Preyatel trembled lightly.

Javor crept forward and peeked around the corner. Slumped against the wall, head hanging loosely, was Brother Isaac. Beside him, the door to a cell swung open.

Javor carefully leaned around it. Empty.

He turned and hurried back up the corridor, the stairs and the tunnel. The outer door seemed farther away than it had when he entered, but at last he emerged into the frigid winter night. He found his cloak, threw it over his shoulders and started back to the wall.

Noise behind him. He turned to see monks and novices, some

carrying torches, rushing across the courtyard. One corner of the wing of the Abbey, the one that held the classrooms as well as the secret library, burned. The monks tried to form a fire brigade.

Javor could not resist his curiosity. He crept through the shadows toward the gibbet. What he saw when he got close confirmed in his eyes what he already knew in his heart.

The body hanging at the end of the row of bodies on the gibbet.

*Malleus.*

He turned and ran to the wall, jumping to grab the top and pulling himself over.

I hope these books are worth the lives of three men.

Halfway home, he realized his face was wet.

*Malleus. Dead. How many men have died trying to be my father?*

Part 5

# Giorgia

*Year 610 Christian Era*

# Training day

Andrina's squeal echoed off the walls of the peristyle garden. Javor caught her, bent his knees and flexed to toss her into the air. He caught her again and put her on the ground. He fell to his knees and raised his fists, ready to fight. Now almost ten, Andrina assumed a perfect fighting stance, her left shoulder toward her father, feet planted wide apart, knees flexed, fists in front of her face. She frowned then launched a flurry of punches at her father's face, which he blocked with open palms.

Javor fell back, holding his hands up to protect his face against the torrent of blows his daughter rained on him. Rolling on his back, he could not hold in his laughter anymore as Andrina punched as hard as she could. He rolled forward, grabbed his daughter and threw her in the air again.

"Javor!" Calanthe called from her couch in the garden. "Be careful."

Javor caught his daughter again and rolled over to pin her under him. A punch on the end of his nose shocked him, sending him rearing back. He grabbed her little fist in his hand and looked at her as blood dripped over his lip.

"Javor, look at you," Calanthe said. "Now you are bleeding. I warned you about this."

Javor hugged his daughter close and looked at his wife. Calanthe reclined on a sofa, holding four-month-old Giorgia to her breast. Her twin sister, Charita, slept in a tiny crib at her mother's side.

He remembered a day six months earlier, in the winter. Calanthe, her belly bigger than Javor had seen in three previous pregnancies, had waddled out of her bedchamber, where she had been speaking with a midwife. "She predicts I will have twins," Calanthe announced, beaming.

The midwife had predicted accurately.

Today, however, Calanthe was not beaming. She frowned at her husband as Andrina stood up in a boxing stance again. "Look at her. You should not be teaching our daughter to be so violent. You should be teaching Adam that way."

Javor rose to his feet, dabbing a handkerchief at his bloody nose. He tousled Andrina's dark hair. "Oh, I will, Calanthe."

"Nonetheless, Andrina is a girl. You should not be teaching her how to fight," Calanthe said.

Javor bent to hug Andrina, then came to Calanthe, bending to kiss her. "Get away from me!" she said, turning away. "I don't want to kiss a bloody face."

Javor wiped his face again and looked at the impressive blood stain on his handkerchief. He rubbed baby Giorgia's head, then bent to kiss it. "She doesn't seem to mind."

"Javor! Don't get your blood on the baby!"

Javor knelt in front of Calanthe and drew his daughter into his arms. He squeezed her and kissed her cheeks. She kissed him back.

Adam ran in from the kitchen, chewing on something. "Fight me, Papa!" Javor crouched to box him, then pretended to fall back, sprawling. "You have defeated me!" he cried.

"That is good with Adam, but you are teaching our daughter as if she were a boy," Calanthe complained.

"I am teaching her to defend herself," Javor replied. "The world is a dangerous place. Especially Constantinople."

"Then she needs a husband to protect her."

Javor looked closely at his daughter for the hundredth time. She looked more like her mother than him: dark hair and eyes, the shape of her face and chin, but like him, wide shoulders and long legs. Adam, on the other hand, looked more like him, with fair, light-brown hair and blue eyes.

Javor looked at his wife. Still young, she was now twice the weight and size of their wedding day. Three chins wobbled as she spoke. He looked down, briefly, past his flat belly to his sandaled feet. "I think she is too young to be thinking about a husband," he said.

"You're impossible," Calanthe said, pulling her baby daughter off her breast. The baby began to whine, waving her little hands. "Lydia!" she called. The wet nurse appeared from under the shade of the peristyle roof. "Take her. I am tired."

Lydia gathered the baby into her arms and faded into the shadows of the awning around the peristyle garden.

Calanthe fixed an accusatory gaze on her husband. "You are encouraging our daughter to act like a boy."

"Good," Javor replied. "Boys know how to defend themselves."

"That is not fitting for a girl!" Calanthe exclaimed. She picked up a cup of rose water and sipped delicately.

"When I was a boy, the girls knew how to defend themselves against the boys," he said.

Andrina wrapped her arms around his thighs for a few seconds that warmed Javor's heart. Then she reached for a piece of cake on the platter near Calanthe's elbow. Calanthe swatted her daughter's hand away. "You'll spoil your lunch," she said.

Adam grabbed his older sister, and the two began a mock sparring match, neither actually hitting the other as their parents watched.

Calanthe popped a piece of cake into her mouth and looked up at her husband. "When you were a boy, you lived in a barbarian village. Our daughter is not a barbarian."

"Definitely not," Javor replied, picking Andrina up. "Like her parents, she is a cultured Roman girl ..."

"Good. No more fighting."

"...who knows how to defend herself."

Calanthe's nostrils flared, pressing her lips tightly together. But before she could retort, Gaetan rushed into the garden. "My lord, Lord Mauricius has arrived."

Calanthe's father strode in, followed by her mother and a small crowd of slaves. "Good morning, son and daughter!" came booming out of his mouth. Mauricius took Javor's shoulders in his hands and kissed him on both cheeks. Then he bent to kiss his daughter.

Calanthe's mother followed suit, then picked up Andrina and kissed her. The little girl wrapped her arms around her grandmother's neck.

"What are you doing here?" Javor asked.

"Why, we've come for Saint Anthia's day," Mauricius answered. He bent to kiss Adam's cheeks.

"Whose day?"

Mauricius laughed, looking at his wife as she cuddled Andrina. "Can I not come to visit my daughter and grandchildren when I want to?"

"Well, of course, but...," Javor stammered.

"Javor, look how dirty Andrina is," Anna exclaimed. "How can you let this happen? What have you been up to?"

Javor dusted his hands. "Just playing. It is good for children."

Mauricius settled onto a couch in the sunshine. One of his slaves put a goblet into his hands. "Good for the children? You are treating my granddaughter as if she were a boy." Andrina squirmed out of her grandmother's grasp and ran to him. He settled her onto his knee.

Anna bent over Charita in her crib. "Javor, Andrina is your oldest *daughter*. You must teach her how to be a proper woman."

"A proper woman? She is only ten," Javor said.

"Javor," Mauricius said, his voice smooth and calm. "We must not excite the sensibilities of our girls. You must teach my granddaughter how to be a proper lady."

"Your granddaughter? She is my daughter."

Mauricius took a deep swallow of wine from his cup, then leaned close. "You must teach my granddaughter properly. Otherwise, I will not come to visit."

"Then don't," Javor said. His face felt hot.

"Javor!" Calanthe yelled. "Do not argue with my parents."

"I am sorry. You are always welcome, Mauricius and Anna," he said, repeating a formula that Calanthe had taught him. "But please, tell me, what brings you here today?"

"To visit our grandchildren, of course," Mauricius replied. He hugged Andrina. She wrapped her arms around him, giggling as he tickled and kissed her.

Anna went to Lydia and lifted Giorgia from her breast. "My, this one is big. She takes after her father. Look at that fair hair and those blue eyes."

"And little Charita is the image of her mother, just like Andrina here," Mauricius said. He put Andrina on the ground and pretended to steal her nose. She yelled in protest, grabbed her grandfather's hands and tried to pry her nose free. Laughing, Mauricius pressed his thumb on her nose. "All right, little one. No need to yell. Do you see what I mean, Javor? You must teach her gentleness and respect."

"I am," Javor protested.

Anna gave the baby back to Lydia and sank onto a couch. "Come over here, Andrina." Another slave passed her a cloth bag, from which she took needles, thread and pieces of cloth. Anna patted the couch beside her. "Come and sit with me and we'll do some needlepoint."

Andrina pouted. "I do not want to do needlepoint now," she whined. "I want to play with Papa."

"Do not argue with your grandmother," Calanthe scolded. "Sit and learn to be a little lady."

Andrina looked at her father. Javor forced a smile. "Go on. It is always good to learn new things."

"But I know how to do needlepoint already. It's *boring*."

"Your stitches are quite wide apart, my dear," Anna said, patting the couch again. "Come now." She held out a threaded needle and a square of mesh cloth.

Andrina gave her father a resentful look, then trudged to the couch. She took the needle and cloth and, pouting, slowly started stitching. Anna pointed out her errors, gently instructing her. Mauricius watched, smiling and sipping wine.

One of Mauricius' slaves held out a goblet to Javor. "You must be thirsty after all that rough-housing with Andrina," Mauricius said.

Javor wiped sweat off his forehead. He took the cup and swallowed a big mouthful. "It is a hot day." He reached for the plate in front of Calanthe and took a piece of bread and cheese. All the cakes were gone. Calanthe wiped the last crumbs from her lips with a silk kerchief and gave it to one of her father's slaves. "I am hungry. Mama, would you like some lunch?"

Anna opened her mouth to answer, but a howl came from Andrina. Javor knelt in front of his daughter to see a needle sticking out of her fingertip. He pulled it out as she wailed. A tiny drop of blood appeared and Javor kissed it away, smoothing Andrina's hair as he pulled her close. "There, there. You are fine. It is just a tiny pin-prick. Literally."

Andrina sniffled, smearing tears against Javor's neck. He kissed her finger again, then her cheek. "See?" He showed her the wounded finger, now clear of blood. There was no sign of a wound. "All better. Come on. We will eat lunch and then I will take you riding."

"Javor!" Calanthe scolded. "You will do no such thing."

Javor rose, his hand on his daughter's shoulder. "Of course I will. We will go outside the city walls and enjoy the fresh breeze. You can come, too."

"I will take the wagon."

But in the end, Javor rode his horse through the Xylokerkos Gate out of Constantinople, Andrina astride the horse's neck in front of him, Adam clinging to his back. Javor stroked Andrina's dark hair and directed the horse south, up a slope past the amphitheatre outside the gate.

The breeze off the Propontis Sea cleared away the stink of the city. Javor breathed deeply, feeling tension drain from his shoulders.

"Look at the flowers, Papa," Andrina said, pointing to weeds growing along the edge of the road. "That's my favourite part of going riding with you. When we see all the flowers."

Javor bent to kiss the top of his daughter's head. They rode past informal markets of rickety stalls, pausing to buy some apples. Andrina fed one to the horse and delighted in the softness of its nose. They rode past fields of tilled earth, watching farmers and slaves seeding them.

At a small stand of trees near a crossroads, they dismounted. After Javor had taken the saddle and bridle from the horse, the three of them sat under the shade of a tree to eat their apples. Javor drank some wine from a skin, and let the children taste a little. Andrina wrinkled her nose and stuck out her tongue. "I don't like it, Papa," she said.

"I do," Adam said. Laughing, Javor pulled the wineskin from his son's hands.

Javor took two small wooden swords from a saddlebag. "Show me your stance," he said to his children.

Andrina took the sword and assumed the initial stance: right foot forward, right shoulder turned toward her father, left arm out behind her, wooden sword pointed ahead. Adam copied his sister. "Very good, children," Javor said, smiling. He corrected a few points of their posture. "Now, show me a lunge."

Andrina demonstrated a perfect little lunge, thrusting the practice sword forward with all the strength her ferocity could muster.

Adam lunged, too, surprising Javor with the perfection of the move. "Excellent. Andrina, show me what I have taught you."

Andrina went through some basic sword-fighting moves: jabs, slashes, parrying imaginary foes. When she was panting, Javor told her to stop. "Your turn," he said to his eldest son. If anything, his form was even better than his sister's.

Javor stopped him with a hand on the boy's shoulder. "Excellent." He gathered his children in his arms and sat on the ground again.

"Papa," Andrina asked when she had her breath again. "Why do Mama and Giagiá and Pappoús not want me to fight?" meaning her grandparents.

Javor sighed. "They do not think it is proper for a girl to fight."

"But you think it is proper?"

"Yes. The world is a dangerous place, and everyone, boy or girl, needs to know how to defend themselves."

Andrina frowned, her lips pursed. "Even at home?"

Javor pulled her closer. "Our home is safe. I will make certain of that."

*Should I tell her about the amulet and the dagger? No, not yet. She is still too young. Soon, though.* "As long as I am with you, my daughter, my love, you are safe."

Andrina squirmed out of his hold and looked him in the eye. "But Papa, sometimes you go away. For a long time." Her eyes filled, glistening.

Javor pulled her closer again. "I will never leave you in danger, my love." And he wondered whether he was lying.

# Rioters

Preyatel started to vibrate. *Not because of Andrina, surely,* he thought. She ran at him, fists raised, and slammed into his stomach. Of course, Adam was right behind her.

Javor pretended to fall from Andrina's blow, and saw from an upside down perspective as Adam tackled his big sister and they rolled over and over beside the columns of the peristyle garden.

Javor laughed until Gaetan burst into the garden. "My lord! There is trouble in the city."

Preyatel continued to buzz. It was annoying. "What trouble?"

"The *demes* are rioting against the Emperor. They say the Exarch's son is marching on the city."

Javor rose and lifted Adam off his sister. The seven-year-old wriggled out of his grasp, then helped Andrina up, too.

"Barricade the main gate," Javor instructed. "Withdraw all the servants into the atrium."

"The gate has already been barricaded, my lord. I have set the menservants to stand watch from the roof."

"No need. Tell them to shelter in the atrium with us." He heard collected shouts, a tumult of running feet, squealing oxcart wheels, clashing metal and smashing glass beyond the outer wall. A low rumble seemed to roll from the direction of the harbour.

"But my lord!"

"There is no need to expose them to unnecessary danger," Javor insisted. "It is not as if they could make a difference if the mob attacked, not even the Greens. We will all shelter together."

Gaetan's face wore an expression of doubt combined with superiority. "But my lord—the servants with the noble family?"

"Are you questioning me?" Javor spat, surprised at the way his upper lip began to twitch. "Do what I tell you."

Gaetan gave a peremptory bow. "Yes, my lord."

"Adam, go help Auntie Tiana come to the atrium," Javor said. The boy ran toward Tiana's chamber.

Preyatel vibrating hot under his clothes, Javor took Andrina's hand and ran down the hall to the atrium. He found Calanthe, the baby twins and other servants had already gathered. Lydia, the wet-nurse, had Charita on one breast. Uncharacteristically, Calanthe held Giorgia on her round belly. Her eyes were wide open with fear, and the baby began to whine.

Andrina stood beside her mother, one arm around her shoulders. With her free hand, she stroked Giorgia's head.

Michael came in, wearing his apron and carrying a long wooden spoon. Kyriake was behind him. Then Adam walked in slowly, supporting the limping Tiana. He led her to a long couch and held her hand as she sat down.

Andrina took Adam's hand and led him to the edge of the impluvium in the middle of the atrium. They sat down together, watching the front entrance.

The pitch of the tumult outside the walls grew. They could hear glass breaking, pottery and stone shattering. A collective shout rose, followed by a deeper sound of creaking and something big breaking into pieces.

Charita continued to suckle the wet-nurse, unconcerned.

"Take her. Take Giorgia," Calanthe groaned, holding the crying baby up. Javor gathered her into his arms, rocking her gently to calm her.

Calanthe groaned as she heaved her bulky body from the chair. "What is all the noise?"

Over the wall, Javor could see lurid orange light dancing on the walls of surrounding houses and buildings. A repetitive chant arose.

Calanthe wrapped her arms around her husband and child, and cried. Her tears wet Javor's shoulder. "Hush. It will be over soon. These things always are short-lived."

"They're calling for the death of the emperor!" Calanthe wailed.

"They're not calling for our deaths," Javor reminded her. He rubbed her back in small circles.

"But the emperor," she wailed again.

*What to tell her to reassure her? Is it worse to say I have no loyalty to Phocas, or that we could be at the mercy of the Imperial troops? I suppose it depends on which side the Imperial troops choose to support.*

*How can anyone predict that?*

Gaetan appeared at Javor's elbow. "My lord, his grace Mauricius is at the front gate."

"What? Let him in, for gods' sake!"

Gaetan hesitated for a shadow of a moment before bowing. "My lord," he said and disappeared down the corridor again.

Something outside crashed and people screamed. Charita released Lydia's nipple to wail.

Mauricius entered the atrium. Andrina ran to him and threw her arms around his legs. He bent, picked her up and kissed her forehead.

Anna appeared behind him, her dark hair flowing in concert with her dalmatica. Somehow, she looked dramatic and purposeful in the chaos of the noise beyond the courtyard. She scooped Adam into her arms and squeezed him close until he complained and squirmed. "Hush, child. Grandmother is here."

"Are you well, son-in-law?" Mauricius demanded over the noise of the babies' crying and the tumult outside.

"We are all safe, father-in-law," Javor responded. "Perhaps if everyone did not act so much like they were in danger, the children would not be so afraid."

Mauricius glared at Javor as he put Andrina back on the ground. The girl ran off toward the bedrooms, earning a "Child! Return!" from her grandfather.

Javor put his hand on his father-in-law's shoulder. "She will be all right, Mauricius."

"Where is she going?"

"She has a strong mind and great courage," Javor answered. He turned as Calanthe wailed. The twins wailed in return.

"Give her to me," said Tiana, her voice hoarse. She gestured with upraised arms, and Lydia did not hesitate to put the baby into them. The older woman gathered the baby close as she sank onto a cushioned couch, shushing and rocking her gently. Lydia tucked her breasts into her blouse.

Martha took Giorgia in her arms, trying in vain to calm her. The kitchen servants clung together, one of them weeping quietly.

"Great courage is fine for a boy, but your daughter is a girl," Mauricius reminded Javor, his brows drawing close.

Before Javor could think of a response, a loud crash sounded from the front courtyard. Gaetan ran in again. "The mob is trying to knock down the front gate!"

Calanthe wailed again, prompting howls from the twins. Even Anna cried out when another blow struck.

"What shall we do, my lord?" Gaetan cried.

Andrina returned to the inner courtyard then, carrying a large bundle in one hand and dragging something else behind her in the other. It scraped along the stone floor, adding an irritating note to the clamour from beyond the villa's walls. "Papa!" she panted, before dropping her burdens with a clamour.

Javor knelt in front of her. "Your armour, Papa," she panted. She held his steel helmet in the crook of her arm. The bundle was his lamellar cuirass, greaves and arm protectors. But she had not brought several other essential items.

*It must have taken all her strength to carry it here.*

"Mauricius!" Javor called, loosening his great-grandfather's dagger in the scabbard he always wore on his side. "Take care of Andrina."

"I want to help you, papa," Andrina said before Mauricius swept her into his arms and passed her to one of the slaves he had brought. She struggled until she slipped out of the slave's arms.

Javor put his hand on her shoulder. "You can help me by staying here with the others and showing them how to be brave. Adam," he called to his oldest son, "you help your mother stay calm." Adam nodded and went to Calanthe, who had collapsed back onto her couch. He hugged her and wriggled to find a place to sit on her lap.

Javor picked up his helmet and the armour that his daughter had dragged in and nodded at Gaetan, who followed him to his study in the very centre of the domus. There, he quickly took out the rest of his armour. He pulled on the felt cap that went between his head and the helmet. Gaetan, flinching at every sound from the front gate, helped him with the cuirass and arm braces, then held his long sword as Javor fastened his greaves.

Taking the sheathed sword in his left hand, Javor strode down the corridor to the front courtyard. He took a firm stance in front of the little lemon tree as the pressure on the gate splintered the thick board that, held in place by iron brackets, formed a secure lock.

With a final sickening crack, the gate burst open. A group of young men in ragged tunics, shock on their faces, stood just beyond it.

"Rich man," said the one in front. He grinned, a gap black in his teeth. He had thick black hair and blood on his cheek, dully illuminated by a flaming torch held by the young man beside him.

"I do not want to kill any of you," Javor announced in a firm, steady voice. "But if you take one more step, I will." He drew the long sword with a ringing sound. Under his shirt, Preyatel's vibration decreased to a dull tickle against his chest.

The gap-toothed man stepped inside, grinning. He raised a heavy wooden club. "There are many of us, rich man," he said, and spat at Javor's feet. "Let us take what we want and maybe we will not kill you." The other men behind him stepped closer, too, but not as far as their leader.

The lead man's eyes flicked to a vase with gold leaf on its edges, sitting in a little alcove on the wall. "Take that," he said, and a thin teenaged boy behind him ran up and grabbed it. "What are you going to do about that, rich man?" the leader teased.

Javor moved his right foot behind him, presenting a narrow target to the mob. He scanned them. A number held blazing torches, others pikes, heavy clubs or knives. None of them looked like former legionnaires.

*What does a former legionnaire look like?*

*Shut up, brain.*

The leader barked a laugh. "I knew it. Didn't I tell you, boys? These rich men have no balls. That's why I father all their children!" Behind him, some of the others laughed.

"Take the vase," Javor said. "Go home. No one else needs to die tonight."

The leader laughed, and the followers behind him echoed.

Javor stepped closer. If he leaned forward, he could sever the leader's head. "One warning. You cannot harm me." Preyatel thrummed against his chest in agreement. "But I can hurt you. If I have to, I will kill you. But I do not want to."

The leader laughed again. Preyatel leaped under Javor's shirt, hot as the torch in the hand of the man beside the leader.

Fast as flame, the leader swung his club at Javor's head. But faster was Javor's sword into the man's neck. His amulet vibrated, filling his head with a keening song. Blood spurted, covering Javor's face and cuirass. Before he could control it, his sword found its way into two of the men with torches. It sang a death song as Javor followed, dancing into the mob, led by the blade and the amulet's direction.

When he halted in the middle of the street, the mob streamed away down the side alleys. Javor drew his breath slowly, calmly, his sword comfortable in his grip. Light from two sputtering torches on the cobblestones illuminated one side of a single face, trembling before him.

Overhead, the moon filtered through smoke.

"Please," said the half-face. The cheek below the wide eye glistened wetly.

"Go. Tell the others," Javor said, shaking his sword.

The eye blinked, then vanished. Javor heard slapping footfalls fade into the distance.

Javor stood in the street for a moment, scanning left and right. Then he turned and walked carefully past his broken gate, to find his father-in-law in the outer courtyard.

"No damage that cannot be easily repaired," Mauricius said.

"Just the dead," Javor replied.

Mauricius did not even bother to shrug. "A few commoners and slaves. Easily replaced."

Javor looked again at the blood stain at his feet. He could not begin to formulate an answer.

Mauricius directed his slaves to put up a temporary barricade at the gate, while Javor, sword limp in his hand, trudged to the inner corridor. He found Andrina standing at the entrance with a small knife and a grim expression, another of Mauricius' slaves—*Basil*, Javor remembered—standing beside her with clenched fists. Tiana held the twins on her lap, while Calanthe stood surrounded by Javor's servants. Adam stood defiantly, holding his grandmother's hand.

Andrina gasped at the sight of blood on Javor's face, helmet and armour. He knelt in front of her. "It is all right. I am not hurt."

Andrina flung her arms around his neck. She kissed his cheek, smearing blood across her mouth. "Oh, Papa. I was never afraid, Papa. I knew you would not be hurt."

# Interlude 6

# The Tyrant Deposed

*Year 610 Christian Era*

The news spread across the city on a clear, warm day in early October. The people of Constantinople watched a fleet of warships sail into the Golden Horn, flying the flag of the Exarch of Africa, Heraclius.

The people, the senators, the aristocrats, the merchants and slaves, Blues and Greens, all knew the dire situation that the Empire faced. In the north and west, barbarian Avars and Sklavenes raided with impunity, looting and killing at will. Sklavenes took land from farmers who had lived for generations within the safety of the Empire's borders, settling it for themselves.

Worse, in the East, the Empire's borders had been shattered by the Sassanids. Seeing the weakness of the Roman Empire after the murder of Emperor Maurice, their generals had conquered Armenia, Syria and Palestine. They had sacked Antioch, again, and their armies had penetrated as deep into Roman territory as Chalcedon, across the Propontis Sea from Constantinople itself.

The people of Rome knew who was to blame for the string of disasters: Phocas, the usurper, the Centurion who claimed the Imperial diadem and purple robes, and butchered the true Emperor Maurice, and his family.

Phocas had not stopped there. He systematically eliminated every one of Maurice's relatives who had an official position, and every senator loyal to him, replacing them with his own brothers and cousins. Brave men, but men with no administrative experience, no knowledge of the world or how to feed the great city.

Phocas dealt with the multiple conspiracies against him with unprecedented cruelty. Torture, blinding and mutilation became common. Constantinopolitans became inured to the sight of the heads of once prominent men and women on sticks along the walls of the city.

In the Year 609 of the Christian Era came word that Heraclius, the Exarch of Carthage, had revolted. He declared himself and his son, also named Heraclius, as Consuls. His nephew Nicetas led an army overland and took Alexandria, the Empire's second city. This cut off the essential grain supply for the capital. Starvation would be inevitable. Nicetas continued north, scattering Phocas' armies.

Then Heraclius, the son of the Exarch, sailed a fleet into the Golden Horn.

Heraclius the son did not need to storm the capital. The people of the city opened the gates. The commander of the city guard deserted his post. The Green factions found the commander's hiding place and killed him, then set fire to the Harbour of Theodosius.

The palace guard turned on the usurper and brought him to Heraclius' flagship.

Heraclius the Younger, tall and glorious, his blond hair shining in the sun, stood on the deck as his men forced the former Emperor Phocas to his knees.

"Is it thus," the young conqueror asked, "that you have governed the Empire?"

Phocas raised his bloodied face. His once fiery hair and beard were crusted with filth and blood. His voice, though, was firm. "Will you govern it any better?"

A steel sword appeared in Heraclius' hand faster than the eye could see. It flashed once, severing Phocas' right arm, but the erstwhile emperor made not a sound as his blood spurted across the deck.

Heraclius' next move severed his enemy's head.

That afternoon, Heraclius entered the Great Palace. In the chapel, his wife, Fabia, was crowned as the new Augusta Eudocia. Then the Patriarch placed the imperial crown on his head and named Heraclius the Emperor.

It was the beginning of renewed hope for Rome. The people of the Eastern Empire hoped for re-established security. Some dared to look forward to renewed glory.

Either would require a long war with the rising power to the east, the Sassanid Persian Empire.

# Andrina and Adam

*Year 611 Christian Era*

"Try this," Mauricius said, handing Javor a cup he had just filled with wine from a small jug. "It is from Cyprus."

Javor sipped and savoured the rich, fruity liquid. "It is good."

"Good? It is wonderful!" Mauricius exclaimed. "Even your barbarian tongue should be able to discern that, son-in-law."

"I admit, it is much better than retsina."

"Pah! I should hope that you do not partake of that swill. Suitable only for the lowest echelons of society."

They sat in Javor's *tablinum*, the room in the centre of the house that served as both a study and a place for Javor to receive visitors. Open to the front and back of the house, it afforded a view of most of the domus, forward to the atrium and front gate, and from the open rear door, the peristyle garden, the kitchen and the servants' quarters at the back.

Drinking the surprisingly good wine, Javor surveyed his wife, Calanthe, lying on a couch and eating grapes beside her mother, Anna, who pinched and cuddled the two-year-old twins. Martha, the nurse, fussed and fetched milk sweetened with honey. Aunt Tiana rested on a couch in the sunshine, reading a scroll. Behind them, Michael worked at preparing a meal, and Kyriake scrubbed clothes.

The sky was high and the deep blue of May. Birds sang in the trees in the garden, a gentle breeze blew over the walls and Javor drank excellent wine.

*It is a good day.*

A smile spread across his face as he watched Adam and Andrina, his oldest children, race each other the length of the garden, jumping over potted flowering plants and bushes. At the back, they started climbing the wall, racing each other up until Gaetan warned them, "Children! Come down before you hurt yourselves." Pausing in mid-climb, they looked toward their father. Javor nodded, and they dropped, rolling on the ground to cushion the impact.

They ran to the kitchen. "I bet I can lift this amphora, and you cannot," Adam boasted.

"I can lift that," she retorted. "There is no way that you can."

Adam wrapped his arms around the narrow clay jug for wine and struggled to lift it.

He is going to break it, Javor realized, and stood. Adam managed to raise it off the floor before Michael turned and pushed it back down. Javor could not hear what he said before the two children scampered out of the way of the cook's ladle.

At eleven years old, Andrina was surprisingly tall. "She takes after her father," her grandparents often said. She had long legs and broad shoulders for a girl. She still kept her thick black hair short, despite her mother's dismay and frequent complaint.

Adam, three years younger, was almost as tall as his sister and, if anything, even more broad-shouldered. He, too, had long legs and arms, which had a habit of reaching things that Javor wished they would not. Unlike his sister, though, his hair was blond, like his father's, and his nose equally prominent. His knees were always scabbed or scraped, his face usually dirty unless Martha or Anna was close enough to wipe it.

"This wine is made from the Mavro grape," Mauricius said, bringing Javor back into the tablinum. "Despite producing an excellent wine, it is completely unknown here in the capital. As a result, I was able to obtain a substantial quantity at a cheap price. And because of its quality,

I anticipate selling it at a premium to the wealthiest, choosiest of the senators. You see, that is how trade is accomplished, Javor: buy cheap, sell dear."

"But what if another merchant starts to sell the same wine, but at a cheaper price?" Javor asked.

"That is the second rule of the successful merchant: protect your sources," said Mauricius. "I made an agreement with the vintner in Cyprus to sell only to me. No other merchant can buy his product."

"Can you trust him?"

"It is not a matter of trust, my boy. It is a matter of a mutually beneficial agreement. He has only one sale to make with me. He does not have to carry his amphorae to multiple ships or markets. And I am paying him a premium price over what he was used to earning in his local markets — a price that is still less than I would pay for a lower quality wine from the established vineyards in Anatolia or Thessalia. So you see, we are both making more coin than before."

Javor could think of no argument to that.

Since he had refused to go on any more missions for Gracian, and given up on the Order, Javor had more time on his hands than he could tolerate. He filled it by taking an interest in his father-in-law's business. Mauricius' trading ships sailed the Euxine, Propontis and Aegean seas, trading wine, silk, spices and other products from the provinces to the capital.

During the tumultuous days of the usurper Phocas, Mauricius' business and income suffered. The Sassanian King of Kings, Khosrau II, had invaded, claiming to avenge the Emperor Maurice, who had helped him regain his throne years before. Of course, it was a good excuse to recapture land lost to the Roman Empire in Armenia, Syria and Mesopotamia. Khosrau did not stop there, either. His armies, led by the legendary generals Shahr-Baraz and Shahin, overran Anatolia and reached Chalcedon, across the Propontis Sea from Constantinople itself.

With the Imperial Navy concentrating on keeping the Sassanians from crossing the sea to Europe, pirates operated without fear. Antioch and other rich trading ports were occupied, as well.

Even with the accession of the Emperor Heraclius, Persia remained in control of large sections of the Empire. Mauricius had had to adjust and find new routes and new products with which to restore his fortune. His ships now concentrated on the northern routes across the Euxine, as far away as Kerch, and along the Aegean and Mediterranean coasts.

Javor's interest in matters of trade and money gratified Mauricius. He was happy to lecture the younger man on the fine points of commerce and trade. This day in late May, he had come with bundles of scrolls and codices, records of transactions and other information, and spread them on Javor's desk while Anna visited her daughter and grandchildren.

Javor's attention was diverted again by high pitched screams from the garden. Andrina and Adam were now wrestling, arguing about who was stronger. From what Javor could see, they were pretty evenly matched.

Anna could hold in her grandmotherly alarm no longer. "Do you see that, Calanthe? Do you see, Mauricius? Andrina behaves more and more like a boy than a girl every time I see her. It's beyond time to reign her in and teach her to be a lady, or she will never find a husband from a good family."

"A marriage is still far enough away," Mauricius replied without looking up from his scrolls. "Let the children enjoy themselves."

At that, Andrina pounced, rolling across the tiles and pinning her brother to the floor. Adam grunted and struggled, then with a heave that surprised Javor, pushed his still-larger sister into the piscina, the basin in the middle of the peristyle garden that collected rain water for cleaning and cooking. The splash reached their grandmother's skirts and dainty shoes. She let out a little cry.

Andrina rose to her feet, water streaming from her head and body. She laughed and launched herself at her brother again.

"Do you see, Calanthe?" Anna shrilled. "Now I am wet, and your daughter is soaked to the skin."

"Calm, wife," Mauricius said. "It is only a few drops."

"Mauricius, this is finest silk, all the way from Qin."

"I know, Anna. I paid for it."

"And these shoes are the finest leather. Water will ruin them!"

"Yes, Anna. I paid for them, too."

"Oh! You are impossible. Men!" she huffed.

Adam and Andrina rolled on the floor, crashing into a decorative bush before Adam jumped to his feet and ran to the back of the garden.

Calanthe swung her bulk on the couch to face her husband in his study. "My mother is right, Javor. Andrina is such a handful, and she will not listen to anything I say."

"She listens to me," Javor answered.

"Of course she does, because you never tell her 'no!'"

"It is a father's prerogative to spoil his daughters," Mauricius advised. He finally put the scroll down. "But Javor, it is also your duty to discipline your children."

"Yes, father. I know," he replied.

"Are you still teaching Andrina to read?" Mauricius asked. He shuffled through the pile of scrolls before him.

"She already reads very well," Javor said. "She has also written some poems." Aunt Tiana had accepted the role of teacher, and was delighted with Andrina's progress in reading and writing. Tiana had lately begun teaching Andrina the basics of arithmetic and geometry, and Andrina drank it all in.

Adam, however, was another case. He did not display the quick uptake of his sister, even though he seemed to be growing physically even faster.

Javor considered showing his parents-in-law the poems his daughter had written. Then Mauricius answered his inner question. "Waste of time, teaching a girl academic subjects," he said.

"It cannot hurt," Javor said.

"Perhaps not yet, but sooner or later, such things will only distract her from her womanly duties. Best get a needle and thread into her hands as soon as you can. Not to mention getting her into some proper clothes for a girl."

He opened another codex and unrolled a new scroll. "Now, pay attention here," he said, moving the papers into better light. "I want to show you some discrepancies in the records. This can be an indication of, at best, sloppy errors by one's crew. At worst, however, it can be a sign that someone is cheating you."

# Javor's dream

*Year: 612 Christian Era*

Javor floated. He rose above the great city. Cresting the great Walls of Theodosius, he caught a glimpse of the sun setting, angry red below clouds orange and black.

Below, the lights of the city flared, dull yellow and orange behind dirty window coverings. Brighter lanterns of the guards shone in small circles along the walls.

Beyond the walls, there were few lights in the suburbs and settlements, none among the fields and farms.

The sun sank lower as Javor turned. Something moved, beyond the city, beyond the Golden Horn and even the Euxine Sea far to the east.

*How can I possibly see that far?*

Darkness came from the east. But it was not the fading of night. A roiling blackness swept forward, sliding under the higher clouds.

A black mist fell lower as it approached the city, blotting out the view of the lands, of the Bosporus and the Golden Horn. The mist reached the sea walls and flowed over them like poisoned water flooding a dam.

The mist flowed over the city, blocking Javor's view. The lights on the sea walls disappeared first, then the bright lamps in the Great Palace. It kept coming, swallowing the greatest city in the world. The eastern districts vanished.

*Is that Mauricius' house?*

A sound at the boundary between hearing and imagination. Moaning, keening, crying that faded, then rose again in waves.

The blackness covered the city now. The only light came from the faint fires to the west and the very last rays of the sun, which vanished, as well.

In the blackness, he searched for a sign of life. Nothing.

He felt himself sinking as a warmth reached him from the benighted city far below. As he descended, the heat became more intense. But not on his feet, not on his face, either. No, this was heating his chest, right in the centre, over his heart.

He was falling now, faster and faster, and he had no way of knowing where in the city he would come down.

Javor woke with a start. He was lying on his back, and Preyatel, lying on the middle of his chest, vibrated so intensely it felt hot.

*What is it, old friend? What are you warning me about?*

He looked to his left, where Calanthe snored softly. He wondered at the time. The room was so dark, he could not see the outline of her hip on the bed.

Preyatel continued to vibrate. Silently so as not to wake his wife, he rose, took his dagger from its hiding spot near the bed and padded out to the corridor.

He felt as if Preyatel were guiding him toward the smallest bedchamber, the room that had once been for some of the servants and was now the twins' room. But as he reached the door, he heard another faint sound from the back of the house.

He paused, listening. Whispers, indistinct. He moved silently toward the kitchen, hand on the hilt of his dagger, invisible in the gloom of the house. Preyatel quieted as he approached the kitchen door.

More whispers, but he could not make them out until he heard a soft giggle. He came around the corner, staying in the deepest shadow.

The open back door between the kitchen and the garden let in only the dimmest light from the city's lantern, but compared to the darkness of the rest of the house, it was enough to make out a female shape beside the door and someone else beyond it.

Another giggle. "Quiet. You'll wake up the whole house."

The form outside moved closer, and the two shadows merged. A wet, sloppy sound, and then the forms separated with a long sigh.

A low murmur, followed by a whisper. "Yes, tomorrow. But earlier this time. At the usual place."

The form inside turned and the door shut with a soft click. Javor watched her fit the wooden bar across it to secure it, then stepped out of the darkest shadow into dimness in the middle of the kitchen.

He recognized the slight form with one arm smaller than the other. "What are you doing, Lydia?"

Lydia, the wet-nurse, cried out and jumped back until she hit the door. "Who? Oh, my Lord, you frightened me."

"Lydia, why were you out so late after dark? Do you not know how dangerous it is on the streets at night?"

"I—I—"

"Who was that?"

Lydia stammered some more. "Who do you mean, my Lord?"

"That man at the door. Who was he?"

Light appeared on the walls and floor, swaying back and forth. Javor heard bare feet slapping the tiles and turned to see Gaetan stomp into the kitchen, a flickering lamp in his hands. "What is this? My lord, my apologies. Lydia, what are you doing? Why are you not sleeping in the stable where you belong?"

"Nothing, sir. Nothing at all."

"Then why are you in the kitchen? You were sneaking out with that Licinius boy again, weren't you? Whore."

Lydia stammered incoherently. The lamplight showed tears streaming down her face.

From deeper in the house, Javor heard a baby start to cry. Seconds later, a second joined.

"Now you've done it," Gaetan snapped. "You've woken the babies."

"Quiet, Gaetan, or you'll wake everyone else," Javor said. "Lydia, see to the twins."

At his words, Preyatel jumped under his tunic.

"My lord, she is not fit to care for your children," Gaetan protested. "She is a whore. You should turn her out of the house immediately."

"Not in the middle of the night. And who is going to quiet the twins? You?"

Preyatel vibrated harder, heating up again.

What is going on? At that moment, he heard a woman's scream from somewhere in the city.

More yelling, tumult, indistinct noises. "See to the twins, Lydia. Gaetan, make certain all the doors are locked." Javor strode to the closet where he kept his armour and suited up. He took the ladder to the roof of the house and scanned the area.

Nothing seemed out of the ordinary. A few dim lanterns burning, the guards' lights moving slowly along the walls that he could see.

But somewhere, down the slope toward the harbour, people were screaming. More and more every minute joined them.

Preyatel continued to vibrate. Javor stayed on the roof until the sky greyed in the east, but did not see a single person on the street.

And Preyatel continued to tremble.

The dark swelling appeared under Lydia's arms two days later.

Martha was the first to notice the wet-nurse's flushed face and groans. She staggered carrying one of the twins out of the bedroom. Martha dashed up to catch the baby as she rolled out of Lydia's arms. The baby wailed.

"What's wrong with you? You nearly dashed her head onto the marble tiles," Martha hissed, bobbing the baby against her shoulder to quiet her.

"I'm—I'm sorry, Martha," Lydia whispered. She leaned against the wall and heaved. "I just feel weak, and so tired today." She took a deep breath and straightened. "Maybe I am with child," she whispered even more softly.

Martha shifted her arm on the child so she could place her other palm on Lydia's forehead. "Not with a fever like that. I do not care how much you've been fucking that Licinius. Stay here," she ordered, backing away. "I mean it. Do not move." Still rocking the baby, she rushed to the room where Javor and Tiana sat on couches, reading old books and scrolls and talking in low voices.

Javor looked alarmed. "What is wrong, Martha?"

"It is Lydia. She is very ill. Please, sir, keep her away from the babies. From all of us."

Javor sprang to his feet, brushing past Martha and baby Charita to the atrium. Lydia sat on the floor with her feet in the impluvium, the shallow drain pool that collected rainwater for the house.

Javor knelt beside her, careful to leave some space and not to touch her. "Lydia, are you ill?" he said softly.

Preyatel stirred, trembling under his tunic.

He could hardly hear her voice. "I was cold before, but now I feel so hot," she complained. She dropped the thin shawl over her shoulders and slumped forward until her chin nearly touched her chest.

Javor swallowed though his mouth was dry. Slowly, he reached toward the wet nurse, Preyatel's vibrations getting stronger as his hand got closer.

To facilitate nursing babies, Lydia wore a loose garment with an opening in front. Careful not to touch her body, he pulled the garment open, exposing her thin chest and swollen breasts. She did not protest, but Martha did. Not to protect the wet-nurse's modesty. All in the household had seen her chest many times. "Master, please do not get close," she warned.

Javor gently raised her smaller left arm. Under the armpit was a dark swelling, almost like a bruise.

But it was no bruise.

"Plague," he breathed.

Martha wailed and Charita started to cry again. From the bedroom, her brother joined her.

Javor did not notice the sounds of feet running to the atrium. "Javor, what are you doing?" Calanthe demanded.

"Papa, what is wrong with Lydia?" Javor looked up from Lydia at Andrina's voice. She stood a few paces behind him, holding her brother Adam's hand.

"She is very sick. Please stay away, Andrina."

Gaetan arrived in the atrium. He strode up to Lydia, grabbed her tunic and hauled her to her feet. "Whore!" he roared. "This is God's punishment for your sins. Leave this good house immediately!"

Javor put his hand on Gaetan's arm. "Stop it, Gaetan. There is no need for that. She is sick. And she is a slave. We cannot turn her out."

"Master, you must," Martha said, rocking the still-whimpering Charita. "I have seen this before. Plague. It seems cruel, but for the sake of the rest of us, we must remove her. Plague spreads."

"Don't be ridiculous, Martha," Gaetan snarled. "Plague is visited on sinners as punishment. It does not...spread from one person to the next like oil on one's hands." He was still holding onto Lydia. She swayed slightly, her eyelids fluttering.

"But it does, sir. It does," Martha insisted. "I have seen it. Twenty years ago, when I was young, the plague came to the city. It was always the same. First one person in the home would have the signs, the weakness and the fever and the buboes under the arms or between the legs. In a matter of days, two others in the household would show the first signs, and the first one would die. Then everyone would get it, first the youngest and the elderly. Almost none recovered once they had the signs. The bodies piled in the streets because there were not enough left to bury them, no room in the cemeteries. Please, sir, protect us."

"If what she says is true, it is doubly certain that we must get her out," Gaetan said. "She is a wanton slut, bringing sin and disease into this house."

At that, Lydia heaved and vomited onto Gaetan's chest, a thin, mucous stream. He cried out, letting go of the wet nurse and stepping back quickly. Lydia toppled to the floor, her hands slapping against the marble.

"Gaetan!" Javor yelled, dropping to a knee himself to pick Lydia up. "How could you drop her like that?"

Andrina ran to her father's side and pulled on his arm. "Papa, you should not touch her," she pleaded.

"Master, please do not let your skin touch her mess," Martha advised. "Please, sir, step back."

It was the look in her eyes that convinced Javor. He looked up at Gaetan, who was trying to wipe vomit from his clothes. Behind them, the rest of the household watched with wide eyes and gaping mouths: his wife, Calanthe, Michael the cook, Kyriake, the servant, and Paulus, the groom. Aunt Tiana stood with one hand on Adam's shoulder, the other on a cane.

Javor looked again at his eldest daughter, at the wide, pleading dark eyes. "Very well. Gaetan," he turned to the head servant. "Clean yourself. Because you have been so cruel, you will take Lydia by wagon to the xenon," using the Greek word for hospital, which literally meant "house for strangers."

He arranged Lydia as comfortably as he could on the tiles, careful not to touch her skin or the vomit on the floor. To Martha, he said, "The twins will need a new wet nurse."

"They are more than old enough to be weaned, sir," Martha answered. "If there is plague in the city, we should not allow anyone new to touch them." She turned to Michael. "Come, let's prepare something for them to eat. They're upset.

"Kyriake, get a mop and cloths and clean the floor, but do not touch it with your hands. And afterward, throw out the rags and mop, too. Better yet, burn them." The maid hurried away.

Javor turned to Gaetan to catch him glaring back. The head servant quickly softened his expression and looked at the floor. "What are you waiting for? Take the poor girl to the hospital, and when you return, bring the physician with you."

"Yes, sire," Gaetan mumbled. He went toward the stable at the back of the house, ordering Paulus, the groom, to come with him to prepare the wagon.

Gaetan returned two hours later with a physician, a short, tonsured man in a black robe and white chiton, carrying a leather bag on a strap over one shoulder. "This is Zacharias of Alexandria," Gaetan introduced them.

The physician bowed and set his bag on the table in Javor's study. "Let me examine the babies first," he said in a surprisingly high-pitched voice.

Martha brought them one at a time. Zacharias took off their coverings and examined every part of their bodies. He sat each on the potty, which had trained Andrina and Adam, and waited until they peed, then poured the urine into beakers. In turn, he held them up to the light, squinting, before sealing them and putting them carefully into a special wooden holder.

He called Gaetan to him, ordering him to strip. Reluctantly, Gaetan pulled off his clothing except for the linen braies, or underwear. Zacharias prodded him under the jaw and examined under his arms and in his groin.

Next he examined Martha, who stripped down to her chemise, a thin dress that served as underwear. As with Gaetan, he looked under her arms and, to her mortification, between her legs. He prodded under her fleshy chin and sniffed her breath.

He then turned to Calanthe, examining her in the same way as he had Martha, albeit with more care and letting her keep her dress on. Then he turned to the children, Andrina and Adam, then Tiana and finally Javor.

He gave each of them a small ceramic jar. "Urinate in this and bring it to me." Calanthe's face turned bright red at that. Adam pulled out his penis and poured forth in front of the physician. The rest went to another room to produce the needed sample, and Zacharias sealed each jar and placed them with the vials containing the babies' urine. "I will examine these using special techniques at the hospital. I will send you my results in two days' time. In the meantime, watch the children carefully. Bathe them twice a day in warm, not hot water. Keep them dry otherwise. Do not go outdoors more than absolutely necessary. Fill the house with sweet-smelling flowers. Everyone should eat apples soaked in vinegar." Andrina wrinkled her nose at that. "And say prayers to Saint Cosmas and Saint Damian."

The physician continued his instructions as he packed his bag. "If anyone should develop a fever, diarrhea or vomiting, bring them to me in the xenon immediately for blood-letting. Now, if you will call your man to take me back to the hospital..."

"But Zacharias," Javor blurted. "What about the others? Michael, Kyriake ..."

"Slaves? You think I should examine the slaves?"

"They are not slaves. Only Lydia, the wet-nurse, was a slave, and I did not own her."

Zacharias looked confused, but then apparently dismissed the feeling. "Still, there is no need to examine the servants."

"You examined Gaetan and Martha."

"Because they had direct contact with the sick girl."

"Does that mean that the disease can spread by contact, as Martha said?" Calanthe asked, a tremble in her voice.

"We in the medical class are not certain, but it is possible."

"Is it plague?" Javor asked.

Zacharias sighed. "Again, we cannot be certain yet. We must examine the girl's humours. There have been no large outbreaks of plague in the city yet, however."

Javor let out a sigh of relief. "Still, please examine the servants. If they are affected, they might spread it, too."

Zacharias' lips and nostrils contracted, but then he sighed again. "Very well. But I have no more jars to collect their urine. I can only examine their bodies. Send the others away."

Martha led the children away, while Gaetan accompanied Tiana back to her room. Javor remained, watching as the physician in turn examined Michael, Honorius and Kyriake. He only made them remove their outer garments and perfunctorily looked at their underarms and groins. "No sign of any symptoms. However, once again, if they do show any signs of illness, take them to the hospital immediately."

Javor gave the physician a gold coin, and told Honorius to take him back to the hospital.

Javor sat with Aunt Tiana in her room. "I had a dream last night. A great black cloud covered the city and blotted out all the light. I woke to a scream from somewhere outside."

Tiana nodded slowly. "You have told me of your prophetic dreams before."

Javor closed his eyes against the pain of the memory he now expressed. "I dreamed of great claws in the sky, the day before Avars attacked our village, killed an old man and kidnapped two girls."

"You have told me of the Avar raid and how they took the girl you loved then," Tiana said. "You never described the dream before. Do you dream on other nights?"

Javor shrugged. "Yes. Often. Silly things. Sometimes I dream of running through the streets. Sometimes I dream of ... of making love to Danisa again. But nothing ever happens. I dream she is with me, she and I want to do it, but there is always something stupid preventing us from touching. Things like that."

"But nothing prophetic or prescient?"

"No."

Aunt Tiana looked out the window long enough for Javor to wonder how long it had been. "It seems that some...thing, some force or entity is communicating with you at critical times," she said without looking at him. "Let me consult some of the codices you rescued. I want to confirm something before saying any more."

The next morning, Preyatel woke Javor again with intense vibrations against his chest. At the same time, he heard a loud wail from outside.

Pulling on a robe, he found Gaetan in the atrium. The head servant was pacing in front of the impluvium, his face white and beaded with sweat. "Plague, sir," he said. "It is spreading through the city."

In the streets of Constantinople, people staggered, sweating. Dark spots appeared on their faces and arms. Buboes, swellings under their arms and in their groins, grew fat and blue. Victims vomited in the streets. Open sores oozed blood and puss.

The day after that, Gaetan began vomiting, running out into the street so as not to let it contaminate the house.

He was too late. The twins woke early with fever, vomiting and crying. Their buboes came fast. Calanthe shrieked when she saw them, and ran for her room.

Javor knelt by their bed, wiping their hot skin with a damp cloth. His tears mixed in the bucket of water and splashed onto their reddened skin. He sent Kyriake for fresh, cool water, but the front door burst open before she could leave.

Mauricius strode in, his cloak billowing behind him. "Javor, gather your family. I have prepared a ship to take us to Heraclea."

Calanthe ran into the bedroom and wrapped her arms around her father, sobbing.

Javor wiped his face with the back of a hand. "Yes. Calanthe, take Andrina and Adam with you. I will stay with the twins."

"Javor, your man-servant lies dead in the street in front of your house. Of course you are coming with us," Mauricius said.

Javor rose to his feet. "You are leaving to escape the plague. Taking the twins will just bring plague with you to wherever you go. I have survived this before. When—" He choked, sniffed and wiped his face again. "When the twins recover, we will join you."

Mauricius' eyes were wide. He looked from Javor to the twins, mewling weakly in their beds, then back to Javor. He swallowed and nodded, then left, holding his daughter's shoulders.

The babies were not about to get out of their beds, so Javor followed his wife and father-in-law to the courtyard, where Paulus was already loading bags into Mauritius' handsome wagon. The horses stamped their feet, tossed their heads and snorted, nervous.

Martha led Andrina and Adam to the wagon. Weeping, she climbed into the wagon with Mauritius. Honorius loaded a case into the back of the wagon and climbed in with it.

Javor bent to help lift his daughter in, but she resisted. "No, Papa, I want to stay with you," Andrina pleaded. Tears brimmed her hazel eyes and her lower lip trembled. "I want to help you look after Charita and Giorgia."

"Me too, Papa," Adam chimed in. His face was already wet.

"No. It is too dangerous for you. You could become sick, too, if you stay."

"But what about you, Papa?"

Javor shook his head. "I already faced this when I was your age. My brother and sister had this same sickness," he said, although his memory of that time, so many years before, was foggy. He could not recall whether his older brother had the swollen sores under his arms or the black spots on his face. He had a clear picture in his mind of Young Swat's red, sweaty face, his weak coughs, blood leaking from his mouth with every breath. *Is this the same pestilence?*

There was no way to know. "I will be well. Do not worry about me. When the twins recover, we will all join you. Until then, it is best that you get away from this sickness while you are still healthy." He lifted his firstborn daughter and son into the wagon without further argument.

"What about the wet-nurse?" Mauricius asked.

"Dead," Javor answered.

"And your cook? What was his name?"

"Michael. He is either with his own family, or dead as well."

Mauricius gave Javor a hard look, then leaned close and spoke in a low voice. "Leave the babies, Javor. There is nothing more you can do for them."

Javor felt the shock down his back to his heels. "No. I...I will tend to them. They may recover. I knew children in my village who recovered from plague."

Mauricius gestured out the open gate to the street. Javor could see Gaetan's body, still lying where he had collapsed. Beside him was a stiff rat. Beyond, infected men and women staggered or slumped against the walls, panting, their clothes stained, their skin dark. "Look, Javor. The infected do not recover. The hospitals are overflowing with the dead. The city workers cannot keep up with the bodies in the streets. Do not deceive yourself."

"They say the Emperor Justinian recovered from plague."

Mauritius nodded. "The Emperor Justinian was installed by God our Heavenly Father as his vice-regent on earth. And he had the best physicians and nurses in the Empire to care for him. Where is the physician caring for your babies?"

"Either overwhelmed at the hospital, or dead himself."

"There is no recovering from this, Javor. Please come with us."

Javor shook his head, then jumped a little as Kyriake laid her hand on his arm. "I will stay with him to help care for the babies," she said. "And for Auntie Tiana. The Master is a kind man. And I, too, survived the last plague. If it did not take me then, it will not take me now."

Mauricius shook his head one more time, then nodded at the driver. He slapped the reins and the wagon rumbled through the gate. Javor watched it until it turned a corner on the narrow street. His daughter looked back at him the whole time.

The rest of the day, Javor did little other than tend the baby twins. He tried to feed them, even holding their little mouths open as he spooned milk into their throats. They vomited it all up, and more, minutes later.

Kyriake came in and out with fresh buckets of cool water and different concoctions of milk and cereal she prepared, but the babies would not eat anything.

Their whimpers turned into whispers as they weakened. By the end of the day, they breathed no more.

Tiana put her arm around Javor. Kyriake wrapped the twins in blankets and covered their faces.

Javor drove his wagon himself to the cemetery beyond the Justinian Walls. The attendants paid him no attention as he gently lowered the tiny bodies into a grave he had to dig himself. Kyriake pushed a cross she had taken from the house into the ground as a marker.

The three of them, Javor, Tiana and Kyriake, waited as one of the monks eventually walked past the grave, sprinkled it with water and mumbled a perfunctory prayer. He then went on to a mass grave where men had dumped a wagonload of bodies and prayed more.

# The spark

As soon as the twins were buried, Javor took Tiana and Kyriake to join his family at Mauricius' country home, near Heraclea, forty miles along the Propontis coast. The family embraced and wept over their losses. The twins, Charita and Giorgios. Gaetan, their grumpy yet faithful head servant. Lydia, the slave wet-nurse. Michael, the cook.

So many friends and neighbours in Constantinople.

That night, Javor followed Calanthe to their temporary bedchamber. Without a word, he pushed her to the bed, pulling her nightgown over her head. He lowered his head to her, and she kissed him hard, pushing her tongue into his mouth. Her hands scrambled to pull his clothes away, her legs spreading apart.

Tears streamed down their faces even as Calanthe pulled Javor into her. They pressed as closely as they could, Javor's chest mashing into Calanthe's breasts. She bit his neck until he cried out, thrusting hard. His fingertips dug into her buttocks. Sweat mixed with tears dripped onto her face.

Her panting moans became repeated little screams, but neither of them noticed Martha coming to the door with a candle in hand, then leaving.

He climaxed hard. Calanthe moaned long, louder than he had ever heard in years of sex with her. Javor collapsed, falling to the bed beside his wife, panting in time with her. His skin was coated with sweat. He reached for her, his palm sliding over her sweaty skin.

She rolled over, kissing Javor's neck as she climbed on top of him, surprising him as he slid into her again.

She rode him hard and shrieked her climax as she fell onto him, panting. Javor felt an urgency, an energy he had never felt before. He rolled over, and his hips battered hers, making wet slapping noises. He roared out another orgasm, smashing as deep as he could as Calanthe's thighs slid up his side and she screamed out.

Then they held each other, weeping quietly until they both fell asleep.

The next evening, Tiana and Javor sat on a balcony overlooking the Propontis Sea and talked in low tones.

"I have been thinking about your dream, Javor. I believe it portended your loss."

Javor gulped down a full cup of wine, then poured more into his cup from the jug that Mauricius' slave had left for them. "How?"

"You have had prophetic dreams before, Javor. This one was a warning. You said you saw a dark cloud coming from the east, across the Euxine Sea, then descending on the city.

"The cloud was the way your dream interpreted the plague. It afflicted the whole city. I do not know how many it will kill, but Justinian's plague, eighty years ago, killed close to half the inhabitants. The population has never recovered."

"Does it mean anything that it came from the east?"

Tiana looked across the Propontis for a time, as the red sun sank lower. "Once, I was known as Te-ma-arun-Vd-A, the high priestess of Tabiti, the queen of the gods of the Scythians."

"Is that not what Kriemhild said on the mountain, all those years ago?" Javor asked. "She said you were a Solar priestess."

Tiana nodded. "I was a priestess of Tabiti, but she is not a Solar goddess. That was a long time ago, before I came to Constantinople. Before I learned that all mythologies, in their essence, are the same. That they are all equally wrong, and equally correct."

"How can that be? Every religion insists it is right, and everyone else is wrong."

"That is not what is important right now. What I am telling you is about the religion of my people, the Sarmatians, part of the broader Scythian nations. We lived on the great plains north of the Euxine Sea and were renowned for our skill as mounted archers. Even the women were great riders and warriors." She paused to catch her breath.

"Since the Huns conquered the plains and shattered the Western Empire, my people have declined. Today, there are only small communities scattered among the new nations, the Goths, Huns, Romans and, of course, the Sklavenes. One of those is near the city of Kerch, the easternmost extent of the Empire, at the far end of the Euxine Sea."

"What does this have to do with my dream?"

"The priests of the Scythians are known as the Enarei," Tiana said. "It means 'man-woman.' The priests are all impotent men, and they dress in women's clothes."

"You mean, eunuchs?"

Tiana shook her head. They paused as one of Mauricius' slaves brought out a lantern just as the last of the twilight faded. When the slave was gone, Tiana answered.

"No, not eunuchs. They claim that they are divinely impotent because of their worship of the goddess of love. But this is the most important part, Javor. The last community of Enarei that I know of clings to existence in a small camp outside of Kerch, where they are despised by the local Christians."

Javor thought for a long time. When his cup was empty, he refilled it and Tiana's. "So you are saying that these priests, these men-women, sent the plague that killed the twins?"

"Please, do not shout, Javor." Tiana had used most of the little strength she had. She panted as she reached for him, spilling wine, but he stood and she could not reach his face. "There is no evidence—"

Javor did not hear another word. He only heard roaring in his ears.

All he saw was red.

He was gone the next morning, on a boat to Constantinople, and from there, to Kerch.

# Part 6

# Beatus

*Year 612 Christian Era*

# Kerch

There is Kerch, my lord," the sailor said, extending a ropey brown arm over the left side of the front of the ship. The port side, Javor reminded himself. *Not much to look at. Not compared to Constantinople.*

A steep slope led up from the smooth sea, or rather the strait the ship was rowing into. The Cimmerian Bosporus, Javor remembered, connected the Euxine to the Maeotian Lake or Sea. Scores of sea birds flew and cried over the water and the ship, and hundreds more sat and walked on the shores of the strait.

Strange to call it almost the same name as the strait at Constantinople. As if the Euxine Sea must have a "bosporus" at both eastern and western ends.

The sailor lowered his arm. Javor glanced at him once more, trying and failing to remember his name. He was shorter than Javor, with shaggy black hair, matted with sweat. His brown skin glistened with sweat in the late-morning sunshine, even though the wind chilled Javor. The sailor held Javor's eyes for a long moment, then scoffed, and shaking his head, stalked off to whatever duties awaited as the ship pulled into port.

The ship rounded a point into a broad bay. Ahead, Javor could see wooden docks extending into the water. Behind them, the land rose more gently than to the south, to a remarkable flat tableland covered with brown, withered-looking scrub. Above, scattered grey clouds raced ahead of a wind that Javor did not feel on the surface of the sea.

*No rain today, nor tomorrow. Maybe after, though.*

The city's walls were low, little higher than a man, Javor estimated, although from this distance it was hard to be certain. They seemed to have been made by piling pale rocks on top of one another. *Not very useful against an attack by a determined enemy.*

The oars along both sides of the galley lifted in unison and the ship glided closer to the wharf. At a barked command from the pilot, the oarsmen shifted to a back-row to slow down. Sunburned men on the wharf ran to catch ropes thrown from the galley.

Javor watched, fascinated by the quick, efficient movements of the men onshore and on the ship as they secured the vessel along the dock and immediately began unloading bundled cargo.

Javor turned to see Pelagios, the captain of the galley, crossing the deck. He pointed to a small, open gate in the walls where the wharf met a dirt road. "The inn is at the top of the hill, there," he said, with an accent that Javor still had not gotten used to.

"The inn? There is only one?"

Pelagios grinned over his shoulder. "Only one I would want to sleep in." He turned away again to shout orders as his men unloaded the boat.

Ignoring the gangplank, Javor pulled his pack onto his back, checked that his sword and dagger were securely strapped, stepped onto the gunwale and jumped to the dock. He landed next to a man coiling rope over his shoulder, who ignored him.

*At least I am finally off that damned ship.* Throughout the ten-day journey from the Golden Horn across the Euxine Sea, every man aboard, from Captain Pelagios to the oar-slaves had treated him with undisguised contempt, sneering as they answered every question and laughing when he turned away. The food had been disgusting, mostly salted, tough meat and hard, twice-baked bread that tasted to Javor like fish.

Javor dodged ropes, nets and canvas-wrapped bundles being loaded and unloaded onto the vessels tied up along the dock. Two armed guards sat on a bench beside the entrance to the city, their spears across their thighs. They gazed listlessly at the activity on the wharf, ignoring men, animals and carts passing in and out of the town.

But one stood as Javor approached, pushing himself up with his spear. Javor barely understood his Greek as he barked "What's your business in Kerch?"

Javor slowed but did not stop. "I come on business of the emperor."

The other guard stood and stepped in front of Javor, forcing him to a stop outside the gate. Javor noticed that it would still be possible to swing it shut, locking him outside.

The guard who had spoken leaned close, sneering. "Where are you from?"

Javor forced himself not to back away. He took a deep breath. "Constantinople."

"Sounds like a barbarian," said the second guard, looking Javor up and down. "Like a Slav."

The first guard scoffed. "What business for the emperor?"

"What business is that of yours?" Javor took another deep breath to calm his rising anger. Preyatel was still, so he knew he was in no danger.

"We don't let armed barbarians into Kerch," said the second guard.

"I am sorry, I did not understand your accent," Javor replied, keeping his voice level.

The guard's expression went from a mocking smile to a frown. He stepped back and lifted his spear.

*He is wide open. A single kick to his knee will bring him down before he could even bring the spear point toward me, and then I'd have my dagger at his partner's throat.*

Instead, Javor held a silver coin to the first guard. "I am pressed for time, friend." He stepped around the second guard and entered the city.

The inn had no name, no sign over the door. The only way Javor found it was by following Pelagios' directions straight up the slope, then asking passers-by. One man wearing a turban pointed at a dilapidated, two-storey wooden house.

Javor knocked on the battered wooden door, which was at the same level as the dirt street, no step nor courtyard. After a long wait, the door opened on a wizened, bearded man in a tattered but clean cloak. His greying hair hung down around his shoulders, merging into a grey beard that extended over his chest. Bushy black eyebrows drew together as he glared up at Javor.

They stared at each other. Javor felt his heart beating. When he felt he had looked into the man's black eyes for too long, he said "Do you have a room?"

The small man's expression did not change. He stepped back and looked Javor up and down like the guard at the gate. Then he took Javor's gaze again. "Who are you?"

"Javor. From Constantinople," he stammered. "The capital."

"Twenty nummi," the innkeeper growled.

"What? That's double the price in Constantinople!"

"Then stay in Constantinople."

Javor bit back his rising anger. *He is taking advantage of me. But I can afford it.* He reached into his purse and tossed a small, tied sack at the innkeeper, who caught it without breaking eye contact. "That's enough for three nights. I want your best room, a jug of ale in the evening and wine in the morning."

The innkeeper whistled, and a thin teenaged boy with a dirty face appeared at his side. "Take him to the big room, overlooking the courtyard," the innkeeper growled, and stalked to the back of the inn.

The boy tugged on Javor's sleeve. "This way, lord." He led Javor up a creaking staircase and down a dark hallway before opening a door.

The room inside was surprisingly large and bright. The shutters were open, letting in the afternoon sunlight. The wooden floor was swept spotless. The walls had been painted a light tan colour, and although faded and scraped in places, also clean. A table bearing a large ceramic jug and bowl for washing stood in one corner, next to a wide bed. Another table stood beneath the window, with a wooden chair in front of it.

*Simple and rough but very clean.* Javor let out the breath he hadn't realized he'd been holding and slipped his pack from his shoulders.

"Meal time is after—" and the boy added a word that Javor had never heard before. Seeing his confusion, the boy tried another expression foreign to Javor, pointing out the window. After some exchange, during which the boy pointed at the sun and then at the church spire in the distance, Javor understood that supper would be in the main room downstairs after the church bell rang for evening prayers, and the sun had dipped below the roof of the basilica.

Javor thanked him, and the boy left. Javor checked the simple bolt, noting that the gap between the door and the jamb would make it easy for the innkeeper, or a thief, to slide a blade through and push the bolt open. He pulled his pack onto his back, loosened his sword and dagger in their sheaths, and left to search for the answers he had come to Kerch to find.

The market was a miserable, dusty, smelly and noisy place. In other words, not unlike every other market Javor had ever been in, just smaller than those in Constantinople. Men in every manner of robe, cape, tunic, hat and other headdress stood behind tables and under awnings, shouting out their wares and haggling over prices with women and men. Some of the people were dark, others fair with hair almost as yellow as Javor's. But no one was as tall.

Behind the tables and awnings, pens and cages held chickens, ducks, geese, mules, horses, sheep and cattle. Javor passed two men arguing over the price of a goose even as one chopped off the bird's head and began plucking feathers.

Javor stopped at a stall and bought a full wineskin. At another, he bought a loaf of bread, and at a third, meat cooking on an open grill. As he passed a bronze coin to the thin, dark-skinned man with a cloth headdress wrapped around his head, he asked, "Do you know where the Enarei are?"

The man looked at him intensely, eyes narrowing. He glanced left, right, over his shoulder. "Never heard of them," he said in an accent that Javor could barely understand.

"The priests of Agrimpasa." The vendor shrugged. "Tabita?"

The meat seller put on an exaggerated display of crossing himself. "I am a faithful Christian. Go away, pagan." He then locked eyes with the customer beside Javor.

Javor hitched his pack higher on his shoulders and moved out of the market. At the last stall in the row, he asked an old man about the Enarei, and earned only a glare in return. As he stepped away, the old man leaned over and spat on the ground.

It took Javor half the day to wander from one end to the other of the miserable little town at the eastern edge of the Roman Empire. But despite the number of times he forced himself to speak to strangers, he failed to learn a single thing about the people he sought, the priests of the ancient Scythian love goddess.

When the sun got low, bathing the city's stone and wooden walls with deep yellow light, Javor trudged back to the inn. He dropped his pack to the floor of the common room and unbuckled his weapons, putting them where they would be in close reach as he sat.

The innkeeper did not even look his way, but the serving boy hurried to bring a jug and cup. Javor gave him a few bronze coins and gulped down a mouthful of ale.

He could smell food cooking somewhere and finished his second cup of ale as the boy began lighting candles on tables and in sconces on the walls. Outside, church bells tolled the evening prayers and people began to appear in the inn's common room, sitting at tables and benches.

Preyatel trembled as the last of the sunlight disappeared from the window. The innkeeper's boy closed and latched the shutters and lit more candles. Javor looked to the door when a stout man came in. He was stocky but appeared powerfully built, with a thick, muscular neck. He wore a calf-length tunica, trousers similar to Javor's, leather shoes and a cloak. A heavy pouch hung from the belt at his waist. When he pulled off his soft cloth hat, his bald head reflected the candlelight.

The man scanned the common room and when he saw Javor sitting at his table, made a beeline for him. He sat heavily on the bench beside Javor. Preyatel vibrated gently under his tunic.

"Are you the one asking about the pagan priests?" he growled. His voice rumbled in Javor's chest.

"Who are you?" Javor asked, edging back so that he could face the strange man more directly. He made certain his weapons were in easy reach.

The stranger leaned closer, eyes shining bright under heavy, furrowed brows. "You're the one from Constantinople, going all over town asking questions no one should be asking." His Greek was grammatically perfect, if tinged with the accent Javor had come to associate with Kerch.

"I never said where I was from. And neither did you."

The stranger's eyes flicked left and right before locking again on Javor. "My name is Stavros. I come from this city. And I am here to warn a stranger against stirring up trouble."

To hide his alarm, Javor poured another cup of ale. "Why is everyone so afraid of talking about the Enarei?"

Stavros pointed a thick, hairy finger at Javor. "Because they're pagan. Idolaters. Devils, every one of them," he spat. "Stay away from them. Don't go around poking your nose where it doesn't belong."

Javor took another gulp of ale. "I'm just asking questions."

"And I told you to stop. In fact, I'd advise you to get on the next ship out of here tomorrow morning. The tide goes out mid-morning, so you'd best be on board soon after sunrise."

"Strange, that a port city like this is so nervous about strangers."

Stavros leaned even closer. "We like travelers just fine so long as they know better than to cause trouble. If you know what's good for you, you'll be gone before you ask another god-damned question. Understand?"

Javor finished his ale. "I understand that no one in Kerch is going to help me."

Stavros stood. "You're damned right, no one in this town is going to help you. So get out."

Javor stood, too, towering a full head above Stavros.

"Have a meal, have a sleep, take a whore if you like," Stavros growled, craning his neck upward to meet Javor's eyes. "Then get on a ship and get out of here." He turned quickly and stalked out of the inn.

Javor watched the door for a long moment until Preyatel quieted. His concentration was only broken when the innkeeper's boy tugged on his sleeve. "Another jug of ale?" he asked.

Javor turned the question over in his mind. *I cannot tolerate speaking to another person tonight.* "No. Red wine. Good stuff. Bring it and my meal up to my room." He picked up his weapons in one hand, his pack with the other, and strode up the creaking stairs.

The boy pushed the door to Javor's room open a short time later, while the last of the sunlight limned the rooftops of Kerch. He held a tray in his hands, on which a jug teetered next to a flickering candle.

Javor took the tray quickly and set it on the table near the window. "What is your name?"

"Michael, my lord." He leaned out the window much farther than Javor thought safe to pull the shutters closed. When he was safely back on the floor, Javor gave him three bronze coins.

The joy on Michael's face quickly clouded. His eyes darted around the room as if he were looking for threats. "My lord—" he stammered.

"Call me Javor."

"My lord Javor, you should not be asking questions about the pagan priests."

"Pagan priests? Do you mean the Enarei?"

Michael squeezed his eyes shut and trembled. He crossed himself. "Yes. That is their hateful name."

Javor sat on the bed, bringing his face closer to Michael's eye level. "Why are they hateful, Michael?"

"They are pagans." Michael leaned close, his eyes wide, arms stiff.

"Devil worshippers. The bishop warns us against them all the time, for they can steal a Christian's soul!"

"Really? How could they do that?"

Michael looked at the door, then at the shutters over the window, as if afraid that the Enarei would come through them at any moment. His voice dropped to a whisper. "The priests are all men, but they dress in women's clothes. They hold their rituals on the flat ground above the smelly water. When a pagan in their community dies, they slaughter his horse and bury it with him. And on their unholy days, they cut willow branches and hold devilish rites above the sea. They worship the devil of the underworld and the sea-God."

"Willow branches?"

Michael shook his head. "I know not why. But they say that the Enarei cut willow branches and throw them on the ground to predict the future." Michael leaned closer, his face distorted with disgust. "They say the priests, all men, then take off their clothes and...consort with one another in great groups."

Javor suppressed a laugh at Michael's distress. "And they perform these rituals here in the town?"

"No!" Michael recoiled. "Christians could never tolerate that!" He looked over both shoulders again before leaning close to Javor and whispering, "They have a place, west of the town, where the flat land comes down close to the smelly lake. Underworld and sea-god together, you see?"

"Yes, I see," although Javor did not. What does flat land have to do with the underworld? He put a hand on Michael's shoulder. "I have something to tell you that you must not repeat to anyone. If you do, you place not only yourself, but the very Empire itself at risk, the Kingdom of Christ on Earth. Do you understand?"

Michael's eyes grew so wide, Javor thought they might roll out of his face.

Javor leaned in so their noses were almost touching. "I am here on a mission from the emperor himself." Michael nodded. "The Enarei are...

part of my mission here to Kerch. I need to know how to find them."

Michael drew back. "But...but why?"

Javor beckoned him closer again. "I am not permitted to tell you that. My mission depends on secrecy. So you promise me not to breathe a word of our conversation. Tell no one I am here on the emperor's mission, nor that I am looking for the Enarei."

Michael thought about that for a moment, then squinted his narrow-set eyes. "But...you have already told everyone in town you are looking for the Enarei."

Javor had to think for a moment, himself. "Yes, and I have been warned against it. So you must not tell anyone else that I continue to do so. Do you understand?"

*People are aggravating.*

"Now tell me, and tell no one else, Michael: how do I find the Enarei?"

# The Enarei

The setting sun lit the canvas in the Enarei camp in yellow and pink. It had taken Javor far longer than Michael had promised to ride a hired horse to the spot the boy said the Enarei lived. Javor dismounted, unable to take his eyes from the encampment.

The tiny Scythian community, now outcasts in what had once been their home, consisted of a tiny village some distance west of Kerch. A long, narrow spit of land extended to the north, separating the Maeotian Lake from a body of brackish water that stank of rot.

The smelly lake.

The community itself seemed to consist of tents erected on the backs of wagons, arranged in circles along the shore. Somewhere beyond them was a corral for the horses or mules that drew the wagons, or so Javor surmised from the smell that came occasionally from that direction.

One thing that Javor did not see was people. Nor dogs, not even a cat. Not a sign of life anywhere in the encampment.

*These are the Scythians, the legendary horsemen of the steppe? The warriors who could shoot their arrows from the back of a galloping horse, and never miss? This is what is left of them?*

But when the edge of the sun touched the surface of the smelly lake, something moved among the tent-wagons.

Javor loosed his sword and his dagger in their sheaths and moved deeper into shadows as other shadows gathered together in the centre of one of the wagon circles. Gradually, he heard a rhythmic chanting.

Javor moved closer, careful not to make any sound. As he reached the wagons, the chanting people filed out through a gap between two wagons, marching to the shore.

As they filed through the gap between two wagons, Javor noticed something they had in common. They're all dressed in women's clothes. Like the rich ladies in Constantinople, the senators' wives.

They wore long silk gowns, brocaded with gold and silver and decorated caps. Silk lace veils hung down to their waists and red leather slippers cushioned their feet. Every layer of each cloak and cape was trimmed and embroidered.

They lined up along the shore of the stinking body of water, raising their arms as they sang. The clouds parted for the last of the sunset, and in the reddish-yellow light, Javor could see they had outlined their eyes with dark pigment.

*What are they chanting?*

Preyatel told him.

"Death to Rome.

Tabita, we pray to you, deliver us from the scourge of Constantinople.

Crush the enemies of your true faith.

Drown the unbelievers, then men of the west.

Bury the invaders.

May your great storms flood their cities and pastures,

May the breath of the underworld bring down their wealthy

May their high and most wise lose their children at once,

May they suffer unbearable woe.

Oh, Tabita, Queen of the Earth,

Call upon Apgrimpasi to kill the Empire of Rome ..."

Javor could tolerate no more. He swept his sword out of its scabbard and stepped in front of the line of priests, his foot sinking into the mud. He brought the point of his sword to the throat of the nearest priest. "Who are you?" he demanded, in Greek.

The Enarei's arms went up over his head, along with those of the cross-dressed man beside him. His eyes were wide, reflecting the yellow sunset." Please," he whispered in Greek.

But down the line, the chanting continued. "Bring woe upon the children of Rome...Breathe death on thy enemies in Constantinople..." The cadences were alien to Javor, but the meaning was clear in his mind. Yet, Preyatel remained still.

Javor closed his eyes, until a vision of his twins appeared behind his eyelids. Giorgia and Charita, limp in their nurse's arms, with Calanthe's tears dropping onto their faces. He had to open his eyes again, so that the fearful face of the Scythian priest pushed away the horrible memory of his children's deaths.

"Who are you?" he repeated, pushing the sword closer to the priest. Blood trickled down the man's neck.

"I am Palakus, priest of our Queen, Tabiti," he rasped. "Please, take your sword away."

Javor let up on the pressure, but kept the tip of his sword close to the priest's throat. "Why are you praying for the death of Roman children?"

Palakus' eyes darted left and right, locking briefly with the priest beside him. Farther down the line, the chanting continued, growing gradually louder. "Because Rome has destroyed our culture, our temples, our people," he stammered. Javor could see beads of sweat on the priest's head. "We once ruled the steppes. Now, we suffer daily under the yoke..."

Preyatel trembled on Javor's chest as the chanting to his right drew louder. "Queen of the Earth, sovereign of the seas, protect us. Send your champions, send your giants, deliver us from threat and danger..."

Preyatel nearly jumped out of Javor's tunic. It felt hot, afraid.

At the amulet's unheard suggestion, Javor glanced over his shoulder, where the surface of the stinking water began to churn and boil.

"What are they saying now?" Javor demanded, although he knew.

"They...they are praying for...aid," the priest whined.

Javor touched the point of his sword against the priest's neck. Palakus leaned forward, forcing the tip of the blade into his neck. Blood flowed and he made a choking sound.

Javor pulled his sword away. "What are you doing?"

"My death brings to life my revenge on you, my murderer," Palakus rasped. Blood bubbled at his lips with his words.

Javor could barely make out the priest's words over the violent frothing of the water behind him and the crescendo of chanting to his right. "Tabiti, breathe death to the children of Constantinople, the bastard inheritors of Rome. Send your champions to defend your faithful..."

Palakus fell to his knees. Javor kept his sword aimed at his chest. The priest on his left knelt with him, holding his arm in support. The rest of the priests continued their chant.

Javor screamed, "Why are you praying for death to Roman children?"

The other priest screamed back, "For revenge. To destroy Rome that we may be free again. To strike back against the celestial god who ravishes Mother Earth!"

Javor looked back once more. A form rose from the churning water, dark against the last red light of the setting sun. The priests' chanting grew louder, faster, almost frantic. *Ecstatic* came to his mind.

The sword in Javor's hand moved. When Javor turned again, he saw that Palakus had grabbed the blade in both hands. Blood streamed between his fingers as he pulled the sword into his chest.

The setting sun flashed red one last time as it sank beneath the waves. Palakus screamed "Death to the children of Rome," and threw himself onto the sword. Blood erupted from his mouth.

A sea-deep groan rumbled behind Javor. He yanked his sword from Palakus' body and turned as the second priest screamed "Behold your death, Roman."

The form in the water rose, straightening into a monstrous, man-like shape. Weeds and leaves hung from broad, misshapen shoulders. Arms as thick as an ox rose, dripping water and muck and the rotting ends of plants.

Javor heard Palakus' last breath rattle out of the bloody hole in his chest as the giant in the water raised its head. Beneath a heavy brow ridge, a single eye opened, a dull yellow light gleaming behind it.

The priests on the shore kept chanting. "Defend us, Tabiti, Queen of the world. Avenge us, Thagimasidas, god of the seas. Join us to the agent of your will."

"Roman fool, you have only eased Palakus' path to vengeance," the second priest sneered. "Killing us will make our *mazan* more powerful. The better to kill you all!"

Javor ended the tirade by slashing the priest's throat. As the man crumpled to the muddy shore, the giant stiffened, then straightened to its full height, more than twice Javor's. Beside it, the water boiled again, and a second dark shape began to rise.

The priests' chanting rose to a frenzy as a second giant rose from the putrid sea. The priests' chant became a ceaseless scream.

Javor closed his eyes in a vain attempt to block the sound, and saw again his twin daughters lying dead in his arms. Something dark inside him broke open. Sword in both hands, he lunged down the shore, swinging wide. A red tide flooded his vision. He swung and slashed, and stopped only when the chanting ended.

His throat was raw. When he lowered his sword, he realized he had been screaming.

A sound like a great tree falling into the water made him pivot on one heel, sword high. Two giants waded out of the water, their steps mashing the corpses of the Enarei priests into the mud. Monstrous hands reached for Javor. He ducked, stepped in under their reach and stabbed upward.

The tip of his sword struck straight and true, but instead of penetrating, caught on the creature's hide. The blade bent, then broke in the middle, the shock wrenching the hilt from Javor's grasp.

With astounding swiftness, the creature grabbed the broken pieces before they hit the ground. It squeezed, then opened its hand, and twisted bits of metal fell to the soft mud.

The hand reached for him then. Javor dropped to the ground, rolled away and sprang up when he hit the fetid water. His great-grandfather's dagger in his hand, he faced the giant as it reached for him again, the immense palm and fingers curving around him.

Javor felt the amulet pulse on his chest. The fingers stopped closing, trembling as an unseen force pushed them back.

Preyatel, he knew. As always, the amulet protected him.

He took the dagger in both hands and slashed with all his might. For a moment, he did not know whether the curved blade had touched the monster. Then the hand fell into the water at his feet, followed by a torrent of black blood that stank like rot.

Javor looked up at the giant's head. Slowly, a hideous maw split it open, and Javor could just see rows of needle-like teeth. It made no sound, but Javor felt waves of astonishment and anguish in his mind.

The second giant leaned over the first's shoulder. Again, Javor heard alien words in his mind, words that he somehow understood. *You have severed a bone of the earth. How came you to bear the sacred weapon?*

Javor listened for a warning, but Preyatel was still. No danger.

"I am the rightful bearer," he answered. "Who are you?"

*We are mazan, called to serve Tabiti, Queen of the world, and Thagimasidas, god of the sea. Despite this wound, we will fulfill our mission.*

"What is your mission?"

*We will strike down the enemies of Mother Earth. We will strive against the Sky to restore balance.*

"Who are the enemies of Mother Earth?"

Hesitation, and then: *The followers of the new celestial god, the usurper who rose from the deserts to the south, who takes many names.*

Preyatel trembled and Javor's heart thudded in his chest. He heard a roaring in his ears. "What names?"

Hesitation again. "What names?" he screamed.

*El,* he heard in his mind. Then the giants turned and strode into the stinking water, sinking to their waists, creating waves of thick, black water and rotting vegetation.

Javor ran after them, but had to stop when the water reached his thighs. The smell was too much to bear. His chest heaved and he spat before turning and struggling his way to shore.

The giants had disappeared into the inky night.

# Pursuing the cyclopes

In the end, Javor found himself doing as the bully in the inn had demanded, if a day late.

He urged the nag he had hired at an inflated price, exhorting it to go as fast as it would. It was nearly midnight when he reached the gates of Kerch, and he had to pay another bribe to get in. By dawn, he was standing on the wharf, asking anyone who would pause for the first ship bound for the mainland of the Empire.

For passage, he paid three times the fare from Constantinople to Kerch. The ship he boarded looked faster than the vessel that had borne him on his outward journey, if smaller. He had to share the cramped cabin with the first mate. But by noon, the coast of the Tauric Peninsula was shrinking behind the stern.

Javor spent the next few days pacing the deck, watching the horizon, stumbling over the crew until the captain brusquely ordered him to sit on the foredeck, "and stay the hell out of the way."

Finally, the horizon ahead of the bow darkened, and by the end of the eighth day out of Kerch, Javor could see the coast ahead. "Helenopontus," the captain said. "We'll make port by tomorrow."

Helenopontus was a province along the southern coast of the Euxine Sea. It was not near Constantinople, but it was as far west as the captain was ready to take Javor. He had no choice but to get off the ship at the first port.

"Port" was a pathetic thing, a tiny wooden wharf outside a miserable little fishing village without protective walls. The crew unloaded a few bales as Javor pulled his pack onto his shoulders and went into the town to find another poor, overpriced horse. Again, he paid far more than he thought it was worth, and worried briefly about his supply of coins.

It was only when he rode along a muddy track beyond the town's wooden stockade that it occurred to him that the ship he had travelled on as the sole passenger must be smuggling, finding a port out of sight of Imperial customs collectors.

He had a bigger worry: how to find the one-eyed giants before they reached Constantinople.

That was not difficult. An hour's ride south of the port town, he came upon a village where the rude wooden homes had been flattened, as if a monstrous foot had stepped on them. What had once been a chicken coop was now splinters mixed with mud and crushed bodies of birds. A dead child lay in front of the remains of a hut, its chest crushed and bloody.

The land became hilly as he rode southward. He stopped and dismounted beside a small, thin man who knelt in mud, praying in front of a mound. A rough wooden cross stuck out of the mud at the far end.

"What happened here?"

The small man looked up at him, eyes unfocused. "Giants," he rasped. "Two giants walked out of the sea. They towered over the houses, smashing them with their great feet."

"When did this happen?" Javor asked, but the man did not answer. He hung his head and began to tremble and weep.

Javor moved on. The giants' trail was not hard to follow: flattened grasses in the pastures, enormous footprints, dead sheep and pigs in the farms. Javor slapped his horse's flank for greater speed, always westward. East-south-east. The hills got higher and steeper as he continued, cliffs rising reddish-brown from the green fields and woods.

*Why are they not heading for Constantinople?*

*To gather allies?*

He urged the horse on, stopping in a dilapidated inn after dark. No one there, innkeeper nor other guests, spoke to him more than necessary. Instead, Javor saw them turn their eyes away when he looked at their faces.

By sunrise, he was moving southeast, following a trail of trampled farms, crushed roofs and shattered walls.

Four days on, he was riding up a steep, narrow valley carved by a swift river. Ahead, the valley opened out. Farms and orchards dotted with houses and small churches covered the relatively gentle lower slopes of the river's bank. On the opposite side, walls of cut stone rose straight up from the bank, squeezing a small city against the grim face of the mountain.

In a cleft between two knees of the mountain nestled a citadel made of more of the stone, so that it looked almost as if it grew out of the rock. As he rode closer, Javor could see activity at the high gates that overlooked the city far below.

He urged the nag to a canter. It snorted in protest, but sped up until they reached a tiny village, just a collection of rude wooden buildings nestled next to a bridge that crossed the stream. One of the buildings had been smashed to bits. Two men and an old woman stood talking in front of the ruin, shaking their heads. They closed their mouths and stared at him as he rode up.

"What happened here?"

No response. The group squinted up at him, jaws set and lips thin. The old woman pushed her scarf back a little, and one of the men shaded his eyes. "Where do you come from?" he growled, stepping in front of the horse.

"Constantinople," Javor said, noticing blood smeared on the shattered timbers of the house. "What is this place?"

"This is Amasya, capital of Helenopontus," said another man, younger, standing on one of the broken timbers. He was dark and small, and wore a ragged tunic.

*That means I have reached the road to Constantinople.* "What happened?" Javor asked, although he knew.

"Two giants came, monsters, ten times the size of a man," the young man continued, his hands waving wildly. "They came up the valley, smashing down homes and farms. They didn't even stop when they smashed down the church! Then they went on to attack the city. They are demons from Persia, sent by that fire-worshipping Khosrau to defile Christendom," the young man said.

They are not that big. Maybe three times the size of a man. Most men. "Persia is east of here. The giants came from the north, beyond the sea," Javor argued. "Did they not damage the bridge?"

"They walked across the river bottom. They sank only to their chests," the young man answered.

"More like to their necks," the older man said. "And they were not just giants. They were cyclopes, with a single eye in the middle of their heads." He turned to Javor. "Are you an equite, then?" He demanded. "If it's a fight you're looking for, warrior, why don't you do something about the devils that did..." He waved his hands to encompass the destruction around them. "...this."

"That is why I have come."

The woman stepped up, squinting even more. She pointed over the bridge. "Then go, warrior! They are attacking the citadel. They have already killed two people here, and one was just a child. It's a fine thing to come now, after the damage is done. Where were you when—"

Javor kicked his horse to a run over the bridge, its hooves clattering loudly on the stones.

*Not just giants. Cyclopes. Powerful beings from mythology come to life.*

*Archons.*

*They called themselves bones of the earth.*

*What am I doing?*

Across the bridge, one of the city gates lay on the ground next to the road, its twisted iron brackets sticking up. The other had fallen into the river.

Javor charged the horse up the steep street toward the citadel, plunging into the shadow of the mountain. Soon he could see the high gates of the fortress, and in front of them, two enormous man-shapes.

One rammed its head repeatedly against the bronze-and-wood gate. Every blow echoed across the plain, shaking the earth and vibrating in Javor's chest.

As Javor urged the horse closer, he could see one cyclops pummeling the wood with a fist and the stump of a severed arm.

Its sibling reached its long arms upward and tore out chunks of stone and brick from the wall. Slowly, a gap appeared near the top.

When a huge chunk of masonry fell and shattered on the ground, Preyatel shook against Javor's chest. The horse jammed its front legs still, skidding over the ground. Thrown forward, Javor's feet flew up over his head and he found himself airborne for a sickening second. Preyatel vibrated again, and then he landed heavily onto his feet. Somehow, his dagger was in his right hand.

He glanced back over his shoulder to see the horse bolting fifty yards away, then turn to look at him. It neighed, stomping the ground with its front hoof and nodding, as if to say, "Run! Get away!"

The cyclopes continued to hammer at the gate and wall of Amasya. He could see archers leaning well over the edge of the wall, shooting arrows that bounced off the attackers' hides.

With every cyclopean blow against the wall, at least one man fell to his death.

The cyclops that still had two hands reached up and dug clawed fingers into the wall. Cracks spread like spiderwebs between and through the blocks. One of the archers toppled off the wall on the outside of the citadel. Somehow, he stood up again until a falling piece of masonry as big as his chest crushed him.

Javor ran toward the monsters, Preyatel vibrating so hard it felt hot. The dagger in his hand thrummed in response, almost singing.

He did not realize he was screaming as he leaped, the dagger in both hands high above his head. He brought it down at the apex of his jump, and it bit deep into the back of the giant at the wall, opening a long fissure that oozed a thick, black, stinking fluid.

Javor landed at the giant's feet, the dagger still in two hands, dripping black liquid. The giant staggered and turned slowly, reaching around its back. High above, its mouth opened so wide, it seemed to split its head in two. A deep, grinding roar issued, yelling anguish and pain. Its body bent at the middle and Javor saw the arms coming around again. Before they could reach for him, he swung his dagger sideways. It sliced through the giant's thick leg as if it were made of bread.

Javor jumped back as the cyclops fell flat on its front. He jumped up onto its back when the monster reached for him. Then the dagger leaped up, pulling his hand upward as he jumped. Javor saw the point of the blade dig into the outstretched remanding palm of the second cyclops. It recoiled, the dagger pulling free of the claw, and Javor fell back to the ground and rolled away.

The first cyclops struggled to rise, black liquid flowing from the wound in its back and dribbling from its maw. Its partner, meanwhile, leaned forward, swinging its stump to smash the tormentor.

Javor stepped forward, ducking the blow. A sweep of the dagger sliced the prone giant's head off. He continued forward, rolling between the remaining cyclops' legs. Jumping to his feet, he swung the dagger behind him, feeling it bite into something.

High above, the cyclops howled in rage and pain. It staggered away from him, focusing its single eye on its dead companion. It bellowed again and turned its singular gaze on him. *Why do you turn the bones of the earth against us, its servants?*

Javor's mind whirled.

*I am the last incorporation of Palakus,* the monster said, its voice a rumble in Javor's mind. *You have slain the final embodiment of the Enarei, the priests of Tabiti. Why?*

Javor thrust the dagger at it, but the cyclops stepped beyond Javor's reach. Its long legs bore it faster than Javor could hope to run, even on a horse.

Then men in leather armour were all around him, slapping him on the shoulder and shouting. It took him some time to understand their words. *Greek*, he realized. *They're speaking Greek.*

The cyclops disappeared in the distance. Javor turned to see the body of the other changing, turning from a dark brown to a dull grey. Its skin disintegrated into ash. Its arms crumbled like a burned log. Soon, all that was left was a pile of dark grey soot that smelled of rot and death.

The wind came up then, lifting the ash in a grey cloud that dispersed into tendrils toward the west.

# Luxury

He let the city's defenders pull him through the gates and into a dim building that smelled of old smoke and candles. When someone pushed a mug into his hand, he realized it was shaking. He collapsed onto a bench and raised the mug to his lips. *Wine,* he thought. He gulped it down without tasting it. When he lowered the mug, he realized a man sitting on the bench next to him had asked the same question at least twice.

"Javor," he said, his own voice sounding strange in his ears. "From the North. But now I live in Constantinople."

The man slapped him on the back. "Javor from the North, that was the bravest thing I have ever seen a man do. I have never beheld cyclopes before. To tell you the truth, I thought they were all gone from the world, if they ever existed outside of old stories."

He sighed. "We lost a number of good, brave men today. Nicephorus, for one. He was the first to see the cyclopes, and shot his arrows to no avail. When those monsters started banging on the gates, he fell from the wall and one of them stepped on him. I thought they would kill us all."

"How did you come to save us just when those ... things came?" asked a small, thin man with a beard. Javor recognized the clothing that marked him as a Jew.

He downed the last of the wine in his cup, and someone refilled it from a jug. "I chased them across the sea," he said.

The Jew scoffed. "Across the sea? Did they swim?"

"As far as I know, they walked on the bottom," Javor answered. "They came from the Tauric Peninsula.

"Did you walk, too?" the Jew demanded.

"Oh, shut up, Joseph," said the man sitting beside Javor. "Is it not enough that he saved the city?"

The light dimmed momentarily as someone new came into the guardhouse. Javor looked up to see a fat, bald man in an ornate tunic and cloak, with a large golden chain around his neck. On each side stood men in full steel armour and scarlet cloaks.

The man with the chain stepped forward, holding his hand out. "Is this the hero of the day?" he said.

"This is the one, my lord," said the man beside Javor, slapping him on the back again. "This is Javor from Constantinople, the man who chased the cyclopes, killed one and drove off the other, and saved us all."

The man in the chain bowed low, hand over his heart. "On behalf of the people and the city of Amasya, sir, I thank you." He straightened and stepped closer. "I am Basil Cauconus, and I am Dux of Helenopontus. No, please do not get up. We are deep in your debt. Please allow me to offer you the hospitality of the city. You will join me for the evening meal, and rest in the ducal palace for the duration of your stay in our city."

"Thank you," Javor replied, finding the mug in his hand refilled with wine. A slave girl appeared at his side with a platter of bread, cheese and meat. "But I cannot stay. I must pursue the cyclops, Palokus."

"Nonsense!" The Dux exclaimed. "You must be tired after your battle with those monsters. I heard all about it. Yours was an exploit worthy of the heroes of legend. You will require rest and restoration."

Javor became conscious of a deep weariness in his limbs. His hands no longer shook, but he felt as if he could not keep his eyes open for much longer. He sighed and rose unsteadily to his feet. "Thank you, Dux. I accept your offer."

"Wonderful!" Cauconus clapped his hands. "Gather our hero's belongings and bring them to the palace. And send word to have accommodations prepared suitable for a hero."

People began to move about, looking busy to obey the governor.

"My belongings..." Javor thought for a long moment. His mind felt clouded. He sipped more wine. "My horse...It's still outside the walls. I think it's waiting for me. It has everything I brought, other than what I am wearing."

Cauconus clapped again. "Dispatch men to find his horse, immediately!" Two men ran out of the guardhouse, shouting. The governor turned to Javor. "What did you lose, sir? All of the resources of the city are at your disposal. You need but ask, and we will strive to accommodate your needs."

Javor found it was getting harder to think. *This must be my last mouthful of wine until I get some food.*

He picked up a wedge of cheese from the platter and bit off a great hunk. "Armour. A helmet. Clothes. A cloak. Some food for the road. A new pack that I only just bought some days ago in Kerch."

"Kerch!" The governor scoffed. "We can supply you with far better gear than any in Kerch. And we will treat you far better than those stingy near-barbarians."

*That will not be difficult,* Javor thought.

A short time later, wearing only the amulet on its silver chain around his neck, Javor lay back in a tiled basin longer than he was tall, sunk into the floor of richly decorated apartments in the governor's palace. Mosaics on the walls depicted stags running across a field. On the opposite wall, a silver goblet sat on the edge near his left hand, filled with wine. Near his right lay his dagger in its sheath, the belt attached.

An older male slave poured steaming water from a jug into the basin, warming the water that lapped over his chest. A slave girl came in carrying sponges. Standing at the edge of the basin, she raised her arms over her head and dropped the shift she wore. Even drunk as he was, Javor marvelled at her flawless beauty. She could not have been out of her teen years, her brown skin unblemished, her breasts small and high, her large nipples a dark brown. Her long black hair hung down to the small of her back, brushing two dimples.

She stepped into the bath, kneeling between Javor's legs. She submerged a sponge, then brought it over his head, squeezing so that water ran over his head and face and shoulders. She gently scrubbed his face, neck and shoulders with a sponge before moving below the surface of the water. The sponge felt slightly rough, invigorating as it swept over his skin. The water began to froth from the soap he had not noticed before.

The slave girl said not a word as she brought the sponge lower. When she caressed his thighs, Javor began to feel the thrill of arousal.

She moved down his legs, then massaged his feet. She moved back up, dragging a delicious path up the insides of his thighs. Her expression did not change as her bare hands spread a little soap on the length of his erect penis and swirled over his testicles.

Javor trembled.

The girl straddled Javor's hips. She put her small hands on his shoulders and pulled him forward until his nose nestled between her small, high breasts. He felt warm water streaming from the sponge down his back. The girl scrubbed gently, her hips getting lower as her hands reached down his back.

He drew a hissing breath through his teeth as her body grazed the tip of his penis. Her hands came slowly up his back to rest on his shoulders, and Javor looked deep into her dark brown eyes. Her face was expressionless as she sank lower.

Javor closed his eyes. *Calanthe,* he thought, but the face inside his eyelids was not his wife, but of another woman.

*Danisa.*

He opened his eyes and gently pushed the slave girl away. "Thank you, but no. I am married." *She is a slave, compelled to pleasure me. I do not want that. Besides, I cannot fuck another strange woman every time I leave Constantinople,* he thought, remembering Miriam at the inn on the road to Antioch.

The slave girl looked at him, the tiniest hint of a smile at the corners of her full lips. "Married," he repeated. "Wife."

She smiled and stood. Javor could not take his eyes from her perfect breasts as water dripped from them. She climbed out of the pool, picked up her shift and walked, naked hips swaying, out of the bath room.

The male slave watched her, too, then turned to beckon Javor out of the bath and to sit on a bench. As he scraped water, soap and dirt off Javor's skin with a curved metal tool called a strigil, Javor wondered why the image of Danisa had come to his mind when he thought of his wife.

"Was the slave girl not to your satisfaction, my lord?" he asked as he wrapped Javor's body with soft, thick cloths.

"She was...wonderful. Thank you."

"Thanks are for my lord, the governor of Helenopontus," the slave replied.

"Yes, well, thank you. Thank him. Tell him 'thank you' from me."

"Very well, my lord. He also commands me to tell you that your horse and belongings have been found."

"Good. But stop calling me 'my lord.' I am not a lord."

"Very well, my lord."

The blare of a trumpet made Javor jump as he entered the governor's big dining hall in the centre of the palace. "His honour, the Lord Javor of Constantinople!" someone shouted, and the hundred or so attendees cheered.

The Dux, the military governor of the province who had found Javor at the guardhouse, had sent sumptuous clothing after Javor's bath: a long tunic with a brocaded border, a heavy cloak, fastened at his shoulder by a copper brooch, soft leather shoes.

A slave with a scar across his nose led him to a table, and as he prepared to sit, he heard another fanfare. "His Highness, the Dux Basil," the slave bellowed. The governor strode in, followed by two guards in full armour and a gaggle of other men.

"Sit, sit," the Dux said to Javor. "It is you we honour this evening."

Javor sank onto a low couch, and the Dux sat on another beside him. Slaves poured wine for them both. The Dux popped a fig into his mouth. "I trust you found the accommodations to your satisfaction, Sir Javor?"

"Very comfortable, sir." Javor took some bread from a slave holding a platter.

The Dux arched his eyebrows. "And the bather? She ... satisfied, as well?"

Javor felt his cheeks get hot. "Y—yes, sir. She was...wonderful." *I do not want to get her into trouble.*

Dux Basil slapped Javor's knee. "'Wonderful'!" He turned to the servant or acolyte or whatever he was to his right. "Did you hear that, Timoteo? He finds the Persian girl 'wonderful.'" He slapped Javor's knee again. "I must say, I heartily agree. I have always enjoyed her fully, myself. She always satisfies." The Dux turned to Timoteo again. "What is her name, again?"

"Negina, my lord," Timoteo said.

"Yes, that's it. Negina." He ate another fig and chased it down with a hearty mouthful of wine. "Oh, and I must tell you, I have more good news for you: your horse has been found, with its supplies. It is now stabled comfortably, and your gear has been brought to your quarters in the palace. But I must tell you, sir, that is a sorry nag. Permit me, on behalf of the province of Helenopontus, to give you a much better mount. A horse fitting for a great warrior such as yourself."

Javor felt uncomfortable about the gift. "Thank you, my lord, but what about the horse I had?"

The Dux shook his head. "Worry not, Javor. It is a poor, old animal, suited only for feeding the dogs."

Javor's stomach lurched. "All the same, I would prefer to keep her. To carry things, so the new horse only has to bear me."

The Dux slapped Javor's knee and roared with laughter. "Clever fellow! Did you hear that, Timoteo? He accepts our gift and makes it even better! Very well, Javor, you may keep your nag as well as a spirited warhorse from the finest breeder in all Pontus." The Dux then sat up straight, leaning close to Javor. He felt his amulet tremble. "Now, you must tell me, Javor of Constantinople, how came you to our rescue today? I have been told that you said you pursued the Cyclopes across the Euxine Sea."

*How much should I tell him? About how the Enarei summoned them out of the muck? No.*

Preyatel quieted with that decision. "I first saw them by a swamp, or a marsh, near Kerch," he said. "They threatened the empire, and in particular, Constantinople. Then they walked into the sea. So I found the first ship I could to take me to the southern shore in hopes that I could intercept them. Fortunately, they were not hard to find on land."

"No, I dare say not!" Dux Basil guffawed. He looked Javor directly in the eye. "But tell me, young sir, what brings you from the capital all the way to far-off Kerch? It certainly does not offer the comforts and amenities of the great city. Even modest Amasya, here, is a shining metropolis in comparison to Kerch."

Preyatel stirred again, a warning.

*Do not worry, my friend. I will tell him only what he needs to know.* "My father-in-law is a merchant in the capital. His ships regularly sail the length of the Euxine Sea."

"A mighty warrior like you, and you married the daughter of a mere merchant?" Basil exclaimed, eyebrows rising high. "I hope he is very rich."

"He is quite wealthy, yes. Perhaps you have heard of him? Mauricius Macedonius?"

The Dux shrugged and sipped wine. "As a military man, I concern myself not with the affairs of commerce. Except insofar as they bring me the things that I need. But I have people to look after the details. My duty lies in protecting the borders and enforcing the emperor's will."

*Military man? With a belly like that?*

"But please, tell me more about yourself," Basil Cauconus continued. "You say you come from Constantinople, but I would wager gold coins that you were not born there—not with fighting skills such as you demonstrated. And judging from your colouring, I would wager further that you come from the North. I dare say, and please do not take offence, but you resemble the northern barbarians, or perhaps the Sarmatians or even the Circassians."

"The Circassians are more often red-haired, my lord Dux," Timoteo interjected.

The Dux scoffed, waving the comment away.

Javor felt as if someone were choking his throat. "I…yes, originally, I came from the lands north of the Empire. I crossed the border as a very young man and settled in the capital."

Dux Basil Cauconus pushed himself up on one elbow, leaning closer to Javor. "And what brought a … brought you to the capital?"

The answer popped into Javor's mind from a place he could not guess. "Jesus Christ. I came to learn about the True Faith."

The Dux's face relaxed and he nodded.

Javor wanted to bring the conversation back to the slave girl. First, though, he needed more wine. "How long have you…had Negina, Dux Basil?"

The governor looked toward Timoteo again, who shrugged. "Oh, I suppose about…two years, now. We acquired her, along with her mother and many other slaves, during a raid on the Saracens. Do you remember that adventure, Timoteo? Glorious!"

"Indeed, Dux," Timoteo agreed.

Javor took sliced meat and a large piece of cheese from another platter. He chewed, but the food seemed to have little flavour. "Her mother?"

The Dux looked confused. He gulped more wine, and a slave refilled his cup. "What about her?"

"You said you took the girl and her mother as slaves at the same time."

The Dux tossed his head, laughing. "Oh, yes! We took hundreds! That was a very profitable adventure, let me tell you."

"And where is her mother, now?"

The Dux shrugged and drank more wine. Timoteo leaned over. "We put her to work on a farm, somewhere. She was not so pretty. The daughter, Negina, as you saw, is quite comely. So we keep her in the ducal palace for bathing and pleasures of the flesh."

"She seems...very young. Even more so if you've...owned her for two years, now."

Timoteo shrugged, an eerie imitation of his Dux. "That's what slaves are for."

Javor could eat no more that evening.

# Pursuit renewed

Javor rose with the dawn the next morning. The male slave from the night before insisted on helping Javor wash and put on the fresh clothes sent by the Dux, and then brought him a huge breakfast of bread, fruit and milk.

By the time Javor got down to the stables, the sun was already above the city walls. As he waited for yet more slaves to bring his horses, he could not help but wonder how long he had been away from home now.

*How long ago was it that I first saw the giants in the Tauric Peninsula?*

*How long since I murdered the Enarei priests?*

*How long since my twin babies died?*

He pushed the thoughts down. He had a new mission, now.

A familiar form hurried across the palace courtyard toward him. Timoteo, accompanied by two servants or slaves, stopped in front of him, puffing. His cloak hung crooked on his shoulders, his belt was loose and sweat beaded on his high forehead. "Sir Javor...I only just learned... that you are..." He put his hand on his narrow chest and panted. His face got redder. Gradually, he regained control of his breathing. "I have heard you plan on leaving us today."

Javor glanced to the right, to see a slave leading the mare from the coastal town, bulging saddlebags already slung across its back.

"Yes, as quickly as I can."

"But so soon? Please, stay for a few days so that we can properly thank and honour you."

Javor shook his head as he glimpsed another horse exiting the stable. "I cannot. I must find the remaining cyclops before it causes much more harm, or worse, recruits help in its mission against the Empire."

"Please, then, accept our gifts of thanks." One of the slaves behind him stepped forward, holding out a cloth bag with bulges that spoke of coins within.

Javor took it and tied it to his belt, tucking it into the folds of his over-tunic. "Thank you." He turned to see two slaves leading the most beautiful horse he had ever seen. It was bigger than any animal he had ever ridden, a bright white colour with a golden mane that moved like water under the sun. It held its head high and stepped high.

Its bridle and saddle were made of heavy black leather, with fittings that shone golden in the morning sun. Hanging from the back of the saddle were a sword and a shield, both polished to a blinding sheen.

The slaves halted the gorgeous stallion in front of Javor. It lowered its great head to look at him, its eyes calm and intelligent. It snorted, tossed its head and stamped its feet.

"What is this?" Javor asked.

"This is the horse that the Dux promised you last evening," Timoteo answered, still puffing. "Three years old, bred and trained in the finest stables in Pontus."

Javor reached out and brushed the horse's face, lingering over its unbelievably soft nose. The horse snorted again, softly. "He likes you, sir," said the slave holding the bridle.

"As you can see, his Highness the Dux has also given you a new sword and shield, fitting for a hero," Timoteo continued. He had regained most of his control over his own breathing and dabbed a white cloth to mop up the sweat on his forehead.

"Thank you," Javor said. He grabbed the saddle and vaulted onto the horse's back. It stepped a little, tossed its head and snorted, but overall its reaction was less than the mare's.

The slave tied the mare's reins to a loop on the stallion's saddle. Javor knocked his heels against the animal's flanks and it cantered toward the gate.

Timoteo ran to keep up. "Please, won't you reconsider? The Dux is planning a special day in your honour."

"Every minute I stay here, the giant gets closer to the capital."

"Will you at least wait long enough for us to arrange some legionnaires to accompany you?"

Javor reined in, making the stallion snort again. Timoteo bumped into the horse's side and recoiled. "No. Absolutely not. I must do this alone."

"Why?" Timoteo wheezed.

"Because almost every man who has ever accompanied me on a mission has died." He flicked the reins and rode through the open palace gate.

As he had found on landing on the Euxine coast, the giant's trail of destruction was not hard to follow: crushed houses, dead animals, broken bones and weeping children. But the trail surprised Javor by bending to the south, instead of west toward the capital.

The first sign was the spot where the first cyclops fell. There was no trace of the grey ash left, but the place where the giant had fallen was now overgrown with a thick, rich garden of grass, flowers and other plants.

The stallion needed little guidance to follow the path that the remaining cyclops had crushed through fields of grain. They passed farms and villages. The giant—*archon*, Javor reminded himself —had avoided larger towns and the smooth roads the Romans had laid down.

When the sun passed the midpoint of the sky, Javor paused to feed the horses, and himself, from the supplies the Dux had given him. He sat on soft grass and looked up at the high blue summer sky. His eyes followed wispy clouds toward the south.

It occurred to him that his current chase was similar to his first quest, when he had followed the old mystic, Photius, to hunt down the monster that had killed his parents.

*No—that was my second quest. The first was when I went to rescue Elli and Grat from the Avars.*

The monster of the second quest had been similar to this one. Big, man-shaped. Ghastog had come for Preyatel, Javor's amulet, when he had left it behind in his parents' hut.

He had not known, then, how important the amulet could be. He had not learned about its protective power, had not named it then.

He had not felt its voice in his own mind.

Somehow, it felt important to recall the events in the order they had occurred. Javor thought back to that day—*how many years ago, now?* His sixteenth birthday, the summer solstice in his home, far to the north of the borders of the Roman Empire.

It had been the solstice celebration, the *kupalo*, when his people prayed for a bountiful growing season. They had gathered near the stream, vulnerable in their finest clothing and flowers, when the mounted raiders had ridden in, trapping them outside their little stockade.

*Although that would not have been much protection against the Avars.*

The raiders had maimed the village hetman and killed another man, whose name Javor could no longer remember. Then they had stolen food and supplies, and taken the two prettiest young women for their amusement.

One of them had been Elli. Javor loved Elli, even though she seemed to alternately despise and fear him. Javor tried to picture her in his mind, but it was hard now, so many years later. He remembered what she had looked like on his brief visit home—*how many years had passed since then? It had been before Adam was born. Or maybe while he was being born.*

But Javor struggled to remember what Elli had looked like when she was 16, like him. *Thin,* he remembered. *Not that she got much heavier after having children.*

*I wonder, if she had lived in a city like Constantinople, and eaten well every day, would she be fat as Calanthe?*

*Concentrate on that day, Javor.*

The Avars had taken the two girls, and the adults of the village had let them. Just watched as they had thrown Elli and Grat over the backs of horses, tying them as if they were pigs, and ridden away.

Javor had gone to his parents' little hut, and found the weapon his mother had shown him only days earlier. This was your great-grandfather's dagger, his mother had said. He took it from a giant he killed in the far-away mountains when he was in the army of the Roman emperor. The dagger was unlike anything Javor had ever seen before. The curved blade, engraved with whorls and angles and strange shapes, the dark colour, unlike any metal he had ever seen, before or since, the handle shaped like a fish.

He realized his hand was stroking the handle, his fingertips tracing the edge of the sheath.

He had taken the dagger and followed the trail left by the horsemen. His only friend, Hrech, had come with him, more to try to persuade him to give up the futile quest than to help.

It had felt hopeless: two young men, boys, really, on foot, chasing mounted steppe archers. But the trail across the grasslands was obvious. After dark, when Hrech was exhausted almost to the point of collapsing, they had arrived at the Avars' camp.

He remembered how they had found the two girls, tied, naked, huddled together under a tree, weeping. He remembered cutting their bonds with his great-grandfather's blade.

He remembered finding the Avars. The severed head, still wearing a helmet, rolling under the high full moon.

The dismembered bodies scattered on the ground.

The naked fear when he saw that their bodies had been pulled apart, the way he pulled a roasted chicken apart.

And when they had returned, finally, to the village as the sun rose again, how he found another scene of destruction.

The stockade knocked down.

The dead bodies and the crippled people who glared at him.

He forced his mind's eye forward. To his parents' home, smashed down into the earth.

His father's broken body in front of it, still holding a scythe as a weapon.

His mother under the broken roof, her neck snapped.

Tears had dripped onto his hands when he had lifted his mother's tiny body from the ruins of her home, and Javor realized that his face was wet again. He blinked, clearing his vision, and wiped his face with his sleeve.

*Time to get moving again.*

He packed up, readied the horses and was moving southward again in only minutes.

# Into the cave

The cyclops' trail led due southeast for days. It skirted the larger towns, but stamped through small villages. Javor rode past shattered houses, trampled pig pens, bodies of chickens and children mashed into the ground, mothers wailing beside little graves.

Every so often, Javor saw clues that told him he was slowly catching up with the giant. The footprints in the mud looked fresher, wetter. Dead animals and people seemed fresher.

And then there were the seared, blackened circles on the ground, bare soil or spots of burned, shriveled grass or grain. After a few days, he realized that these were the spoor of the cyclops' blood, the black ichor that withered everything it touched.

One large spot stood out: a black hole filled with dead branches and leaves. In the centre stood a wide, low bush covered in broad, deep green leaves with serrated edges and blood-red flowers. Unlike the surrounding plants, these flowers thrived.

*What does that mean?*

He sheltered in a farmhouse that bore the scars of war on a day when storms chased each other across the sky. He knew the following day would bring a steady drizzle. In the morning, he brought out the preparations he had made for days like this: light canvas that covered both rider and horse.

On the tenth day, he caught up to the cyclops where the trail plunged into a canyon carved by a narrow stream. The giant limped along, smearing black ichor on the rocky cliff.

Javor urged the beautiful gift horse faster, but it balked, snorting and tossing its head. The pack horse behind bumped into them, clattering the gear strapped to its back.

Javor kicked his heels against the horse's sides and shook the reins. The white stallion cantered ahead a few steps but stopped again, its hooves scattering loose stones. It whinnied, the sound bouncing off the cliff walls on either side of the stream. Javor had to hold onto the saddle horn to keep from falling off as the white horse backed up, jostling him when it bumped into the pack horse. It stomped its hooves in response.

The archon's back straightened. It turned to look back over its shoulder and quickened its pace, moving at an astonishing speed along the narrowing path.

It stopped where the stream frothed out of a sheer rock face. The cyclops looked one-eyed at Javor. The stallion screamed, tossing its head. Javor fell against its neck when the pack horse bumped into its hindquarters, getting a mouthful of mane.

The cyclops picked up a rock the size of the horse's head and hurled it toward Javor. Javor felt the amulet tremble, and the boulder's path curved. It splashed into the stream behind him, and rolled away, harmlessly.

The cyclops blinked slowly, once, then stepped into the rushing stream. The water surged white over its ankles. It bent, slumping its shoulders, and melted into the rock face.

*Where did it go?*

Javor kicked his heels into the stallion's sides, but it refused to move. "Ah!" he cried as he dismounted. He loosened the dagger in its sheath and took the stallion's reins, pulling it upstream. The stallion tossed its head, snorting, but let Javor lead it up to the rock face. Behind it, the pack horse came calmly.

It was only when he stood next to the cliff that he saw that the stream curled out from around a high wrinkle in the rock face. Behind the wrinkle was an opening to a deep cave, high and wide enough for a horse. With the rushing water came the smell of wet rock and rotting leaves. The only way in was to wade.

Javor peered in, but could see no farther than the length of his arm. It was as if the cave ate the daylight that entered it.

He unsheathed his dagger and stepped into the stream. He felt a shock travel all the way up his leg and his back as the frigid water surged over the top of his boot. He clamped his jaw and stepped farther, fighting the current that pushed him back.

But when he stepped into the cave, his left hand was wrenched back so hard, it hurt his shoulder. The white stallion whinnied in protest, refusing to enter the darkness.

Javor turned to take the reins in both hands, awkward because he still held the dagger. The wide-eyed stallion screamed and pulled, tearing the reins out of Javor's hands. Hooves splashing in the stream, it backed away until it could turn around, then squeezed past the pack horse and bolted down the narrow path.

Javor emerged from the cave, wet to his waist, to see the stallion's hindquarters disappear behind a boulder. The pack horse looked after it, too, and snorted. It turned to look at Javor.

"You are right. What a coward," Javor said.

He sheathed his dagger, and then realized that the amulet, Preyatel, was still. No danger ahead.

He took the pack horse's reins, and it followed him without protest into the cave.

The light from the opening faded quickly to near total blackness. The sound of rushing, gurgling water filled the space and echoed in Javor's chest.

He stepped slowly, placing his feet carefully into the water to find a solid landing. The current pushed him back, swirling over his knees and into his boots.

When the last of the light from the cave mouth disappeared, Javor realized he could still see. A faint radiance revealed a bend in the stream bed ahead. He looked up, but there was only blackness.

*How high is this tunnel?*

Around the curve, the light was brighter. The source of the phosphorescence seemed always to be behind a boulder or a fold in the cave wall, but he could never find it.

After a few more steps, he could see that the stream narrowed, and there was a relatively flat area of the cave floor beside it. He gratefully stepped onto the drier ground, surprised to feel sand under his feet. He led the horse out of the water, then leaned on a convenient boulder to pull his boots off and dump the water out.

He looked up again, but still could not see the roof of the cave. He thought about riding the horse instead of walking, then discarded the idea. There was no way of knowing when the cave roof would get too low.

That was the moment he heard the whispers.

He shook his head and pulled his wet boots back on. *It's just the sound of the water swirling over the sand.*

"Why Javor ..."

*Just the water.* He tapped his foot to confirm the floor here was sandy. *Water moving over sand sounds like a whisper.*

"Why Javor..." so soft, at the very edge of audibility, so low he wondered whether he imagined it. "Why Javor?"

He took the reins and led the horse up the path. It grew wider, as the stream became wider and shallower and the light grew brighter.

The whispers grew stronger, as well. "Why Javor? Why Javor? Why Javor?"

"Why what?" His call echoed off the rock walls.

No more whispering.

Javor looked back, into the inky blackness. The light behind him, where he had come from, had faded. He turned: the light ahead glowed brighter, beckoning him. He took a firmer grip on the reins and walked on, reassured by the slow clop of the horse's hooves.

Around another bend of the stream, the path widened out yet more. The light concentrated into a single source ahead on the path: a shimmering, shifting blue-green shape that slowly coalesced into a human form.

Preyatel vibrated softly: Danger.

Javor and the horse continued. The diffuse light along the rock walls faded as it concentrated. When he was perhaps ten paces from it, Javor could see it was a woman.

*No. Three women. There are three women in this tunnel.*

He did not bother wondering where they had come from, for he recognized the face of the woman in the middle.

Hekate, who had come to him at Vorona's hut in Sklavenia, and again at the gate to Antioch.

The women on either side of her faced away, one to the left, the other to the right. To his right, Hekate's left, was a girl of perhaps 15 or 16 years. On the right, an old woman, her face bearing deep lines, her hair hanging limp and ragged to her shoulders.

Hekate looked at him, her face at once impassive and intense. As she had before, she spoke in his mind, without moving her mouth.

JAVOR. WHY DO YOU PURSUE AND KILL MY SERVANTS?

"Your servants? Do you mean the cyclopes? They brought pestilence to my city. They killed my babies."

THEY DID NOT. This voice seemed to come from the young woman to his right.

THEY ROSE FROM THE FERTILE MARSH AND YOU ATTACKED THEM IMMEDIATELY.

"They were summoned by the pagan priests, the Enarei. They were called to bring disease to Romans," Javor argued.

This time, the voice came from the crone.

THEY WERE SUMMONED BY THE ENAREI TO PROTECT THE WORLD FROM ROME.

"I heard them praying for plague," Javor countered. He did not notice that the horse was backing away slowly.

THEY PRAYED FOR RELIEF FROM THEIR OPPRESSORS, SAID THE MAIDEN. THE BISHOPS OF THE CELESTIAL GODS PERSECUTE THEM.

"What has that to do with my children?"

This time, the woman in the middle spoke without moving her lips.

YOU WERE TOLD, YEARS AGO, THAT YOU ARE CAPABLE OF WONDROUS DEEDS. YOU WERE SUMMONED ONTO A PATH. BUT YOU HAVE STRAYED FROM THAT PATH TO SERVE THE CELESTIAL ARCHONS.

The blue-green light swelled around the women, and Javor could see beyond them that the tunnel divided into three openings. As one, the women slid to the side without moving their limbs.

CHOOSE YOUR PATH, JAVOR. CHOOSE WISELY TO RESTORE BALANCE AND END THE STRIFE AMONG THE GODS.

The light moved from the three women into the tunnels, illuminating each one a short distance. In front of Javor's eyes, the women faded, became transparent and dark.

"Wait! Where is the cyclops?" Javor reached out to the centre woman, but touched only the damp air of the tunnel.

He shivered, cold from his wet boots.

*Three paths to choose from. Only one is the right choice.*

The opening on the left was the widest of the three, broad and high enough for two horses to pull a cart or a chariot. The floor looked smooth, as far as Javor could see, with a slight downward slope. Javor pulled the horse toward it to peer a little farther, but the horse pulled back, snorting.

In the centre, the path was narrower, but still wide enough for Javor and his horse—even high enough to ride, for a short distance at least. The floor was not as smooth nor as straight. In the bluish light, the tunnel seemed to curve slightly, descending for a short way and then rising again.

Javor moved to the right-most opening. This one was too narrow and low for the horse, and it rose steeply. The bottom and the walls were rough, strewn with rocks that looked loose and treacherous. But the light was stronger, and the air seemed to bear a faint fresh breath.

*Which to choose? The one on the left will be easiest. The one on the right means I'll have to leave the horse behind.*

He shrugged. *Then the middle, it is.*

*But how am I supposed to end the strife among the gods?*

# The middle path

It was only after Javor had walked for some time along the middle tunnel that he noticed the stream was no longer a part of it.

Had it ended—or rather, begun where the three tunnels branched off? Or did it come from that narrowest cave that led upward?

Whatever the fate of the spring, the path that Javor led his horse along continued smooth, gently rising and falling and bending easily left or right.

*How long have I been in these tunnels?* he wondered. *Is it still daytime above ground?*

He recognized then that he felt thirsty. The horse must be thirsty, too.

*Hekate, or whoever that was, told me to choose wisely. But she didn't tell me whether the water from that stream was safe to drink.*

*Gods are useless.*

The light grew stronger as he went, becoming slowly warmer, more yellow-green than blue. The air began to smell fresher, cleaner. The scent shifted gradually from stuffy, wet stone to rich, damp earth.

The tunnel opened out and Javor found himself in a wide open space. He wondered briefly again about how deep underground he was and how long he had been in the earth, until his attention was overwhelmed by what he saw.

He stood at the outer ridge of a great space. The only thing in his experience that he could compare it to was the immense hippodrome in Constantinople.

*This is bigger. Thrice the size? Ten times?*

Ahead of him, the floor of the natural theatre sloped gently downward. To either side, the curving rock walls arched away from him on either side, fading into darkness.

Warm, diffuse, greenish-yellow light emanated from below. He walked forward, the horse pacing him. The reins hung slack between his hand and the horse's bridle.

The light came from an immense glowing lake. Wavelets lapped at the stony shore, creating ripples in the light and shadows on the walls high over his head. The water was clear, but he could not see the bottom farther than a pace from the edge.

His eyes scanned the surface from the rippling shore, outward, farther and farther until they reached a looming shadow that rippled with yellow-green light. He realized he was looking at land rising out of the middle of the underground lake. On the left side of the island, a ledge extended outward. To Javor, it looked like a gigantic shoulder and the side of a neck that rose high, disappearing into darkness at a height he dared not guess at. He could not see the other side of the neck, nor the opposite shoulder.

There was a confusing shadow, though, on the shoulder of rock. He came closer to the shore, puzzling at what he saw. He did not let his feet touch the water at the edge, and watched to make certain the horse did not drink, either. The moving, rippling yellowish light moved over the horse's flanks, but it did not bend its neck.

*It is smart enough not to risk drinking,* Javor realized.

A shadow reached from the shoulder of rock in the lake all the way across to the shore. As he came closer, he could see that it was a huge column of black rock, a pillar that had broken at its base on the island, and toppled. It had stood so high that it now reached across the lake.

Even farther: pieces stretched in a broken line up the rocky shore, disappearing where the yellow-green light of the water faded into darkness. As he came closer, Javor could see that the pillar's surface was rough and pitted.

What he saw beyond the toppled column made his heart stop for a second.

The cyclops stood waist-deep in the water, holding the pillar with its remaining hand. It turned its one-eyed gaze to Javor, then slowly, maybe even sadly, turned to look across the underground lake.

Javor needed another moment to comprehend the shadow spreading in the water below the giant.

*The light comes from the water, from below. So it would not cast a shadow downward.*

*Then what is that dark stain in the water?*

Understanding was a shock from his heart to his fingertips.

*It is dissolving.*

As if it heard his thoughts, the giant turned to Javor again. The yellow light behind its single eye glowed brighter for a moment as its thoughts reverberated in Javor's skull. *Farewell, warrior. When we sensed you arriving in Taurida, we expected you to be our ally. We do not understand why you turn against Mother Earth.*

"What is happening?" Javor asked, his voice a coarse whisper.

The cyclops sank lower into the water as its body continued to dissolve. A dark stream of suspended grit drifted toward the unseen centre of the lake.

*I return to Abzu, the parent of all life. I bring the spirits of Palakus and the other Enarei, to combine our waters with the source of all waters.* Javor watched it sink slowly into the glowing water, its body dissolving into a cloud that streamed away. Slowly, the yellow light in its eye dimmed, then went black as the surface of the water touched it.

The giant was gone.

Javor felt dizzy. He reached out to steady himself against the toppled pillar. Too late to stop him, Preyatel began to vibrate, so hard it buzzed against his chest.

At the moment his palm touched the rough, black surface of the column, Javor jolted straight. His eyes closed and his mind filled with visions.

*No. Memory.*

# Ullikummi's dream

Javor did not see what happened. He remembered.

Waves dashed white at the base of a beautiful cliff of white and green and blue that rose from an endless blue-green sea. The waters roared as they hit the cliff, hissed as they sank down its curves.

Wind pushed white clouds over the cliff's green top, rustling Javor's hair, filling his nose with the scent of saltwater.

The light shifted, dimmed. Shadows deepened across the cliff face, revealing an undulating surface that gleamed in the nearly horizontal light. Rain began to fall, making the marbled cliff glisten.

A man rose from the sea. No, not a man: a god, an exaggerated version of the ideal human physique. Immense, shoulders far wider than Javor had ever seen, a beard that hung down over his chest. Leg muscles bulged as it strode, ankle-deep across the sea.

Horrifying in its beauty.

His genitals were all out of human proportion, huge and heavy. The god pressed himself into the rock face. Hips and buttocks flexed and the cliff face rippled, shimmering in ecstasy.

Lightning flashed. Rain came down hard, driving against the cliff face. Wind whipped the waves against the god's ankles and the cliff's feet.

The god's hips thrust one more time. The wind sighed. Or was it the cliff?

The god pulled away from the cliff face, turned and sank into the sea. The wind died away, the waves calmed. The cliff face shimmered once more, and then slowly, slowly, sank lower. The top tilted back, reducing the sheer face to a steep slope. A long shadow appeared down the face, then darkened. Deepened. It split, slowly opening. A shape rose from the opening, a pillar of dark rock that grew, and grew, rising skyward.

The god reappeared and took the pillar in its arms. Although the pillar was several times longer than the god, he carried it like a baby.

The god carried the pillar to a lake with water that glowed yellow-green. It walked across the surface of the water to a rocky island in the water, where a mountain bigger than anything Javor had ever imagined rose to the sky.

The god placed the pillar on a flat space on the rock, which emerged above the level of the water like a shoulder, before ascending to heights that Javor could not guess at.

The god vanished, and the rock pillar grew higher and higher. It rose past white clouds to a great palace, larger than even the emperor's Great Palace in Constantinople.

The black pillar burst through the palace's floor, into a great chamber where another god, man-shaped too, with long black hair and a short beard, sat on a throne the colour of the sunrise. He held three thunderbolts in one hand and an axe in the other. Beside him on a twin throne sat a goddess with long, dark hair and a sky-blue gown.

The black pillar smashed the walls of the great golden palace, the noise echoing across the skies. It tore open great rents in the marble floors. Huge chunks of marble tumbled through the blue sky, shattering as they plummeted to the earth below.

The long-haired god sprang to his feet, roaring in pain and anger. The sky went from blue to black. Lightning flashed, thunder vibrated in Javor's chest and feet. Rain gushed onto the black pillar, to no effect.

The golden palace shattered with a sound like a landslide and heartbreak. The god and goddess fled.

Javor saw the god and goddess approach another god, man-shaped as well but tall and thin, with a long, pointy beard that reached his waist. The thin god dove into the glowing water. He swam to the bottom and picked up a long tool with teeth along its length.

The thin god attacked the bottom of the black pillar. He sawed through the base and Javor felt the stabbing, tearing agony in his ankles.

Javor opened his mouth but he could not scream. He could not move.

Javor's vision went black as he felt himself teeter. He felt teeth inside his legs, ripping his flesh until he felt himself topple.

After a time he could not measure, vision returned. The pain in his ankles became a searing memory. He looked down: his legs, his boots were intact. No blood.

Motion caught his attention. On the flat rock, the black pillar fell over, across the glowing water. Its top hit the far, rocky shore, shattering into pieces.

Waves surged outward over the lake. Somehow, Javor could see them travel across the seas, all around the world, drowning shorelines, washing away villages and seaports.

Javor's sight returned to his own eyes. He was looking at the pillar that his hand rested on. Beyond the pillar, on the shore, the pack horse stood, tossing its head.

Before he could decide what to do, the pillar vibrated under his hand.

He understood the vibration as words. I AM ULLIKUMMI. KNOW ME.

I AM THE OFFSPRING OF KUMARBI, THE KING OF HEAVEN, WHO FATHERED ME ON THE CLIFF, SERTAPSURUHI, WHEN TESHUB, MY HALF-BROTHER, REBELLED AGAINST OUR FATHER. OUR FATHER PLACED ME ON THE SHOULDER OF UPILLUMI, THE DREAMER.

"I knew it looked like a shoulder!"

MY DESTINY WAS TO UNSEAT TESHUB, THE SKY GOD

WHO HAD USURPED MY FATHER'S THRONE. I DESTROYED TESHUB'S PALACE, IMPERVIOUS TO HIS LIGHTNING AND RAIN. TESHUB FLED WITH HIS WIFE, THE QUEEN HEBAT. HE SOUGHT THE HELP OF ENKI, THE CLEVER GOD, WHO BROUGHT THE TOOTHED WEAPON FROM THE BOTTOM OF THE MOTHER OF ALL WATERS. ENKIL SEVERED MY FOOT, TOPPLING ME.

"Did Teshub resume the throne of the gods?"

I KNOW NOT. I HAVE BEEN LYING HERE, SENSELESS THESE AGES, REMOVED FROM THE SKIES, BUT NOT IN THE ETERNAL WATERS OF LIFE. YOU MUST ASK UPELLURI, THE DREAMER, WHO HOLDS THE SKY ABOVE THE EARTH AND OBSERVES EVERYTHING IN HEAVEN AND EARTH.

"Upelluri." Javor looked across the glowing lake to the mountain where Ullikummi's base rested. He turned to look at the horse, which seemed to have calmed.

He removed the pack and other gear from the horse's back. "It seems we have to part ways now. Thank you, horse. You are a true friend." He patted its nose, gently.

The horse snorted, then lay down on its stomach on the ground, folding its legs beneath it. Javor put on his helmet and the burnished armour the Roman Dux had given him. He checked his dagger was secure on his belt, tightened his straps, and then climbed up the uneven surface of Ullikummi.

He stood on top, on what had been the pillar's side when it had stood on the shoulder of the mountain god. Preyatel was still, assuring him that he was in no danger.

He took a careful step forward, then another. The pillar's rough, uneven surface helped make it less slippery, safer to walk on.

And then he began the journey over the glowing lake, the mother of all waters, keeping his eyes on the far side, the mountain god named Upelluri.

# Upelluri

As Javor carefully stepped along the length of the broken pillar that was Ullikummi, Preyatel began to vibrate.

*Danger.*

*We need answers. Information, old friend.*

The glowing water fascinated him, drawing his eyes downward. He forced himself to watch his feet as he slowly made his way across.

By the time he reached the far end, his knees wobbled with exhaustion. He sighed in relief as his foot touched the broad stone on a far side.

*Hold, human.* The voice came from every direction at once, so loud that Javor felt vibrations in his chest. He fell to his knees, hands over his ears.

He looked across the glowing lake and saw the horse step into the water. "No! Go back!" He waved his arms, but the horse waded in and began swimming.

As it came, it accelerated. Waves rippled ahead of its chest, fading in a v-shape behind it. As the horse got closer, the waves at its chest began to froth white. By the time it climbed out to stand behind Javor, it looked young again, strong, muscles rippling under its short hair.

*How?*

YOU HAVE REACHED THE SOURCE OF LIFE, the voice echoed

through Javor's body. Javor clapped his hands over his ears again, swaying against the pain. DRINK, HUMAN.

Javor looked up at the mountain rising into darkness over his head.

DRINK AND LIVE.

At that moment, he saw Tiana in front of his eyes. Tiana, looking older than he had ever seen her. Thin, her face drawn. Weak. She smiled a little and nodded at him before the vision faded.

Trembling, Javor cupped his hands and scooped water from the underground lake into his mouth. It was warm, gentle, and clear.

*It tastes like the purest water I have ever drunk.*

STAND, HUMAN, said the voice of the god on whose shoulder he stood. Its volume had not decreased at all, but it no longer hurt. LOOK AROUND YOU.

Javor would never be able to understand it or even describe it. He could see the entire world as if from an immense height. Still, the glowing lake stretched out before him.

He turned around, seeing mountains and seas and rivers. Cities of men, ships crossing water, armies marching. Vast plains of ice and snow gleamed at the farthest reaches of the world, north and south.

And scattered across the world, glowing beings struggling against shadowy ones.

"What ... what is this?"

BEHOLD THE EARTH.

Javor looked up at the towering mountain that was the god Upelluri.

"Are you one of the Bones of the Earth?" Javor asked.

I HAVE HEARD THAT PHRASE, BUT RARELY. IT IS...AS CLOSE TO A VALID METAPHOR AS YOUR KIND CAN COMPREHEND.

THE HURRIAN HUMANS CALLED ME THE DREAMING GOD, BUT I AM NOT DREAMING. I SEE EVERYTHING. I HAVE SEEN THE RISE OF MOUNTAINS AND THEIR SLOW WEARING AWAY. I HAVE SEEN CONTINENTS MOVE, RIVERS SHIFT, SEAS FILL AND DRAIN.

I HAVE SEEN THE RISE OF THE SPECIES CALLED HUMAN. I HAVE SEEN YOUR KIND RAISE CITIES AND SMASH THEM DOWN. I HAVE WATCHED YOUR CONSTANT WARS AND THE RIVERS OF YOUR OWN KIND'S BLOOD YOU HAVE SPILLED.

I HEAR THEM, TOO. I HEAR THEM CHANT AND SING AND PRAY TO IMAGINED GODS THAT ARE MERE SHADOWS OF THE TRUE POWERS OF THE WORLD. AND I HAVE SEEN THOSE POWERS OCCASIONALLY RESPOND.

"Do you mean the Christ?"

Another pause.

THE CHRIST...WOULD BE DIFFICULT FOR YOU, A HUMAN, TO UNDERSTAND. CHRISTOS IS ONE OF THE FIRST EMANATIONS FROM THE PLEROMA. WHAT YOU HUMANS CALL 'THE CHRIST' IS AN APPROPRIATION OF THE TERM. THE HUMANS WHO WORSHIP THE CHRIST CALL IT 'THE SON OF YAHWEH.' THAT, TOO, IS AN APPROXIMATION OF THE TRUTH. BUT TO UNDERSTAND, YOUNG HUMAN, TURN TO THE SOUTH.

*South?* Javor turned, looking far down at the curving surface of the earth. He turned around to see more mountains that suddenly swept down to a green plain. Two broad rivers twisted in rough parallels to a deep inlet of the sea.

*The Euphrates and the Tigris.*

Beyond them, the land became steadily more brown, drier, until it became a desert, an ocean of sand.

And in the midst of that desert, where the parched sand met a dark blue, narrow sea, a city of sand stood. Hanging in the air above it, a god in the image of a dark-haired person, its sex indistinguishable, arms over its head, robes fluttering around its body.

The god turned and glided north, to a city on the banks of a river that flowed down to a black lake.

Above the city, another god hovered, also human-shaped, also androgynous but smaller, dimmer. Its eyes were intent on the city below, watching as people cooked, ate, worked, had sex, bartered and prayed.

The southern god glided through the air high above the curved, uneven earth toward the dimmer one that watched it get closer. The two reached out, touched hands. They glowed bright, so bright Javor's eyes smarted, but he could not look away. The two gods melted into one another, became one, then rose higher, brighter every moment until they spread across the sky like a great, glowing cloud.

"I don't understand," Javor said in a small voice. "Was that...God?"

WHAT YOU HUMANS CALL 'GOD' IS SIMPLISTIC AND VARIED. TO PUT IN TERMS YOU CAN COMPREHEND, YOU HAVE WITNESSED THE ACTIONS OF ARCHONS.

"I know about archons."

Upelluri's voice made Javor's chest vibrate.

THEY ARE EMANATIONS OF THE FULLNESS OF THE UNIVERSE, AS AM I, BUT PARTIAL, IMPERFECT. ARCHONS REFLECT OR CHOOSE PORTIONS OF THE FULLNESS. THEY HAVE ALWAYS INHABITED THE MATERIAL WORLD, ALTHOUGH THEY ARE NOT OF IT. THEY ARE FROM THE CELESTIAL REALMS BEYOND THE MATERIAL UNIVERSE. THEY MOVE, THEY DIVIDE, THEY UNITE CONSTANTLY.

SINCE THE EMERGENCE OF HUMANKIND, MANY HAVE INTERACTED WITH WOMEN AND MEN. THEY HAVE APPEARED AS GODS AND ANGELS, DEMANDED WORSHIP, LOVED AND HATED HUMANS. THEY HAVE ENCOURAGED WARS, REVEALED WISDOM. OFTEN, THEY HAVE TAUGHT AND AIDED HUMANS. SOME HAVE REVEALED THE TRUE NATURE OF THE UNIVERSE, EVEN THE FULLNESS.

"Fullness...what Tiana calls the 'pleroma'?"

THAT WORD IS ALSO AN APPROXIMATION OF REALITY. REMEMBER, YOUNG JAVOR, THAT THOUGH I, OR ANOTHER ARCHON MAY SHOW YOU THE TRUTH, THE HUMAN MIND CANNOT GRASP THE EXTENT OF THE FULLNESS,

THE UNIVERSE. THE FINITE MIND OF HUMANITY FAILS IN THE FACE OF INFINITY. THAT IS WHY EVERY HUMAN CONCEPTION OF THE NATURE OF THE UNIVERSE, EVERY RELIGION IS A SHADOW OF TRUTH.

Javor felt dizzy. "So...the Christian God is an archon masquerading as the creator of heaven and earth?"

THE CREATOR OF THE MATERIAL UNIVERSE, INCLUDING ME, IS AN AEON OF INCOMPREHENSIBLE POWER AND AGE, EVEN TO ONE SUCH AS MYSELF. THERE ARE ARCHONS WHO HAVE REVEALED THEMSELVES TO HUMANS IN THE REGION OF THE WORLD WHERE THE FIRST CIVILIZATIONS AROSE, PLACES THAT HUMANS CALLED EGYPT AND UR. AND NOW AN ARCHON IS ACTIVE IN A DESERT CITY, MEDDLING WITH THE PEOPLE THERE. YOU WITNESSED IT MERGE WITH THE ARCHON IN JERUSALEM. HOW HUMANS WILL PERCEIVE IT AND REACT IS NEVER PREDICTABLE, BUT I FORESEE GREAT STRIFE AMONG HUMANITY.

"Why did you show me this?"

YOU HAVE BEEN SHOWN THIS BEFORE, BY THE ARCHON YOU CALL SARBOX.

"Sarbox showed me the bones of the earth, how the earth grew up. How the different generations of the earth grew."

THE BONES OF THE EARTH ARE THEMSELVES ARCHONS. WE ARE EMANATIONS OF THE AEON THAT CREATED THE PHYSICAL WORLD.

"The Demiurge."

THAT IS WHAT SOME HUMANS CALL IT. IT IS A FLAWED CONSCIOUSNESS. AN EMANATION OF SOPHIA, WISDOM, THE FIRST EMANATION OF THE PLEROMA. THE DEMIURGE CREATED THE PHYSICAL WORLD. ITS EMANATIONS ARE THE ARCHONS.

THE BONES OF THE EARTH ARE THE EMANATIONS OF

THE PHYSICAL WORLD. OTHER EMANATIONS SPREAD THROUGHOUT THE UNIVERSE THE DEMIURGE CREATED. SOME OF THOSE HAVE COME TO INHABIT THIS WORLD.

"Are there other worlds, too?"

THERE ARE INFINITE WORLDS, YOUNG HUMAN. LIFE AS YOU KNOW IT, ALL LIFE, IS THE PRODUCT OF THE ARCHONS OF THE EARTH, LIKE ME, AND ARCHONS FROM BEYOND EARTH. MAINTAINING LIFE IN THIS WORLD REQUIRES THE BALANCE OF BOTH ORDERS OF ARCHONS.

"Earth and sky..." Javor mumbled, remembering the words of an old woman in a shed over the Euxine Sea, years ago.

A woman that warned him against the archons.

A woman named Sophia.

A woman who protected him against the archons.

"Sky once loved Earth," he whispered, repeating Sophia's words on that windy night overlooking the Euxine Sea. "'Sky has turned away from Earth, and seeks to suppress her...and all the great civilizations have turned away from her, too.'"

THE ARCHONS, EMANATIONS OF EMANATIONS OF EMANATIONS, HAVE COME TO EARTH TO ATTACK AND CONQUER. TO SUBJUGATE AND CONTROL THEY ARE ALSO EXHORTING HUMANS TO CARRY OUT THEIR WILL. ONE BY ONE, EVERY CIVILIZATION HAS TURNED TO WORSHIPPING THE SKIES, THE SUN, THE EMANATIONS FROM BEYOND THE WORLD. ROME, PERSIA, THE EMPIRES EAST OF HERE IN LANDS YOU DO NOT IMAGINE. EVERY TIME THEY OBEY THOSE ARCHONS, EVERY TIME THEY SUCCEED IN TAMING SOME OF THE LIFE ON EARTH, THEY WEAKEN THE WEB OF LIFE.

"What do you want from me?"

YOU WERE GIVEN GREAT KNOWLEDGE OF THE BONES OF THE EARTH, AND THE ARCHONS OF THE SKIES. YOU WERE MADE CUSTODIAN OF IMMENSELY POWERFUL

GIFTS. ONE YOU CALL YOUR FRIEND.

"Preyatel."

THE OTHER IS A WEAPON THAT CAN NEVER BE RESISTED AND CAN NEVER BE DESTROYED.

"My great-grandfather's dagger."

THESE ARE GREAT GIFTS THAT WERE HIDDEN FROM HUMANITY FOR GENERATIONS OF YOUR KIND. THEY ARE MORE THAN ARTEFACTS. THEY ARE PART OF US. OF EVERY ONE OF US. NOW YOU USE THEM AGAINST US.

"Against you?"

YOU HUNT AND DESTROY THE EMANATIONS OF THE EARTH. THE DRAGONS. THE GIANTS WHO ROSE FROM THE FERTILE SEA. THE GUARDIANS OF THE DEEP PLACES OF THE EARTH. THEY ARE THE GUARDIANS OF LIFE. TELL ME, JAVOR, WHEN THE WATER NO LONGER FLOWS AND THE ONLY POWER IS FROM THE SUN, HOW LONG DO YOU THINK LIFE WILL SURVIVE?

Javor's answer surprised even himself. "How long will we survive? How long do we survive now?" His voice rose of its own accord. "You live forever. We live for a few years."

IT IS THE LOT OF LIFE. HUMANS DIE SO EASILY. YOU DIE BECAUSE OF TINY LIFE FORMS YOU DO NOT KNOW EXIST. MOST OFTEN, YOU SLAUGHTER EACH OTHER.

"Who killed my children?" Javor screamed up at the mountain. "Who decided they should die as babies?"

GO NOW, YOUNG WARRIOR. GO BACK TO YOUR HOME AND MAKE WAR ON THE EARTH NO MORE.

Javor felt himself fall, farther and faster than he had ever moved before. He did not have time to scream before he plunged into the glowing water below the god's shoulder.

The water was not cold, not warm, but invigorating. He felt no need to breathe, no urge to struggle for the surface, nothing but rushing, the motion through the water, faster than he had ever moved before.

Preyatel was still—it almost felt thrilled to be experiencing this fast journey. He rushed through the glowing water, then into a black, narrow tunnel, twisting and bending.

He felt no need to breathe, no discomfort, just the rushing.

The water became colder, darker. He felt the tunnel getting wider, even though he could see nothing.

Then he was moving up, faster and faster. He felt the need, now, for air, and tasted salt on his lips. When he thought he would have no choice but to breathe seawater into his lungs, his head burst through the surface. He flew out, up, over, landing with a thump and a clatter on a wooden dock. Startled men yelled. A donkey brayed.

Javor rolled onto his back and sat up, to see the sea walls of the harbour of Constantinople. Beside him, the horse staggered to its feet and shook water off its skin like a dog.

*I am home.*

# Interlude 7

# An Imperial wedding

*Year 613 Christian Era*

Mauricius tapped his foot on the floor as Calanthe fussed over Andrina's clothing. *Time is getting on.*

Calanthe smoothed Andrina's scarf over the back of her dalmatica and tucked loose hair under it. It was difficult with such short locks.

Andrina squirmed and stepped away from her mother's reach. "Do you have to do that?" she whined.

"It is not every day that there is an imperial wedding," Calanthe retorted.

"And, if we are lucky, we will not see another for a long time," Anna put in. "Please, Andrina. Hold still. It will make your mother happy."

"What difference does it make what I look like? No one is going to be looking at me," Andrina protested.

"Of course, people will look at you." Calanthe adjusted the dalmatica on her daughter's shoulder. "People we know will see you, so you need to look your best."

Andrina turned to Mauricius. "Papaoús, please tell her to stop."

"Calanthe, she looks fine. Let her be," Mauricius said.

"What do men know?" Anna insisted. She undid the brooch holding her granddaughter's cloak at her shoulder, made a minute adjustment in the way it draped, and re-fastened it. "There. That's better." She squinted at the folds in the heavy, brocaded cloth.

"I am ready!" resounded across the atrium. Adam bounded into the atrium, wearing his best clothes.

"Adam, your dalmatica is fastened on the wrong side and your hat is backwards," Calanthe said. She relented on Andrina to direct Martha, who unpinned Adam's brooch, flipped his cloak over and adjusted his clothes.

"What is so special about this day, anyway? Why do I have to wear all these stupid clothes?" Andrina whined.

"The emperor is getting married," Calanthe said, again.

"Who cares? People get married every day."

"It's the *emperor*, stupid," Adam said, hiking up his trousers.

"Like you know," Andrina said. "The 'emperor.' Who cares? He is just another man."

"Andrina!" Calanthe scolded. "He is the emperor. God's vice-regent on Earth. Do not forget that he freed us from the tyranny of Phocas, the usurper."

"I did not forget. But what does that have to do with putting on these stupid girlish clothes and going to his stupid wedding?"

"You will enjoy it, dear. The emperor is a mighty warrior," Calanthe said. "He is a strong, handsome man."

"Not as handsome as Papa," Andrina retorted. "Nor as strong, I will wager. Nor as brave."

"Andrina!"

"I wish Papa was here," Adam said. "Then we could prove which one is stronger."

"That is not only impractical, it could be seditious, grandson," Mauricius said as he helped Adam fix his clothes.

"I don't know what...'sedjus' means," Adam said. His hat fell to the floor. "It's just that Papa has been gone so long." He picked up his hat and let his grandfather place it properly on his head.

"I wish the twins could see this," Andrina said, surrendering finally to her mother's ministrations. "They would have liked to see the parade with all the horses and carriages."

Calanthe's hands dropped from her daughter. Her eyes fell, too, and her lip trembled for a moment. "They are in heaven, now," she said with a sigh. "Where there is no plague, no pain, no strife. Our Lord Jesus Christ and His holy Mother Mary watch over them. As they watch over us." She took Andrina's chin in her hand. "That is why we must all be good, now. So they will be happy with our behaviour."

Mauricius saw tears in her mother's eyes, and felt them in his own.

Mauricius took Calanthe by the shoulders and turned her toward him. "Daughter, you look beautiful. You do me proud on this day of an Imperial wedding."

Calanthe forced a smile. "Thank you, Papa."

"Giagiá," Adam piped up, addressing his grandmother. "You look so...pretty."

Anna preened. "Why thank you." She adjusted the hennaed hair that showed beyond her scarf. Her jewelry, newly polished, flashed in the sunlight. "And you look very handsome, yourself."

"He is the image of his father," Mauricius said. "Are we ready to go? The service starts soon. Calanthe, I have to ask you: what are you *feeding* these children? Look at the size of them!"

Calanthe surprised everyone with a little laugh. Despite her scolding, she looked proud of her surviving children. At thirteen, Andrina was already as tall as her mother, with broad shoulders and long legs, like her father.

Two years younger, Adam was nearly as tall as his sister. While he was covered with several layers of dress clothes now, as young as he was, Mauricius knew his grandson's arms and legs showed ropey muscles. He could excel his older sister now in climbing, running and jumping. But he was no match against his sister in lessons with Aunt Tiana.

"We are ready, Papa," Calanthe said.

Among a lot of shuffling suggestions, comments and orders, the group made their way to the carriages in front of the domus. Mauricius helped Aunt Tiana, who wore a simple grey gown and dalmatic and relied on her cane to walk.

"Will we see the Excubitors?" Adam asked his grandfather. "I hope so."

"I am sure we will, grandson," Mauricius said. The Excubitors were the elite of the Roman army, the personal bodyguards of the Roman emperor.

After close to an hour of pressing through the crowds, the little group made their way into the Hagia Sophia, the Church of Holy Wisdom in the middle of the oldest part of Constantinople.

An hour later, Mauricius heard his granddaughter whisper "This is so *boring*."

"Hush!" Calanthe hissed. "What do you want? You are watching the coronation of a new Augusta."

"We cannot even see her, nor the Patriarch," Andrina continued, her voice a hiss. "All I can see is the backs of these stupid people's heads."

"'These people' are the best of Constantinople!" Calanthe hissed back. "Lady Martina is kneeling before the altar, and the Patriarch is behind the iconostasis."

"What is the point of going behind the iconostasis? I have never understood that," Andrina persisted. "No one can see him!"

"Settle, please, granddaughter," Mauricius whispered. Andrina rewarded him with close to a quarter hour of peace, until he heard his Calanthe complain again in a whisper. "What are you doing?"

"I am sharing a snack with my brother," came the answer.

"In *church?* In the Hagia Sophia? During a coronation?"

"We are hungry!" Andrina hissed.

"When we get home, I swear..." Calanthe hissed.

"Hush. That is all for now," Mauricius said. "We will talk about this later."

Adam opened his palm. On it was a little sweet bun, baked by Martha. One of Adam's, and his grandfather's favourite snacks.

"Thank you," Mauricius said.

Adam winked.

Finally, the Patriarch emerged from behind the decorated screen called the iconostasis that separated the unwashed, yet blessed people of the Church from the altar, and placed a diadem on Martina's young head.

Then the Augustus, Basileus Heraclius, the new emperor, strode forward. He knelt for the Patriarch's blessing, and the marriage rites began.

Andrina stood on tiptoes. "How old is she? Sixteen?" she whispered. "And he is, what? Forty?"

"A hundred," Adam whispered, and giggled. Mauricius could not suppress a smile.

"Hush!" Calanthe ordered, and the lady in the pew in front of her turned and frowned.

Another eternity passed. Finally, the Augustus and new Augusta rose as the Patriarch chanted new blessings. They proceeded out of the cathedral.

As soon as they could, the family pushed out of the cathedral and hurried to a spot on the Mese, the main avenue of the capital city, and waited for the wedding procession to pass them.

Mauricius suppressed a smile as he watched Adam show off. The boy bent, pushed his head and shoulders between his sister's legs and rose, so that she was sitting on his shoulder. "There they are!" Andrina exclaimed.

People cheered as the new Augusta Martina and the Augustus Heraclius rode in a gilded chariot down the Mese, pulled by white horses.

A man with a face reddened by drink spat into the road ahead of the new emperor and empress. "Disgraceful! Go to hell!" he said, although his voice was drowned in the tumult. Only those next to him could hear.

"What's wrong? That is the Emperor!" Adam asked.

"Pig! Marrying his own niece, and the true empress is not yet cold in the grave," the man said.

"What are you talking about?" Andrina asked from atop her brother's shoulders.

"'Emperor' Heraclius dishonours the Church by marrying his niece, a year after his wife's passing," the man snarled. "Close your mouth, you little slut."

"Hey!" Adam protested, wobbling a little under Andrina's weight. "That is my sister."

The man spat at Andrina. Adam swung a fist, connecting with the man's chest. Andrina toppled from his shoulders but landed on her feet, crouching.

Calanthe gasped. "Children! What are you doing?"

"You little brats," the stranger snarled, raising a clenched fist.

Adam jabbed the man's midriff, and he staggered back. The people behind him pushed him up, and he came back, face red. "You little devils! I will whip your—"

Mauricius stepped in front of him. "Those are my grandchildren."

The red-faced man snarled. "The whelp looks like a barbarian."

"Shall I let my grandson beat you?" Mauricius asked. From the corner of his eye, he could see Adam in a defensive boxing posture. "Or my granddaughter? I think you need a lesson taught you by a girl."

The man snarled again and spat on Mauricius' feet. Adam hit him in the nose.

The red-faced man cursed as he struggled to his feet. Adam hit him again, and this time the man sprawled on the pavement. He let out a string of curses.

"Stop this *now*," Anna ordered.

Mauricius turned to see a red-cloaked excubitor wading through the crowd, a hand on the hilt of his sword. "Is there a problem here?"

"No problem, sir," Andrina said sweetly. She stepped forward, helping the red-faced man to his feet. "This gentleman just stumbled." As the man wobbled, a hand to his face, Andrina leaned toward the Imperial guard. "I think he had too much to drink."

"You little—" the red-faced man began, then saw the look on Adam's face. He fell silent and looked at the ground.

The Excubitor surveyed the scene. "All is well, sir," Andrina said. She brushed dust off the red-faced man's tunic.

The red-faced man nodded, but did not meet the Excubitor's eyes.

After a beat, the excubitor shrugged and moved on. Mauricius let out a breath and turned back toward the procession. The emperor and empress were long gone, and the crowd began to disperse.

The red-faced man began to say something, but Andrina stepped forward and punched him in the stomach. He crumpled to the cobblestones.

Adam stepped up. "Do not try anything. If you do, you will answer to me. And I'm stronger than my sister," he said.

"Oh, you are not," Andrina said.

"Am so!"

Calanthe pulled her children away. Once surrounded by her parents, she said, "I have never been so embarrassed. In front of the emperor and empress, no less!"

"Do not worry, daughter. I am certain the emperor and empress did not notice," Mauricius said. "Come. Let's go to my house. We will have some good wine and dinner."

Calanthe's lip trembled. "I have never been so embarrassed."

Mauricius put his arm around Adam's shoulders and squeezed. "I have never seen a child hit so hard. Well done, grandson."

# Homecoming

Javor led the now-young horse through the gate into the outer courtyard of his house. Seawater still dripped from them. The sun was bright, but lower in the sky than Javor expected.

Andrina came running when he dropped his helmet onto the atrium floor, Adam close behind her. He was almost as tall as his older sister, and his blond hair hung to his shoulders.

Javor went down to one knee to embrace his children. "Papa, why are you all wet?" Andrina demanded.

"You were gone so long, Papa," said Adam, helping him unstrap his armour.

Javor realized he had no idea what the date was.

*How long was I underground?* "How long have I been away?"

Andrina looked into his eyes, worry in hers. "Nine months, Papa."

Javor's mind reeled. He sat down on the floor. *How is that possible? The boat to Kerch, the time there...the ship to Anatolia, the journey across the plain and into the mountains...nine months?*

"So much happened while you were gone, Papa," Andrina said.

"So many bad things," Adam put in. Tears spilled down his cheeks.

Javor rose. *Nine months* echoed in his mind. The children looked bigger. Adam was now only a little shorter than Andrina, despite the two years between them—and Andrina was tall for a girl.

"What happened? Where is your mother? Where is Tiana?"

Adam's lip trembled. Andrina's gaze dropped. "Aunt Tiana is sitting with Mama. Mama is in her bed. She has hardly gotten up since... since—"

"Giagiá and Pappoús are dead!" Adam wailed, meaning his grandparents, Anna and Mauricius.

"What? When?" He did not have to ask, "How?"

"About...two months ago," Andrina answered. "It was the same day, the day after the emperor's wedding. Everyone in their house died. All their servants, all their slaves. So are Martha and Kyriake, and all our other servants. They died of the plague, one by one." One tear found a path down each of Andrina's cheeks, but her voice was firm, her eyes resolute.

Javor took his children into his arms and held them tight. One image filled his mind: the giant he killed in Helenopontus, its body dissolving into dust. Dust that blew away in the wind. Westward. Toward Constantinople.

Calanthe staggered into the atrium. "Javor," she sighed.

Her belly was huge, hanging low, and her skirts were wet.

"Calanthe." Javor stepped toward her just in time for her to fall into his arms, and staggered under her weight.

Tiana emerged from the hallway, leaning on her cane. "The baby is coming, Javor. The midwives are all dead. It will be up to you and me to deliver this child."

"No," Andrina said. "I will help. Papa is only a man."

Straining, Javor picked his wife in his arms and carried her to her bedchamber.

"Light more candles," Tiana instructed.

"Andrina, bring a jug of wine," Javor said, although he had no idea what good it would do.

"Adam, light the stove and heat up some water," Tiana added. Adam dashed out.

Javor took his wife in his arms, but he could not repress a question. "Tiana, did you tell me to drink the water in the cave?"

Tiana nodded.

"How long ago was that?"

Tiana shook her head. "Not now, Javor. We have something more important to do."

Calanthe screamed, sending pain through Javor's ear. "He's coming, Javor!"

Andrina returned at a run, a jug in one hand and a cup in the other. Javor poured wine into the cup and held it to his wife's lips. She took a small sip, but then pushed the cup away.

Javor drained the cup into his own mouth.

Adam came in with a handful of burning candles. He dashed around the bedchamber, lighting all the other candles in the room, then the brazier in the corner. "The water is warming," he reported.

Andrina wiped her mother's face with a damp cloth. *Why is she so capable? She is only twelve years old. No, thirteen. I have been gone nine months. I missed her birthday.*

He looked at his wife, lying on the bed, knees up, thighs spread as wide as they would go. Calanthe alternated between screaming, groaning and panting.

She shrieked one more time, arching her back more than Javor thought possible. "The baby is here," Tiana said. "Andrina, help your mother hold her legs apart."

Andrina reached between her mother's legs. "Push, Mama."

*How does she know that? Has she witnessed the other births?*

Adam was back then with a big, steaming jug. He put it on the table by the bed and handed Tiana another cloth.

"Wipe her face, gently," Tiana said. "And be ready."

Calanthe shrieked again. "Now! The baby is coming now."

"Now," Javor realized, was hours long. Hours while Calanthe screamed and panted. Hours while Adam and Andrina ran back and forth to the kitchen to reheat the water. Hours while Tiana encouraged her and wiped her brow. Hours while Javor helped her sip wine.

Javor watched his wife grow weaker. Her breath came faster, shallower, softer. Her screams less frequent, less loud. Her back relaxed onto the bed. Her eyes closed. Her knees fell, limp to the sides.

"Mama, mama, don't give up!" Andrina cried.

Tiana leaned close to Javor's ear. "There is a problem. The baby is breached. It is coming feet first."

Even Javor knew that was a problem. "That is wrong. It is supposed to come head first."

"Really?" Adam asked. "Why?"

"Mama, push!" Andrina pleaded.

Calanthe groaned and sighed. Desperate, Javor reached out and pushed down on his wife's belly.

That elicited a shriek. "Papa, what are you doing?" Andrina cried.

"Just trying—trying to push the baby..."

Calanthe moaned. Her eyelids fluttered.

"Well, don't do it again," Andrina ordered.

Javor swallowed and stepped back from his daughter's glare.

Tiana reached between Calanthe's thighs again. "Please, lady, push."

"Please, Mama," Andrina urged.

Calanthe groaned. Andrina reached between her mother's legs. "I have one foot. Take the other, Adam."

Adam lay across his mother's leg and reached between her thighs. "I can't. It's too slippery."

"Try harder!"

Javor lay on the bed and reached around Calanthe's shoulders. "Push again, my love."

Calanthe's eyes fluttered.

"I have the foot!" Adam said.

"Pull!" Andrina said.

Javor could see his children struggle to pull the baby out of their mother. Adam's hand came away. "Try again," Andrina ordered. Adam reached again with both hands.

The brother and sister strained. Calanthe sighed again and her head slumped to the side. Tiana muttered prayers and wiped the mother's face with a cloth. Javor sobbed. He reached forward and pushed again on her belly.

He heard a wet sound and then Andrina and Adam slumped back. Each held a tiny leg in one hand. Between them was a bright pink, wet shape.

That did not move.

Andrina took the newborn into her arms. "Papa, he is not breathing."

Javor took the baby into his arms. The wet shape lay still, quiet. He squeezed it gently, shook it softly. He put his mouth to the baby's and blew, feeling air flutter out over his cheeks.

He blew again, and again. Nothing happened. His face was wet, but he did not know whether that was from the baby or his own tears.

He felt a hand on his arm. "Papa, let me." Andrina gathered the tiny body in her arms and put her open mouth over the baby's mouth and nose. She blew, raised her mouth and took a deep breath, then put her mouth over the baby's again. Three times she blew, and then Javor saw the baby's leg twitch.

Andrina breathed into the baby one more time, and this time when she raised her face, she was rewarded by a thin wail.

Javor looked at his wife. Adam cradled her in his arms, weeping. But Javor saw her eyelids flutter. Her chest rose, and then a little squeak escaped her lips.

"We are very fortunate, and Calanthe is very strong," Tiana said. "It is rare for baby and mother to survive a breech birth."

Javor fell to his knees beside the blood-soaked bed and took his wife in his arms. The little family wept together in relief and released joy.

Part 7

# Nicolas

*Year 615 Christian Era*

# Conception

Javor woke to Preyatel trembling on his chest. A single candle entered his bedchamber. In the flickering light, he saw a silhouette, a stout woman with long, wavy hair.

"Who?" he slurred, his voice rough from sleep.

Beneath his nightshirt, Preyatel continued to vibrate.

Calanthe, in a nightgown, put the candle on the nightstand and slid under the blanket beside him. Her hand stroked his face. It felt rougher than he remembered.

He no longer felt the amulet vibrating.

"What is it?" he whispered.

In answer, she kissed him on the mouth, softly at first, then becoming more insistent. Her hand lingered over his throat, then traced down his chest and belly.

It was the first time in a long time she had kissed him. The first time she had ever come to his bedchamber. Until now, he had always come to hers.

It was the first time she had ever initiated lovemaking.

"Calanthe..."

"Hush," she breathed and kissed him again, deeply, pushing her tongue into his mouth. Her hands moved lower, found him hard and stroked him.

His arms went around his wife's body. He pulled her body close, and then felt his amulet tremble between their chests.

Calanthe pulled away, sitting astride his thighs. He no longer felt his amulet. She pulled her nightdress off, revealing the body of their wedding night. Her breasts high and round, her dark hair thick, spilling over her shoulders in rich curls. Her belly flat and firm, creased at her navel.

*Calanthe has never taken her nightclothes off for making love.*

He reached for her breasts, held them in his cupped hands.

Javor flexed his hips up, pushing deeper into his young wife. Calanthe groaned. She tossed her head back, her eyes closed. She flexed her hips, spreading wetness over his thighs, and with a gasp he was inside her.

*Calanthe almost never gets on top.*

He watched her ride him. The candle glowed brighter, illuminating her riding him, eyes squeezed shut, thin lips parted, her brown hair hanging down in soft waves past her shoulders. Her long arms and long fingers splayed on his chest.

Her eyes opened, shining for a moment before the candle dimmed again.

*Danisa. Why do I imagine Danisa when I am making love to my wife?*

He did not last long. His hips bucked uncontrollably and he climaxed, moaning, squeezing Danisa's breasts.

*My wife's breasts.*

Danisa—no, Calanthe—threw her head back, arched her back and shuddered before rolling off of Javor. She lay on her back for four panting breaths, then got out of bed.

The candle died, leaving the grey light from the door the only illumination in the bedchamber. Calanthe, stout again, picked up her nightdress, which was now a cloak, and walked out the door without putting it on.

Javor blinked.

*A dream. I dreamed of my wife.*

*Wine. I need wine.*

He swung his feet to the floor and padded out to the corridor.

*Why am I naked? Where is my nightshirt?*

His heart went cold.

*Where is Preyatel? Where is my amulet?*

The amulet had not left his chest in twenty years.

A crash and Andrina's scream launched him full-speed, naked, to the atrium. Somehow, his dagger was in his hand, blade drawn. But at the door to his bedchamber, he felt as if he had run into waist-deep water. He struggled to move forward, brandishing the dagger.

Andrina cried out again. There was another crash and the sound of a hand striking flesh. Finally, he reached the atrium, where a candle lay on the floor, casting a tiny glimmer of flickering yellow light.

He recognized his daughter's silhouette as she struggled to rise, as if she were lifting a great mass on her back.

Another silhouette lay still, sprawled in the impluvium. A third form lay beyond it.

A feminine form stood, arms raised, at the entrance from the street. The light was dim, grey, but he could never forget that silhouette, the long hair, the long nose, the small breasts and flat waist, the narrow hips that no baby had ever passed through.

*Danisa.*

Javor struggled forward against unseen resistance.

"Thank you, Javor," she said, her voice deeper than he remembered. "You have helped me fulfill my mother's original plan. What should have been her plan, that is, if she had been able to see what I can see."

And she disappeared.

The resisting force vanished with her and Javor stumbled forward.

"Papa!" Andrina cried. He turned to see her, cradling the body beside the basin.

Javor sank to his knees and saw whose body Andrina held. He reached out, trembling, to touch his son's face.

The boy's right hand held a small sword. Javor took it and laid it aside on the tiled floor.

"He is not breathing," Andrina said.

Javor took Adam's body from his daughter, cradling it. He pulled off the nightshirt, ran his hands over the boy's arms, torso, legs, but could find no wounds, not even a blemish. He was perfect.

But he was dead.

"I am sorry, Papa. I heard a noise. I tried to get out of bed, but it was as if something was holding me down. When I finally came out of my room, I saw Adam fighting a legionnaire with a sword. He fought so well, Papa, he defeated the legionnaire. He killed him. And then he turned to that, that...woman. He lunged at her, once. He did it perfectly, Papa, the way you taught us. Then he collapsed into the impluvium. He did not move after that.

"I tried to come to him, but something, I don't know, something knocked me down to the floor. I could not see what it was, it was too dark, and I could hardly move. I am sorry, Papa. I could not help him." She sobbed. "I could not save him."

Javor laid his dead son's body on the floor as gently as he could and went to the body of the legionnaire, lying prostrate on the ground. He grabbed the shoulder and rolled the body over, then recoiled when he recognized the face.

Darko. Danisa's brother. The boy he had brought down from the mountains eighteen years earlier, when he had been called Ana-Kui. The boy who had enlisted in the Legions, with hope of joining the excubitors.

The hilt of a knife stuck out of his chest.

*He helped his sister attack us. He tried to kill my son. He helped Danisa steal my amulet, my oldest friend.*

Javor leapt up and ran to Calanthe's bedroom. He halted at the door.

The shadow on the bed lay still and silent.

Javor reached out a trembling hand. His wife's chest did not rise, nor fall. No breath tickled his fingers held under her nose.

He struggled not to vomit as he turned to the dark, silent crib behind him. Beatus lay on his back, still. No breath came from him, like his mother.

Sobbing, he ran further back into the domus, to Tiana's room. The wise woman lay spread on the floor, her legs splayed, blood spreading in a growing pool under her head.

He fell to his knees to gather her into his arms. Tiana's eyes fluttered. "Javor," she whispered. "Danisa. It was Danisa." Blood bubbled in her mouth. "You are a seventh son. You can save your son." She drew a last breath that gurgled in her throat. "Then you must restore the balance." Her eyes closed and her body went limp.

He went back to look at his son's beautiful, perfect body. His face looked quiet, calm, sweet.

For the first time in his life, Javor had no more rage left to feel.

He only felt empty.

*Save my son, she said. Which one?* He gathered Adam into his arms again and kissed his warm forehead.

And felt something.

Not a stirring, not a twitch nor an intake of breath. But a vibration. *No. A flow.*

He moved and kissed Adam's mouth. And felt it, stronger. A flow of energy from himself into his son. He trembled and Adam's body trembled, too.

Javor opened Adam's mouth and then blew into it. Remembering how Andrina had saved baby Beatus, he put the boy's open mouth with his own and breathed into Adam.

And was rewarded with a twitch.

He breathed out again, then released the boy to take in more air.

"That's it, Papa!" Andrina said. "Do it again."

Javor pressed his mouth against Adam's and breathed hard again. He felt the boy's chest expand and came up to let him exhale.

"Again, Papa!" Andrina cried.

Javor breathed life into his son again, and when he came up this time, he heard Adam's exhalation.

Andrina pulled her brother's body from her father's arms and laid him on the floor. "You have put breath into him again. Now we must get his heart beating again." She put both her palms on the middle of Adam's chest and pushed down, over and over again.

Javor watched his daughter push on Adam's chest in something like a heartbeat's pace. He could not breathe and could not take his eyes from his son's smooth, pale face. Time passed as Andrina pushed, grunting with effort.

Javor sighed. His sons were dead. He leaned forward to kiss his son goodbye for the last time.

And felt energy flow from him into Adam. Like water in a river, like the flow of the Bosporus itself. Adam's body stiffened. His back arched. His fingers flexed.

Javor felt himself weaken as energy continued to flow into Adam, but kept his mouth on his son's as Andrina kept pushing on Adam's chest. Finally, the boy surged to a sitting position, pushing his sister's arms away. Javor fell onto his side and looked up at his son, panting.

Adam's eyes darted around as he gasped, too. He gagged and fell forward into Andrina's arms. She laid him down on his back again.

"Where is she?" Adam gasped, his chest heaving. "That witch. She—"

"Hush. She is gone," Andrina said. "Rest."

Javor did not have the strength to do anything but look at his children.

Andrina wrapped her arms around Javor and pressed her wet face against his chest. If not for the pressure of her arms, the sweet and firm feel of her hands against his skin, Javor would have felt nothing.

# Inheritance

New dreams began the night after Calanthe's burial.

They began with the vision Sarbox had shown him. The birthing of the earth, how the sun stirred life on its surface and deep within, the rise of its oldest, deepest powers.

How those powers grew, changed, mated, birthed new powers that themselves grew and grew the earth with them.

How other powers descended from the light-sparkled blackness above and surrounding the earth, sparking new powers in new forms.

How life rose in a splendid and terrifying panoply, a range far beyond the reach of Javor's imagination.

How humans arose on a broad, grassy plain and spread across the world to inhabit every clime and landscape. How they changed the landscape, changed the kinds of life there. How their cities rose and decayed. How armies marched out and slaughtered each other.

How still newer powers rose, glowing bright about settlements of men, how they met and struggled and merged and devoured one another.

He would wake quickly, sweating and panting.

The death of Calanthe's parents created complications for Javor.

Mauricius' possessions passed to his only living child, Calanthe.

They included his small fleet of ships, a lease on a warehouse and dock at the northern harbour, and its contents of spices, wines, honey and other goods.

Her inheritance also included a significant amount of debt. And with her death—her murder—those ships, trade goods and obligations all became Javor's.

A group of creditors called at Javor's domus one day. All men dressed well in colourful dalmatics and kerchiefs pulled across their faces. The leader—or at least, the one who stood in front, at the front gate but not daring to enter—was a head shorter than Javor and as wide as he was tall. "As the inheritor," he said after introducing himself and the others, "You have inherited Mauricius' debts, as well. Given the circumstances, we are calling in our debts."

"I buried his daughter, my wife, only yesterday," Javor answered. "Come back some other time."

"Now is the time," the leader said, and Javor could not remember his name. "The debts are substantial."

"How much?" Javor growled.

The leader mentioned a sum that left Javor's mouth dry. Several times the total sum he spent on his servants' wages—or used to pay before they all had died. It would even put a substantial dent in the gold he had taken home as a reward from the Kobolds.

After some argument, Javor convinced the group that he would need time to gather the money. Grumbling, the masked group left.

*Two days. How can I arrange that much money in two days?*

Javor strode across the city, to the docks and Mauricius' warehouse. The calls of gulls competed with grunts and calls of men on the docks.

Javor found Theo, Mauricius' warehouse supervisor, counting stock. "I thought you would be here days ago," he said on seeing Javor at the door, his voice deeper than a bear's.

"My wife passed," Javor answered, looking around. The warehouse looked full, shelves piled high with cloth and casks. Dust floated in the beams of light that shone through the high, unglazed windows near the roof. The space smelled of dust, spices, wet wool, spilled wine and seawater.

"May God have mercy," Theo said, his voice flat. His eyes showed too much experience with death. But the lines around his eyes and mouth did not move. "My parents and my four children all died a month ago. My wife died on the first day of the plague."

"I am sorry," Javor said. "But I have to look to my father-in-law's commerce now."

"That's why I expected you earlier. Of course, I heard all about his passing, and I knew his daughter would be the only one to inherit."

"It looks like things are going well. The shelves are full."

Theo shook his head. "That's because there's no one left alive to buy anything. The market is deserted. No one needs honey or spices, and they're only buying cloth for shrouds. And not even the rich senators are bothering to buy silk these days."

"Oh. I admit, I do not know much about commerce. Buy cheap, sell dear, right?"

Theo squinted at him for a long moment, then grunted and returned to counting.

"How much money do you have?" Javor asked.

Theo turned to him again. "Why?"

"Mauricius' creditors called on me. They want their money."

Theo nodded. "Makes sense. The old man dies, they get nervous about getting their investment back. How much do they want?"

Javor told him. Theo shook his head.

"So, how much did the...old man have?"

Theo shrugged. "You'd have to ask the argyropratēs."

"The who? What is an 'argyropratēs'?"

Theo grunted again. "The man who holds Mauricius' money for him."

"He holds his money?"

"What do you think—he carried it all around in his purse? Enough to pay all the sailors, buy food for his slaves, pay me every month? Not even a giant like you could carry that much gold and silver around." Theo's eyes narrowed. "Don't tell me you don't have an argyropratēs. What do you do with your money? Keep it in your house?"

Javor felt his face get hot. "Of—of course not. Never mind. Tell me who Mauricius' argyropratēs is."

"You should also talk with his notary and find out about his will. What did he want to do with his possessions? Sure, it makes sense that his only child would inherit it all, but rich people often do strange things. Like give large properties to the Church. But that's usually the very rich, the senators and landowners, not a simple merchant like Mauricius."

*It seems I have several more people to talk with today.*

At almost 16 years, Andrina was nearly as tall as Javor himself. She had broad shoulders and long legs, like her father, and long muscles were visible in her arms. Two days after the creditors' visit, she helped her father set three couches and a small table just inside his front gate. She filled three cups with the best wine left in the pantry.

Javor's first two guests arrived early, just after the few living shopkeepers opened their shutters on the main street. Javor bade them sit and drink.

The creditors came shortly later, still in their formal cloaks and scarves over their faces. Javor remained seated.

"Are you ready to settle your debts?" the leader said.

"They are not my debts, they are my late, honoured father-in-law's," Javor answered. "And before we go any further with settling any debts, I demand to see the faces of the men who claim them."

The group looked at each other. Then, slowly, the leader lowered his scarf. "You understand, we are trying to protect ourselves against the plague."

"And you understand that I must know whom I am giving money to," Javor answered. "Now, where is your proof of these debts?"

Another of the group stepped forward with a bundle of papers. Javor passed them to one of his first guests. "This is Romanus Glycus, the argyropratēs who handled my father-in-law's money."

Glycus examined each paper, his face intent, for long enough that the creditors began to shuffle and murmur. Javor sipped his wine and looked up at the high, clear summer sky. The air was already hot, the sunlight fierce on his head, but he did not let his expression betray his discomfort.

Finally, Glycus handed the papers back to Javor. "They are correct. The sum Florus Staurakius said is correct, and it matches my records, as well."

"Very good," Javor said. He indicated the second guest on his right. "This is Lucas, Mauricius' notary. He has explained Mauricius' will to me, and our assumptions were correct: my father-in-law's assets and debts passed to his daughter, Calanthe, and after her death, to me. Lucas has executed the will and registered the transfer.

"My late, honoured father-in-law was a shrewd man of commerce and trade. As a result, his assets are far more valuable than his debts. However, I am not a man of commerce. Thus, to settle those debts, I have made some decisions. Please, Lucas, you can explain better than me."

Lucas drained his cup of wine. "The late Mauricius Macedonius owned four ships and a long-term lease on a warehouse on the harbour," he said. He suppressed a belch. "In settlement of the debts of the estate, we are transferring to the creditors three of those ships, including their slave crews, as well as the warehouse, its staff and slaves. However, this does not include the docking rights of the fourth ship, which will remain in the possession of our master, Javor Sklavenius." He flourished another bundle of papers. "These are the deeds of ownership."

"But," sputtered the leader, Florus, "the amounts owed to each of us vary. Other than me, no one here is owed more than the value of a single ship, let alone a warehouse."

"You can work that out among yourselves," Javor said. "The value of the property is more than just under the circumstances."

"What circumstances?"

"A plague. You men are lucky to be alive to bother me with this matter. You should be pleased to receive three ships." He did not say that he had kept the newest, fastest ship, and the best captain and crew of the fleet.

Florus sputtered some more. The men behind him argued and muttered.

"One more thing," said the banker, Glycus. "As Sir Sklavenius said, the value of the ships and warehouse are greater than the total debt Mauricius owed. You now owe sir Javor the sum of two hundred solidi."

Florus and the men behind him erupted at once, tossing arguments faster than a cat kicking dirt. Fed up, Javor stood, towering over the group, one hand on the hilt of his dagger. "That is all, sirs. My final word. Unless one of you wishes to challenge me."

Florus looked up at Javor and swallowed visibly. After a long moment, he frowned. "Very well. It is a...reasonable offer. We will return with one hundred solidi tomorrow." He reached for the papers that Lucas held.

*This man has balls.* "Very well. One hundred solidi. You will get the papers tomorrow when I get your gold," said Javor. "Goodbye." He slid the gate closed before any of the creditors could say another word.

Andrina, at his shoulder, kissed his cheek.

# The daughter's dream

*Year 616 Christian Era*

Javor held his baby in his arms. So tiny. Only his head and one hand stuck out of the blanket. The head with its thin, soft covering of dark fuzz, the impossibly small fingers reaching and grasping. The baby's mouth opened and closed, looking for milk.

*Beatus. Blessed. Because you have blessed me after my twins died of the plague.*

Javor kissed the baby's forehead. *A baby's head smells so good.*

*Thank you, God. Or Pleroma. Or whatever you are.*

He put the baby into Calanthe's arms. Calanthe, naked, her long dark hair loose and lustrous as on their wedding night.

*She is so beautiful.*

He turned to see his babies sitting beside the impluvium, Charita and Giorgia, two years old. Both sat on the floor, naked as their mother. He scooped them into his arms and held them against his bare skin.

Bare skin. He realized he was naked, too.

Even his chest.

His amulet was gone, but he felt no fear.

Before he could wonder about that, two pairs of arms wrapped around them: Andrina and Adam, both naked, both tall, fit, pressing their faces against his body.

And behind them, another boy, perhaps two years younger than Adam. His hair was dark, cut in the Roman style.

He knew who it was. Austinus, Calanthe's third child, his second son, who died before being born.

*At last, we are all together.*

*Is this paradise? Am I dead?*

*Are the Christians right?*

He looked up. There was an older man, tall, with long, dark-grey hair and beard. He wore a long black robe, trimmed with silver, and a heavy silver chain hung around his shoulders. Austinus, the Comes of the Order when I first arrived in Constantinople.

Beside him, another tall, thin, older man whose face was deeply lined. He wore long, shabby grey robes and a shapeless hat. A sword was strapped around his hips. Photius, the man who brought me to the Order.

*But you are dead. I saw you die, dissolved in a dragon's venom.*

On the elder Austinus' other side, a shorter man, thin and wiry, with dark skin. He wore tight black trousers and a light coloured tunic. A sword hung from his hip, too, and a dagger on the other side.

*Malleus. My friend. Who tried his best to kill me the first time he met me.*

*You are dead, too. Murdered by Gracian. I saw your body hanging from the gibbet.*

The arms around him disappeared. The babies were no longer in his arms. He turned to see Adam lying, facedown in the impluvium. Andrina was nowhere to be seen. He thought he heard her voice, calling from far away.

And in Calanthe's place, a naked Danisa, holding a baby. Not a baby with thin, dark newborn fuzz on its head, but thick, blond hair.

*Like mine.*

"Papa," a voice repeated.

*Andrina. Where are you?*

"Papa, wake up," Andrina said.

Danisa faded. The baby faded. Austinus, Photius, Malleus, the twins, his stillborn son Austinus, all gone. Replaced by a red-tinged darkness.

Something pressed on his arm. Someone shook him.

"Papa! Wake up," Andrina urged.

Javor bolted upright. His daughter, his oldest child and the only one left alive, stood in her nightgown, holding a dim candle.

"What is it? Where is your—" He stopped himself from saying "mother."

*She is dead. Like the rest of them.*

"You were dreaming, Papa," she said, sitting on the foot of his bed. "You were calling out names: Mama's, and Beatus, and Adam. Others, too. Malleus, Austinus. And...and Danisa."

Javor shuddered. The room was cold, the brazier dark. "I am sorry for waking you," he said. His voice was hoarse.

"You did not wake me, Papa," Andrina answered. She put the candle on the table and wrapped her arms around her father. "I had a dream, too."

Javor held his daughter tight and kissed her head. "Do you want to tell me?"

Andrina took a deep breath, then pushed back from her father. "It was about Danisa, too. She had a baby, Papa. Your baby."

Javor pulled her close again. "It was just a dream."

"No, Papa. It is true. It is real. I know it." She extricated herself from his grasp for a second time. "You know it is real. That is why you dreamed of her, too. Do you know what else I dreamed of?"

Javor knew, but feared to admit it.

"Your amulet, Papa. Preyatel. Your friend. 'Preyatel' means 'friend' in Sklavenik, does it not?"

"How do you know that? How do you know about my amulet?"

She smiled through pain. "Oh, Papa. I have always known. Since I was a little girl, I knew. You never took it off. You were always protective of it.

"I know it spoke to you. It spoke to me, too. Many times. Where the riots came close to the house. And that night," she whispered, leaning close. "That night, when Danisa came. And that legionnaire—that was her brother, was he not?" Javor could only nod. "She cast a spell on you, Papa. She kept you from rising, from taking action as she seduced you. She stole your seed, while her brother murdered my mother.

"She took your friend, your amulet, Papa. When she pulled it from your neck, it called out to me. It woke me up. I came out of my room and I saw that legionnaire coming out of Mama's bedroom with a bloody knife in his hands. And I saw Adam jump on him. He fought him, Papa. He took the legionnaire's knife and killed him.

"And then I saw Danisa come from your room, Papa. She saw Adam and me. Then I could not move. I tried to protect Adam, but I could not. Danisa looked at me and I felt...frozen. Paralyzed.

"And then she looked at Adam. She looked at him and raised her hand, and Adam fell to the floor. He was dead. She killed him, Papa. Killed him with a look!" In the dim candlelight, Javor could see her face was wet.

Andrina drew a sobbing breath. "You have not been the same since that day, Papa. When the twins died, you were so angry. I had never seen you so angry. And you went away for such a long time, and when you came back, you were still angry.

"But since that night, when Adam died...when Danisa murdered him ... since then, Papa, you have been so sad. You almost never leave the house. You never go to the market, never go to church."

"The church has nothing for me, Andrina."

"Papa, there are days when you barely get out of bed. Yes, you made the arrangements to bury Mama and her parents, but since then...you have been so unhappy."

Javor sighed. "You are the one thing in this world that makes me happy, my love."

She smiled sadly again. "Thank you, but that is not true, Papa. Nothing makes you happy."

"I have lost so much, Andrina. Five children, one of them just a baby. A wife. Aunt Tiana. Malleus..."

"Papa, you have another baby," Andrina announced.

Javor blinked. He realized tears were running freely down his face. "That was just a dream, Andrina."

"No, Papa. I told you that Preyatel called out to me that night. And it called to me tonight. And to you, too.

"That night was ten months ago, Papa. Danisa has your baby. He is now one month old. Your seventh child. They are in the mountains to the west, in the lands of the barbarians."

"Sklavenes," he corrected her. "We are called 'Sklavenes.' It means 'people who speak.'"

"No, beyond them. The Goths. Danisa is not a Sklavene. She is a Goth. And she has retreated to the land of her mother.

"Your son is alive, Papa. He is in the hands of the woman who murdered your wife and your other son. Your oldest son. And your beloved 'aunt,' Tiana.

"We will find him, Papa. We will find Nicolas."

"'Nicolas?'"

"That is his name, Papa. The name that Danisa gave him. 'Victory.' We will save him, Papa. You and I will travel west and bring your son, my brother, home."

Javor knew better than to argue with Andrina.

# About the Author

Scott Bury is a journalist, editor and novelist based in Ottawa, Canada. After more than 20 years of writing for magazines and newspapers like Macworld, the Financial Post, Applied Arts, the Ottawa Citizen and Graphic Arts Monthly, he turned to his first writing love, fiction. He published a children's story, "Sam, the Strawb Part" in 2011 and donated all the proceeds to an autism charity. Later, he published a short story for grown ups that might fall into the "urban paranormal" category, called "Dark Clouds."

The Bones of the Earth, a historical fantasy, came out in 2012. It was followed in 2013 with One Shade of Red, an erotic romantic spoof of the inexplicable bestseller, Fifty Shades of Grey.

The Eastern Front trilogy tells the true story of Maurice Bury, a Canadian drafted into the USSR's Red Army in 1941, just in time to face the German invasion of the Soviet Union in Operation Barbarossa. It comprises Army of Worn Soles (2014), Under the Nazi Heel (2016) and Walking Out of War (2017).

In 2018, he launched the new Wine Country Mystery series with Wildfire.

In 2015 and 2016, he was invited to contribute to three Kindle

Worlds, a project that was cancelled in 2018. He wrote seven titles for them. He plans to revise and republish them over the next year. Torn Roots is the first of these, introducing the Hawaiian Storm series.

In between writing books and blog posts, Scott helped to found an author's cooperative publishing venture, Independent Authors International. He is also President of an authors' professional association, BestSelling Reads.

You can find out more about Scott Bury and contact him through his website, www.writtenword.ca, his blog, Written Words, and on Twitter @ScottTheWriter.

# More from Scott Bury

**THE EASTERN FRONT TRILOGY**

***Army of Worn Soles:*** A Canadian is drafted into the Soviet Red Army just in time for Nazi Germany's invasion in 1941. Caught between Nazi and Communist forces, Lieutenant Maurice Bury keeps his men alive as they retreat from the German juggernaut. But will they escape from the hell of the POW camp before they starve to death?

***Under the Nazi Heel:*** For Ukrainians in 1942, the occupying Germans were not the only enemy.

Maurice Bury joins the resistance, to protect the country against enemies on all sides.

Experience this seldom seen phase of World War 2 through the eyes of a man who fought Under the Nazi Heel.

***Walking Out of War:*** The Soviets draft every remaining Ukrainian man for their final push on Germany. Canadian Maurice Bury, is thrust once again into the death struggle between Hitler's Germany and Stalin's USSR.

Maurice plans to survive until Nazi Germany dies, to return home to Canada. But to do that, he'll have to elude Stalin's dreaded secret police.

## HISTORICAL MAGIC REALISM

***The Bones of the Earth:*** In the darkest time of the Dark Age, barbarians have destroyed the Western Roman Empire, while volcanoes, rising seas and new plagues threaten the rest. A young Sklavene searches for answers. What is the link between Javor's heirlooms, his lover and his enemies? And why is the Earth wiping out human civilization?

## OTHER WORKS:

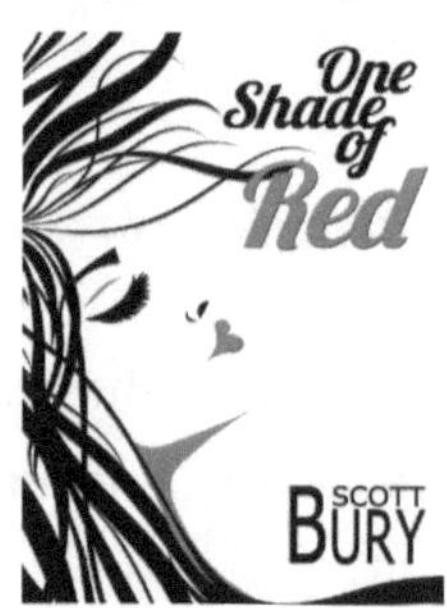


***One Shade of Red:*** When university student Damian Serr discovers a rich, beautiful woman with a voracious sexual appetite, he doesn't try to improve on perfection. All he can do is hold on for the ride.

Alexis gives Damian an intense education, pushing him to his sexual limits. The only question he has is: will she break them?

***Sam, the Strawb Part:*** A thin boy dresses as a pirate, attaches a jolly roger to his bicycle and starts to hijack strawberries.

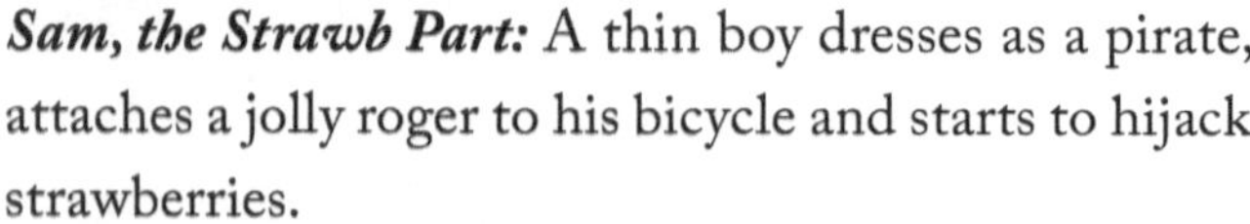

The evil fruit monopoly doesn't take kindly to pirates. They hire notorious pirate-killer Commodore Tiberius J. Swinkill, to hunt Sam down.

This swashbuckling tale of fury and fruit is for children, parents and everyone who loves strawberries, children or pirates.

***Dark Clouds:*** The Witch Queen's Son, Part 1: Matt always knew when his mother was on the way: the wind would swirl from all directions at once and dark clouds would mass in the sky.

Matt and his pretty wife, Teri, try to get out of the way. But only they can stop the Witch Queen's plans—and the price for that is blood.

**THE HAWAIIAN STORM SERIES Mysteries with FBI Agent Vanessa Storm.**

***Torn Roots:*** Vanessa Storm's first case in Hawaii is to find a kidnapped woman. When she gets to Maui's jungled south coast, she finds the kidnapped woman is also suspected of arson.

Throw in a dispute between resort developers and a loud environmentalist, a taciturn geologist, a laid-back local police lieutenant and a rogue Homeland Security agent, Vanessa has to find her way through this labyrinth without triggering an international incident.

***Palm Trees & Snowflakes:*** In Honolulu, where the palm trees are strung with holiday lights, FBI agents Vanessa Storm and Alan Terakawa have their hands full trying to stop the deadly flow the newest designer drug. Faulty intel brings the agents into a firefight, which yields only more puzzles.

***Dead Man Lying:*** With lush rain forests, black sand beaches, and a laid-back lifestyle, Maui offers the perfect retirement location for once-famous country singer Steven Sangster ... until he ends up dead.

As the killer, or killers, strike again and again, FBI Special Agent Vanessa Storm must untangle the lies spun by the singer's associates, friends, family — and the singer himself before the music dies.

***Echoes:*** The Kahuna—"wizard" in old Hawai'ian—was the only one who could surprise Vanessa Storm when she was a teenager. When she's an FBI Special Agent, though, things are different. She's no longer a girl impressed with small-town bad boys.

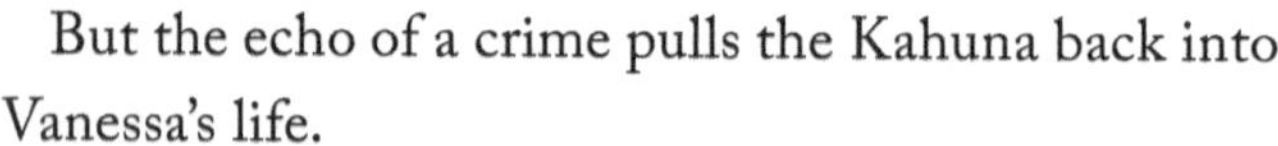

But the echo of a crime pulls the Kahuna back into Vanessa's life.

Coming soon!

www.ingramcontent.com/pod-product-compliance
Lightning Source LLC
Chambersburg PA
CBHW030350030726
47497CB00002B/269

* 9 7 8 1 9 8 7 8 4 6 2 4 9 *